THE
PLEASURE
ZONE

Dear Reader:

Cairo has created another erotic page-turner and it's all about pleasing. Nairobia Jansen is the ultimate pleasure goddess. The former porn star is now a sleek entrepreneur who reigns over The Pleasure Zone, an upscale, private club that is truly for the uninhibited. Everything goes in this adults-only paradise geared to the freaky and rich who seek no-holds-barred satisfaction.

Nairobia, a vixen born of a Dutch mother and Nigerian father, is a seductress like no other as she's viewed as irresistible by all those she encounters. She maintains an icy persona with her show-stopping looks and takes pride on not being vulnerable or serious about relationships while ensuring she's forever sexually gratified. She's vowed to never let another man capture her heart and end up falling into their love trap. No, she's all about full control of her life.

Nairobia was first introduced in *Between the Sheets* along with the powerful married couple, music mogul Marcel and publishing exec Marika, whose story is also featured in *The Pleasure Zone*. Check out an excerpt in the back of this title.

As always, thanks for supporting myself and the Strebor Books family. We strive to bring you the most cutting-edge, out-of-the-box material on the market. You can find me on Facebook @AuthorZane or you can email me at zane@eroticanoir.com.

Blessings,

Zane

Publisher
Strebor Books
www.simonandschuster.com

ZANE PRESENTS

THE
PLEASURE
ZONE

WITHDRAWN

A NOVEL BY
CAIRO

SBI

STREBOR BOOKS

NEW YORK LONDON TORONTO SYDNEY

SBI

Strebor Books
P.O. Box 6505
Largo, MD 20792
http://www.streborbooks.com

ISBN 978-1-59309-661-8
ISBN 978-1-5011-1963-7 (ebook)
LCCN 2015957580

First Strebor Books trade paperback edition February 2016

Cover design: www.mariondesigns.com
Cover photograph: © Keith Saunders/Keith Saunders Photos

10 9 8 7 6 5 4 3 2

Manufactured in the United States of America

For information regarding special discounts for bulk purchases, please contact Simon & Schuster Special Sales at 1-866-506-1949

The Simon & Schuster Speakers Bureau can bring authors to your live event. For more information or to book an event, contact the Simon & Schuster Speakers Bureau at 1-866-248-3049 or visit our website at www.simonspeakers.com.

THIS BOOK IS DEDICATED TO
All the Facebook beauties 'n' cuties and cool-ass bruhs
who make this journey mad fun.
Thank you for being open-minded enough,
bold enough, and adventurous enough
to share my love of hotness in the sheets with you.
Keep wavin' ya freak flags!

ACKNOWLEDGMENTS

What's good, my freaky peeps? *The Pleasure Zone* isn't simply about a sex club. It's about exploring and discovering your own pleasure zones. It's about an unyielding determination to be as sexually fulfilled as humanly possible without regret, without shame, without making excuses. It's about unleashing your own hidden desires. It's about sexual freedom.

Special shout-out to Jeffrey Roshell: Congrats on the release of ya first joint, *ThornHill High School*. I haven't read it, but wanted to wish much success to you, playboy!

Mad luv to my cyber-boo, Markisha Harris; my cyber-wifey, Dierdre "Miz Wigglez" Mitchell; and my cyber-side-piece, Zanetta Davis!

Sara Camilli: I am forever indebted to you for all that you do.

To Zane, Charmaine, Yona and the rest of the Strebor/Simon & Schuster team: *Danke, Gracias, Grazie, Merci, E dupe…Bedankt…* there are not enough languages in the world to thank you for supporting, encouraging, and believing in *me*.

And, as always, to the naysayers: Fourteen books and still climbing. Lick balls, *muhfuckas!*

One luv—

Cairo

ONE

Desirous.

Hedonistic.

Orgasmic.

Drenched in exotic beauty, Nairobia Jansen was all of those things, then some. She was Kama Sutra. A dangerous combination of... seduction and sin.

She was good pussy.

Good fucking.

She was sweet surrender.

And the gray-eyed, half-Dutch, half-Nigerian beauty knew it. After all, she was every man's wet dream. And over the years she'd become the forbidden fantasy of her share of women as well. No. She wasn't a lesbian. But she didn't consider herself heterosexual, either. In fact, she hated labeling her sexuality. She found it constricting, and goddamn boring. She refused to live her life confined to someone else's definition of who she should or shouldn't be. She fucked whom she wanted, when she wanted, however she wanted, with abandon.

But it was no secret she loved the taste of pussy. Hell, most of the world had probably seen her with her face pressed between the thighs of a slew of women during her porn-star days. She was Pleasure back then. It was unbelievable how that time in her life felt like a lifetime ago. Still her reputation followed her. She was a legend in the porn industry. And she was certain many men had jacked off watching her get fucked from the back, her ass bouncing up and down on a long dick making it disappear, while she tongue-fucked another woman. Pussy was heavenly. She loved licking into its wet folds, sucking on its plump golden lips. She loved the way its scent stained her tongue. Loved the heat of another woman's cunt melding into her own, grinding clit-to-clit, creaming out an orgasm.

However, make no mistake. She loved the wet, juicy, slosh-slosh sound her pussy made every time it was being deep-stroked by a long, hard, throbbing cock more. So—hell no, she could never be a lesbian. She loved dick too much.

Nairobia drew in a deep breath, and resisted the urge to wince at not having had some good pussy since the death of her...well, the only woman who she'd once ever considered sucking and fucking exclusively. *Marika.* The thought of her being gone was still too much to give thought to. And tonight wasn't the time for gloom.

No. It was a celebration. The grand opening of her latest adventure, a club—nestled inside what used to be a lesbian club—in the midtown section of New York. Its sole purpose was to cater to the carnal desires of wealthy men and women who stepped foot through its doors. She'd bought the space a little over a year ago as an investment to add to her already impressive portfolio. And now her dream of opening the doors to one of the world's most erotic sex clubs would become a reality.

Tonight.

Nairobia stared at the wall of water cascading behind the sleek, curved bar before her eyes locked on the bartender. She was scandalously dressed, as always, in a form-fitting, sheer linen gown, a front and back slit crawling up to the crack of her luscious bare ass, and golden sweet pussy.

A Chopard diamond necklace, with over a 140-carats of tear-drop-shaped diamonds, cascaded around her neck and dripped down into her cleavage. Her shoulder-length hair was pulled up in what she liked to call a *naughty girl* chignon. Her hair pulled back, twisted into a loose bun, then loose strands of hair pulled out, framing her face for that freshly "just-fucked" look.

The messier the better, that's how she liked it. Like sex, she liked it wild.

"What's your poison, Mademoiselle?" the bartender asked over the music. Silk's "More" melted out through the world-class sound system.

She glanced around the club.

Chic.

Sophisticated.

Heated marbled floors.

Swathes of billowy ivory silk covered the walls on the first floor.

Candles of enormous sizes flickered about the expansive space.

Gas-lit torches lined the walls.

Draped candlelit booths.

Oversized white leather sofas and armless chairs.

Massive floral arrangements perfumed the air.

She looked up at the vaulted ceiling, then fluttered her gaze back to the milk chocolate Adonis in front of her, his eyes dancing over her body. Every muscle in his sleek torso bunched, and her pussy clenched.

Goapele purred out of the speakers about being ready to play. And Nairobia was more than ready. She stayed ready. Always wet, always ready. She thrust her pelvis to its beat, then reached over the bar, positioned in the center of the floor, and pulled him into her by his spiked collar. She kissed him on the mouth. Sunk her teeth into his plump bottom lip. Then nipped at the small diamond hooped earring in his left ear. There was a panther's head tattooed on the back of his neck. And her mouth watered to bite it. She resisted the urge.

For now…

Save for his collar, the six-foot-four bartender's sculpted body was naked, dusted in gold as was every other wait staff, server, and bartender. He grinned as Nairobia leaned further over the bar and her hungry gaze slid down his body and fastened on the meaty dick hanging between his muscular thighs.

Mmm.

Josiah.

Josiah.

Josiah.

He was drool inducing as was everyone else who would work the club, including the deejays and the bouncers. It was a mandatory requirement—to be beautiful, to be sexy, to be…fuckable, whether you were dressed or undressed. And, oh how he was so, so very *fuckable.*

Nairobia knew she would feed the staff her pussy and she'd feast on their hard dicks, and weeping cunts. But rule number one: she would not, ever, indulge the patrons' libidos. No, no, no. Sexing the clientele would make for bad business. And fucking over good coin was not how she'd managed to brand her name, and her delectable talents. No matter how many thousands of dollars would pour into her club tonight—or on any other night, no matter how many loins would ache for her loving touch, she wouldn't cross the axiomatic line. Not with the patrons.

She fixed her gaze on the sight before her. The swells of Josiah's biceps made her clit tingle, but fucking him right this very moment was the farthest thing from her mind. She wanted his long tongue on her clit, in her pussy.

She whispered in his ear, "My poison tonight is, *een natte tong op mijn kut.*" A wet tongue on my pussy.

He smiled, then replied huskily, "Your every wish is my command, Mademoiselle." His bulging chest muscles and abs rippled. Even the sight of his thick forearms, lined with wide veins, made her pussy churn in delight. She imagined him using her naked body as his human bench-press, lifting her up over his head the way one would a set of one hundred-pound barbells.

Nairobia inhaled deeply and held it. She rubbed a smooth hand over his rock-hard pectorals, right before pushing out a warm gush of cinnamon-scented breath, slipping her tongue into his ear and telling him how her pussy whispered from beneath her gown, how it longed for his long, thick tongue. *"Mijn poes verlangt naar uw tong."*

He understood nothing she said, which made it that more alluring. *He will submit to me,* she told herself. *As they all will, offering me his tongue…and his big, thick cock, if I so desire it.*

Josiah disappeared from sight as a rich, sexy ballad filled the air. Nairobia blinked. Then a sly grin eased over her lips as she prowled around the bar. There he was. Lying on the tiled floor behind the bar on his back, his hands behind his head, his dick lying languidly across his rippled belly. He waited for her as the DJ played a song that opened up with the sound of a rainstorm and a female moaning.

"What is this he is playing?" she asked once she made her way around the other side of the bar. "Feelin' This," he told her. By a group called Profile, spelled with a *Y* instead of an *I. Profyle.* That it was played in some movie. "Motives," he added. She didn't know the movie, but she liked the seductiveness of the song.

Mmm.

She purred low in the back of her throat, hiking her gown up over her curvaceous hips. "Yes. Feel this wet *kut.* Taste it." She squatted low. Straddled his face. Lowered her quivering pussy onto his waiting tongue. Then slowly rocked her hips. She murmured in her native tongue, "*Maken graag miijn kut. Voeden mijn poesje je tong. Ja*, my darling, *jaaaaa*." Then she repeated herself in English. "Yes, my darling, yessss. Make love to my cunt. Feed my pussy your tongue."

He groaned into her trembling slit.

A spasm wracked her entire body. Nibbling, licking, sucking on her clit, his teeth lightly grazed it before capturing it between his lips. She moaned.

His fingers spread open her wet lips and he greedily tongued her, suckled her, flickering over her clit, feasting on her wet pussy. "Mmm, *ja, ja, ja*…" She spasmed around his tongue and fingers, her nectar coating his tongue. "Yes, yes, yes. *Mijn natte kut likken*…" She demanded he lick her wet pussy.

And he did.

He licked. Licked. Licked. Licked.

"Fuck," he muttered against her lust-flared labia. He sucked on her lips. Wickedly kissed her *kut*. Breathed it in. Tongued her clit. Her hips rocked in sensuous rhythm. His stiff tongue speared her pussy. And she moaned as he made a growling sound that echoed along her silken walls. "Aaaargh, aaaah, aaaah…"

She glanced over her shoulder. He was fisting his thick cock. Her mouth watered, her pussy got wetter. She smothered him in her wetness as he fucked her with his tongue.

"Oh, yesss, oooh…mmm…so wet…*uw tong*…mmm…*zo fijn*…" Your tongue…mmm…so good…

She threw her head back, eyes rolling in the back of her head. Peaking toward orgasm, she swallowed, her breath hitching a bit. Nairobia bucked against Josiah's face, her clitoris swollen and achy, her cunt roiling in pleasure. Seconds later, liquid heat squirted out of her. With low moans, he drank her juices, swallowing, swallowing.

She grinded into his mouth, riding another wave, wrenching out one last orgasm, before lifting her hips and pulling his wagging tongue from the wet space between her thighs.

She stood.

Satiated.

For the moment...

She always needed more.

Always wanted more.

Always.

Josiah shot to his feet, and Nairobia reached for his collar and pulled him into her. She licked his lips. Then kissed him, tasting her on him, his tongue, his mouth drenched in her juices.

She broke the kiss and stepped back from him.

"Have I pleased you, Mademoiselle?"

"Oh, yes, my love, yes. Your mouth and tongue are heavenly." She reached for his plump dick. Grabbed it in her hand. "I will have you in my chambers. And fuck you into my cunt, my darling. Soon." She stroked him. He dipped at the knees. Allowed his hips to roll, his dick thickening, lengthening, in her grasp.

The bulbous head of his dick swelled. Sticky nectar streamed from out of its slit. His mouthwatering cock stretched to enormous proportion, causing her firm grip to stretch, to loosen. She grabbed him with both hands. He became fevered with lust as she stroked him. Brought him to the edge. Taunted him. Slowly fucked his cock into her two-handed fist, her wrists twisting in delight as she stroked him to nirvana.

His muscles tightened.

Brows drawn tight, he groaned in anticipation, in...heated need.

She could have easily dropped to her knees before him. Devoured him. Drained him. Bathed him with her tongue. Sucked his scrumptious cock into her mouth, the length of him sucked down into

her throat, the head blocking her airway. But she wouldn't dare.
Not tonight.

She could feel the swelling of his nut right below the crown.
And she imagined him saying—*if* he spoke Dutch, *"Zuigen mijn dick teef."* Suck my dick, bitch. She moaned at the thought. "Mm. *Ik wil voelen van deze grote lul in mijn kont."*

He groaned. "Aaah, yes. Whatever the fuck it is you said, yes, yes, yes. Aaah…aaarrgh…" She translated for him. Told him she wanted to feel it in her ass. He grunted his approval, leaking onto her hand. Furiously thrusting his hips, he wanted relief. Craved it.

His balls tightened.

She lazily glided her moist tongue over her lips.

Oh how she could milk him to release with her hungry, wet mouth. Or bend over the bar and offer him the inside of her pulsing pussy.

But she wouldn't.

The Weeknd sang about a girl being worth it when she finally let go of Josiah's throbbing cock and he took it into his own eager hand, fist pumping away.

She smiled watching him watching her with hazy eyes. She told him to come for her, to get lost in the pleasure. After all, this is what her club was all about. Pleasure. Sweet release. A split-second later, he was growling, throwing his head back, roaring over the music, bellowing.

And then…

Heat jetted out from his cock, his milky seeds spilling out onto the bar's floor. She stalked over to him. Lifted his hand to her mouth, and licked his thick fingers clean, sucking them into her mouth—one by one, before easing up on her tiptoes and kissing him ever so lightly on the lips. Then offering him her tongue. He sucked it into his mouth, and their tongues danced in the remnants of his juices and hers.

"Allow your balls to fill, my love," she said, finally pulling away from him. "And prepare for opening." And then she was gone, stepping into the glass elevator, ascending to the second floor. The doors slid open, and she stepped off. She looked down over the elaborate gold railing, taking in the spectacular view. The club was certainly a breathtaking sight to behold.

Red-bottom-heeled models—a dozen or so, beautiful women she'd hand-selected from around the world to work in her establishment—wore pasties shimmering in Swarovski crystals and matching thongs and elaborate, bejeweled masks. Their male counterparts, sun-kissed, chisel-chested male models, were donned in loincloths and wore silk domino masks. Chords of muscle in their powerful thighs, big dicks and big, heavy balls were prerequisites.

Oh how she loved big dick. Its taste, its feel, stretching her mouth, stretching her walls, stretching her ass; the delicious burn, causing her to cream and mewl in deliciousness.

Mmm.

Nairobia squeezed her inner walls as she swept a gaze around the mostly empty club, then up at the three large, white Persian-carpeted cages suspended in air by thick ropes of metal chain. In a matter of moments, each cage would lower and two female models would step in one; two males and one woman would endeavor into another; and, in the final cage, two women and one male would venture inside. Then the cages would rise midway. And the caged lovers would hover in the air fucking and sucking, feasting on their anonymous lover's eager sexes.

Huge statues, along with life-size erotic paintings of men and women in coitus, depicting threesomes and cunnilingus, and a variation of other lusty positions were situated throughout the club under the glow of sultry lighting.

The whole vibe oozed sensuality.

It dripped sex.

Rose petals scattered about, a spiral staircase wound up to the second and third and fourth and fifth floors, where there was a bubbling fountain in the center of the second floor, flames dancing across the water's surface, and more oversized sofas. The third floor held stadium-style seating for live shows. And behind a set of double French doors was The Playground, a room filled with every type of sex toy imaginable, exclusively from her adult-toy line, *Nasty*.

The fourth floor featured two large stages for the male and female exotic dancers, along with another bar and DJ booth. Down the hall there was a cognac lounge and humidor area that was equipped with a full cigar bar stocked with the most exquisite brands, where aficionadas could smoke their favorite cigars and sip some of the world's finest cognacs.

There were floor-to-ceiling windows and transparent floors looking down the club's five flights. Each top floor had spectacular views of the Hudson River. The fifth floor opened up to a five thousand-square-foot rooftop garden with retractable walls and roof, along with an enclosed penthouse lounge.

The spiral stairs also descended down into the basement level, or the Love Tomb, as Nairobia called it. Gas lamps lit the way to a Roman-style sauna with polished wood benches stretched along the walls; a heated pool was on the other end for those who wanted to frolic in the sparkling blue water. Several passageways led to numerous chambers beneath the club, where patrons who craved their sex with a bit more kink could indulge their fetishes.

Each floor offered a condom and lube station that was set up like a candy station, with every type of condom in large crystal bowls—in every imaginable color and size—for those who preferred to play safe.

Although every member had to be tested and was required to retest every three months—and provide written documentation—if they wished to remain a member in good standing. Patrons had the option to fuck raw…or wrapped.

The choice was theirs.

A variety of lubes were also at the ready for those who might tap out after a few rounds or who simply weren't blessed with the juiciest cunts and needed a little something to keep from scraping up a man's cock. There was nothing worse than sandbag pussy, and a man having to go home with a chafed dick.

Rihanna's "Skin" poured out of the speakers as Nairobia looked over the railing one last time. Bare-footed, naked bodies airbrushed in gold paint—long dicks, voluptuous breasts, and colossal asses on display for all to see—sauntered around the club in tune to the beat, preparing to take posts throughout the exquisite space as human statues. They'd be holding gold candelabras, lighting the way to nirvana.

The lights dimmed.

Oh, yes, in less than an hour—hidden behind thick mahogany doors, a decadent sea of pleasure awaited everyone who stepped across its threshold.

The sign above the doors that opened up into the club's Italian-marbled foyer read: ENTER IF YOU DARE. LEAVE BEHIND YOUR APPREHENSIONS. SURRENDER TO YOUR DESIRES…AND STEP INSIDE THE PLEASURE ZONE.

Nairobia smiled wickedly.

TWO

The sweet notes of "Send Me Out" by Kelela played as flames swayed across the stunning fountain's water on the club's second level. The song was sexy. The artist's voice poured out of the speakers like warm honey. And it made the air around Nairobia thicken with sexual energy. She skimmed a hand down her neck, then allowed it to glide down over her pulsing body.

The club's grand opening had exceeded her wildest expectations. It was close to midnight, the bewitching hour—the freak hour, and the club was packed with hard-bodied hunks and curvaceously heeled women thrust in the throes of decadence.

Nairobia's tongue slid across her teeth as she gathered the drool that formed in her mouth, and swallowed. Salacious thoughts and forbidden desires bloomed into sinful realities right before her and she was…well, she was shamelessly wet.

Sweet pussies slid down hard dicks. Thick dicks pushed through swollen cunts; balls pushing against asses, while wandering hands skated up bodies to cup bouncing breasts. The music and the delicious sounds of orgasms echoed around the club. Permeated its walls.

And Nairobia was floating.

On lust.

On mounting desire.

Nipples peaked, her gaze swept around the sensual space, her arousal heightening. The luminosity of the flickering firelight from the gas lamps reflected beautifully off tiled mosaics of notoriously lusty satyrs and maidens. The walls illuminated by the fire's glow and its dancing flames gave the illusion that the satyrs were moving, their hips *thrusting*.

She felt herself growing lusciously wetter.

Not from the room's ambiance, but from the sight of a mocha-colored, mink-lashed vixen being ravaged by three delectable, broad-shouldered chocolate hunks. She was straddling the one with the braids, his long legs stretched out along an oversized burnt-orange leather sofa as his hips thrust up in her, slicing into her cunt. Another, dark chocolate with dreads, was in back of her, his large hands on either side of her ass cheeks, the ring of her anus stretched around the head of his jumbo-size dick as he eased himself in and out of her, loosening the way inside her tunnel. The third hunk, bald, caramel-coated bliss, stood with both his hands on his hips, his legs spread wide, his balls dangling over Mr. Braids' face as Mink Lash licked the head of his dick.

Nairobia felt the urging need to squeeze her thighs together, and she did.

There was a deep throb, a sweet aching, spreading through her pussy as she watched the four lovers in the throes of unadulterated pleasure. Her cunt caught fire, enflaming her slickened lips. She could feel the flames quickly spreading through her asshole, swirling up and around her clit. Her whole body became engulfed in heat.

And she needed relief.

She needed something long, hard and thick to hose down the inferno raging inside her.

She needed to be…*fucked*.

And the hedonistic sounds of hot, raw, sweaty *fucking* only coiled her desires tighter and tighter, squeezing her soul helpless until she found herself nearly breathless.

Nairobia knew she needed to turn on her heel and flee to the comforts of her plush office and watch all of the *fuck*tivities from the safety of monitors that gave her a bird's-eye view of every wicked, every sordid, every salacious act performed in every part of her establishment before she broke her rule and joined in. Temptation was gnawing away at her resolve.

Yet, there she stood.

Fixed on the glorious sight before her.

Mink Lash opened herself to her three stallions, giving into the dick and the heat. She moaned loudly over the music. There was a delicious rhythm all three cocks found, thrusting and retreating, fucking into her holes. Pure bliss coated Mink Lash's face as she grunted and groaned and writhed around each thrusting cock.

Nairobia knew all too well the delicious feeling of being penetrated in all three orifices, pussy and ass and throat stuffed balls deep. She almost envied the busty vixen as she captured their meaty cocks in her greedy holes.

Bitch.

Watching the foursome was slowly uncoiling all her self-control, and Nairobia knew it. She felt it. But she wasn't ready to leave. No. Not yet.

So she prowled closer.

The voyeur in her wanted—no, *needed*—to see more. They knew she was watching them and they fucked with wild abandon, wanting to be seen. Wanting to be heard. Wanting their wet, scented heat to be savored.

Nairobia seductively licked her lips, breathing in the aphrodisiac. She wanted to bite into the air and swallow up the musky heat.

"Yes, my loves," she rasped, edging over toward the sofa. "Stretch her to the hilt. Fuck into her soul." She stalked around the sofa. "Fuck *haar ademloos...*" Fuck her breathless.

She found herself taking a slender, manicured finger and ever so lightly sliding it down Carmel-Coated's spine, then over the globes of his muscled ass. She reveled in its magnificence. Next to a long, thick dick, a man's beautiful muscled-ass was another one of her weaknesses.

He thrust hard into Mink Lash's mouth and then slowed. "Open your fuckin' mouth," he ordered. She did what she was told, and he slid his dick gently over her tongue, rubbing the tip over her lips before plunging back inside the wetness of her juicy mouth. Mink Lash gagged. "Suck that dick," he growled.

Nairobia smiled. Mink Lash was a good, greedy bitch. She knew how to submit to the dick. Nairobia admired that. And obviously so did her three lovers. Her pussy and ass and mouth were spread wide with cock. Caramel-Coated feathered a hand over Mink Lash's cheek, then took her head and held it in place, thrusting, deeper, pushing every inch of himself to the back of throat.

"Yes, my love," Nairobia whispered in his ear, "clog her throat with your hard cock. Crush her windpipe, my darling." Spit splashed out of Mink Lash's mouth, her eyes watered. Nairobia slapped Caramel-Coated's ass and he let out a groan.

The freak in her wanted to drop down, spread her warm hands over his sweat-glistened gluteus and reward him with a tongue lick or two along the crack of his ass.

But she resisted.

She preyed around him. Moved on to Dark Chocolate. She allowed her hands to stretch out across his thick shoulders. She stood in back of him, her body practically pressing into his, and marveled in the feel of his muscles as they fanned out. She ran her hands along his traps. Then caressed his delts, before spreading out over his back again. Her hands slid down to cup his ass and her mouth watered. Unlike Caramel-Coated's smooth, hairless ass, his was lightly covered with hair along the seam of his crack. Nairobia gripped it and he thrust himself deeper, his cock getting lost inside the warmth of Mink Lash's ass.

Mink Lash mewled, her big bouncy ass sucking in his dick as Nairobia glided her hands underneath him and cupped his low-hanging balls. She lightly bounced them in the palm of her hand. They were heavy. And hairy. As was his cock. And it looked scrumptiously heavy as it disappeared in and out of Mink Lash's ass; the thick, curly hairs at his groin brushing against her flesh.

Nairobia's own ass clenched in want. Desire settled in the pit of her cunt and spread along her inner walls, tightening viciously around her clit, spreading like a wildfire.

Her voice heavy with lust, she muttered words in Dutch. Told him to shove his cock deep in her ass, to fuck her shitless.

He groaned in response. She moved on to Mink Lash. "Yes, my darling," Nairobia whispered, leaning into her ear as she gurgled and clutched around a mouthful of cock. "Surrender to the dick. Worship it. Let it own you, my love. Or," she sweetly warned, "I'll put a crop to your ass, my darling."

She reached for one of Mink Lash's taut nipples, and pinched it. Twisted it.

Mink Lash screamed. Cried out as her three lovers impaled her with their engorged cocks. They fucked her mercilessly. She struggled for breath. Then cried out again. Her yell was sharp, echoing out across the room as they savagely shredded her throat and ass and cunt to pieces.

Arousal hummed through Nairobia's veins. She felt her entire pussy quiver and tingle with need. There was no way she would get through the night without clutching a dick into her cunt and orgasming around it.

Oh, how she would love the feel of a warm nut coating the walls of her pussy. The thought only fueled the fires of lust enflaming her.

She was ready to come. Not later tonight. Not tomorrow.

Right *now*.

And she would.

THREE

"*Ja, ja, ja,*" Nairobia hissed over her shoulder, taking in the sight of Josiah's sweat-glistened body as he spread open her ass and pierced the back of her cunt with his engorged cock. "Fuck me, my love…yesss…take my *kut*…mmm…oooh …aaah…*ja, ja, ja…*"

The club's fucktivities had her libido in overdrive. She couldn't—*wouldn't*—go another second without the stretch of a cock inside her. So she summoned Josiah to her office. And now he was in back of her pleasing her, fucking into her cunt like a wild, horny bull. She clenched around him, and he groaned in pleasure as she orgasmed around his cock.

She was deep. Wet. Hot. And tighter than Josiah remembered. It made him sizzle. Everything about Nairobia was overwhelming, her body, her pussy. She was potent. God, how he loved her pussy. He loved the way it spoke to him; the way it wetly sucked and slurped in his dick, her ass clapping around him with every demanding thrust. He felt himself drowning in her silken heat.

His neck lolled back, his eyes rolling up in his head as she handled the heavy length of his cock with ease, her silky walls bringing him closer to the edge of climax. Neck straining, abdominal muscles tightening, he cried out, "Aaah, fuck!"

He didn't want to come. Not yet. He'd just gotten inside her. And it'd been weeks since she'd given him her pussy. So he needed to savor it, needed to linger in it for as long as humanly possible.

But her clenching walls and endless wetness were making it difficult to keep from exploding inside her.

He pulled out, leaving Nairobia empty, the crown of his dick slick and swollen, the condom already filled with pre-cum. He wanted to feel her naked pussy on his dick, skin-to-skin. But she wouldn't allow it. Said he needed to earn her raw cunt.

He sank to his knees and tongued her ass, greedily licking the puckering rim as he slid two fingers into her pussy. His tongue lashed over her hole, then darted around it as his probing fingers found her spot, and stroked on its swollen heat.

Nairobia mewled. Clawed at her desk, her nails raking viciously over its surface. "Suck my clit," she demanded, her need rolling out into a whisper. She arched her back. Spread her legs wider. Reached back and pulled open her ass cheeks. Allowed him access and privilege to all of her swollen sex.

Josiah took in the magnificence of her cunt, her labia, her slit, her scent, then positioned himself beneath her, her sex hovering over his face. He opened his drooling mouth, and latched onto her clit and sucked in.

"Oooh, *ja, ja*…bite it," she pushed out, panting.

He slid his tongue from her core to her clit. Then, with teeth and tongue, he nipped at the swollen bud, then grazed it, scraping her with pleasure until, finally, biting into it. Heat and sparks shot from Nairobia's clit, then gushed out from her slit, soaking Josiah's face with her liquid desire.

Nairobia cupped her breasts. Tweaked her nipples until they ached. She closed her thighs around Josiah's head, and rode his face. He groaned. Grabbed his cock and slowly stroked himself. Her pussy was so luscious, so heavenly. Lost in the throes, he licked and sucked and nibbled and bit.

He ravished her sex, filling her with desire; her sweet body tightening, then going slack, then rigid all over again with need.

Euphoric.

Intoxicating.

Another climax crashed against Nairobia's walls, splashing out in heavy waves of bliss as expletives filled the room, and her body convulsed, her pussy melting into her young lover's mouth.

Mouth curling up in a satisfying smile, Josiah was ready to plunge back inside her wet, slippery heat. Blood hummed in his body for release, for her. He needed back inside her. *Now.*

Quick on his feet, his sheathed erection bobbed up and down in anticipation. An instant later, Josiah's cock was at the opening of her slit again, his head aching for entry past swollen tissues, back into her juicy flesh.

Nairobia drew in a breath as Josiah touched her, using his fingers to open her wide, making her more needy, more aroused. Then she inhaled, feeling the plump head of his cock at her entrance— all slick, all ready—wanting him, waiting for him. Her pussy clenched emptiness. She longed to have him back inside her.

"Bury yourself in me," she said, in a voice heavy with lust and heat. "Lose yourself inside me, my love."

Josiah groaned. Oh how he wanted back inside her so desperately, lost in her sweet heat. Without words, he gave her what she asked for. Between gnashed teeth, he gave himself what he craved. What they both craved.

His dick sank deep.

His toes curled. Nairobia grew wetter, her swollen lips wrapping around his shaft with each thrust into her body, her cunt quaking with joy. Exploding. Clenching. Cock drawing out, then plunging in, drawing out, then plunging in. In. Out. In. Out.

Rhythmic pounding lifted Nairobia's body up with every thrust. Her walls tightened. Delicious pleasure soared through her body, clutching, crashing and colliding into Josiah's own crippling need. "Feel that," she rasped. "My wet heat for you? My needy cunt greedy for you."

He moaned. "Yes, baby, yes…aaah, shit, yeah…" He thrust deeper, faster. "Shit!" The friction and heat were making him mindless. Nairobia pushed back against him, her ass slamming against his groin.

"Harder."

Josiah groaned, bucking faster, sawing his cock back and forth, in and out, his swollen shaft pillaging her core. Nairobia heard herself crying out in pleasure. Heard the slap of Josiah's body against hers.

"*Ja, ja, ja*…you like this wet *kut*…you love how it makes your cock crazed, no? Mmm. My *kut* is so wet for you…fuck *meeee*, my love…"

And then—oh thank God—Josiah slipped his hand between their bodies to stroke her clit, more pleasure swirling in brilliant heat. Wet flames engulfing him. And her.

Josiah quickly pulled out. And moments later, Nairobia was up on her desk, her legs pulled back, her knees pressed toward her breasts, gazing up at Josiah as he snatched off his condom and fisted himself over her creamy cunt.

"Yes, my darling, yes," Nairobia cooed, pulling open her sensitive folds. "Come all over my *kut*. Let me feel your heat…"

"Aaaah, aaaah, aaah…ohhhhh, fuck…" Dazed at the sight of her pink insides clenching and quivering, her juices pooling out, Josiah choked back a yell as heavy ropes of scorching cum gushed from his cock, lapped against her labia, and singed her clit.

Over and over, he pumped himself, squeezing his cock, releasing ribbon after ribbon of his seeds, emptying his swollen sac. He pumped himself, milked out every last drop, until he had nothing else left.

Nairobia moaned as he laid his still-hard dick over her slit and slid back and forth over it, before sliding its head over her sex and slathering his warm, milky seed into her flesh.

"Lick me," she hissed, her hips slowly undulating.

Tongue out, Josiah leaned in, and buried his face between her thighs, licking her clean.

She melted all over again.

FOUR

"Yo, what's good, my beauties, cuties, hookers, hoes, pimps, and playboys...this is ya boy, Mar*Sell*, coming at you live with another steamy segment of 'Creepin' 'n' Freakin' After Dark.' All of my peeps who get down with me know how I like to serve it up: Hot, raw 'n' ohhhh so nasty. And tonight will be no exception as I introduce to you one of the world's sexiest women alive. So drop them drawz, sit back...relax...light a candle...pour yourself a glass of your favorite wine and let me mentally lick you into climax..."

Nairobia shamelessly eyed the radio host, licking her lips, as he adjusted his headphones. Dark-chocolate skin melted over ropes of thick muscle. Long-lashed eyelids wrapped around smoldering dark-chocolate eyes. Full, luscious lips made for pussy sucking. Long, thick, manicured fingers. Everything about this man was... deliciously *big*. From his feet to his hands and scrumptious dick, he was six feet eight inches of heavenly perfection.

Marcel Kennedy.

Her pussy moistened at one of many sweet memories. His dick wrapped around her plump, juicy lips. Her tongue swirling over and around its thick, plum-shaped head, licking up and down the thick-veined shaft. His fingers lovingly stretching her cunt, stroking her insides until she felt her asshole clenching and her uterus starting to shake.

She could still hear his deep voice, coaxing her, urging her, to suck him into her wet, velvety mouth. One inch…two inches, four inches…then six. She cupped his heavy cum-filled balls—she felt them swelling with want and need in her hand. Her mouth glided back up to the head of his dick, suckling the head, nursing it in the way a hungry newborn would its mother's nipple, before gliding her mouth back down over his thick, pulsing shaft, sucking in eight inches of dick…nine inches…eleven inches…

She moaned inwardly.

Two fingers became three fingers, getting lost in her wetness, the slickness of her pussy, making it easy for a fourth finger to ease its way in. And then there was another set of hands, soft and gentle, pulling open her ass. She felt the heat of their touch on her skin, the heat of breath caressing her asshole, then the tip of a wet, heated tongue sweeping over its opening, teasing her, taunting her.

She gasped in ecstasy, sucking in the remaining two inches of dick as his sexy wife tongue-fucked her asshole.

Marika.

God rest her beautiful soul.

Marika and Marcel had been the perfect couple. Open and loving. Bold and daring, both with voracious sex drives that allowed the other to openly indulge in surreptitious sexual encounters while the other either watched or, more often than not, participated in. Oh how they were the epitome of uninhibited lovers. Behind closed doors and between the sheets, Marcel and Marika were everything Nairobia could have ever hoped for. They were as close to sexual perfection as it could ever get.

Almost.

Nairobia sighed inwardly. She still couldn't believe it was a year since her unfortunate death, no…*murder.*

How tragic.

Killed by some crazed bitch. A one-night stand turned obsession that cost them everything. Marika lost her life. And Marcel lost his soul mate, his lover, his whole world crumbling down around him by the pull of a trigger.

Nairobia had attended the closed-casket funeral. Hundreds and hundreds and hundreds of celebrities, professional athletes, and mourners flocked to pay their respects. Her heart broke into a thousand pieces seeing Marcel so broken, so lost. Beset with grief. And regret. And guilt.

He was inconsolable for months after Marika's death. He'd cut himself off from the world. Cocooned from the prying eyes of the press and media. Practically vanishing.

And here he was now, one year later...looking more desirable than ever.

So, so...*fuck*able.

"...She's an author, model, and one of the most desired women around the globe..."

Nairobia blinked, catching Marcel's burning gaze on her flushed face.

"...That's right, my freaky peeps...tonight's guest is a woman who has graced the covers of both *Playboy* and *Penthouse*; is the CEO of her own production company, Sweet Pleasures; and, has built a multimillion-dollar empire with her exclusive adult toy line, *Nasty*. Just how we like it..."

I am good pussy.

I am good loving.

I am unforgettable fucking.

Nairobia smiled, slowly crossing one sultry leg over another, then clasping her hands in her lap.

"Without further ado, Tri-State, I introduce to you Nairobia Jansen..." There was the sound of applause coming from in back of her. There were several dozen guests in the studio who'd been invited to tonight's live show. They would all be given a basket of sex toys and edibles from her latest collection, along with an autographed copy of her book, *Good Pussy*.

Nairobia adjusted her headphones. "Ooh, thank you, my darling," she said seductively, while trying to temper her Dutch accent without completely disposing of it. She reached over and touched Marcel's hand. "It's so good to see you, my love. Thanks for having me on the show."

"Nah, baby, thank *you*. It's damn good seeing you, too. And, yo, trust. I *see* you, baby." His gaze slowly roamed over her. "Yo, my peeps…I wish you could see what I'm seeing right now…" There was howling and whistling in back of them from the studio's male guests, and even some of the females. "This beauty is mad sexy, yo. Spellbinding. She smells good. Looks good. She's damn intoxicating, my peeps. I can see why so many muhfuckas have been turned out. You got mofos drooling all over the place."

Nairobia glanced over her shoulder and smiled.

Always known for flaunting her most famous assets—her voluptuous breasts, curvaceous hips, and beautiful round ass—in scandalous wears, tonight was no exception.

She was scantily sheathed in a diamond net mini-dress with a neckline that plunged below her navel and a slit that crawled up to her bare pussy with an open back to match, leaving nothing—and I do mean, *nothing*, to the imagination. She stood. Placed a hand on her hip, and slowly turned, giving everyone in the room an up close and personal view of her body. She had an ass like two basketballs, and men loved seeing it bounce. She was tempted to bend over, grab her ankles and make it shake in Marcel's handsome face. But that would be tasteless. She was a lady, after all. Classy.

"Damn, baby," Marcel said low and husky wiping fingers over his brow. "It's getting hot in here. Yo, Tri-State, this beauty has ya boy sweating like crazy."

She smiled, taking her seat. "I take that to mean you like, no?"

"Do I *like?*" He licked his lips. She was sure it was subconsciously done as his lusty gaze scanned her body again. She had that effect on many. "Yo, let's just say you're starting to awaken the beast."

Her cunt clenched. "Mmm," she purred, reaching over and running a manicured finger along the inside of his thigh. "And does this beast bite?" she teased.

Marcel let out a low groan. "Nah, nah, baby. As long as you're petting it and keeping it wet, it's good." She gave him a knowing glance. And good it was. Her finger traced the length of his ever-growing cock. Then, before she wrapped her hand around the stretched fabric of his pants and groped it, she snatched her hand away—acutely aware of the audience in back of them, even though she *loved* being watched.

She feigned disappointment. "Too bad, my darling. *Ik hou van zijn gebeten.*" I love being bitten.

She watched his Adam's apple bob up and down as he swallowed. "Damn, baby, there you go talking that sexy shit." His crooked grin, followed by dimples, and a glint of mischief dancing in the pools of his eyes, had her slowly melting.

Damn him.

"*Arrêtez d'essayer de me tourner.*"

He told her in his smooth, honey-rich voice to stop trying to turn him on. Lucky for her—and to her world travels, she understood French. She smiled. "I'd never do anything you wouldn't want done," she confessed, flirting with the fantasy of a good fucking.

"Aiight, aiight. I heard that," he said, shaking his head. "Don't tempt me. Word up, yo. But before I get sidetracked wit' tryna chain you to this desk 'n' having my way with you, let's jump right into tonight's interview."

She nodded and smiled. "Yes, let's."

"Aiight. You've modeled. You've done porn. You've graced the covers of magazines. You've written two best sellers. You've created your own sex toy line…" Nairobia nodded as he listed her accomplishments. "And now you've opened your very own club in Manhattan. Tell us about it."

"Yes, my darling. I am a woman of many talents…" She shifted in her seat. Uncrossed her legs, spreading them open, teasingly, then closing them, crossing her legs at the ankles, revealing her thigh, and the whole side of her soft, bouncy ass.

Marcel struggled to keep focused. Struggled to keep from fucking her right here, right now. Nairobia saw the hunger in his eyes and wondered how long it'd been since he'd plunged his colossal dick into some pussy. Good pussy.

Before Marika's death, she would have spread open her thighs and welcomed him inside her wet, silky walls, while her mouth made love to his wife's clit, her tongue sinking into her cum-sodden cunt.

But, now…?

So much had changed.

She'd changed.

He'd changed.

Those clandestine encounters between the three of them were now bittersweet memories to be tucked away, and savored.

Marika was gone. Dead.

Still…

She fought from rocking her hips in abandon as the memory of him sucking her engorged nipples, one at a time, between his lips, into the waiting heat of his mouth; his wet tongue lashing, his teeth grazing each—

Marcel cleared his throat, pulling her from her lustful reverie.

She shifted in her seat. Crossed her right leg over her left.

Their gazes met and, in that moment, she imagined him standing. Then unzipping his pants to drag the heavy length of his cock out, it straining toward her own waiting, hungry mouth. She could almost taste the sweetness of his semen on her tongue.

Almost.

A moan caught in the back of her throat as she swallowed down the thought of him flooding her mouth with nut. Her leg bounced over her knee in a failed attempt at cutting off the budding ache between her thighs.

Marcel parted his lips to speak. But she didn't, she wouldn't, allow it. "The Pleasure Zone, my darling, is a club like no other," she said, her tone coated with the slightest hint of her Danish and African ancestry—her mother was Dutch, her father Nigerian. "It's an ultra-chic, upscale, private, For Adults Only club, where hedonistic desires unfold under one lavish roof."

Marcel groaned. "Damn. Sounds like it's gonna be hot 'n' poppin'. But, yo, let's pause for a moment. Let's rap a lil' about your joint, *Good Pus*—bleep—*sy*, real quick. Why'd you write a joint like that? And what makes pus—*bleep*—sy good pus—*bleep*—sy?"

Nairobia licked her lips. "Well, my darling. Good pus—*bleep*—sy is what every woman likes to believe she has. But, unfortunately, it's more than a state of mind. It's a state of being. Good pus—*bleep*—sy is a mixture of things. It's the sound, the taste, the feel all wrapped around the ability and the want to indulge in its partner's inner-most desires. It's wet, juicy, tight…built for every stroke, every inch, giving you limitless access. Good pus—*bleep*—sy pulls you in; it's not just milking the dic—*bleep*, it's gripping and sucking out a man's soul, it's emptying out his balls. It's snatching his breath.

"Good pus—*bleep*—sy makes a man clutch the sheets and cry out and brings him to his knees. It makes an already unstable man lose what's left of his mind, having him busting out windows and stalking you. Good pus—*bleep*—sy, my darling, speaks to the dic—*bleep*…"

"*God*daaaaayum, baby." He licked his lips. "Yo, you hear that, Tri-State? She said good snatch speaks to the dingaling. Damn. Tell us what it's saying, baby, when we're balls deep in that ish?"

Nairobia slowly opened her legs. Gave Marcel a sneak peek of her smooth, honey-coated cunt. "It's saying…beat me. Fuc—*bleep* me. Dic—*bleep* me down. Make me cum…"

She closed her thighs.

Marcel stared at her. She knew what the fuck she was doing to him. And it had his balls bubbling, his dick rock-hard. "Damn," he breathed out, then quickly told his listening audience that they were going into a commercial break. He eased back from his microphone as Miguel crooned "Pussy Is Mine" over the air. The producer Nina walked over to them smiling. "Girl, you're about to cause a riot up in here. The testosterone level in the back is through the roof. It's crazy right now. I'm loving it."

Nairobia smiled. "I aim to please, my love."

Nia blushed. But she couldn't help herself from sliding her gaze over the slopes of Nairobia's breasts, her protruding nipples, before catching Nairobia's eyes staring up at her. Nia's face flushed shamefully. Nairobia smirked, standing up to give her—and the burning gazes in back of her—another full view of all of her lusciousness. She reached for Nia's delicate hands and placed them up to her firm, upright breasts.

They were real. Beautiful. And always ready to be fondled.

The audience went wild watching the station's producer sensually cup Nairobia's breasts. The act surprised Nia and made her instantly moist. She'd never felt another woman's breasts before, though she'd had her share of bi-curious fantasies.

Nairobia leaned in to Nia's ear and whispered, "My hot, silky cunt feels even better." She winked at the shocked producer, then let her hands go. Another time, another place, she might have been compelled to offer Nia a taste of her nectar. Or maybe, snatch her by her hair and snap her neck back, shoving her hand in between her thighs, then stroking her trembling sex until it clutched and dripped.

Marcel's wife had once told Nairobia she was the kind of woman who'd capture her heart, if she were to ever fall in love with a woman. Why she thought of that at this very moment, she didn't know. But what she did know—without a doubt, was, she could turn this little young perky tart inside out. One night in the sheets with her, she'd ruin the poor soul so damn good she'd be up late at night prowling the streets for pussy.

Nairobia almost laughed at the visual. Nia nervously muttered something inaudible before scrambling off. Marcel smiled at Nairobia, his gaze studying her as if he knew her wicked thoughts. He pressed his legs shut. Opened them. Then shut them again.

His dick was beyond hard. It was harder than granite and steel combined.

Without him saying it, without her looking down at it, she knew it was.

Marcel's dick was always hard.

He loved fucking.

Almost as much as she did.

It took Nia several moments to catch her breath and pull herself together before she finally signaling that they were back on live in five…four…three…two …one…

"Aiight, aiight…what it do, my freaky peeps. If you're just tuning in to the Tri-State area's hottest radio station, 93.3 *The Heat*, you don't know what you've been missing. Tonight we have the sexy Nairobia Jansen with us. And we were briefly discussing her book, *Good Pus*—bleep—*sy*. Go out 'n' cop ya copy, *ASAP*.

"Now, switching gears for a sec. Let's go back 'n' talk a lil' more about this new club of yours. What exactly is The Pleasure Zone, love?" Marcel inquired. "A gentleman's club? And how can we get put on? I know the listeners wanna know how they can wave their freak flags up in that piece. Isn't that right, Tri-State?"

"Well, my loves," she said into her microphone. "It's where every illicit fantasy you can ever imagine is indulged, and one's wildest dreams become their realities. It's an adventure where anything— and I do mean *anything*—goes." Her gray eyes locked on Marcel's heated gaze. "Entry, however," she continued a beat later, "is tighter than a virgin in a chastity belt." She let out a soft chuckle. "You must be on either the guest list, or own a membership."

"Oh, word. And how much is a membership?" She told him five grand for a silver membership, ten grand for gold, and twenty thousand for platinum. He whistled. "Daaaaaaayum. That's some expensive shit."

"There is no price tag for the ultimate pleasure, my darling. However, the experience alone will be worth every cent."

"Damn. I'm looking forward to coming through."

"I look forward to having you," she said, innuendo hovering over them. "And I promise you. Everyone who steps across its thresh-old will experience a night of decadence. One they'll never forget."

"Aiight. You heard it here, my freaky peeps. The Pleasure Zone is the spot to be. So get ya paper up. And let the freak games begin. Nairobia, mad love, baby. And much success to you."

That was her cue. Her time on the air was over. "Thank you, my love," she said as Liv Warfield's "Soul Lifted" started to float through the airwaves. She removed her headset, standing.

Marcel rose from his seat, then quickly pulled her into his arms, heat covering his body. He stole a kiss, a light brushing of his lips against hers. But he wanted more. He wanted his dick in her, bad.

"Thanks for coming through, baby," he rasped. "It was good

seeing you." His voice rolled over her, making her entire body tingle in a way that caught her off guard, but she didn't deny herself the pleasure. He leaned down and kissed her on the cheek. Then said, "You make me wanna throw you down 'n' fuck the everlasting shit out of you. All I want is to be inside you. It's been too long, baby." Nairobia imagined him naked, dick swinging, balls hanging, as his hand slipped down to the small of her back.

She breathed him in.

She had to capture the moment, feel him one last time.

Her hand curled around the print of his never-ending dick, arousal slowly creaming her slit. She wondered if he could smell her in the air around them.

"Marcel," she said, the words coming out in little more than a breath. In Danish, she muttered, "Yes, it has." She squeezed him one last time. Stroked him. Then stepped back from him, gathering her clutch, and leaving behind his throbbing cock and a burning trail of desire.

FIVE

ENTER IF YOU DARE...LEAVE BEHIND YOUR APPREHENSIONS
AND SURRENDER TO YOUR DESIRES...

Nairobia's lips curled into a devilish grin as The Pleasure Zone's slogan played in her head over and over and over. It rotated heavily in her mind like that of one of her favorite songs in her expansive music collection.

Enter if you dare...

It made her pussy wet and tingly.

She licked her lips.

Caressed her slit. Toyed with her clit.

The Pleasure Zone was more than sordid sex. It was a journey into the unknown. It was exploration. It was a voyage to toe-curling pleasure. It was uncovering passion. It was being tested beyond one's own limits. Completely surrendering.

As far as Nairobia was concerned, entrance into her private club was a privilege, not one's right. Holding partners accountable in bed was a right, as was being sexually fulfilled. But the doors to The Pleasure Zone were for the elite, for the uninhibited, for the freaky.

Shame and guilt had no place there. It wasn't welcomed. They were simply useless emotions. And Nairobia had no tolerance for either. She believed in the motto: live and let live. But she'd be goddamned if she'd ever allow her establishment to be infiltrated by a bunch of pillow princesses, frigid bitches, or prudes who lived their lives sexually repressed because they feared giving into their deepest desires, which is why every member was rigorously screened—once, twice, three times—before offered their exclusive membership.

No, no, fear kept you trapped and stuck in mediocre sex, in unhappy marriages, and screwed-up relationships. It kept you enslaved to misery. And Nairobia knew plenty of men and women who were stuck in sexless situations, or in relationships where the sex lacked sparks, where their libidos remained neglected. She knew men and women who were too afraid to expect that their needs be met in the sheets by their partners. Too afraid to open their mouths and let their mates know what they yearned for.

Mmph.

Sinful.

Her cunt ached and wept for them. *Bless their little clogged, horny souls,* she thought as she slid a hand between her legs, then smacked her pussy, hard. She smacked it again, harder.

"*Slecht* kitty," she pushed out in a whisper. Bad kitty.

She lovingly scolded it for giving a damn. Their neglected loins weren't her crosses to bear. If they wanted to be sexually frustrated, then let them. She'd been demanding good fucking since her days in the porn industry.

Staged scripts or not, she refused to feign orgasms when she was nowhere near the edge. She refused to pretend the dick was good when it was trash. She despised trashy dicks. Despised lazy-dicked men. And she hated rabbit-fucking even more. And lots of her porn-star counterparts—with the exception of Lexington Steele who knew how to fuck, and made her cunt cream every time he'd fucked her in the ass with his eleven-incher—were only good for that. Rapid pounding. Oh no, no, no. No man was going to pull her hair and pound her pussy or slap her ass and bang it out its frame unless *she* demanded it, unless *she* begged for it.

Paid profession or not, she never gave a damn about porn protocol. She'd always been vocal about her needs, her wants, during her whole career as Pleasure. And she'd been known to walk off sets right in the middle of a scene if she wasn't being sexed right.

Just like all women wanted to believe they had good pussy, men wanted to believe even more that they had good dick. Their egos depended on it. But Nairobia refused to stroke either their fragile egos *or* their good-for-nothing dicks. White, black, Latino, Asian—and she'd let her share of them fuck her too (only in the ass though)—it didn't matter. Trash dick was trash dick no matter whom it was attached to.

Why call herself *Pleasure* if she wasn't being pleasured, if she wasn't able to be a pleasure to others, because the dick was attached to a worthless fuck?

She was porn-star royalty. Period. Goddamn you. Thank you very much. And she'd demand nothing less than premium dick and top-of-the-line fucking.

However, in the beginning of her fifteen-year career, she'd been labeled *difficult*. Called a *bitch*. Told she was *hard* to work with. Had been threatened with being *blackballed* from the industry. But in the end, her relentlessness and amazing bedroom skills won out. Her pussy was her prized possession. And many craved it. Her name rang bells in the industry. And she eventually became one of the most sought out porn-stars in the adult entertainment industry, nationally *and* internationally. And she had the numerous XBIZ, XRCO and AVN award trophies in the best actress and best body categories, as well as the many Porn Star of the Year and Twistys Treats of the Year awards, to prove it. And being inducted into the AVN hall of fame in 2013 had really been one of her greatest moments in her career.

Not to mention the fact that she'd won the AVN Female Performer of the Year Award three years in a row. And had snagged the TLARAW Best Sex Toy Award for her two most popular, best-selling sex toys: the Pleasure Deep Penetration Vibrating Pussy and Ass doll, and the Pleasure Cream Pie Pussy. Men paid a pretty penny to fuck her molded genitalia, while fantasizing about having the real thing.

Oh how the imagination could be so beautiful with the aid of good lube and a delectable sex toy.

Nairobia looked up at her eleven-foot ceiling and smiled. She'd been officially out of the industry for the last three years, however, her reputation still followed her. She'd made her mark and had retired from the industry still beautiful, still healthy and—thank God, still sane—and with tons of contacts.

She had a lot to be proud of.

Never one to let good talent go to waste, she took her skills and her most lethal *assets* and founded her own production company, Sweet Pleasures. In the beginning, she'd performed exclusively for her own company for a few years before bringing on other aspiring and well-seasoned porn-stars into the company's fold. Now her company—based in California—had annual revenue of twenty million dollars, with a staff of ten.

Nairobia was thirty-six, wealthy, and so very thankful she hadn't succumbed to AIDS or some other filthy STD or a drug addiction like so many others she'd known during her career.

She shuddered at the thought.

Bottom line, after years of award-winning performances and limitless fucking, Nairobia knew a thing or two—or *three*—about mind-blowing orgasms. And pleasuring.

She swallowed back the recollections of her days as Pleasure just as erotic heat roiled its way to the pit of her pussy. The memory of Lexington Steele was the sizzling source of her budding need for release.

Zoete hemelen (sweet heavens)! She couldn't help herself. Lexington Steele had been her first encounter, and had ripped her ripened cherry to shreds. He'd fucked her senseless. Fucked her inside out and upside down. Then fucked her all over again. And thinking back to the first time he'd plowed his big, juicy black cock in her asshole, making her cream heavy out her cunt, out her ass, all over his dick—had her dizzy with lust. She remembered vividly how she'd gotten her first taste of her ass slathered on his cock, before he'd yanked it from her mouth and shot thick ribbons of his gooey spunk in her mouth, her face, and all in her luscious mane.

Nairobia was eighteen.

My how time flew. Eighteen years later, and she was a well-seasoned, well-fucked, multi-orgasmic, dick-riding goddess. Her tongue slid over her lips. Then curled into a sly grin. She made a mental note to give Lexington a call. Just to say *hallo*, of course.

Thoughts of him made her horny. She spread her smooth thighs, wide. Slid a hand over her hungry sex. Toyed with her clit. Teased it ever so lightly until her nipples peaked and goose bumps lined her skin, and her body began to shudder.

Mmm.

Her free hand glided over her taut belly. Then up over her left breast. She pulled at her nipple. Lightly pinched it. Then let go.

A delicious orgasm needed to simmer, slowly. And she decided to wring hers out slowly. It would be sweet torture, but well worth the wait.

She reached for her crystal flute, taking a slow, deliberate sip of her Moët & Chandon. She swirled the bubbly around in her mouth, allowing it to settle on her tongue, savoring the elixir, before she swallowed.

Whap!

Shuddering at the thought of not being completely fulfilled

sexually, she brought her hand down on her sex again. Her clit throbbed from the biting sensation. She couldn't figure out for the life of her why she was feeling bad for the sexually neglected when it was by their own doing. It was a choice. Settling, that was. And that's what they had chosen to do. Settle.

Ze neuken.

That's right. Fuck them. She smoothed her hand over the sting, caressing her pretty pussy—the cunt that had launched a thousand or more hard dicks into her pleasure zone, and wrenched out an infinite amount of orgasms from each of them; the cunt that had brought her share of men to their knees, crippling them of their free will.

Oh yes. Like in her book, *Good Pussy*, she was good pussy. And she knew it. And good pussy, like that of a good tongue—or good dick—should never go to waste.

Ever.

Nairobia pressed a button on what appeared to be a remote control. Moments later, Josiah appeared walking into the room in his naked glory, his dick swinging with purpose. He was exquisite. Heat bubbled in her veins just looking at him.

So young.

So virile.

So hard.

So willing.

So, so full of thick, tasty cum.

She licked her lips. And he grinned sexily at her, his gaze honed in on her rich with promise. And understanding. She felt the ache inside her sizzle and spread. The sight of him, the thought of his mouth and tongue on her pussy, obsessed her to no end.

"Come, my darling," she cooed, spreading her legs wider. "Lick me to orgasm."

"Your pleasure is my pleasure," he rasped, moving quickly toward her.

Nairobia smiled.

She'd trained him well. Taught him how to pleasure her with abandon. He'd been just an inexperienced boy trying to be a man when she'd met him—twenty, to be exact. But he'd been eager to have her, when he'd approached her with his boyish charm, good looks, and pussy-melting body.

Damn him for being so relentless. He'd pursued her during her entire stay on the beautiful island of St. Lucia. Though he was Dominican and Haitian, his family owned a home in Castries— the island's capital, where he'd been staying for the summer while working at Jade Mountain, an exclusive resort, where she'd been vacationing—*alone*.

A week into her stay, she'd given into his advances, a mixture of curiosity and wanton need making the decision to fuck him that more easy. Seeing him naked had been like staring into a kaleidoscope bursting with vibrant colors. He was breathtaking. And his thick-veined cock was mouthwatering. But he'd come disappointingly fast and hard the first few times she'd mounted him and rode him down into the resort's plush mattress. So what if he'd been able to become erect again quickly? Quickies were not wanted, desired, or celebrated in Nairobia's world.

It made her pussy angry.

Her cunt needed long, deep stroke sessions. It needed staying power. It had a mind of its own, and it became enraged when it wasn't fucked with the utmost care. It was insatiable. And not many could rise to the occasion of keeping it—or *her*—satisfied. So she'd tossed him out of her suite numerous times in the wee hours of the night. And, yet, he'd return the following evening, scratching at her door like some sex-starved puppy, eager to learn, eager to please, willing to be fired from his job. And she'd sneak him in and let him try all over again.

It had been his limitless enthusiasm that had won Nairobia over. Now, look at him. Four years later, he'd matured, evolved, into a sexual beast, her very own human sex toy.

He lowered himself to his knees. Breathed her cunt in. Licked his lips. Then leaned into her glorious slit and tasted it. She moaned low in the back of her throat as he lapped at it with his tongue. Then he swept his tongue into her cunt. And the low sound he made with his greedy wet licks gave Nairobia the most delicious sensations. Slick sounds mingled with her breaths while he rubbed circles over her greedy clitoris with the pad of his thumb. Nairobia's hips slowly rocked up to his touch, to his mouth. He ran the tip of his tongue over her clit, then dipped it inside, before sliding it over her throbbing pussy lips.

She gasped in pleasure. It was always about pleasure, always about multiple orgasms. And Josiah had her teetering at the edge, had her clinging on to the toe-curling sensations. "Yes, yes, yes, my love," she cooed. *"mijn kut likken…"* (lick my cunt) *"…het plagen…"* (tease it) *"….maken het graag…"* (make love to it).

He had no fucking clue what she was saying, but he loved hearing her speak in her native tongue. It sounded hot. And it made him hotter. Made him harder. He held in a curse. Goddamn, shit, fuck.

"Mmm, baby…you taste so good," he murmured, his voice vibrating over her labia. He licked her slowly, savoring every part of her sex; her exotic scent rising, her slick juices pouring out over his tongue and fingers.

Oh God…his tongue. His lips. His mouth. The way he caressed her pussy with loving care made her want to talk dirty to him. She felt the pleasure escalating. She looked down at him between her legs and licked her glossed lips. He looked so delectable kneeling before her, praising her, worshiping her.

It was a glorious sight to behold, him pulling her lips apart, capturing her clit with his mouth, his eyes closing as he reached between his own thighs and began to stroke himself with one hand, bringing himself to the edge, while his other hand, fingers pushing inside her, stroked her to sweet bliss.

Josiah loved her pussy. And he loved pleasing it. Eating it. Fucking it. If he could crawl in and spend the rest of his life in it, he would. That's what he'd told her once. And those words stuck with her. She wasn't in love with him. She lusted him. Deeply cared for him. But love? No, no, no. She loved his tongue. Loved his touch. Loved his cock.

Nairobia's scent was stronger, sharper with arousal. A blast of heat shot over the crown of his cock as he stroked himself. He groaned, desperate to hear her beg him to fuck her. More blood rushed through his shaft. His dick was thick and hard and aching, impatient. Nairobia inflamed him. She unraveled him. He wanted to rise up and push himself inside her, wanted to fuck himself into her sweet channel, become engulfed in her wet flames.

But only if she demanded it, only if she—

She moaned. Spread her thighs wider, offering more of herself to him. He slid his hands beneath her, cupping her ass, then brought her cunt up to his mouth like a bowl filled with liquid cherries. She gasped in expectation, in burning want. Then he stuck his tongue in her ass and licked her on the verge of an orgasm, before running it up the slit of her pussy to her clit.

Two fingers entered her as he licked over her clit.

"Yes, my darling, yes…mmm…aaaah…oooh, *ja, ja, ja…!*"

She closed her eyes, inhaling her sweet scent as Josiah pulled her open and stroked his fingers back inside her wetness, then slow pulling out and smearing his fingers up and down and over her clit, before sucking it into his mouth.

Nairobia gasped. An orgasm sizzled hot in her belly. This beautiful specimen before her, between her legs, tongue wedged between her sweet, puffy lips, was about to bring her to ecstasy. She was right there, hanging on the cusp of a delicious orgasm when her cell rang. She cursed it a thousand times over.

But instead of allowing it to roll over to voicemail, she answered it, breathlessly, without looking at the number. *"Ja?"* she rasped, a mixture of annoyance and delight coloring her tone.

"Hey, beautiful," the voice on the other end crooned.

Nairobia moaned in the back of her throat and melted into her boy-toy's hungry mouth. The sound of her caller's voice used to always made her weak with want. *"Ooh, ja, ja.* Mmm..." Josiah licked her pussy with deep, long strokes. *"Hallo,* my darling, Mar*Sell*..."

He laughed. "Damn, baby. Sounds like I caught you at a bad time. What are you doing?"

Nairobia moaned again. *"Met mijn kut gegeten."*

Marcel didn't know much Dutch. But he knew enough to know it had something to do with her pussy. Fuck, fuck, fuck. He missed the feel of being inside her. His dick stirred in his Armani slacks. It had been over a year since he'd had Nairobia's pussy stretched over and around his dick. Her pussy was like heated velvet. Silky, wet walls that lovingly gripped and pulled and milked a hard dick, his dick, to orgasm.

Seeing her in his studio over a week ago, after so many months, had him wanting her, had him needing her. Since his wife's murder, he hadn't needed or wanted release with anyone as bad as he wanted, needed, it from Nairobia. He wanted to get lost in the heat of her insides again. Bad. He'd fuck her raw. Nut in her sweet, tight cunt, then lick her clean.

If only for a night.

She moaned again. "Damn, baby. What, you getting fucked?" he asked, feeling his dick stretch and come alive.

She panted. "Yes, my love…with…oooh…mmm…a long…*ja, ja*… thick…mmm…tongue…uhhhh…oooh, *ja, ja*…lick my *kut*…" She grabbed the back of Josiah's head, pushing his face, his mouth, his tongue deeper into her wet, hungry sex. She wanted him smothered in her juices. "Tongue my pussy, my darling."

Marcel groaned on the other end of the phone. "Damn, baby… is he eating that pussy right?"

"Yes, my darling, yes…he's a good pussy eater…mmm…"

Josiah looked up at her, a smile eased over his cunt-juiced lips. He licked her wet seam, then slid a finger inside of her, felt around in her heat. Fucked into her core. Searched for her pleasure zone. Then, when he found it, wedged a second finger in. Nairobia gasped. He loved the sound of her juices. Loved the way the folds of her pussy flared. Her pussy was heaven for him.

He tugged her succulent clit between his lips and softly sucked, nursing on it until it swelled and throbbed against his tongue. Nairobia was on the verge of coming. She dropped her cell, forgetting…

Marcel who?

Marcel what?

He could listen to her cries of pleasure from the floor for all she cared. Her pussy fluttered around Josiah's tongue and fingers.

And then she came.

SIX

The following afternoon, Nairobia pulled into the subterranean parking garage of her apartment building and was greeted by one of the valet, Ethan. He greeted her with a smile as he opened her door and helped her out of her Lamborghini.

She returned his smile and thanked him, before sliding him a twenty-dollar bill. She didn't have to tip him, but she found the blond-haired, blue-eyed attendant adorable. And she saw how he always looked at her every time he was on shift. With eyes filled with curiosity and heated want.

A part of her wanted to indulge his desires with a dose of good pussy. But she knew fucking him would more than likely ruin him. She didn't want that on her conscience. Being responsible for turning out yet another, horny manchild.

Josiah was more than enough.

Before him, there had been her young Spanish lover, Felipe. And the one before Felipe had been her Italian Stallion, Carlo. And then there'd been Javier, Zeus, Adam, Mark, Lewis…in that order.

Nairobia never kept any of them around for longer than a year, however. There was no need to. All her lovers ever needed was, a year of good-fuck training from her. She saw it her duty, her sole mission in life, to deliver them toe-curling sexual experiences by teaching them how to be good in bed, how to be open-minded and sexually adventurous. The more open-minded, good lovers there were in the world, the less likely for women to be sexually unfulfilled.

She believed you had to train them—potential lovers—up while they were still young...and *teachable*. Legal age of, course. Still, you had to get them while they were ripe and ready for the picking, or you might end up with another sexually challenged—or *worse*, a selfish lover. Nairobia found most men were too set in their egotistical ways and too difficult to open their minds and free them of their sexual repression. Unlocking their inhibitions was more of a challenge than it was sometimes worth.

So she'd rather seduce them while they were young. Fuck one young cock at a time. Turn him out. Then send him out into the world. Hard cocked and horny, prepared to make a woman's toes curl, fucking deep inside her pleasure zone.

Surprisingly, she'd still kept Josiah around.

He was her special one.

"Enjoy your evening, Miss Jensen," Ethan said, cutting into her reverie.

Nairobia raked her gaze up and down his body, taking in all five feet, eleven inches of him. He was too meek for her. And way too short. But he had a lean, muscular build. And he had a strong jaw, strong nose, angular face, and high cheekbones. He wore his thick golden-blond hair longish, the ends brushing past his collar. And he had a deep, powerful voice to be so young. Oh he was young. But he was so ripe and ready to have his cock in her.

Oh if only he were a bit more aggressive. She found the meek ones to be...well, let's see...potentially hazardous. They had the potential to become stalker-*ish* after a dose of good pussy. That was the last thing she needed on her hands, some sex-crazed man-child pestering her for more pussy. She knew the aftermath of such foolishness. She'd been there, done that: the harassing phone calls, the gifts, the stalking.

Nairobia had no interest in drama.

She shuddered at the memory. "Thank you," she said. She licked her lips and leaned into Ethan. "I'm sure I'd enjoy you more, my love. Perhaps one day." Then she kissed him on the cheek, keenly aware by the lump in his pants that she'd aroused him, once again.

Designer bag dangling in the crook of her arm, Nairobia sauntered off, while Ethan struggled to keep his eyes off her as he always did. Yes. It was no secret. He had a burning crush on her. And he kept a hard-on in his pants for her. All the time.

Shit. She was Nairobia Jansen after all.

He'd been working part-time at the luxury high-rise building for close to three years, but the minute he'd found out who she was, he'd gone and ordered every porn movie she'd ever starred in. He even had clips of her on his smartphone for those midday moments when he wanted, needed, release.

As if she could feel his eyes on her, Nairobia glanced over her shoulder and caught him staring at her ass.

Busted.

She winked at him, then sassily strutted toward the elevator, leaving behind the faint trace of her floral perfume. She smiled, and swung her hips to give him a little show. He was so aroused, his balls heavy, his cock aching. Every time he saw her, she made his body hot and sizzling.

He inhaled. Suddenly he could smell her. Just her. Among the exhaust fumes and rubber, somehow Nairobia was the only thing he breathed in.

God, what a horn dog he was. He couldn't help himself. No matter how hard he tried, he couldn't keep his eyes off her. Couldn't stop lusting her. Couldn't stop imagining the feel of his hands caressing her body.

A sly smile slid over her lips as she envisioned Ethan in back of her, still staring at her ass. One time she'd caught his gaze locked on her protruding nipples, and she'd asked him flat-out if he wanted to lick them, suckle them in his mouth, if he wanted to tease them with his fingertips.

Oh, and there was the time she'd brazenly asked, whispering the question low enough for only him to hear, how big his cock was, causing the twenty-one-year-old NYU student's cheeks to flush.

Another time, she slipped out of a pair of lacy thongs—on one of those rare occasions when she wore underwear—right in front of him and slipped them inside his pocket. "Take me to bed with you tonight, my love," she'd said, low and sultry.

He'd almost come on himself on the spot.

But those sweet panties were in his hands and up to his nose way before he'd ever made it home. He spent his whole hour lunch break sniffing her, licking the inside of her crotch wildly as he watched his favorite porn movie of her, *Cum Snatcher*.

And there had been a few other awkwardly enticing moments…

Nairobia's gaze lingered on the young valet's face, and he blushed, not sure if he should turn his own gaze away or run over and press her up against the elevator door and fuck her.

He had nice-sized balls, but God, he wished he had bigger ones to do it. He'd fuck her good, too. Or at least try.

Nairobia placed the palm of her hand up against the security panel, and the elevator leading to the top floor slid open.

She blew him a kiss, and Ethan swallowed as the elevator closed behind her. He stood a moment longer, then, before he slid behind Nairobia's car's wheel and drove off to park it in its designated spot, he looked around the parking garage, then slyly leaned in and sniffed her seat. He licked over the leather where he believed her pussy and ass had been. He imagined she tasted like honey and felt incredible. *Fuck, yeah, baby.* He fantasized about having his long cock in her. She was nothing like the campus sluts he rammed. Nairobia was a grown woman. Experienced in the art of fucking. And he wanted to be covered in her heat. Painted by her warm juices.

She was his ultimate fantasy.

One day he'd drum up the courage to make it a reality. He knew he'd probably bust fast. Of course he would. In most of her five-minute movie clips, she'd been able to make the male actors in them come quick. And they were pros for Christ's sake!

Ethan groaned inwardly. He'd never last with her.

He'd have to take two Viagra pills and a Red Bull.

And invest in a cock ring to keep up with the infamous Pleasure.

SEVEN

S he leaned back against the brass handrail, and glanced up at the surveillance camera mounted in the corner and mouthed, "Lick my *kut*." She enunciated the words as if she were speaking them directly to someone. She felt like being naughty. Felt like giving whatever horny soul was on duty today a peep show. But she licked her lips instead, and pulled out her ringing smartphone. She didn't recognize the number, but answered anyway.

"Ja?"

"Bonjour belle." Hello, beautiful.

Nairobia caught a glimpse of herself in the elevator's mirrored walls, and smoothed her hair over her shoulder. She had to admit, she looked remarkably stunning for a woman who'd only had three hours of sleep. Beauty was only skin deep. Nairobia knew that. And she knew once the physical beauty faded, if you didn't have good character, if you didn't have a good heart, then you had nothing. She'd known over the years beautiful people who were downright ugly on the inside.

Nairobia ran a hand through her hair. "Mar*Sell, mijn liefde. Bonjour.* To what do I owe the pleasure of this call?"

"I was thinking about you, baby," he said in his rich baritone voice. "What are you doing tomorrow?"

"I'm not sure." The elevator dinged, announcing the arrival to Nairobia's floor. She stepped out into the marble foyer when the door slid open. "You know I live for today, my darling. Why?"

"Well, baby, how about you live for tomorrow and let me whisk you away for the day?"

"Oh, no, no, my love." Nairobia placed her palm against a wall-mounted security pad. "You call me from a private number, then want to kidnap *me* for the day?" The smooth mahogany doors slid open automatically. And Nairobia stepped in.

Marcel chuckled. "I'm not tryna *kidnap* you, baby. Simply tryna spend the day with a beautiful woman on my arm."

Nairobia dropped her bag and keys on the credenza, then headed to the kitchen. She grabbed a bottle of coconut water from the massive stainless steel refrigerator and popped it open.

"Flattery will get you almost everywhere," she teased.

Marcel smiled. "Ah. Then *permettez-moi de vous ai...*" Let me have you. *"Pour la journée."* For the day.

She took a sip from her water. *"Mmm,"* she moaned, leaning up against the kitchen's marble island. She had a state-of-the-art kitchen, but couldn't tell you where most of the cookware or cutlery were. "You know I love when you speak in French. Keep it up and I may lose myself to you."

"Then come lose yourself, bébé. Come to Rhode Island with me."

"Rhode Island? Why on heaven's earth would I want to go there?"

"Because I'd like to be in the presence of your company," Marcel said firmly.

"And you've called me from a private number, no? You call me private like I'm some stranger to you, no?"

Marcel shook his head. "Definitely not. My bad, baby. I'll text you my number if that'll make you feel better."

She feigned a pout. "It is too late. Damage already done."

"Nah, it's never too late, baby."

He'd forgotten to unblock his number when he'd called her as he had the few other times he'd called her. He'd had his number changed and blocked shortly after Marika's death. Too many people had had his number, and the phone calls had been overwhelming—from those wishing to extend their condolences to the nosey-asses wanting to know what had happened to the relentless reporters fishing for a story. It'd been too much for him to deal with, so he changed his number, cutting off everyone's direct access to him.

Less than a second later, Nairobia's phone pinged.

"Did my text come through, yet?" he asked.

"Yes," she said as she opened the text with his number. "Now, tell me. What exactly is in Rhode Island?"

Marcel smiled. "Laila Reynolds is giving a free concert in Providence," he stated in a matter-of-fact tone. As if she would have known this already.

"Oh," was all she said.

Nairobia liked the R&B singer. She even had both her albums. Autographed. But that did not mean she stayed abreast of the sultry songstress' tour schedule. However, she did enjoy a good show. "When? And where?"

"Tomorrow afternoon. At India Pointe Park. And I want you to attend with me."

Nairobia took another swig of her water. "And why would I do that, Mar*Sell*, my darling? So you can hold me hostage, then have your way with me?"

Marcel laughed. "I assure you, baby. I won't do anything against your will. *Je le promet.*" I promise.

"Very good. Now what time shall I expect you?"

Marcel grinned. "My driver should be there around ten."

"Okay. I'll be down in the lobby waiting."

"We'll be outside waiting. See you tomorrow, beautiful."

Nairobia smiled. "Oh, and Mar*Sell*, my darling…"

"Yeah, what's up?"

"*U krijgt geen kut.*" You will get no pussy.

Marcel knew what kut meant, so he knew that whatever she said had something to do with her pussy. He groaned. "Damn, baby. What did you say about that beautiful pussy of yours?"

Nairobia repeated herself. "I said you would not get any of it. You will not taste, or feel the insides of my *kut. Comprendre?*"

Marcel let out a hearty laugh. "Aiight, baby. I understand. Whatever you say. But how about some of those sweet kisses instead?"

Nairobia felt her body warming. There was something deliciously irresistible about him. But she would not allow him to become a distraction for her. Period.

"You have done nothing to earn my sweet kisses, my darling."

He groaned. "Then I'll have to fix that."

"Best wishes, my love."

Marcel laughed. "See you in the morning, baby."

She disconnected the call, smiling.

EIGHT

T en a.m. sharp, Nairobia stepped out of her building to find Marcel's driver waiting. The moment he saw her, he tipped his hat and smiled as he opened the rear door.

The car smelled of leather and *him*.

Dial soap, a hint of cologne, and a dizzying amount of testosterone. She slipped inside the car and leaned over and kissed him on the cheek once she was safely inside and the door shut. She hadn't seen him since the radio interview, and he looked good, casually dressed in a pair of white linen pants and a white linen shirt that was partly opened, revealing a smooth expanse of chocolate chest. No, on second thought, he looked better than good. He looked...damn good, fucking good—and everything else in between.

He had his iPhone and iPad both on the bench beside him.

"Hello, beautiful," he said, his lips slowly curving into a sensual grin. "It's good seeing you."

"And you as well, Mar*Sell*, my love," she said, settling back in the seat across from him. This was the first time the two of them—not counting down at the radio station—were alone, together... without Marika.

For some reason, the space in the cabin all of a sudden felt smaller, the air between them thicker. She shifted in her seat.

"How's the club going?" he asked, cutting into the awkwardness that had seeped in around them.

"Deliciously sinful," she said, her tongue gliding over her lips. "You should come indulge your curiosity."

Marcel smiled, his undivided attention on her. "I may do that."

"And so you should."

There was that awkwardness again.

But why?

He was no stranger to her, or she to him. So what was the problem?

Marcel's phone rang. It was one of his many assistants, Arianna. He reached for it, and picked up. "Mar*Sell* here."

"Hi, Mar*Sell*. It's me. Arianna," she said as if he didn't already know.

"Yeah. What's up?" he asked calmly, his gaze dancing up and down the length of Nairobia's body.

"I know you're on your way up to Rhode Island. So real quick. I need to know where you put the contracts that were on your desk yesterday."

He stroked his chin. "Oh. They're locked in my desk, bottom left drawer. Why?"

"Lance asked for them," she told him. Lance Green was one of MK records' attorneys, and Marcel's fraternity brother.

"Oh, aiight. Make sure you lock my desk when you find them."

"Already done."

"Aiight. Hold it down until I get back."

"Always, Boss. Have fun at the concert. And bring me back something. Nothing cheap, either."

He laughed. "I'll see what I can do." The call ended and he set his phone back on the bench. He looked over at Nairobia. "Now, back to you, beautiful lady. I'm all yours for the rest of the trip."

Nairobia glanced out the window and noticed that they weren't headed toward any of the airports. She blinked. "Um, we are flying, no?"

He shook his head. "Oh, I didn't tell you. My bad, baby. We're driving up."

Surprise flickered in her eyes. "Driving?"

"Yeah. It's only a three-hour ride. I thought it'd be a nice leisure drive. Give us more time to spend together, before the concert…"

She blinked. He expected her to travel *three* hours in a car? Cars were made to sit in for travel under an hour; anything else required flying. What was this world coming to? She could have flown and met him there.

"And *when* do you expect to have me back?"

"Tonight. After the concert." She flashed him a "you-have-got-to-be-kidding-me" look. Amusement curled his lips. "Don't worry, baby. We'll fly back by helicopter."

She glanced at her watch. Laila's concert had better be worth the trip.

Nairobia couldn't stand it any longer. She had to ask, "How have you been holding up, Mar*Sell*, really?"

"I've been good, baby." He smiled. "I'm even better now that I'm in the company of a beautiful woman."

She blushed. "Thank you. But that's not what I'm speaking of. I want to know how are you?"

He knew what she meant. His smile faded and he stared intently into her eyes. She saw the muscle in his jaw twitch.

"The truth, Mar*Sell*," she insisted. "How has it been for you *without* Marika?"

He sighed, dragging a hand over his face. Then took a deep breath. He hadn't been willing to talk about this—Marika's death—with anyone. Not even his boy, Carlos.

He took a deep breath, and pushed out, "It's been hell, baby."

She gave him a look filled with compassion. She couldn't identify with losing a life partner, but she knew the pain of losing someone you loved. She'd felt that crushing pain right after her mother had died. But that was totally different. Her mother hadn't been murdered. Her death hadn't been tragic.

Marika's was.

Marcel felt his chest tighten. "Some days are better than most now," he continued. "But overall, I'm making it."

Nairobia nodded. "It gets better, no?"

He stared at her, his eyes glistening, then shrugged one shoulder. "Does it?"

Nairobia reached over and grabbed his hand. She shook her head. "No. Not for a long while does the pain start to not feel so numbing."

He swallowed. "I don't think it ever leaves you," he said solemnly. "I'll probably end up carrying mine to my grave."

She cringed. "No, Mar*Sell*, my darling. You can't let it."

He cast his eyes downward, then turned his head, and stared off somewhere far. "I don't know how to." His voice came out low and hoarse. "It's all I have left."

She reached over and placed her finger under his chin, and turned his head to look at her. "No, my love. Look at me." Reluctantly, his eyes met hers. "You have so much more."

Nairobia stared into his gaze, and saw something in him she hadn't seen before. Vulnerability. Sadness. He was still haunted by that night. The night Marika was murdered over the airwaves, the entire nightmare unfolding over the radio before hundreds of thousands of listeners. Never in a million years would Marcel have thought one sexual encounter would turn deadly.

But it had. Thanks to that Ramona bitch. She had fucked his whole world up, all because she couldn't have him to herself. He knew without a doubt he had good dick. That he was a phenomenal lover. And before marrying Marika he'd had his share of crazies stalking him for the dick. Wanting him to wife them up. But he'd always found a way to shake them off. But Ramona had been relentless. And the craziest of them all.

"I want you to tell the whole world out there listening about our night together... Tell them how your wife fucked me in my ass while I rode your dick. Tell them how this bitch ate my pussy while I sucked all over your long, black...tell your listeners how you and this bitch took turns fucking me and how much I loved it... No man has ever made me come the way you did, MarSell. Your dick is so big...And you ate my pussy better than any man I've ever been with...I have never had tongue make my whole body shake..."

And then...somewhere in between the pleading and begging... it was over.

A shot was fired.

Fear slashed through Marcel's heart as he leapt from his seat, cupping his hands tightly over his headphones.

The gun went off twice more. Then there was a deadly, crippling silence over the airwaves.

Marika was dead.

He still hadn't fully forgiven himself for it. He still blamed himself for her death. Yet, he wanted desperately to get back to living, to move on with his life. But it wasn't easy.

Nairobia saw Marcel's eyes brimming with tears. Tears he fought to keep at bay, and they pulled at her heartstrings. He hadn't talked about that night, or about the loneliness he'd felt thereafter, with anyone.

"Marcel, my darling," she said, her heart filled with compassion and warmth. "You have to forgive yourself. No matter what you think you did, or didn't do, you have to let go of it. Holding on to guilt will only eat away at you."

"It already has," he said, inhaling a sharp breath. His tears fell.

Fuck. He hadn't wanted her to see him getting emotional. Shit. He squeezed his lids shut, pinching inside the corners of his eyes.

Seeing him pained hurt her. She wanted to be there for him. But wasn't sure if she knew how to be. She wasn't the emotional kind of woman. She couldn't be being in the adult film industry for as long as she had. She had to pretend to be detached. And over the years, she'd become an empty vessel filled with hard cock.

Nairobia leaned over in her seat and wrapped her arms around his neck. She hadn't expected anything more than him hugging her back, but, to her surprise, he burrowed his face in her neck and wept. She hugged him tightly.

At that moment, something came over her. She wanted to ease his pain.

So she did what any respectable, caring woman in her position would do. She slowly slid to the car floor—inching between his hard thighs, her hands gliding up over hard muscle—and nuzzled her way upward until her jaw rubbed up and down over his crotch, until she felt him grow beneath her.

She glanced up and looked at him through dark lashes. His eyes became wet volcanoes as he looked down at her; his gaze suddenly flaring hot as she lowered his zipper, then pulled open his belt. He didn't try to stop her. Maybe he should. But he didn't want to.

And Nairobia didn't want him to, either.

She wanted to do this—pleasure him—for *him*.

Just this one time, give without getting.

She reached into his silk boxer briefs and dragged his cock out over his pants—smooth, warm chocolate flesh, beautifully thick and ready.

A droplet of pre-cum shimmered on the very tip, and Nairobia's mouth watered as she licked over the slit as one would their favorite ice cream cone. Blades of carnal hit sliced through Marcel's body as Nairobia moaned over his cock, her wet mouth loving over its crown.

His head lolled back.

She eyed him through her lashes, then tightened her soft lips over the swollen head, and flicked over and around it. Marcel hissed. "Aah, shit. *Sucer la bite, bébé.*" Suck that dick, baby.

One hand gripped her hair, urging her, prodding her, to open wider for him. Slowly, he moved his hips, forcing his hot, heavy, enormously thick cock further into her mouth. Nairobia flattened her tongue and extended her sweet offering to him as he filled her mouth with more of him.

She would not let him stretch her neck, no. Not today. She would allow the head to hit the back of her throat and push past her tonsils—into her upper throat, but that was all she would allow him to have. She would take nine inches of him and use her skilled hands to slowly stroke the remaining four inches of him.

She'd suck him until his cock lodged in her throat and robbed her of her breath, then she'd pull out over the length of him, leaving behind trails of spit while stroking her hands up over where her mouth had been, so that her lips could suckle his head again, before spreading over and sucking his large, chocolate, cream-filled balls into her mouth.

Nairobia closed her eyes and sucked Marcel as she focused on delivering him the most exquisite pleasure with her mouth. He shuddered and fisted her hair, and she let out a long, erotic moan over the length of him, sending him further toward the edge of release. Nairobia glided her two thumbs up and down the underside of his wet dick as she drew her mouth away, licking over his head again, before she sucked his head into her mouth again. Marcel's ragged breathing and the slow grind of his hips told her that she was taking him there, bringing him toward an orgasm as she worked his head between her tongue and the slick roof of her hot mouth. She suckled him there for what seemed like an eternity.

Marcel emitted a low growl of satisfaction, then muttered words in French, and Nairobia grew wet in response, dampening the red silk thong she'd worn. The harder she sucked him, the harder he became. The pleasure slowly building became overwhelming.

Marcel had needed this.

Like he needed air.

And Nairobia was giving it to him. Without being asked. Without being prompted. She'd felt his pain, and had wanted to bring him pleasure, to comfort him—lovingly, with her mouth, lips, and tongue. He groaned in deep appreciation as his cock stretched her mouth wider.

"Nairobia, baby…mmm…yeah…like that…give it to me wet…"

The sound of her name in between his manly moans made her pussy burn hotter. The longer she sucked him, the wetter her mouth, the wetter her pussy, became. Her outer cunt lips slickened, causing the air around them to thicken sweetly with her musk.

Breathing in, Marcel groaned. "Oh fuck." Her scent was driving him mad.

Nairobia licked over the crease of Marcel's balls, then dipped her tongue along the center of his ass, then slid it back up the underside of his cock, while her hand cupped over the head of his dick, and milked it, her thumb flicking over his slit.

"Aah, motherfuck, baby…*ta bouche*…aah…yeah, *bébé…est…donc…* aaah…*humide et juteuse…*"

Nairobia smiled over Marcel's cock. Yes, her mouth was wet and juicy. And so was her cunt. So, so very wet.

"Nairobia, baby…aah, shit," he whispered, his fingers tangling in her hair. "Aaah, baby, I'm getting ready to nut for you. Aaah, yeah…uhh…you want this big load, baby…"

Fist pounding either side of the bench, thick, muscular neck stretched back, Marcel groaned low, then growled as his orgasm spread through him like a wildfire.

Nairobia moaned as she sucked, cupping his balls and slowly massaging them, kneading them, tugging them. She wanted to give Marcel release. Wanted the taste of him. She bobbed her head faster, stroked his shaft harder, and squeezed him rhythmically until he exploded inside her mouth, fierce and wild—his heated seeds hitting the back of her throat.

Nairobia sucked with more vigor, momentarily draining him of his pain. She sucked him until he went soft in her mouth, then eased up to meet his hazy gaze and covered his mouth with hers, until their tongues swam and mingled in the heat of his sweet milk.

NINE

Three days later, a crowd of paparazzi was on the ready along the velvet rope outside an extravagant club in Las Vegas. A private party was being hosted in Nairobia's honor for the launch of her new fragrance Sweet Desires.

Hair in a messy updo, the fashionably late beauty hit the red carpet—which was awash with models, actors, and reality TV stars—causing a frenzy of flashbulbs to *pop, pop, pop* as she stepped out of her limo wearing what looked like a strip of gauze around her breasts and hips with a pair of pencil-thin heels. Perfection at its best, she was a paparazzo's dream.

Her hips led the way as she gracefully sauntered up the red carpet, strategically stopping every so often—hand on hip, blowing a kiss, or looking over her shoulder to pose for a zealous photographer or two. She'd thought to bring a date, but then—at the last moment—decided she didn't need to be on the arm of any eye candy tonight.

Josiah could simply wait in her suite for her return.

"Nairobia! Nairobia! Over here, darling!"

"Oh, Nairobia, *dahling!* You look simply delicious! Love your outfit!"

"Nairobia! Over here! Congrats on the release of your new fragrance! Love the samples!"

Wearing a naughty smile, Nairobia struck a suggestive pose.

More cameras clicked.

All the paparazzi were shouting for her, wanting her to turn in their direction, hoping she'd give the gossip hounds something lewd and dirty to salivate over.

She simply waved for the cameras.

"How does it feel to be immortalized?" one of the paps yapped, speaking of the life-like wax figure dozens or so celebrity friends watched Nairobia unveil of herself not less than twenty-four hours ago in Madame Tussaud's Wax Museum at the Venetian Resort, making her the second personality from the adult entertainment world to be enshrined in wax. Jenna Jameson having been the first.

It'd been an auspicious occasion, for sure. And Nairobia was still floating on clouds of joy to be esteemed in such a way. Her attraction would be displayed next to Jenna Jameson's—the porn industry's international superstar—and Playboy Publishing founder Hugh Hefner's wax figures.

She was deeply honored. The gesture was humbling, to say the least.

But tonight was Nairobia's launch party for her new fragrance Sweet Pleasure and she didn't want anything overshadowing that. Not even talk of her fabulous life-sized wax figure.

"It feels heavenly, my love," Nairobia cooed, gliding down the red carpet as though it were a runway.

Once inside the club, music vibrated the walls and a cascade of flashing lights nearly blinded Nairobia as she sashayed her way through a throng of partygoers and ardent admirers. Drinks flowed in abundance. The club was packed to capacity with women wearing shimmering miniscule dresses and men blessed with bodies that appeared straight off the cover of *Men's Health* and *GQ*, while scantily clad models walked around with bottles of Nairobia's sexy and sensual perfume—packed with floral notes, vanilla and jasmine petals—on shiny silver trays, along with the night's specialty drink, Sweet Pleasure.

It was a beautiful sight to behold.

Nairobia plucked a drink off the tray of a passing cocktail waitress, wearing a G-string and glittery pasties. She took a slow sip and winded her hips to a Drake song. She smiled at the cages that hung from the ceiling with body-painted dancers. The scene reminded her of her own club. The bass thumped and the dancing crowd gyrated in time with the frenetic beat of the music.

Red lights splashed over the crowd, and the giant tiles of the dance floor were lit from beneath. Ice sculptures sat on pedestals around the room. But in the center of the club's dance floor was a larger-than-life ice sculpture of a naked Nairobia holding a bottle of her perfume.

On the second level, a gigantic penis adorned with two humongous balls carved out of dark chocolate erupted in the center of the VIP section, spilling rivulets of mouthwatering milk chocolate lava from its dickhead. Nairobia licked her lips at the sight, imagining herself undressing and sliding her body down into the basin of warm chocolate. She decided she wanted one for The Pleasure Zone.

Every second person who sauntered past her, stopped for either hugs and air-kisses—and the occasional, "Let's do lunch," or simply to congratulate her, or to take photos with the statuesque diva. Graciously, she smiled and posed for the cameras.

Eventually, Nairobia hit the dance floor and allowed the music to take over. She shimmied and gyrated her pelvis, teasing the crowd, even dancing provocatively with a few admirers—bumping and grinding into them, feeling their cocks grow painfully hard. Men took turns cutting in, trying to get their thrills for the night, and Nairobia welcomed their roaming hands and warm kisses—on her cheek, of course. Then she graciously moved on to the next.

Across the room she spotted a deliciously dark man standing there, amusement sparkling in his eyes, watching her. His masculine face illuminated every time the lights flashed, and Nairobia noticed how breathtaking he was.

He licked his lips. Nairobia wasn't sure if the sensual gesture was directed at her or not, but she battered her thick lashes over her hypnotizing gray eyes and gave him a mischievous smile—anyway, before slowly pivoting on her "fuck-me" heels, giving him her ass to stare at.

Two hours into the festivities—after all the kisses and good wishes, Nairobia stood by the chocolate penis sliding a finger into the basin, then sucking her chocolate-coated finger into her mouth. Her nipples peaked. She felt eyes on her, so she knelt and licked on one of the gigantic balls, giving onlookers something to fantasize about, before sinking her teeth in and biting out a chunk of chocolate.

Cameras flashed at the erotic sight.

Seconds later, Kelly Rowland's "Motivation" started playing. Nairobia stood and noticed the same man from across the room walking through the crowd toward her, carrying a magnum of Dom Pérignon in his hand. He was the color of rich, black silt. Donned in all white, around his thick neck hung a diamond cross on a thick platinum chain. He was six feet two inches of chiseled magnificence and Nairobia's gaze stayed fixed on him as he approached her.

Her pussy clenched, and she wondered what'd taken him so long to come to her.

She eyed him sexily as he leaned in her ear and said over the music, "Dance with me, beautiful." It wasn't a question, but a command that blanketed over her senses. And she felt a rush of desire flow through her veins as his deep sexy voice brushed her skin. Oh yes. He had a scrumptious bedroom voice and was definitely motivation to get slutty.

She looked up into his big dark eyes and smiled. His eyes sparkled like two black diamonds. Nairobia immediately noticed he had beautiful smooth skin and long, thick lashes. She took in the rest of his face. He had an immaculate goatee framed around a set of full chocolate lips and a head full of thick curly hair.

And then...

He smiled, a crooked but sexy one. And Nairobia felt herself swoon—just a little, when he flashed her a set of perfectly straight, white teeth and deep dimples. Big hands, big feet, a nice smile, a nice ass, and dimples were a few of her weaknesses when it came to men. And this intoxicating mystery man managed to have it all.

His eyes scanned hers curiously, waiting. "Well. You game?"

He grabbed her hand, and he led her to the dance floor, not waiting for an answer. Nairobia smiled as he slid his hand down her lower back and pulled her into him. "Nice party."

Nairobia smiled. "Thank you." She worked her arms up in the air over her head and pulled the diamond pins from her hair, undoing her French twist. Her hair toppled down past her shoulders as she seductively twirled her body. She dipped low, then worked her way back up.

A thick arm went around her waist and Nairobia felt the Mystery Man press himself into her ass. He leaned into her ear, and said, "I know your perfume is sweet, but what about you, baby? How sweet are you?"

His warm breath made her shiver. She could smell the liquor on his breath, and felt herself getting lightheaded. Maybe it was from his cologne, or the three cocktails she'd sipped on, or the fact that he had her pressed into his hard-body, but Nairobia felt suddenly drunk.

She spun free of his grasp and faced him, shimmying up close. "Only one way to know, my love."

A slow grin curved his lips. "You're sexy as hell, beautiful," he said softly, pulling her in closer. "Where you rest at?"

Ciara's "Dance Like We're Making Love" played and Nairobia felt herself melting against him as she worked her body against his. She gave into his body heat, and felt his cock grow against her pelvis. It didn't feel long, but it felt deliciously thick...and heavy. And she wanted nothing more than to unzip his white dress pants and drag his cock out of his underwear to stroke it in her delicate hands.

"Right now, my darling, I'm resting in your arms," she teased. "Or would you prefer to have me resting somewhere else?"

He smiled, and cupped her ass as he bumped his pelvis into her. "Yeah, Ma. In my bed." He pulled her in tighter, his lips at her temple. "But, nah, I'm sayin'. Where you live?"

"California and New York. And you?"

"Oh, aiight. Cool. I rest in Brooklyn, baby."

She looked at him and matched his smile, then tried to dance her way out of his arms, but he refused to let her go, or relinquish her to the three other men who tried to cut in.

Hmm. Possessive, no?

Nairobia was no man's possession. But she would allow him a night of fantasy. Give him the illusion of being in control. She adored men who dared to take charge.

By the time Meek Mill's "All Eyes On You" started playing, Nairobia had learned that her mystery man was single—for the moment (whatever that meant)—and staying in Vegas for the week with his *peoples*. He claimed—Nairobia was used to men *claiming* a lot of things to only later find it to be untrue—to own several businesses in and around New York and New Jersey with an uncle.

"Tell me, my love. Is your uncle as delicious-looking as you?"

He laughed. "Nah, nah. But he got mad swag, though. And he

pulls more pussy than me." He laughed again. Truth was his uncle had the face of a gorilla and a cock the size of a horse's. And the panty-sniffing freak could be ruthless and dangerous when crossed.

Mystery Man pulled her in closer. "Why, you tryna meet him?"

Nairobia looked into his eyes, and imagined him fucking her, fast and hard, until she exploded her cunt juices all over his cock. She was so not interested in meeting an uncle who did not look like him. Who would most likely not wet her *kut* the way he had done.

"No, my darling."

He smiled. "Cool. 'Cause I ain't tryna share you. Not tonight."

"Hmm. Who are *you* here with tonight?" she asked, ignoring his last remark of not wanting to share her. As if he had a say. She wondered why a man as sexy as him would be single. Or was he only single while in Sin City?

Not that it mattered. She'd flirt with him. And even arouse him. But she had no intentions of pleasing him. True, she'd been a porn star, and she loved to fuck. But her *kut* was the crème de la crème. She gave a man her cunt when it needed feeding. And hers was still full from Josiah.

But she'd happily spread her thighs and welcome his warm tongue inside her slit and his beautiful lips on her clit. She swallowed back her lusty thoughts and blinked him in, admiring the way his body moved. He moved his hips like a man who knew how to stroke a pussy.

"I'm here with my peoples," he finally said, moving in close. "And you?"

"With you for now," she said saucily.

He smiled. "Nice. I dig that." He whispered in her ear. "Now what about later? You still tryna be with me then?"

"Maybe. Maybe not," is all she said.

"Oh, aiight. It's all love, baby. I can hold out until it's a *yes*."

Nairobia was pure temptation. And he'd been eyeing her fine ass the whole night, from the moment she'd stepped through the club's door. In fact, he'd come to the event in hopes of seeing her. Yeah, he knew who she was. Who didn't? She was sexy as fuck. A freak. And if he had his way, he'd have her in a dark corner somewhere with his hard-ass dick in her. But tonight he was being a gentleman, hard motherfucking dick and all.

With his body practically glued to hers, his straining erection throbbed in his pants, and Nairobia imagined there being a dampened spot of pre-cum in his underwear.

She draped her arms around his neck and looked him in the eyes, letting him know with her body that she knew *exactly* how aroused he was. He felt her skin heat against him, and groaned inwardly. He knew she was bad as fuck, but God, this was too good to be true. To have her in his arms, up close and personal, was more than a wet dream. It was a potential fuckfest, and a potential disaster in his underwear if she didn't stop grinding her pussy up on his dick. He'd never come in his pants by simply dancing with someone. But, the way Nairobia's sexual heat was warming his dick, tonight would be the night his cock creamed in his drawers.

He closed his eyes and inhaled sharply, sucking in the smell of her as he rubbed his hand up and down her back. Usher's "Superstar" started playing, and Nairobia spun out of his embrace, then raised her hands up over head, seductively dancing to the beat.

Mystery Man whispered into her ear over the music, "You know you got my dick hard, right?" He pressed his hips into her and ground himself on her ass as their hips moved in sync. Nothing more needed to be said. They danced as if they were the only two on the floor, oblivious to the clicking cameras.

Six songs later, Mystery Man's cell phone buzzed in his suit jacket pocket. He pulled it out, and glanced at the screen, before finally letting Nairobia go. "Damn, Ma. Hate to cut this short, but I gotta roll."

He tried to adjust himself, but the bulge in his designer pants was too thick to hide. Nairobia smiled to herself. She was tempted to rub her hand over the front of his zipper, but decided it would be in poor taste. So she murmured near his ear, *"Mijn kut huilt te voelen van je dikke lul."* My cunt weeps to feel your fat dick.

And it did.

Being pressed into his hard body, his heat seeped through her. She could practically feel his heartbeat beating on her back. And the feel of his swollen cock brushing into her clit and up on her ass had awakened her sleeping cunt. Now it purred for a good stroking.

He grinned crookedly. "What was that sexy shit you just said to me, Ma?"

A coy smile drifted across her mouth. "If our paths cross again, my love, I'd rather show you than tell you."

A glimmer of arousal lighted Mystery Man's eyes as his hand slid to her lower back. "Oh, word? Then I think I'd better make sure we make it happen."

"Perhaps you should," Nairobia said sassily. "But be warned, my love. I will be like no other."

Mystery Man smiled again. "Baby, I like the sound of that."

He reached for her hand and took it in his strong grip, then attempted to lead her through the crowd back to where he'd found her. But horny men, hungry for Nairobia's attention, surged around them, like vultures stalking road-kill, trying to feed.

They'd patiently waited, and now they wanted their turn with the beautiful vixen.

A fair-skinned man with hazel eyes grabbed her arm as she walked by holding Mystery Man's hand. "Pleasure, baby. Would you mind taking a picture with me?"

Mystery Man frowned at the inebriated man, but Nairobia didn't see the harm of taking a photo with him. He looked perfectly harmless enough, a bit drunk, but nothing to cause alarm.

"Nah, fam," Mystery Man said, giving the guy a menacing glare. "You see she with me, right?"

"Yeah, but—"

"But nothin', muhfucka. Fall back."

Nairobia's cunt clenched at his abruptness.

Next, a gorgeous, Latino-looking man grabbed Nairobia and kissed her on the cheek, then licked the side of her neck, like some slobbering Saint Bernard.

"Damn, Pleasure, baby," another man said, grabbing her hand. "Loved you in *Slut Season*. Will there ever be a part two?"

"Not with me starring in it," Nairobia said lightheartedly. "But thank you, my darling."

Mystery Man pulled her along.

Another drunk admirer said, "Tell me something, Pleasure. Is that pussy as sweet as it looks on screen? Me an' my dick wanna know."

Nairobia smiled, but it didn't reach her eyes. "It's sweeter," she said evenly. She was used to men getting drunk, then becoming obnoxiously lewd. But when he grabbed her ass with his big hand, and said, "I'd love to take my dick and shove it in this fat, juicy ass," Nairobia slapped the drunken man's hand from her ass, and gave him a scathing look. "Look. Don't touch."

Klootzak!

How dare that *asshole* try to maul her at her own damn party!

Before Nairobia could open her mouth to say another word, Mystery Man stopped and turned his dark eyes to her, his brows drawn tight, his gaze narrowed. "Yo, did that dumb muhfucka just put his hands on you?" A muscle ticked in his chiseled jaw.

His aura turned dangerously dark. Taken aback by this devastatingly handsome man's roguish demeanor filled Nairobia with a dizzying heat. She blinked twice. Her pussy clenched for more. His aggression and raw masculinity suddenly became overwhelming.

Quelling the urge to fan herself, she glanced at the drunken man still leering at her, then dismissively said, "It's nothing to bother with. No harm—"

"Yeah, potnah, no harm—" He wasn't able to get the rest of his words out. Mystery Man's fist cracked into the drunken man's jaw, knocking him to the dance floor in one punch.

Oh God no!

Why had he done that?

And why had no one come over to assess the situation?

Where was security when you needed them?

Nairobia loathed violence, but there was something disturbingly sexy about this mystery stranger wanting to defend her honor. Blood hummed in her body.

Still…this was not acceptable.

Nairobia looked down at the poor drunken soul sprawled out on the floor, a flicker of pity in her eyes, before she turned her gaze to her Mystery Man's. "You didn't have to do that," she said over the music.

"Yeah, I did," he said, his smoldering eyes locked on hers. The club's flashing lights softened his beautifully rugged face, but there was still an edge to his voice. "I don't play that disrespect shit. And the next muhfucka who comes at you sideways is gonna get his jaw rocked."

Mijn heer!

My Lord!

Why was her cunt clutching uncontrollably? Suddenly, her clit ached to be sucked into his mouth. Possessively, he pulled her in front of him, his warm palm resting slightly above the crack of her ass as he escorted her off the dance floor.

They finally made it back to the erupting penis. "Dig, Ma. I wanna see you again," he said, before leaning in and kissing her on the cheek.

Nairobia's clitoris throbbed. She fought the painful urge to take his big hand and shove it between her thighs, maneuvering his fingers over her sex.

She cocked her head, matching his heated gaze with one of her own. "Then I guess you'll have to find your way to me."

He looked at her glossed lips as if he were considering how soft they might feel against his, and—without permission, without care—framed her face with the palm of his hands, then ducked his head and slowly brushed his lips against hers. He eased back, and grinned.

"I'm good at finding what I want. Make sure you're ready for me when I do." He leaned in and, this time, kissed the edge of her mouth. He drew back. "Enjoy the rest of ya night, beautiful. My peoples will be watchin' to make sure no one else comes at you crazy."

His *peoples?* What peoples? And who was this Mystery Man?

Nairobia glanced around VIP, then back at him, giving him a quizzical look. "Who? Where are they?"

"All over, baby," he said. "I got eyes everywhere."

For a moment, she wondered if she should be worried that this stranger had eyes keeping watch on her. She hadn't anticipated being stalked tonight, or any other night, for that matter. But she wasn't in Europe anymore. She was in the United States, for God's sake. The land of the crazies and the deviants.

It hadn't occurred to her, until now, that if she planned on living in the States that perhaps she needed her own security here after all. She touched her Mystery Man's arm. "Thank you for your concern. But, I'm fine, my darling. Besides, there's club security everywhere. I'm in good hands."

His lips curled into a lopsided smile. "Oh, I see. You're definitely fine, baby. And you'll be in even better hands when I get at you again." He glanced at his Rolex. Shit. He really had to go. He didn't want to, but he knew his uncle would keep blowing up his phone all night. Kashmir wasn't the kind of man who took to waiting, on anyone, for too long.

"I gotta bounce. I'ma be checkin' for you real soon. Be ready."

What was she supposed to get ready for? Did he not know she was *always* ready? He had to know who she was, no? Yes, yes. Of course he did. Why else would he be at her private party?

Breathlessly, Nairobia eyed him as he started walking off, then she called out to him. "Wait. I didn't get your name, my love."

He flashed her another award-winning, dimpled smile. "It's Coal. As in black rock."

She slid her finger in the basin of melted chocolate, then shamelessly stuck her finger into her mouth and sucked it clean, wondering exactly how *black* and how thick his rock truly was. He shook his head, smiling. All Nairobia saw when he looked at her—before he turned on his heel and maneuvered his way out of the club—were a pair of eyes that sparkled like two beautiful black diamonds staring back at her.

She watched him vanish into the crowd, leaving her to her salacious thoughts and wondering how he planned on finding her in a big city like New York.

TEN

"Deeper...mmm...yes."

Nairobia's nails raked down Josiah's back as his cock plunged into her pussy. It was creeping past four in the morning and their bodies had been rocking into the bedsprings for over an hour. Her pussy had been severely overheating ever since her encounter with the dark-as-midnight Mystery Man at the club.

Her body on fire, Nairobia had returned to her suite to find Josiah stretched out across the sofa, naked. Waiting for her, his cock lying languidly to one side over his thigh as it always did.

His eyes glazed with sexual hunger, Josiah had crooked his finger at her, motioning her over to him. She'd smiled and licked her lips, then slid out of her skimpy skirt and stepped out of it, before walking over to him and straddling his face, giving him what he'd been yearning for.

A taste of her cunt.

Her melting on his tongue.

Her coming all over his mouth.

He'd licked her and sucked on her clit until she orgasmed. Now she was on her back. She usually took control and rode him. But tonight she wanted him to have the lead, this time. So here she was on her back, her legs wrapped around Josiah's waist, moaning as his cock stroked over her sweet spot, causing her folds to swell beautifully.

She felt so damn good. Too fucking good to be true.

Josiah wanted to come, badly, but not until he'd drained Nairobia. Not until he'd fucked her helplessly dry. He'd been doing his damnedest to fuck her until she stapped out. But he knew the task was wishful thinking.

The longer his cock stayed embedded in her, the longer he stroked, the wetter she became. Nairobia could take more. And the more he gave, the more she wanted. She was overwhelmingly wet as he teased her pussy, pulling out to the head, then waiting for her juicy hole to close around his cock head, before he slammed back in. He spread her mercilessly open, then sunk deep inside her body, losing himself inside her heat.

"Harder." Nairobia gasped, her gray eyes sultry, dilated, and full of fire. "Mmm, *ja...ja...neuk* me...uhh...mmmm..."

She moaned louder, encouraging her young lover to *fuck* her. Hard. Fast.

"Yes, yes...give me more...mmm...yes, my love..."

God he was so long-winded. So good. The feel of him buried inside her, so deep, so right, made pleasure build and multiply with every thrust. Josiah eased up on his arms and moved his dick in and out of Nairobia in fast, fluid motion. His hips bumped into her pelvis, causing him to put pressure on her clit as the head of his dick brushed over her G-spot, then nudged the mouth of her womb.

Josiah felt the liquid fire as it swirled around her walls. He didn't know how much more of her deliciously wet clutch he could stand before he lost himself in her. He let out a low growl, fucking her in deep, hard strokes, his entire body tightening.

Nairobia moaned as he sank deeper. Her body, full of soft need and burning desire, ignited Josiah's blood, making his legs shake. His hands tightened on her hips and he pounded rhythmically into her body, his thrusts rapidly stroking her G-spot.

Nairobia mewled, feeling herself swell and tighten, her body filling with sweet bliss.

Josiah groaned against Nairobia's neck, causing vibrations to ricochet over her flesh. Thank God for her religious pelvic exercises. Five hundred Kegels a day did her pussy wonders. She tightened around him. And Josiah squeezed his eyes shut, reveling in the feel of her, soft and wet, her feminine heat and sweet musky scent overtaking his senses.

He withdrew, then sank back in, his heavy balls smacking the back of her cunt, as her pussy sucked him into an abyss of pleasure.

She felt so fucking amazing. So orgasmic.

Oh how deliciously he fucked her.

Nairobia could feel his cock throb inside her with every thrust, every beat of his racing heart. Josiah's lids went heavy as Nairobia moved with him, meeting his ravenous thrusts with urgency. "You love this *kut*, no? You love how wet it grows around your cock, no?"

"Yes, yes…ahh, shit, yeah… I don't ever wanna stop fucking you."

"Then fuck me until your balls empty, my love…mmm…"

Josiah moaned as Nairobia opened herself wider to him and sunk her nails into the hard contours of his chiseled ass. "Uhhh… aaaaah…oooh, shit…"

Nairobia matched his moan, already close to another orgasm. She'd already come multiple times and now she had him on the edge of exploding as well.

Josiah drew his hips back, then slowly rolled them forward, swirling his cock, drilling it in to her wetness, until his cock reached the bottom of her well. He repeated. Once, twice, three times…

Teasing Nairobia.

Taunting her with his cock.

"Yessss! Fuck meeeee, my love…" Her heart beating in her ears, Nairobia wasn't sure if she cried out in Dutch or English when she spoke. She couldn't even hear her own voice. All she heard was the slap of Josiah's sweat-slick body smacking into hers. All she felt was Josiah as he pummeled deep inside her. His cock. His balls.

"Yes, yes, yes…give it to me good, my love. Yesssss…" Her cunt grabbed at his cock uncontrollably, her walls caressing his shaft as he slid in and out of her.

He gnashed his teeth, hovering at the edge of release. "Aaaah, fuck…you keep grabbing my dick like that…uhh…and I'ma come all in you."

"Come, my love. Fill me with your seeds."

Josiah groaned low in his throat. He was painfully close, too close. But he wasn't ready. Not yet. So he slowed his pace. Rolled his hips, circling, teasing, pulling out barely to the head of his dick, then pumping his pelvis in one stroke back in, deep.

Nairobia was on the verge of another climax.

She was—

Josiah curled his fingers around her right breast and suckled the tip, causing her to arch up from the mattress. He knew how to make her pussy quiver, and he loved the way she loved on his dick. The way she swallowed him whole. The way her silken walls gripped him. He loved the way her body went flush. The way her nipples grew dark and tight when excited.

Their age difference didn't matter. He was fucking turned on by her. But his feelings for Nairobia went beyond lust, beyond infatuation. Her pussy had a switch to his dick that only she controlled. And it drove him crazy with want. Made him hard and wild.

Made him hungry.

Made him want to be helplessly reckless.

He thrust hard and then slowed, sliding almost out of her body again, watching the mouth of her cunt suckle the head of his dick.

"Give me all of your cock, my love. Oh. Mm."

Nairobia clawed his back, and he moaned again. She bit his neck, and he groaned. His muscles bulged as he crashed his mouth over her lips and began kissing her, his tongue sweeping inside her mouth as he stroked inside her body.

The sheets rustled beneath them. Nairobia's breasts bobbed between them as he pounded into her body. Finally, after several moments of heated kissing, Josiah's lips were on her neck, nipping at her flesh. Then his head ducked and he licked at her nipple, before sucking it back into his mouth again, lightly tugging with his teeth. He kept sucking at her breast, his mouth moving from one breast to the other, giving them both equal pleasure as his shaft caressed the slick walls of her pussy.

Nairobia cupped the back of Josiah's head. *"Zuigen*…uh…mmm… *moeilijker…"* Suck. Harder.

Josiah sucked harder. Then licked. Then nipped at her nipple. Nairobia bucked upward, her cunt grabbing his cock. Yeah, she liked that. Her nipples bit. He bit into her other nipple, and she moaned as his teeth sank into the puckered crest. Wet fire swept through her veins.

She slid her hands up to Josiah's chest, searching for his nipples. When she'd found them, she rolled them between her fingers until they pebbled, then pinched.

Josiah growled, his body slamming in to hers.

And then he came, hard, causing everything around him to blur.

Nairobia wasn't his. But she *was* his for the night. All his. And he wanted to savor every wet stroke of her for as long as he could. She'd given him her body, and limitless access to her hot, wet, sweet clutch.

Josiah didn't pull out. He remained buried inside her, slowing moving his hips, enjoying the warmth of her. He knew there were plenty of men who'd kill to be inside her right now. She'd partied all night. And, yet, had returned to her suite…to *him*.

That had to mean something. Right?

Her cunt clutched his cock, causing his orgasm to rip through his body, flooding his chest with warmth.

That was all the answer he needed.

ELEVEN

Back in New York, Nairobia found herself up to her sultry eyeballs in membership applications and invoices. Since opening night, over a month ago, the club's membership had already increased by another two hundred new members. And on her desk there were still another…three hundred and seventy-two applicants from across the world—including that of a Middle Eastern prince—vying for membership in The Pleasure Zone.

Nairobia had known from the beginning that there was a market for a club such as hers. Oh, sure there were other sex clubs in the New York area, but none compared to hers. Besides the club's "Anything Goes Behind These Doors" policy, Nairobia catered specifically to the rich and freaky. No others.

Was it discriminatory? Perhaps. But she didn't give a damn. Have good coin and you could have whatever your freaky heart desired. You could experience sweet bliss and the underworld of taboo sex all under one tantalizing roof, until daybreak.

Nairobia glanced at the time, and smiled. It was almost time for the doors of her club to open. She was pleased of her club's over-night success. But, she'd be lying to herself if she didn't admit that it was overwhelming. Running a club of this magnitude was nothing like hosting her private sex parties around the world.

It required dedication and real commitment, and hard work. A little more than she'd bargained for. Sadly, Nairobia was beginning to think she wouldn't be able to keep up with managing the day-to-day demands. The Pleasure Zone was not to become her life, only a part of it. The last thing she wanted was to be living and breathing to keep a club open. No, no. Her club would be a success. But she would not marry herself to it for that to happen. If she wanted a husband, she'd have one. No, no. She wanted excitement. She wanted pleasure. And she enjoyed seeing men and women receiving it here.

Still, she couldn't help feeling a bit overwhelmed.

The club's doors were already opened three nights a week—Friday, Saturday and Sunday, 10 p.m. to 6 a.m. That meant three sumptuous nights of decadence. Nairobia saw no need to extend sin beyond that. But the club's members thought otherwise. Requests for another night were coming in heavily. Now Nairobia was at her desk, contemplating adding another night, which meant being chained to her club more than what she'd hoped for. She had books to write. Parties to host. And two other businesses to run.

She was the *face* and *body* of pleasure. She was a gypsy soul. Born for living. And fucking. *Not* toiling over paperwork. Yet, here she sat.

Nairobia took another deep breath. *Ik zal niet versloeg.* No, she would *not* be defeated. At some point, she knew she'd need someone to manage her club's responsibilities. Someone almost as freaky as her, someone she could trust. Someone educated, and business savvy.

But *who?*

Nairobia wasn't the most trusting. And she definitely wasn't about to let anyone come up in here and tear her good name down, or ruin her club's success. No, no. She knew all too well about silent haters. The ones who wished you well to your face, but then slithered behind your back to try to do you in.

She would have none of that around her.

No negativity.

No hating.

No jealousy.

No one trying to sabotage her.

So she'd have to ride it out until she was able to come up with a better solution.

Her cell rang, pulling her from her thoughts. She glanced at the screen, before answering. "Pasha, my darling," she purred. "You've received my text, no?" She'd sent her a text late last night indicating she was in need of a few good men to protect *and* serve her.

Pasha was her hairstylist back in California, whom she had fallen in love with the moment she'd stepped foot into her posh Beverly Hills salon over a year ago. Since then, Nairobia allowed no one else to lay fingers through her hair, except for Pasha.

"Yes. I got your text. And I think I have someone for you."

"And how well do you know him, my darling?"

"We're close," Pasha said in an almost cryptic tone. She paused, then added, "I trust him with my life."

Nairobia pursed her lips. "Hm. Old lover, no?"

Surprised, Pasha blinked on the other end of the line. "Very close friends. He stood by me during one of the most difficult times of my life. He's trustworthy."

Nairobia had sent her a text early this morning wanting leads on hiring a security firm that could handle her security needs, particularly having a bodyguard. She already had security for the club. But she didn't feel they were adequate enough.

After what'd happened back in Vegas, Nairobia felt it best if she had protection of her own. Sure she'd spent time down at the range and packed a little heat in her purse from time to time. But, now being here in the States, she felt she needed more.

"I like the men around me sexy, my darling. Security or not, I need to be surrounded by mouthwatering men. He is, no?"

Pasha smiled. "Yes. Very."

"He has all his teeth, no?"

Her stylist laughed. "Yes. All thirty-two."

"Is he uptight?"

"No, not at all. He's very laid-back. And very open-minded."

"Hmm. So far I like. Is he cross-eyed?"

"Nairobia! Ohmygod! You're hysterical. No, of course not. He doesn't have a lazy or wandering eye. He's a very normal-looking guy, and extremely sexy, I might add. I think you'll be quite pleased."

Nairobia purred. "If he's all you say, my love. Then I already am. Where is he?"

"He's here in L.A. He actually has several clients out here that his firm provides security services to. In fact, I believe you've met his partner, Mel. He was here the last time you came to the salon."

Mel was from New Jersey as well, but had moved out to the West Coast around the same time Pasha's salon Nappy No More II opened. She'd had her choice of either him or Lamar continuing to work with her, but Pasha had chosen Mel instead, and he'd been more than willing to hold it down for her.

Nairobia thought for a moment. Then realization came in full, vibrant color. She remembered. Oh how she remembered him. The six-foot-seven mountain of muscle with the thick neck, bulging biceps, and golden-brown skin was not someone easily to be forgotten. Nairobia had found the two-hundred-and-seventy-five-pound giant gorgeous to look at. He bore a striking resemblance to her dear friend The Rock—with his deliciously fine self.

"It's my understanding he'll be catching the red-eye tonight back to the East Coast," Pasha said, pulling Nairobia back to the conversation. "I'll give him your number and have him call you so the two of you can work out all the specifics."

Nairobia clapped. "Perfect, my darling. I'm looking for someone who can start as soon as possible."

"Then he'll be your guy. Hopefully, it'll all work out."

Nairobia smiled. "Hopefully, it shall."

The two women spoke a moment longer, then the call ended.

A sense of relief flowed over Nairobia. She hoped this referral was a good fit for her, and her club. The last thing she needed, or wanted, was someone squeamish or prudish working for her. She'd have to fire them on the spot.

Taking a deep breath, Nairobia glanced at the neatly stacked pile of files on her desk, and decided she would only do what she could until she found herself someone to manage it all for her.

For now, she had a club to run. She had fantasies to fulfill, and orgasms to unleash.

TWELVE

Domineering and commanding, a whip snapped as O.C.A.D's "Muse" pounded through the hidden speakers. The floor alit with burning candles, the stage flashed with red lights and sweet pussy and ass.

Sexy. Alluring. Five feet, eight inches of coca-brown flesh stood in the center of the stage in a black leather corset, black thong, black leather opera gloves, and six-inch, thigh-high black leather Louboutin boots. Her short sassy cut was hidden beneath a long black wig with blunt-cut bangs.

The sexy Scorpion pumped her pelvis, then swirled her hips in a hypnotic circle, her skin shimmering under the glow of the lights. Hands up over her head, she rolled her hips like that of an erotic dancer, and then sensually strutted the stage while her whip cracked against its floor, licking the wood. She stood at the edge of the stage and looked out into the crowd as if she were looking for someone in particular. Someone worthy. Someone utterly debauched and hungered for the whip.

She looked down.

And there he was right in front of her, gazing up at her. Bare-chested. In nothing more than black boxer briefs and Timberland boots. He was a hazel-eyed man with sideburns that curved along his jawline and a crooked smile, leaning over on the stage and staring directly in her eyes as she slowly moved her hips, the leather of her whip snapping mere centimeters from his handsomely rugged face.

Her cunt clenched when he didn't flinch. He emitted a slight gasp, then licked his full lips. A sign that he was clearly turned on. Hungry for the crack of the bullwhip against his caramel skin, starved for release. Her mouth watered to give him what he desired. Unfortunately, she needed access to the Love Tombs. It was the only place where bondage and lashings were allowed.

And she needed entry.

But, tonight, she would push the envelope to the edge. She'd be creative.

Her tongue traced over her cherry-red-painted lips, relieved this fine-looking hunk of rugged, hard-bodied flesh wasn't someone she knew. That had been one of her greatest concerns when she'd initially interviewed for membership at the club. Being recognized.

The owner had assured her that everyone who entered The Pleasure Zone had something to lose, and so, so, much more to gain. No one wanted their sexual proclivities on display for the outside world. So discretion was more than an expectation. It was a requirement. One heavily enforced.

Well, with the hefty yearly membership fees charged *up* front, it just ought to be.

She cracked her whip again.

Nine Inch Nails' "Closer" played as she dropped down and spread her thighs, her crotch inches away from Hazel Eyes. Reaching in, she grabbed him by the back of the neck and ground her pussy in his face, her sweet musky sex, scenting his mouth and lips.

The horny men in the room went wild, barking and whistling. Envy flashed in eyes that ached for her, silently brooding that she'd chosen him out of the others. Without hesitation, Hazel Eyes licked over the leather of her crotch.

The men in the room groaned low, and squirmed in their seats, painfully aroused and watching. Hazel Eyes groaned over her pussy as he bit at the leather, stimulating her clit. Oh, he wanted to play? Well so did she. She reached for his sweet, brown man nipple and pinched it, before leaning back and pressing her heel into his chest.

She felt her orgasm twirling around the pit of her pussy when he slowly lifted her foot and kissed the sole of her boot. Her mouth parted on a silent moan of pleasure. *Yes, yes, oh yes…*she would fuck him tonight. Or maybe not.

Rising up, she lifted herself from the floor, her hands swept up her undulating hips she worked her way backward. Then twirled her body, her pussy pulsing, and her whip cracking wildly as she shook her hips across the stage, bending over and clapping her ass. She reached for a candle, then slowly turned—a sly, seductive grin spreading over her beautifully glossed lips—as she blew the candle out, gyrating her way back to Hazel Eyes.

His breath hitched in anticipation as if he knew before she did it. Splashed the hot wax up his chest, splashing up his neck and over his left nipple. His dick grew excruciatingly hard. She splashed more wax, and a growl so deep, so primal, ripped out from his chest over the music.

She was Pain.

Not her real name. But the one she used whenever she wanted to indulge her dark side. And tonight she was feeling dark and sultry. She loved walking over on the wild side. Loved latex and leather. Loved whips and chains. Loved creating scenarios and role-playing. She loved unleashing her freaky side.

And she loved freaky men.

Masculine. Muscular. Willing. Obedient. Submissive.

Men.

With a masochistic side.

For years, she hadn't ever considered herself a real Sadomas-ochist or a Dominatrix. It had been all play, until two years. After training vigorously under a lesbian Dominatrix who went by the name of Cum Master. She'd taught her the art of the whip. Taught her about the types of whips, and their use. Taught her how to inflict the right amount of pain to bring on excruciating pleasure. Thanks to the Cum Master, she'd learned the art of sadism.

"Men try to be something they can never be…"

Her whip cracked again. She bounced to the beat, and hummed the lyrics in her head. She loved turning the tables on men. They needed to feel what it was like to be objectified. Defiled. Needed to know how to submit to a woman. It wet her pussy. She loved administering pain *and* pleasure. Loved the sound of a whip crack-ing. Loved the sound of a paddle smacking across the muscled-ass of a man, then lovingly licking over the stings, before biting into each ass cheek.

She loved ass-play, licking and fingering and fucking a man's tight ass.

Oh how she loved it. She was team-ass licking. Team-ass fucking. Team freak-nasty. Things she could never be, or *do*, at home. Filthy things her lover would never go for, let alone understand.

So for the last two years, she'd been creeping on her fiancé with men who craved kink. Her latest kinky sidepiece was a married man whom she'd met on an online sex site. He'd been looking for ass-play and prostate stimulation—something his prudish wife abhorred. Pain had responded to his ad with hopes of licking his ass and stimulating his P-spot. And the rest was history. They crept when he wanted his ass slid into with her fingers and tongue, whenever their schedules allowed for it.

This was her first time at The Pleasure Zone. But she already wanted more. She wanted access to more floors. She wanted to indulge more of her desires. Everything about what she'd seen so far made her body throb and her pussy moist.

She was a freak.

She craved hot-nasty fucking.

Lord, God, help her!

If her fiancé ever found out what she was up to behind his back, he'd leave her for sure. She was greedy. She wasn't about to leave him. She loved him too much to let him go. Loved the sex. Mmm. The sex. Oh how magnificent he was in bed, big long West Indian cock and all. But sometimes she needed more. Not emotionally. Sexually.

He was much younger than her, but he was good to her in and out of the sheets. He was adventurous and freaky—to a degree. Hell, he'd fucked her and her two sisters several times before things had changed, before her two sisters became all motherly and matrimonial on her.

And before her fiancé had caught feelings for her, and wanted her for himself.

Before life changed between her and sisters, they'd been sleeping with the same men since their freshman year in college. For years, their rules had been simple: the men they sexed had to be single, willing to fuck all three of them either together or separately, preferably together since that's what turned them on; he had to be over the age of twenty-one; he needed to be able to orgasm more than one round; and, be open and honest about his sexual desires. Something Pain found most men unable to do.

The three freaky sisters had once shared a special sisterly bond like no others could. But Pain...well, she was a different kind of freak. She waved her freak flag a whole lot higher than her fiancé or her now two married sisters.

And she wasn't ready to let go of it.

Pain coiled her whip, and stepped back. She put her right foot before her left and then released the whip with a quick snap. Oh how she loved the sound of it cracking. The Cum Master had told her how whips were good for pain, and good for bondage. She felt her sex swelling with lust at the thought of having this six-foot-something's body wrapped in rope, his skin beautifully welted.

Tove Lo's "Moments" played and Pain drew her arm back and lashed her whip, then swung it over her head, before snapping it to the floor again.

Eyeing the man of her momentary desires, she hooked her leg around a shiny steel pole and twirled herself around it, her hair flying out behind her. When she finally stopped swirling, she held onto the pole with one hand and leaned forward, and her ample cleavage spilled out over the top of her corset, displaying the tops of her luscious breasts.

Oblivious to everyone else in the room, Hazel Eyes licked his lips. And she returned the sensual gesture in kind. Leaning her back against the pole, she dropped her whip as the instrumental to Kendrick Lamar's "Swimming Pools (Drank)" started playing and gyrated her hips to the beat, slowly sliding down the pole, opening and closing her legs, flashing her audience—particularly him, giving him peeks of her waxed cunt. She slid her thong over to one side and bared her clit, then ran a finger over her slit. She swirled her finger over it and stroked herself, closing her eyes and biting into her bottom lip, losing herself in the sensation.

She stuck a finger inside her slick cunt, then seductively stuck her wet finger inside her warm, lush mouth and sucked. Blood rushed to the cocks of every red-blooded man watching, imagining her mouth around them, her slick tongue licking over their balls.

She slowly slid her back up the pole, then spun around it. Gripping it with both hands, she adulated against it. Pressed the seam of her sex into it, holding her head back and sliding up and down, stimulating her clit, teasing her slit.

The men around the stage panted, but she stared and moved her body as if she were dancing for only *him*. Hazel Eyes. The man who had her pussy on fire with just his fiery gaze on her.

She slid the palm of her hand down over her flattened abdomen and slowly lowered it down over her thong, then between her legs. She threw her head back and half closed her eyes, her sultry mouth partly open as her hands roamed all over her body. She slowly turned and bent at the waist, giving all who watched a full-view of her gorgeous ass. She slapped it. Then shook it.

More men found their way up to the stage watching in lust-eyed amazement, their attention fixed on nothing else but her bare flesh, the visual breathtaking.

She stared over her shoulder—her hips rolling, her ass shaking, her wet arousal glistening the back of her cunt—with a fuck-me look that had mouths drooling, tongues wagging. She grabbed the pole again and swung her body around it, before hanging upside down from her knees. Hazel Eyes' groin tightened at the lovely sight.

She wasn't a stripper, by any means. But she and her sisters had once taken pole-dancing lessons and she'd made it her business to master the art.

By the time the instrumental version of The Game's "Holy Water" started playing, Pain was floating on euphoria. She felt so free as she slinked her way up the pole, then leaned back and swung her-self upside down, flashing onlookers a naughty smile.

She flipped upward, then slinked her away down and around the pole. Dropping down, she pumped her pelvis. Tempting *him*. Tempting them. Teasing *him*. Teasing them.

Skillfully, she eased herself to the stage's floor, sprawling her body. She slowly parted her legs, bent her knees, and arched her back. Up. Down. Up. Down.

Then like a panther, she gracefully crawled her way over toward Hazel Eyes. Her soft fingertips brushed over his cheek, causing him to draw his tongue over his upper lip.

"You like what you see?" she said, her voice low and raspy. He wouldn't have heard her over the pulsing music had she not had her lips flush to his ear.

He grinned.

"Yeah, baby. I love it."

"You wanna lick my cunt again?"

He groaned, his dick throbbing, and eased his long tongue out of his mouth, flicking it. "Yeah, baby. Let me taste that sweet chocolate pussy."

"Can I tongue your ass?"

"Aah, shit yeah, baby."

"Can I punish you?"

He let out a low growl. "Hell yeah, baby. Punish me. Make me your bitch tonight."

He was so damn sexy. And those eyes mesmerized her. She wanted to beat and fuck him. Her blood boiled. She loved a masculine man comfortable in his masculinity, in his sexuality, willing to submit.

Hazel Eyes gnawed on his tongue as Pain slid up on her knees, then lifted her body. She shook her hips, sauntering back to the middle of the stage, bending over and retrieving her whip from the stage floor.

She faced the crowd, then crooked a finger at Hazel Eyes, motioning him to come onto the stage. He drew a deep, shuddering breath into his muscled chest, then hopped up on the stage. Pain eyed him. He was fit. Toned. Tall. Bowlegged. Bare-chested. And the bulge in his boxers…oh my!

Her mouth watered as he prowled toward her.

She loved bowlegged men. Loved fat, mouthwatering cock.

Before Hazel Eyes could get any closer, she flung the whip at him. It wrapped around his wrist. Unflinching, he smiled. Yes, he was what she needed tonight.

A man willing to submit, to be on display… Mmm. Exhibitionism was so sexy. She tugged on the whip and pulled it, pulling him closer. His breath quickened as she asked for his other wrist.

She had to be careful not to break any of the club's rules for second-floor sex play, or run the risk of being escorted out and having her membership cancelled. Still, she took his other wrist and wrapped the leather whip around his hands. She wouldn't lash him. But she'd coil him. That wouldn't be so bad. Right?

Pain instructed him to hold his hands up over his head as she secured him to the pole, before expertly tethering his legs. She ran her hand over his cock, and he moaned as she squeezed and leaned into him. "What's your name, sexy?"

A muscle tightened in his lower stomach. His dick throbbed painfully hard. Blood pooled and pumped into his shaft. "Zion," he pushed out, breathlessly.

Pain eased her hand down into the waistband of his underwear, fingered the dark curly thatch around his thick cock. She moaned at the feel of his impressive size. His erection pulsed in her hand, thick and ready. She wanted him. Now. She yanked his underwear down over his hips. Then leaned in and crushed her mouth over his lips, kissing him passionately as she slipped two fingers between her breasts and pulled out a leather strap from her corset.

Hazel Eyes hissed as she stroked his cock with a gloved hand. She licked her lips, then took her other hand and massaged him with both her hands. "I want you deep in my cunt," she said, wrapping the strap around his balls and the base of his cock. "Would you like that?"

He moaned out his answer as she grabbed his erection by the base and slid her gloved hands up and down his shaft.

She brought her soft lips to his neck and bit the skin over his jugular. The bite turned into a sensual lick, then a kiss, then another bite. Pre-cum slid out from the tip of his dick and dripped onto her hand. Pain lifted her hand to her mouth and licked over her glove. Hazel Eyes groaned.

"Mmm," she purred. "You taste like sweet arousal." She stroked him again, roughly, purposefully, milking out another string of glaze. "Taste," she urged as she lifted her hand to his mouth. He licked. Moaned. Then licked over her glove again.

Pain grabbed his balls. Stroked him again until pre-cum streaked her glove. She let go of his turgid flesh, then playfully slapped his face, before sliding in front of him, and rolling her hips until she was positioned directly in front of his perfectly straight cock, pointing rigid like an arrow at its target. She bent over, pulled her thong to the side, then eased back and fucked herself on his dick, raw and filthy, looking out into the crowd.

In back of the dim-lit room stood the shadow of a tall, dark, muscled figure—watching, a mixture of surprise and amusement glinting his dark eyes. Thick arms crossed over a wide chest, his biceps bulging under a body-hugging, black T-shirt, he blinked. Then narrowed his eyes.

Hol' up. Wait. Is that? He shook the absurd thought from his head. *Nah, that can't be...*

Knowing he had to be mistaken, he stepped further inside.

Pain grabbed her ankles and moaned as Hazel Eyes thrust his hips, ramming his dick inside her, sliding in and out of her wetness. Feeling heat sweep over her body, Pain cried out and looked up into the burning eyes of a familiar face from across the room.

THIRTEEN

"Damn, baby, you're still sexy as ever."

Nairobia blinked. Heat instantly washed over her body at the sound of the man invading the space behind her; his panty-dropping voice licked at her libido. She turned to face him. And eight-and-three-quarter inches of thick, mocha-colored cock was what instantly flashed through her mind the minute she looked up into the green, sparkling eyes of one of the sexiest men alive.

He gave her a lopsided grin, taking her all in, starting at her feet and working his way slowly upward. He didn't have his coal-black, wavy hair pulled back in his signature ponytail. Instead it hung past his shoulders in never-ending waves.

"Carlos, my darling," Nairobia cooed, her gaze sizzling over his.

She hadn't seen him since the Annual Music Awards in Monte Carlo, Monaco over a year ago. And he was as gorgeous now as he'd been then. He looked scrumptious in his fitted, short-sleeved white V-neck tee and a pair of torn, white jeans poured on over his muscled ass. The scent of his expensive cologne, mixing with all the testosterone that seeped from his deliciously buffed skin instantly aroused her.

She hadn't had him between her thighs in close to two years. But she remembered the sweet taste of his lips and the way his greedy cock splashed in and out of her juicy cunt. Good dick was hard to forget.

But it wasn't always attached to a good man. Not that Carlos wasn't a good one; he just wasn't one Nairobia would ever have longer than a night—*or* two—in her bed or between her thighs. The green-eyed pretty boy, in all of his fineness, was a notorious womanizer. And the whole world knew he—one of the world's most eligible bachelors—was a manwhore. Nairobia didn't judge, however. And she didn't care.

After all, everyone had a past, and their own story to tell. And she definitely had more than her share of sex tales to share. Still, Carlos had been linked to some of the most beautiful women around the globe. From supermodels to Hollywood starlets and songstresses, the R&B crooner and model was known for his prowess in the sheets, and for breaking hearts. The tabloids had him labeled as an international playboy. And they loved seeing him through their cameras' lenses. He was just so damn sexy to photograph, even in the most scandalously compromising positions. Like the time he'd had a wardrobe malfunction and the drawstring of his linen pants came loose, and so did all of Nature's glory. Dick and balls for all to see, dangling on display.

Yes, yes, yes. Nairobia could attest to his delicious dick strokes and toe-curling tongue licks. And truth to be told, he was almost as good as his fraternity brother and best friend, Marcel. Almost.

She allowed herself a moment to indulge the memory. She'd invited him to her villa in Milan during the 2014 Fashion Week. No questions were asked. The intent was clear. The two of them fucked each other breathlessly, like two sex-starved teenagers, until sunrise. And then came an early morning romp of pussy eating, his tongue laving her lust-filled clit, her cum-soaked cunt, and all over her succulently wet lips, followed by an exquisite ass fucking. *"Me in mijn kont neuken,"* she'd told him. Yes, she wanted it in her ass. And he'd given it to her. He'd fucked her hard because she'd wanted it, demanded it, every controlled thrust bursting with heat and power.

"*Neuk me!*" she'd urged over and over. "Fuck me, fuck me, fuck me…!"

And he'd done just that, releasing his warm, milky load into his condom, still stroking slowly into the heat of her willing, wanting ass until her muscles relentlessly squeezed his dick, and he plopped out.

That night he'd obliged her libido, owned her body, with a hard, thick dick, emptying his cum-filled sac until there was nothing left of him to give. She had been fully satiated when she slid out of her sheets, her anus still humming from the deep fucking, and walked him to the door.

He had wanted her number. But she'd kissed him on the lips instead, then shut the door in his face; a grin painted on her swollen lips from the kissing and heavy dick sucking she'd done.

She smiled.

A mix of Native-American, Italian, and African, Nairobia knew if she dared to let the three-time Grammy-award-winning heart-throb soak the inside of her eggs the way he had his condom, they'd make some beautifully exotic-looking babies together.

She felt a pool of heat building in her stomach, then washing over her uterus.

"Damn, it's so good to see you, baby," Carlos said. And just as he stepped in to wrap Nairobia in his arms, her bodyguard appeared from out of nowhere and slid one long, thick arm between them, pushing him back.

"Nah, fall back, playboy," the bodyguard growled.

Lamar was new to Nairobia's security detail, and had come highly recommended by Pasha. The day after Nairobia had spoken to her, Lamar had come in for an interview, dressed in black, and looking every bit of intimidating, menacing, and, oh so, deliciously intoxicating.

This was his first day on the job. And so far Nairobia was highly impressed. Sure she could have flown in the confined comforts of her luxurious private jet, but she needed to see how this chocolate Mandingo handled the controlled chaos that oftentimes swirled up around her, like this very moment.

Men ogled her. Women eyed her slyly. Cell phones snapped pictures to capture the moment, while heads turned to take in the back of her luscious ass as she sauntered through the airport wearing—over a black Brazilian thong with two-strand diamond chains which wrapped around her hips—a very short, black crochet net dress with a halter silhouette and cutout sides. The hundred thousand-dollar dress, as with the majority of her couture, left many mouths agape...and drooling.

Sure there were some women who sneered and rolled their eyes at her as she passed by. A few even held on to their men, or narrowed their eyes at him as Nairobia moseyed by. But to hell with them! She had no interest in their men.

She almost laughed.

Insecure, that's what they were. They were a bunch of narrow-minded bitches, who more than likely needed a good fuck to loosen them up.

"Can we help you?" her bodyguard said, his steely gaze fixed on Carlos.

"Nah, *playboy*," Carlos said sarcastically, sizing him up. "It's all love over here, Hercules. Nairobia's my peoples." Carlos kept his glare locked on the six-foot-four, dread-wearing bodyguard. Carlos was a pretty boy, but he was far from soft when it came to knuckling up.

"Now, now, my love," Nairobia cooed, touching the beefy hunk's muscled arm. "Play nice. Carlos is a dear acquaintance of mine."

Lamar grunted, then sized Carlos up. "Oh, aiight." He stepped back, but stayed near and kept his eyes locked on Carlos behind a pair of three-hundred-dollar sunglasses.

Nairobia's bodyguard was rugged and thuggish, cocky and slightly arrogant, yet when he'd interviewed for the job, he knew how to articulate himself in a professional manner. She liked that about him. She found his swagger enticing. And, aside from the fact that he had a broad nose, smooth, dark-chocolate skin, and thick lips, she imagined he also had a thick, long, strong tongue and a big juicy cock to match the set of thick long fingers on his hands.

She reminded herself to send her stylist, Pasha, a bottle of champagne and a basket of sex toys from her latest collection, thanking her for the referral. Or maybe she'd take a moment to stop by her salon and drop off the basket of treats in person.

Oh, yes. Her newest edition of eye candy would do just fine.

Carlos smirked at Mr. Dreamy Dark Chocolate, then opened his arms and Nairobia stepped into his embrace. At five-ten, she was naturally tall. But, standing here in a pair of six-inch Jimmy Choos, she stood eye-level, matching the crooner's six-five frame. She pressed herself into him, pressing her pelvis into his groin. She wanted him to feel the welcoming heat of her cunt. Wanted him to know his hard cock held a special place between her thighs.

"Damn," he groaned, before kissing Nairobia on the side of her mouth. "You sure know how to get a muhfucka excited."

"And I know how to bring him to orgasm, too," she muttered in his ear. "Do not tempt me, my darling."

Carlos chuckled. "Oh, have at it, baby. I'm all yours."

"Mmm. Do tell, my love. Is your cock hard for me?" she whispered, sensually rubbing her crotch into his right in full view of the public. Yes. Smack dab in the middle of a bustling LAX airport she grinded herself into him.

She was shameless. And she knew it. She fearlessly explored her sexuality and loved expressing her sensuality through her dress. And she didn't give a damn who didn't like it. She lived to make the world around her uncomfortable.

Besides, it made for great press.

She felt the thickening of Carlos' cock against her clit, then remembered the heavy feel of him on her tongue and the musky smell of him as she'd taken him deep in her mouth. The memory of how he'd enjoyed her wandering tongue wetly loving over every inch of his turgid flesh brought a wicked tilt to the corners of her lips.

Mmm. Got milk?

She swallowed.

Behind her, Lamar's jaws tightened. He'd felt his dick stirring in his boxer shorts as he watched her ass—*literally*, on the low. And no matter how many times he mentally scolded himself for looking, he couldn't help himself. There was no denying it. She was a stunner, sexy as fuck. He didn't know how he'd be able to concentrate on the job, if she insisted on wearing skimpy shit around him. *Fuck*.

At the rate he was going, he'd have to wear bigger slacks and an extra pair of underwear to keep his dick strapped down and from bulging. He was slowly starting to hate himself for taking on this job. He should have handed it over to one of his employees, or his partner.

He sighed, tearing his sight from her plump ass just long enough to glance at his watch before surveying the area. The airport was crowded as fuck and all she wanted to do was stand here dicking around with this…*pretty-ass muhfucka*.

What the fuck is she doing? he thought as his cell phone buzzed in the front pocket of his black blazer. Though he could use the distraction, he ignored it, his eyes drifting back over the globes of Nairobia's mouthwatering booty.

There was no denying it, no matter how hard he tried. First day on the job and there was definitely a raw attraction to the infamous Nairobia Jansen.

Motherfuck. Lamar shook his head. He'd already concluded, as beautiful and desirable as she was, she'd be more trouble than her worth. She was self-indulged. Used to getting her way. Too damned high-maintenance. Thought the sun, the moon—hell, the whole fucking solar system—revolved around her. And she had a ton of starry-eyed mofos falling at her feet.

He wasn't the one.

Though he'd never admit it right out, he'd bust a nut or two to a few of her porn videos back in his day, fantasizing about fucking the shit out of her sexy ass. Hell, he even had a pinup of her when he was, like nineteen, up on his wall.

She was flawless then. And she was more dangerously perfect now.

Now, here he was working for her. He'd have to keep his distance. Keep this shit strictly professional. He'd crossed the line once with his last client. But he wouldn't get caught up again. At least he hoped like hell not. The last thing his security firm needed was to be tangled up in a bunch of drama, like with his last employer. Or worse…some sex scandal.

Lamar looked back over at Nairobia and stared at the back of her head, instead of her juicy ass cheeks. He cursed himself, his dick growing harder against his will. He was hired to protect her, not fuck her. He knew this. Sadly, his dick hadn't gotten the memo, yet. He made a mental note to purchase those jockstraps and baggy pants first thing in the morning, and pick up two more pairs of dark-lensed shades.

Carlos grabbed her hands and stepped back from her, his eyes appraising her. "Damn, baby. Are you coming or going?"

Nairobia licked her lips. "I'm *coming*, my love. And you do know how much I love to *come*, no?"

Carlos grinned. "I already know. Damn. You're starting to make me sweat with your fine-ass. So what brings you out to L.A.? Business or pleasure?"

"*Pleasure*, my darling," Nairobia said saucily as she cast her gaze down to the lump in his designer cut-up jeans. Tonight, she was attending an all-white party at Hugh Hefner's infamous Playboy Mansion in Beverly Hills. Then later in the evening, she'd be hosting one of her very own exclusive, invite-only sex parties at her Bel-Air estate, before flying back to New York just in time for the doors to her club to open.

"And you, my love. Is this business or pleasure for you?"

"Business," he told her. He had a meeting with his PR team, followed by a photo shoot, then he was performing at the Staples Center tomorrow night. "But I am always in the mood for something pleasurable." His eyes gleamed mischievously.

Nairobia seductively licked her lips.

He added, "Speaking of which, I hear you've opened a Manhattan gentlemen's club. I'll have to come through and check it out."

Nairobia cringed at hearing her club being trashed down to that of a gentlemen's club. Yes, there were lots of scantily dressed women, and plenty of happy endings. But there was nothing gentlemanly about her establishment. "No, no, no, my darling. I do not have a nightclub for men. The Pleasure Zone is a den of sinful goodness for the uninhibited."

She removed her diamond hairclip letting her hair tumble down past her shoulders. She shook her head, running a hand through her tousled mane.

Carlos grinned. "Nice. Put me on the guest list."

Nairobia eyed him and smiled. "Enter if you dare, my love…"

"Oh, I'm always up for a dare, baby. How about we start with you coming to my show tomorrow night? Up close and personal?"

Nairobia pursed her lips and pondered the invite. She couldn't remember the last time she'd been to a concert. It'd been years. For some odd reason, the thought of seeing a bunch of star-struck women, throwing themselves—*and* their panties—at the sexy crooner made her that more interested in attending. After several more seconds of thought, she told him she'd love to go.

He smiled. "Cool. I'll make sure my publicist has two tickets for you." He shot a glance over at Lamar, then brought his attention back to Nairobia. "You'll be my special guest."

Legs spread. Arms crossed. Totally still, Lamar cleared his throat, loud enough for the both of them to hear him. She could feel his eyes on her ass behind the dark lenses of his shades. She slid him a sultry glance and felt her pussy tingle. She decided, then, she might one day give him his very own private viewing if he earned one.

But—

A camera flash went off.

They'd been spotted.

"Ohmygod!" screamed a young woman, pointing in their direction. "That's Carlos!"

"Looks like I'm being outed," Carlos said lightheartedly, giving her another hug and kiss on the cheek.

"Yes, my love. Your fans have sniffed you out."

Nairobia quickly stepped out of his embrace just as a gaggle of women surged upon them like a tsunami, causing a number of travelers to get knocked over as adoring fans surrounded them, screaming out Carlos' name, while whipping out their cells and begging for photographs with the R&B sensation.

"Carlos! I love you!" another worshiping fan called out.

"OMG! There's my baby daddy!" someone else yelled, running in the direction of the others, cell phone on the ready for a photo.

Lamar clenched his jaw. He knew this shit was going to happen.

Instinctively, he grabbed Nairobia, pulling her into his hard body, ushering her away from the pandemonium, while struggling to ignore how good her body felt against his.

His dick stretched another two inches down the inside of his thigh.

Shit.

Shit.

Shit.

FOURTEEN

Saturday night came quickly. Laid out on her ten-thousand-dollar bed was an equally expensive gown. The backless, crystal-embellished, see-through gown with a plunging neckline was a Balmain masterpiece Nairobia simply had to have after seeing it in his collection at Paris' Fashion Week. She'd snatch it up first chance she had gotten; now the fabulous piece was in her possession and she couldn't wait to showcase the French designer's one-of-a-kind, show-stopping evening gown.

After applying a glittering body cream, she pinned her hair up into a sleek chignon, then slid in a pair of diamond and ruby studs, followed by a diamond choker with a huge ruby teardrop around her neck. The piece was exquisite, fitting snugly against her skin, the breathtaking ruby dangling ever so delicately in the middle of her slender neck.

She then sat at her vanity and (for dramatic effect) applied a coat of MAC lipglass in Russian Red over her succulent lips. She reached for a bottle of her most expensive perfume, and spritzed her wrists, then dabbed some along her cleavage and along the inside of her thighs.

Finally, Nairobia removed the dress from her bed and shimmied herself into the delicate garment. She stared into her mirror and smiled. The gown wrapped scandalously around every inch of her body, hugging her delicious curves. Underneath, she wore a pair of sequined panties. She decided against baring all her assets to-night. Her breasts and delectable nipples, hidden beneath jeweled pasties, were sufficient enough. She turned to the side and admired her voluptuous ass. Carlos might be the featured attraction at the Staples Center tonight, but Nairobia would definitely be everyone's distraction.

She tucked her diamond-encrusted clutch under her arm, then made her way downstairs to where her *date* for the night had been impatiently waiting. She hadn't planned on asking him to the concert tonight, and it wasn't as if she needed him tagging along, but she had decided at the last minute that she wanted to know more about the sexy hunk whom she paid quite generously to pro-tect her. And what better way to get to know her bodyguard than by seeing him with—what she hoped—his guard down; and, perhaps later (after a few cocktails), his pants. Or if not his pants off, she hoped to get at least a sly glimpse of his cock bulging in his slacks at some point during the evening. She hadn't gotten over how he'd snatched her up in his arms and escorted her out of the air-port yesterday. His body felt hard against hers. And she almost believed she'd felt a hardening in his crotch when she ever so lightly brushed a hand over him when she'd pressed into his body, but she hadn't been for certain.

Lamar paced the tile in the foyer becoming increasingly irked that she'd taken her slow, sweet-ass time getting ready. Almost two-motherfucking hours! He was real close to telling her ass he'd catch her the next time. But, on the low, he wanted to see what the hype around that pretty R&B motherfucker was really all about. Still, he couldn't believe he'd agreed to go with his client to a concert.

Not as her bodyguard as she'd boldly informed him, but as a last-minute substitution for a date. She'd considered him a date substitute, some shitty last-minute afterthought. He couldn't believe that shit. But why should it matter? It didn't. Not really. He wasn't checking for her like that, even if she were one of the hottest broads in the world, bouncing around a big, juicy-ass.

She wasn't the only bad bitch in the universe.

Nah. She's the fuckin' baddest.

Lamar shook his head, then glanced at his watch. It was already 7:30 and the concert started at eight. Women. He slid his phone from his hip, ready to hit up his partner, Mel, on the West Coast to see how life and business were treating him when Nairobia appeared in the foyer. He stopped pacing and looked up from his phone. Goddamn. His breath caught. That fucking dress!

His dick hardened by the heartbeat.

He groaned inwardly as his gaze flicked over her face, then lower. She was provoking him. *That* dress was provoking him. And he didn't like it one goddamn bit. He was pissed he'd taken his shades off.

Nairobia grinned as she followed his glance. At the last minute, she'd removed her pasties. And now her nipples were stiff. "You like, no?" she asked saucily. It was a loaded question for sure.

Fuck yeah, he liked. The way her dress dipped low in the front, almost to her navel, flashing lots of cleavage and the generous swells of her breasts. But he wasn't about to play himself as some thirsty cat. Still, surprisingly, his mouth watered to suck a nipple between his lips and graze the tips with his teeth until they tightened almost painfully. "Yo, muhfucka, snap outta it," he told himself. *Get ya mind right, niggah. She does this shit for a living. Turning muhfuckas on. Dick-teasin' ass!*

Lamar swallowed and took a moment longer to savor the view, then shrugged his shoulders. "It's aiight," he said evenly, almost nonchalantly.

She stared at him, blankly. *It's aiight?* Was that the best this beefy bastard could do? All right was *not* the effect she was going for to-night. She rolled her eyes. "Come," she huffed, sashaying toward the doors. "I don't want to be late."

He smirked. *Oh now she's concerned about being late. Really?* He followed behind her, his eyes on the sway of her hips. And the vision pissed him off more. It made him hard. Again.

Once inside the limo, Nairobia settled back into the soft leather as the driver shut the door the moment her so-called date slid into the luxury cabin. Mirrored shades back on, he sat across from her. Legs open, he tried not to look at her, those mouthwatering nipples, her smooth, silky legs.

Lamar exhaled. He felt himself swinging like a pendulum between agitation and sexual frustration. He looked down to keep from looking at her protruding nipples and made the foolish mistake of looking at her sandaled feet. She had pretty-ass toes on top of every-*fucking*-thing else that was ridiculously sexy about her. His blood heated all over again. This pissed him off even more. Lamar loved pretty feet and toes. Now he had to wrestle with thoughts of sucking each red-painted toe into his mouth.

He sucked in a breath and cursed himself as hundreds of images—of *her*—swirled in his head: her on her hands and knees, him fucking her from behind, in her ass, her pussy; her on top of him, riding him down into a mattress; him eating her pussy while she sucked his dick; her ass in the air, his tongue in her sweet hole. He'd never eaten ass before, but he knew for sure he'd eat her booty like a bag of groceries.

The salacious thoughts running through his head were fucking ridiculous, and had both his heads ready to explode.

Nairobia breathed in as her pussy clenched. A mixture of leather and his intoxicating cologne tantalized her senses. His scent and heat clung in the air making it uncomfortably difficult for her to keep from soaking her sequined panties. She didn't know what it was about the twenty-eight-year-old, dark-chocolate hunk who she'd hired to manage her club's security that had her feeling...so unnerved, so damn needy and greedy. But she wanted a taste of his chocolate. Very thick chocolate, she hoped.

She cleared her throat and willed her pussy still. "So tell me, my darling," she cooed, reaching over and touching his knee. Lamar's body stiffened as the electricity from her fingertips zapped through his core. There was definitely a sexual attraction he cared not to explore, nor acknowledge. He had to keep telling himself to stay focused. To not let anything she said or did unnerve him. Nairobia licked her lips. "Do I make you nervous?"

He frowned. *Why the fuck is she asking me some shit like that?* No she didn't make him nervous. She made him...he shook the thought from his head. "Nah," he coolly replied. But his dark gaze behind his shades skittered away. "Why you ask?"

Nairobia grinned. She knew men. She studied them. She'd been around enough of them—and fucked enough of them—to know when she made a man uneasy. When her sexual energy was too much for them.

For some reason, with *him*, she couldn't tell one way or the other. Instead of answering his question, she eased up from her seat, then leaned over him, her palms planted on either side of him against the seat, and said, "Good. I am precious cargo, my love. I don't want, or need, any man who I am entrusting to *serve* and protect me, nervous of me, or around me."

Yeah, he'd protect her all right. But he didn't like that *serve* shit. The way it rolled off her tongue made him cringe. Unless she was referring to getting *served* a dose of hard dick, Lamar wasn't down with serving a broad shit else, except for a mouthful of his babies.

He swallowed. And started to sweat. *Motherfuck.* He knew he should have busted a few nuts before flying out here with her. His hands itched to slide them through her hair, curling the strands around his fingers as he pushed her face-down into his lap. She could definitely suck his dick if she wanted.

Yo, fuck, man! You buggin' for real, muhfucka! Don't let this broad try'n play you. His toes curled in his boots. He had to fight to keep from telling her what he'd like to see her do with that pretty mouth of hers.

"Yo, check this out," he said, his vernacular going from professional to hood. "Ain't shit soft over here, ya heard? So we good on all that *nervous* talk, ma. You hired me to handle ya security team 'n' keep you safe 'n' that's what I'ma do." His jaw clenched. "But, if at any time you feel unsatisfied with my firm's services, then you can terminate the terms of the contract 'n' me 'n' my peoples can bounce; feel me?"

Nairobia gave him a lingering stare filled with promises of hot nastiness. "I would love nothing more than to *feel* you, my darling. Trail my tongue along the swell of your cock. Then fill your mouth with my cunt. But not tonight, my love."

Goddamn. Lamar felt his pulse quicken. His mouth went dry, but the tip of his dick trickled with desire. Behind the dark lenses, he kept his gaze on her, trying like hell to maintain his cool, calm, collected composure. He felt the heat. Felt her potent sexual energy slowly burning his senses.

His jaw clenched. "Then we good," he bit out.

Oh, yes. They were good, more than good. The only thing Nairobia wanted to see bouncing at the moment was her ass up and down on his strikingly handsome face.

She needed to see *him*. Wanted to look him in the eyes. Wanted to look into the windows of his soul. His hand gripped her wrist when she boldly tried to remove his shades.

Nairobia's mouth watered. She leaned in and placed her lips flush against his ear. She whispered, "The question, my love, is: are *you* good? Is your cock hard for me?"

He fought to not breathe her in. "Nah, my shit ain't hard," he lied, hoping she wouldn't be brazen enough to reach between his legs to feel the truth, that his dick was harder than steel. "And, yeah, I'm good. I'm always *good*…anything else?"

Mmm. A moan caught in her throat. The innuendo wrapped around her like a silk blanket. She licked her lips. Instantly, his breath coming fast, he felt like he'd been punched in the gut.

Nairobia flicked at his ear with her tongue, then whispered, *"Als ik heb mijn weg, mijn liefde, zal ik nemen u naar mijn bed en smelten mijn kut*…all over you. Now. There's nothing else, my darling. For now."

His dick jumped.

She kissed him lightly on the cheek, then eased back in her seat as the limousine rounded the corner onto Figueroa Street, one block from their destination.

Adjusting his shades, he eyed her out of his peripheral vision, his nostrils flaring, as she stared out the window, pretending she had not just been up in his face taunting him with her beauty, with her femininity, her sensuality. He had no fucking clue what she'd just whispered into his ear, but the shit had heat shooting through his balls and blood rushing to his dick. He cursed under his breath. He hoped like hell that by the time they climbed out of the limo, his throbbing erection would be hard to see.

His dick pulsed. Again.

He clenched his fists, and groaned inwardly.

Fat, fucking chance!

Nairobia's lips curled into a smile as she stared out into the night. Yes. If indeed she had her way, she'd have him in her bed, melting her cunt all over him.

And if not…

She had a chest full of sex toys, and a wicked imagination.

FIFTEEN

"Yo, what's good, Los Annnnngeles!" Carlos screamed out into the crowd an hour-and-a-half into his set, shirt unbuttoned and pulled open. An array of multicolored panties scattered at his feet. "Y'all having a good time tonight?"

"Yes!" the crowd shouted.

The twenty-thousand-seat Staples Center was filled to capacity, and the R&B crooner had the crowd melting in their seats, ready to get home and tear it up in the sheets after he and his sexy label mate, Laila Reynolds, had just delivered a seductive, heart-stopping, loin-tingling duet together from off his latest album, *P.O.P.*, which stood for *Pussy over Pennies*. The sexual energy in the air was so thick you could slice it with a knife. There were lots of hard, horny dick and horny, wet pussies in the building tonight down to fuck, and Carlos knew—without a doubt—somebody was getting pregnant tonight.

He was a mixture of Prince, Maxwell, and Eric Benet all rolled into one sensually, seductive man.

"Cool, cool. Ladies, y'all ready for me to slow it down and get real nasty with it?" He held up his microphone to the crowd.

"Yes!" they screamed.

"Y'all ready to get wet tonight?"

More screams. "Yesssssss!"

More panties soared in the air and fluttered to the stage.

"I stay wet!" someone from the audience screamed.

"Yeah, baby," Carlos moaned. "I like it wet."

"We love you, Carrrrrlos!" a few groupies in seats a few rows back of Nairobia yelled out. They were clearly inebriated. And, more than likely, had won their tickets and backstage passes to the show from the many contests the radio station 93.3 had had leading up to tonight's event.

Carlos flashed a smile. "Awww, damn. I love you, too, baby. Now who's ready for me to…" The sultry intro, with the naughty beat, to his smash single, "Lick Her Slow"—from his first album, *Dirty lil Secrets*—started playing. Carlos licked his lips. "Yeah, I know y'all know what that is." He pulled out a big, juicy peach and bit into it. Juices splashed out and dripped down his chin. He licked around his lips, then stuck his tongue out and slowly licked around the peach, before taking another bite.

The crowd went wild.

Bulbs flashed from everywhere.

He slowly chewed, savoring the fruit's juices, then said, "How many of you beauties out there are real juicy?"

Hands flew up in the air. Scantily clad women shot up from their seats, professing to be the juiciest of them all. *Lies!* Nairobia chuckled to herself. Most of them were delusional. She looked over to the right of her and spotted the female rapper Lil' Kim— three seats down from her, waving her hand in the air, too.

Nairobia frowned. Maybe once upon a time, but now…

Nairobia rolled her eyes, shifting her gaze back to the stage. Carlos bent over and picked up a pair of purple panties off the stage floor to wipe the sweat from his chest. The panties were huge. But he wasn't the one to put any of his fans on blast, so he took it in stride. He waved them in the air and the crowd laughed. Then he looked inside for any stains. Certain they were clean, he wiped the sweat from his face with them, then tucked them in his back pocket. "Yo, big girls can get the tongue too," he teased. Then sang, "Close ya eyes, baaaby…let me in between ya thighs…hot tongue…licking all over you…"

He held the mic out to the crowd as they sang out the rest of the chorus, "Tasting all over you…loving all over you…licking it nice 'n' slow…"

Carlos brought the microphone back up to his lips and sang out, "Let me bury my head between ya legs…and get lost in paradise… licking you up 'n' down…"

He stared out into the crowd as if he were looking for someone in particular, still singing, flicking his tongue in and out every so often; driving his female fans wild.

More panties flew in the air. He caught a pink thong mid-air, sniffing it, before sliding the flimsy undergarment over his head. As much as he adored his female fans, some were nasty as fuck, half-washing their asses, or smelling like fish juice. And a few in the past had been nasty enough to toss a pair of filthy, shit-stained drawers up on the stage at him.

Carlos sang a few more lines of his song, then hopped off the stage and that only sent his lusty-eyed fans screaming louder. Women jumped up and down, covering their mouths, and stomping their feet as he walked through the crowd, touching hands, and kissing females on the cheek, before making his way over to the object of his desire.

Nairobia.

Carlos' hungry gaze skimmed down her body as he made his way over to her, singing as if he were singing his song to her, about her, his tongue licking all over her cunt and clit, loving all over it.

She instantly became the envy of every woman there as he took her hand and guided it over his hard cock. Just the sight of her had him aching for her.

"Tongue all up in it…lapping all over it…nibbling all over it… flicking all over it… Givin' your body it…let me lick it nice 'n' slow… Kissing all over it…loving all over it…makin' ya body beg for it…"

His tongue flicked. The women in the crowd watched in wide-eyed lust as he made his long tongue curl, then roll, seductively sliding it in and out of his mouth.

Paparazzi were everywhere. A gaggle of cameras flashing, catching every suggestive move the R&B sensation made.

He took Nairobia by the hand and sang the lyrics to the sensual number as he pulled her up from her seat. Nairobia stood, balancing on five-inch gladiator sandals, giving those in back of her a heavenly view of everything she was made of. The men whistled and clapped as Carlos walked backward, slowly pulling her along with him.

Nairobia swayed to the beat, her hips rolling every so often.

He licked his lips. "Close ya eyes, baby," he crooned. "Me on my stomach…You on ya back…legs spread wide…you maneuver ya hips…to greet my lips…"

Screams from adoring fans ricocheted around the arena. "Yass! Yassss!"

Lamar gritted his teeth and stayed glued in his seat, trying to keep his gaze off her ass while staying on full alert to what was happening around him.

Carlos helped her up on stage, then said… "What y'all think, fellas? Is she bangin' or what…?" He slowly spun Nairobia around, causing the place to erupt with whistles and barking noises.

"Let's give 'em a show, baby," Carlos whispered in her ear, pulling her body into his. He slowly swirled his hips, while singing, "This tongue's making you wet…making ya body weak…" Carlos' female fans kept screaming out his name as he ground his pelvis into

Nairobia's ass causing her to match his rhythm with a slow, seductive wind of her own hips.

He shocked her—and the crowd—when he slowly moved in front of her, while his background singers sang the chorus, and brought himself down on one knee, then pressed his face into the center of her crotch, his hands cupping her ass. If it were up to him, he'd fuck her right there, right then, in front of his adoring fans.

Nairobia, never one to be outdone, slowly eased her gown up over her hips for his (and the crowd's) full enjoyment, showing off her long, sexy legs. She stood wide-legged as Carlos sang a few bars of his song, then nastily licked the satiny part between her thighs. Nairobia gyrated her hips. Pumped her pelvis. Then slowly turned until she had her big juicy ass in his gorgeous face. This only made the crowd wilder, especially when Carlos took a suggestive bite out of her left ass cheek, before standing up and continuing the rest of his song. "Got me loving ya body…licking ya body… against the rhythm of desire…that swells…and rises…and erupts, dripping 'n' trickling down my chin…"

"Give it up, L.A., for the one of the world's sexiest women alive… the beautiful Nairobia Jansen!"

The crowd clapped. Then the whole building shook with wild abandon as Carlos pulled Nairobia into his arms and covered her mouth with his, pushing his tongue past her parting lips.

Cameras flashed. Phones flew up in the air, capturing the moment on video. The paparazzi ate it all up. The sexual display between the two was truly fodder for the tabloids.

Porn-star and R&B pretty boy turning the crowd out.

SIXTEEN

Instagram:

Ohmigod! Loved the concert last night. But I'm so jelly right now!

Yo who else peeped my future BM lettin' Carlos grind up on her fatty?

Yeah, I'm hatin' muhfuckas! Pleasure is my wifey!

Hahahaha! I woulda bust on that, fam!

She a whore! But I'd smash that!

She sexy AF! My dik still hard AF!

Yo word to the mutha! Pleasure can get it all night!

Facebook wall:

Ohmigod!! Seeing Pleasure up on the stage w/Carlos' sexy-azz at the concert last night gave me my whole life back! That bish my idol!

I'm not a lesbian. But she can get it.

Yasss, bish! Yass! Lawdgawd! Pleasure u did me right sugah-boo! U stole the show n tore yo' stank drawz at the concert, gawtdammit! Witcho ole slutty-azz! U made my cootie-coo real soggy! Had to get me some dingaling!

Twitter:

@CarlostheCrooner I love u baaabeee! Itz ya number 1 boo!

@CarlostheCrooner Y u all hugged up with that bish@Pleasure-Zone? She cute tho!

Follow me@CarlostheCrooner! Please! U 2@PleasureZone!

@PleasureZone I can be a freak 2 baby! #PornStarsCanGgetIt2!

Follow me baby @PleasureZone

@PleasureZone *Saw u @ concert! Damn u fiyah! My girl mad I wanna fuk u!*

@PleasureZone *next time u @#NappyNoMoreII Ya ole stuck up azz better speak! Don't do me! @PleasureZone follow me sugahboo!*

@PleasureZone *cum get this nut baby!*

@PleasureZone u stolllll the show! Follow me@PleasureZone! Pretty please!

Lamar shut his iPad. "You an' Pretty Boy are all over social media," he stated, as he strapped himself into the plush leather seat across from her. Nairobia had no interest in flying back to New York on a commercial flight. She'd already tortured herself by flying the friendly skies' public transportation, as she called it, coming to L.A. Something she'd only done to test Lamar's skills—well, *one* of them. And he'd passed with flying colors.

Now she could luxuriate on her early morning flight back to the Big Apple in the comfort of her private jet. She'd summoned her pilot last night to have him fueled up and ready. She glanced up from the magazine she'd been reading, which had a series of ten pictures covering two pages of her and Carlos. Speculation was written across the pages, that somehow the two were lovers, that they were having a torrid love affair. She'd been half-reading the story with the headline: How many kisses does it take to get to next base?

Nairobia shut the magazine and stared at Lamar thoughtfully, before shrugging dismissively at his comment. Although she had Twitter and Instagram accounts, and a Facebook Fan page—which were all managed by one of her production assistants at Sweet Pleasures, she couldn't be so bothered with social media.

She found it too messy, and too trashy.

"Am I not always, my love?" She tilted her head. "Talked about?"

"Yeah, I guess," he said curtly.

"Then it's not newsworthy to know that I am, no?"

Lamar frowned. *What the fuck crawled up in her ass?* Last night she'd been all up his face, taunting him with her sweet, juicy ass and those big, fluffy breasts of hers; now she was coming at him sideways. Moody-ass broads. He sighed inwardly, shaking his head. He wasn't about to let her give him a headache. Not at six in the fucking morning. Shit. He was tired as fuck. He didn't get much sleep.

After the concert, he'd been dragged to some big-shot after-party out in Malibu. And, yeah, he was supposed to be her *date*—as she referred to him—but the shit *felt* more like work trying to keep horny-ass *"muhfuckas"*—as Lamar called them, from swarming her. The whole night was one big headache. They hadn't gotten back to her spot until well after two in the morning. Then, by the time he'd gotten in bed, he'd tossed and turned unable to get to sleep. The pressure building in his dick had become too much to ignore. He had to literally take another shower—a very cold one at that. And, still, that'd done nothing for the heat that he had boiling through his body, or the steely erection that ached painfully for release. He needed some pussy. He needed to fuck.

Yet, the only thing he had at that moment to ease the pressure was his hand, a hand that hadn't been used to jack off his dick in years. Masturbation wasn't Lamar's thing. Fucking and getting head was.

Glancing at Nairobia sideways, behind mirrored shades, Lamar wondered what it must be like to be her. It had to be lonely. Spending her whole life fucking a bunch of random men. It had to do something to her self-esteem. He didn't know. He wasn't a shrink. Maybe it didn't affect her at all. Hell, he didn't care. But, after everything he'd experienced in the short time having her as a client, he surmised he didn't need a college degree to know Nairobia was nothing more than an attention whore who loved to be seen.

He needed a blunt. Bad! He cursed under his breath for stopping one of his favorite "chill-out" pasttimes. Taking a deep breath to relax himself, he surveyed the jet's main cabin. There were ten oversized seats, along with a plush leather sofa, a fifty-five-inch flat-screen, a stocked media console, and an extended dining table. In back of the jet were two suites, each with its own bathroom.

Lamar glanced back at the sofa and wondered how many times she'd been fucked on it, over it. Wondered how many times her pussy had soaked into the leather cushions. He wondered how many babies she'd swallowed right there on that sofa. And then his mind swirled to the left as the nose of the plane rose, wondering what it'd be like fucking her on her own plane.

Groaning inwardly, he scolded himself. "Muhfucka, what the fuck is wrong wit' you? Pull ya'self together." He eyed Nairobia as the jet roared down the runway, the outside world zooming by.

Keenly aware that he was watching her—the same way she'd known, felt, his eyes were on her all last night, burning over her—Nairobia looked over at Lamar.

"Why do you hide, my love?"

He frowned. "Hide? What do you mean?"

"Your eyes. You hide them from others. Why?"

"That's not what I'm doing. I wear them because it allows me to watch others without them knowing I'm watching them."

Nairobia smiled. "Well, my darling. When your eyes are on me, I'd rather *see* you looking at me."

He gave her a head nod. "I'll keep that in mind."

She opened her magazine, and flipped through the pages one last time, before glancing out the window with a smirk on her fine-ass face—as if she knew he'd been thinking lusty shit about her, as if she knew he was sitting on the other side of her with a hard-ass dick.

SEVENTEEN

"I see you were at the concert in L.A. last night," Marcel said low and husky into the phone. He glanced at the photo plastered on the front page of the entertainment section of her up on the stage with Carlos, with her head tossed back as if she were in pure ecstasy; her ass all up on his boy's cock, and his arm wrapped around her, pulling her in close as he sang.

Nairobia smiled. "Yes, my darling. And it was quite delicious."

Marcel raised a brow, then eyed the photo again, before glancing at the next caption. It read: R&B CROONER TAKES PORN-STAR BEAUTY. Beneath it was a candid shot of him with his tongue shoved down her throat. Marcel slung the paper. He knew he had no right to feel slighted. After all, Nairobia was a grown-ass woman free to do whatever she pleased with her body. Still, that knowing did nothing for his deflating ego, or his raging libido. "What was *delicious*, the show?"

No. His cock. "*Ja*," is all she said.

He hesitated, then hedged. "You fuck him?"

Nairobia blinked. None of his fucking business; thank you very much. What or *whom* she did with her *kut* was no one's concern except her own. She answered to no one. She belonged to no one. She wasn't sure why the question unnerved her because she'd had them both between her sheets—at the same time. But it did. And she felt herself becoming annoyed that he dared ask her that.

"Mar*Sell*, my darling. You know a lady never kisses and tells."

He smiled. That's what he loved most about her. Her ability to keep her mouth shut. But today he hoped like hell she'd open it wide for his hard cock.

"Oh, aiight," he said. "Then how 'bout you kiss on this dick, then tell me how good it is?"

"And why would I do such when you have not earned my sweet kisses?"

"Because my dick misses you," he murmured into the phone. He called her for one thing, and one thing only. Pussy. He had no time for games. It had been weeks—shit, longer than that—since he'd gotten laid. And his swollen balls were dangerously full from the drought. Getting pussy wasn't a problem for the music mogul and radio show host. He had access to some of the most exotic, beautiful women from around the world. The problem was, since the death of his wife, his sex drive hadn't been—well, let's just say his dick didn't always come alive when called upon.

But over the last several weeks it'd been throbbing for some pussy—Nairobia's pussy. He was a man who went after what he wanted. And what he wanted at this very moment was to bury his dick deep inside Nairobia's silky walls. He couldn't stop thinking about her. He hadn't stopped thinking about her.

Ever since seeing her down at the radio station during her interview with him, then talking, well, listening to her on the phone some weeks ago—moaning in his ear, then watching her between his legs on the car ride to Rhode Island sucking his dick…well, shit. All he could think about was having her in his bed, her bed, or any other bed. Hell, he'd fuck her over a ledge, up against a wall, on the hood of his Bentley…or wherever else as long as he could feel the inside of her warm guts. He couldn't stop thinking about the way she'd parted her thighs, teasingly, showing him her golden brown pussy lips in the studio. Her pink, creamy center was all that kept flashing through his mind during their interview segment. It had been hard for him to concentrate.

And he damn sure couldn't get the image of her soft, buttery lips wrapped around his dick, licking and teasing its head, suckling it the way a newborn nursed its mother's nipple.

Over the last few weeks, she'd been fucking with him—without knowing it, haunting his thoughts. And he knew the only way he'd be able to shake her from his brain was busting the thick-ass nut he had swelling up in his balls. He'd been saving up this nut for her. And now he was ready to pop off in her cunt.

Shit.

Nairobia was dangerously addictive. And he knew it. And his wife had known it to when she was alive. The two of them hadn't been able to get enough of her. Still to this day, he believed his wife, Marika, had caught feelings on the low for Nairobia, even if she'd never admitted to it.

Hell, he wouldn't have ever blamed Marika for falling for the exotic sex goddess if she'd confessed her true feelings for her. He would have understood. Hell. Who the fuck was he kidding? He knew he'd have welcomed it with open arms, and a hard damn cock, like right now. His dick was bricked. He felt pre-cum seeping from the tip of his dark chocolate-colored dick, wetting his drawers. And all he could imagine at that very moment was Nairobia's beautiful lips caressing his cock, her tongue flicking over his mushroom-shaped head, her soft hands cupping his cum-filled sac.

Marcel glanced at his Omega Skeleton. It was close to seven p.m., and he was still in his office looking over the contracts of three new artists MK Records was signing on. But to hell with work!

He had to stand and stretch his legs. He needed to free his dick from the constraints of clothes. He wanted to fuck. He wanted some ass. Jacking off wouldn't suffice. Getting just head would only frustrate him. He needed the wet grip of a pussy. He groaned inwardly. Shit. His dick was stretched down his leg, its head practically brushing his knee.

Besides his wife, none of their other sexual conquests that they'd shared together during their marriage—with the exception of Nairobia—had ever been able to handle all thirteen inches of him. But like his wife, Nairobia rode his cock like a roller coaster. She was a pro. He loved watching her throw her luscious ass back on his dick, watching her pussy make his dick disappear in her slick heat. She wasn't afraid of a big dick. She'd always welcomed it.

Marika had had some good pussy. No, scratch that. It'd been superb. But Nairobia's was like floating on clouds. Every time he had slid his dick into her deep, wet tunnel, he'd felt like he was fucking his way into heaven. Her *chatte* was simply heavenly.

He knew he should probably fall back and leave well enough alone. But he had to have a taste of her. He needed the warmth of her. The only woman he'd ever begged for pussy from was his wife. And, even then, it was done playfully, knowing she'd give in. Or else he'd take it. But Nairobia wasn't Marika. And he wasn't interested in taking what was between her legs. He wanted her to give it to him willingly. He wanted her to want his dick buried inside her, fucking into heat and desire, as much as he wanted it.

Nairobia purred, pulling him from his lustful reverie. "Mmm. Is that so, my darling?"

He licked his lips and grabbed at his dick. "Straight up. I want my dick deep in you," he said, a thick lusty heat coating his tone. "*Je veux te baiser.*" I want to fuck you.

His erotic words caressed her insides.

She licked her lips at the thought of him stretching her, loving her, fucking her.

"Tell me, my love. What else do you want?"

"C'mon, baby. Let's not play games. You know what I want. I think I already made it clear."

"Yes, my darling, you have." She grinned. "But I want to hear it again, anyway."

He groaned at the ache in his balls. He needed release. "I'm sitting here with all this big, hard dick. I've gotta thick creamy load just for you. I've been saving it up so let's stop all this chitchat and make it happen, baby."

Nairobia moaned, her mouth practically drooling. One of the many things she enjoyed about Marcel was his straightforwardness about sex. He was a man who had no problem telling a woman exactly what he wanted from her. And how he wanted. She found that refreshingly sexy, a man not afraid to express his sexual desires.

Another thing was that he was clean; so, so very clean. And he drank lots of cranberry and pineapple juices, always ensuring he had a sweet, thick, creamy treat for any wet, waiting mouth hungry for his semen.

She despised men whose ejaculate smelled rancid—like the back of a garbage truck, or had spunk that tasted like spoiled blue cheese, or tasted like he'd been licking an ashtray. Smelly sperm was a no, no for her. And she refused to let any of it enter through any of her orifices. And she wouldn't dare allow a facial to be given.

The thought made her cringe.

As far as she was concerned, a man who didn't/couldn't have enough pride in himself to eat right and drink right to provide sweet, nutritious loads of man milk was not worthy of release in her mouth, her ass, or her juicy *kut*.

She thought it disrespectful; an egregious act for any man to boldly offer his cum to her when his insides were rotted to the core.

No. Her pussy would never be contaminated with such nastiness.

Which is why she always milked her lovers to orgasm with her hands—or her feet, first round. She needed to see and smell their excitement before she'd ever wrap her pillow-soft lips around a cock, before she'd ever swallow it to the back of her throat.

She believed a lady never wasted good nut. She gobbled, gulped, and drained it right down to the very last drop. But she dared not ever slosh a dirty, foul-smelling load into her velvety mouth unless she was—(how you say?)—slutty trash.

And slutty trash she was not.

She stepped into a sumptuous pair of six-inch red stilettos and sauntered over to her French carved Trumeau. The eighty-four-hundred-dollar, nineteenth-century antique mirror had been a gift from her late mother before she'd died several years ago.

Losing her mother had been devastating for her. She'd been the only one who had always been supportive of her chosen path as a porn star, whereas her conservative father saw it—and her—as a disgrace. In his eyes, she'd brought shame and dishonor to her family. And he'd disowned her.

Sure, it had hurt her deeply in the beginning, being shunned by her own father. But, thankfully, her liberal-minded mother had been the one to encourage her to follow her heart, live her dreams, and do whatever it was she aspired to do—regardless of who else didn't approve of it. And at that time in her life, fucking (and being fucked) was what she'd wanted to do. She hadn't wanted to escape poverty to be in the porn industry, like so many young men and women she'd known. Nor had she'd been molested as a child. No. She'd been flouncing her gorgeous body naked on Plage de Tahiti— a beach in St. Tropez, France—when a renowned French photographer approached her with his card to pose nude for him at his studio. A few months later, a production company that had purchased some of his works of her eventually recruited her for a softcore DVD.

And the rest was history.

She blinked back the memory, staring at herself. Every time she looked in this mirror and saw her reflection, she was reminded of her dearly departed mother. She smiled, taking in her naked body shimmering in glitter lotion.

"*Allez, bébé*," Marcel said, pulling her from her musing. "I can be at your spot in about"—he looked at his watch—"thirty minutes, so—"

"So you can feel the heat of my cunt, my love?" she inquired, cutting him off. She wanted to be fucked deep and delicious. Wanted to claw at the sheets. And scream out in ecstasy.

But—

"You already know," Marcel murmured.

She cupped her breasts, then made them bounce. She turned sideways and marveled at her magnificent, traffic-stopping ass. She slapped it, then made each cheek pop before turning back full view. She wasn't vain, but she loved her body. She slid a hand between her thighs, and moaned in Marcel's ear. "You want my *kut* smeared all over your big, juicy dick? You want me riding your face, your tongue, like I'm taking cock, until I explode into your mouth?"

Fuck yeah. He wanted to lick, feast, suck, slide his tongue inside her and over her sweet, puffy lips and clit. He groaned. "Yo, you need to stop effen with me, baby. You know you want me stretching that shit."

Nairobia couldn't help but laugh. She loved the sound of his Brooklyn accent, one he'd gotten good at hiding when needed.

"*MarSell*, my *lieveling*. I admit. You make me want to ease out of my panties—wait. I'm not wearing any…"

Marcel pushed out a breath. "Damn. What else is new? When do you ever wear them shits? Let me cover that pretty pussy with my mouth. We can sixty-nine. I don't have to put this dick in you. Not tonight."

Nairobia swallowed. She was tempted. Oh, so, so very tempted. His touch was intoxicating. His thick cock was…mmm…it was delish. But she would not allow herself to be lured into Marcel's burning want. She knew he'd worship her pussy, lave it and love it all night long, fucking her on her back, on her side, on her knees, upside down. He'd give it to her just the way she liked. Yes, God. He'd give her orgasm after orgasm after orgasm with his hands, mouth and tongue, and with his big, juicy dick.

He'd indulge her every whim.

Melting and mewling, Nairobia knew her body would respond to him in every way imaginable. There was no denying it. She adulated Marcel's sexual freedom. She adored his freakiness. They'd own each other's bodies until the sun rose. Then after they'd worn each other out with kink and sex, they'd return to their corners of the world until his loins longed for her warmth again.

So what was the dilemma then?

The problem was, goddamn it…she'd never sexed him without his lovely wife. And, quite frankly, she wasn't so sure she wanted to be bedded down, fucked into a mattress, by Marcel without her.

Marika.

Sex with the two of them had always been full of heat and passion. She just couldn't fathom it being the same without her. Besides, she had to be in the mood for his ginormous cock. She loved big dick, but colossal cock wasn't made for everyday fucking. No, no, no. It was a nice treat on those days/nights she wanted to feel the stretch and burn of her cunt as each inch delved inside her.

Tonight she was hungry for nothing more than ten inches.

"So what's good?" Marcel said, slicing into her thoughts again. *"Papa peut obtenir le qui chatte douce, bébé?"* Can Daddy get that sweet pussy, baby?

Oh yeah. He wanted her. She had him practically begging. She wanted him, too, but on her terms, and on her time. She'd fuck him when she was good and ready to melt her pussy over the length of him. Not when he called on her.

True they had history, a scrumptiously rich one. And she loved the feel of him fucking into the folds of her *natte, sappige kut*. But her wet, juicy pussy wasn't his to have on-call. No, no, no. She wasn't his fuck-buddy. They weren't friends with benefits.

Still…

She was in heat.

She snapped open her bejeweled fan and fanned it over her pussy. Marcel was heating her. She moaned, and closed her eyes. "Mmm. *Zijn stem maakt mijn kut nat.*" There was no denying it. His voice made her pussy wet. Soaking wet. But so what? So did several other men in her life.

Marcel grinned. "So we fucking, baby?"

"*Mijn liefde*," Nairobia said softly. "You know I adore you, my love. And your big black cock, but…"

"No 'buts,' Nairobia. This dick misses you. Let me show you how much. Tonight. I want you to sit on my face while I lick that sweet pussy, baby."

Marcel's dick was about to bust out of his black boxer shorts. He would have pulled it out and stroked it while he listened to her breathe softly into his ear over the phone, but he wasn't in the mood for stroking his own dick—not tonight. Tonight he wanted some pussy. And he was tired of sucking his own dick, something he'd been doing—from time to time—since he was thirteen. A skill he'd haphazardly learned during one of his many jack-off bathroom sessions. He'd leaned in to spit on the head of his dick and realized he was flexible enough—and his cock was long enough—for him to lick it. So he did. And liked it. Licking his own dick eventually evolved into him sucking the head into his horny, wet mouth.

And he liked it.

His wife had loved that about him, being a self-sucker. She'd always said it turned her on. Made her pussy wetter every time he'd give her a show.

Nairobia closed her eyes and—as if she'd read Marcel's own lusty thoughts—imagined him bowing at the crown of his cock, worshipping it with his tongue, pumping it into his mouth, bobbing his head up and down, taking his long cock all the way to the back of his tonsils, sucking himself to the edge of bliss.

She felt her pussy heat as she relished in the memory of watching Marcel suck his own dick. She'd thought the act erotic. Seeing a masculine, rugged, sexy man like Marcel with his cock in his mouth. She wasn't sure how'd she'd personally feel about being exclusive with any man who enjoyed sucking his own dick. But the act had been spectacular to watch as he watched her make sweet love to his wife with a pink strap-on from her Nasty toy collection.

"Look, baby," Marcel said, deciding he'd had enough idle back and forth. He wasn't for a lot of chitchat when it came to wanting to get his dick wet. He wanted to fuck her senseless, but—

"Come *lécher mon minou doux*," she murmured seductively into the phone, her voice sweet and husky.

True she didn't want him fucking her. But it was a woman's prerogative to change her mind as often as she wanted. And Nairobia had quickly changed hers; just like that. Marcel desired her. So why should she not allow him to pleasure her? Why should she deny herself his touch? His lips? His tongue?

He could massage her walls with his long, thick fingers. Caress her clit with his wet tongue. But he could not have her *kut* stretched over his cock…not tonight.

But he could come lick her sweet cunt until the sun rose.

EIGHTEEN

Marcel arrived at Nairobia's building in record time, his dick throbbing the whole drive over. A doorman and security guard, along with surveillance cameras, manned the luxury high-rise 24/7. The minute he stepped through the sliding glass doors, the freckle-faced doorman recognized him and let him in. He smiled at Marcel, his glimmering white teeth sparkling under the bright halogen lights of the lobby.

"Ms. Jansen is expecting you," the doorman said, accompanying him to the elevator. Marcel wondered how he knew whom he was there to see since he'd never visited her there. He first thought it was that the doorman had assumed he was there for Nairobia because she was the only woman of color in the building. But he quickly learned she had texted the doorman a photo of him. In case he turned out to be a psycho. Marcel shook his head, smiling.

He couldn't wait to get upstairs. Nairobia's voice had been unimaginably sexy on the phone, stoking the fires in his loins higher. Until it was an inferno, boiling in his balls. He'd respect her boundaries and not force his dick on her, in her. But by the time he finished fucking her with his tongue and fingers, she'd wish he had stretched her around his wide, long dick.

He planned to have her body begging for him. And he'd gladly reward her with every inch of his cock. Punishing and pleasuring her for making him beg for her, for making him crave her.

Ever since his wife's murder, he'd been extremely cautious about fucking random women. So no. Stray pussy was out. Random pieces of ass were troublesome. Period. The last random fuck had proven fatal. And had cost him his wife's life.

And dating had been a challenge since he'd always find himself comparing them to his wife, dissecting them, pulling them apart, then trying to put them back together again in her likeness. It'd made him crazy. It was too much for him, and for them because he wasn't able to give them what they wanted. Him.

Truth be told, Marcel wasn't sure he was even ready for anything serious with anyone. His balls were full, but his heart was empty. He simply needed a sexual outlet, a fuck hole to lose himself in—and not through some random hookup site, or at some nightclub. He'd even given up jet-setting across the globe to the swanky, invite-only sex parties he and Marika attended religiously over the years. Going would've only reminded him of what he now no longer had. His wife.

When Marika were alive, he'd always seduced her in a way that made it easy for her to toss caution to the wind and freely give herself to him. No matter where they were. He'd known how to keep her aroused, on fire, burning. Just for him.

And she'd done the same.

Giving him unrelenting pleasure.

During their sixteen-year marriage, he'd belonged to Marika. Only her. She'd been everything he'd ever needed. They'd been equally yoked in mind, body and soul. She'd welcomed his sexual yearnings. And he'd openly embraced hers. His wants and desires had been hers as well; each always focused on the other's desires. Together they'd had some of the most explosive sexual encounters during their marriage.

Sometimes, when he inhaled deeply, Marcel could still smell her sweet musky scent; it clung thickly in the air around him, intoxicating him, driving him crazy. He'd loved the smell of her wet pussy. And he missed it immensely with each passing day.

He closed his eyes and breathed in deeply.

Now…here he was.

Needing Nairobia.

Wanting Nairobia.

Yearning for release. In her mouth, her pussy, her ass. He wanted all three holes, but was willing to accept whichever hole she was willing to give him. Tonight, her warm, wet mouth would be his receptacle. His cum dump.

If she were willing.

Otherwise, he was fine with the scent of her on his lips, stained on his tongue. He would feast on her, releasing blissful moans from her, wringing out one orgasm after another until she came in his mouth, until she melted all over his tongue, until he was full from her juices.

Holding the door open for him, the doorman used his key card to swipe for access to the penthouse. "Go right up, Sir," he said, slicing into Marcel's lustful memory.

Marcel glanced at the man's plated nametag. "Thanks, Stewart."

"Hope you enjoy your visit," he said.

"That's the plan," Marcel shot back, then smiled.

The doorman grinned slyly as if he knew something Marcel didn't just as the elevators doors closed. Marcel's dick throbbed harder. His balls ached so bad for release he could nut in his drawers right on the spot.

Nairobia stood naked in a pair of six-inch Louis Vuitton heels in the middle of her elaborate foyer when the elevator door finally slid open. She couldn't wait to feel Marcel's strong hands cupping her ass, kneading over her sensitive flesh. Parting, spreading; his tongue licking the opening of her pussy and nudging inward pulling out to lick over her clit.

She decided she wouldn't be a selfish lover…not tonight. Her intention had been to simply lower her *kut* down over his face and feed him her sweet, juicy sex. But as she waited for his arrival, her desire to taste him—again—intensified. So she now intended to suck his cock into her mouth. Thick veins roped around a big thick dick, she planned on licking up and down the length of him with her tongue, bathing him with her spit and drool and heat.

Marcel watched her smile with feline cunning, before her voice floated over toward him in a husky whisper as she said, "What took you so long, my darling, Mar*Sell? Mijn natte kut heeft gewacht voor u…*"

Yes. Her wet pussy had been waiting for him, for his tongue, for his fingers…for a blissful release. Marcel looked her over from head to toe as he stalked toward her, loosening his tie, unbuttoning his custom-tailored shirt. He knew very little Dutch, but he smelled her arousal, saw the flames of desire swooping up around her, and knew her pussy needed some tender loving just as much as his hard cock did. Seeing her completely naked, ready and waiting to be served up like a delightful feast was what he craved. She was every horny man's wet dream.

Her nipples were erect, plump like two juicy, seedless grapes. And Marcel couldn't wait to taste them, to lick them, to pop them into his wet mouth.

He pulled off his tie. Yanked open the buttons of his shirt. Then pulled his crisp white T-shirt out from the waistband of his slacks and dragged it upward, revealing smooth chocolate skin, flat abdominal muscles. He threw his shirt carelessly to the floor.

"*Je ne peux pas attender de lécher ta chatte,*" he said as he prowled closer. Oh how he couldn't wait to lick her pussy. He wanted to lick her to climax.

He swiped his tongue over his lips.

He was so close that Nairobia could smell the crisp scent of his cologne and the musky heat of his skin. She couldn't take it any longer. This torture, these slow ticks of the second hand. It was all too much for her.

Marcel's manhood swelled and strained against the fabric of his pants. Nairobia's gaze shifted to his crotch, then down the length of his right thigh. There it was. So long, so thick, so, so…snake-like. She couldn't wait to suck its head into her mouth.

As Marcel stalked closer, Nairobia backed up a step, then another, lifting her right breast up, extending her tongue and licking around her areola. Her nipple.

She licked it until it pebbled into a hard bead. Then smiled at Marcel. He groaned, arousal and jealousy swimming in his dark eyes. He wanted his mouth, his tongue where hers had been.

He reached for her. Not a word was said when he pulled her into him, against his hard body. Nairobia's breath caught. His masculinity, his manliness, his powerful existence, overwhelmed her senses. And she felt herself melting against him.

She drew up on her tiptoes. "I will love you with my mouth and tongue," she whispered. She licked at the shell of his ear. "Then capture you in the back of my throat and swallow your sweet milk."

She pressed her lips against his, then kissed him senseless. As she pried his mouth open with her tongue and slid inside, she could taste the hint of peppermint and cognac. Her eyes turned somnolent with desire as Marcel groaned, his lips pressing harder.

Within seconds, Nairobia's hand snaked its way between his thighs and her fingers curled around his cock, stretching to his knee. She'd never quite mastered sucking the entire length of him into her mouth. Eleven inches, the most. But tonight she promised herself she'd choke to death trying to swallow the remaining two inches.

When she broke the kiss, he smiled down at her. Then whispered, "*Ik wil al je pik in mijn natte mond.*" She wanted all of his cock inside her wet mouth. And she found herself becoming crazed with want. She stroked him several times for emphasis, before he removed her hand, then brought it up to his lips. He kissed the inside of her palm. Then let his hands travel along the curves of her body. He grabbed her at the hips, then lowered himself until he was eye level to her sweet cunt.

He bathed her stomach in kisses, stuck his tongue in her navel, and caused her flesh to quiver. "Spread your legs open for me, baby," he urged softly, his gaze fixed on the mocha-colored hood of her clitoris as she opened her thighs. She took her hands and spread herself open to him.

Marcel stared at her glistening, puffy mound.

God, she was stunning.

Then he looked up into her smoldering gray eyes and grinned. His eyes glittered with heat and lust as he said, "Your pussy is so beautiful, baby." He repeated himself in French. "*Ta chatte est si belle...*"

He moved his face in, and lapped at it until her pink clit distended.

Nairobia moaned. Grabbed the back of his head. "Lick me, my love. Mmm...yes...taste me..."

Then, as if she'd willed her juices to flow, nectar trickled out of her slit. And, without thought, Marcel licked that one drop of dew as if she were a piece of ripened fruit, his tongue touching her opening. His hands captured her ass, and he dug his fingers into the globes of her flesh while he stroked her clit and sucked at her. Nairobia threw her head back and moaned his name.

"Yes, my darling, yes...mmm...tongue my pussy, Mar*Shell*... mmm...yes, yes, yes...*mijn zoete kut tong...*"

Marcel's tongue lapped at her labia. Probed between the folds of her opening. Then devoured her, so hungry, so greedy, he licked over her pussy, enjoying the taste of her, savoring it. He fucked her in and out with his tongue, the rapid-fire flickering of each stroke drew moans from somewhere deep as he licked and sucked her in all the right spots.

He plunged a finger inside her, causing Nairobia's back to arch. She purred for him as he stroked her inner walls. She tightened around his finger.

Then one finger became two. And Nairobia slowly rolled her hips, then began to fuck herself down on his oversized hand as the pleasure pulsed through her. She was all slippery heat, her cunt frantically clutching around Marcel's fingers. He groaned, his steel-hard cock aching, his balls throbbing for release.

Fuck. He ached all over for her. He wanted to fuck, to take every hole she owned with force and fiery heat.

Marcel sucked her swollen clit back into his mouth, fucked her with his fingers until they both felt the sweet storm swirling up inside her, rising higher and higher, crashing harder and harder.

He had her right where he wanted her. On the edge.

She mewled, her nails digging into his scalp. Her eyes became half-lidded, the gray becoming smoky as Marcel licked and licked, his tongue feeling like wet flames against her clit. Nairobia was on the verge of coming all over his face, drowning him in her juices.

She cried out in pleasure. Spoke vulgar and dirty to him in her native tongue. Told him over and over to fuck her with his fingers, his tongue. To lick her pussy, tongue her ass. She cursed him for having such a luscious greedy mouth, for being such a splendid pussy eater. She cursed him for lavishing her cunt and clit with so much sweet affection all the way to the crack of her ass.

Right at this moment, she hated him for being so goddamn good. But she loved his wickedly talented mouth.

Oh, God, how she loved…his sweet licks.

Marcel's dick jumped furiously, impatiently, wanting to feel the warmth and wetness of her mouth, the soft touch of her hands, the greedy need of her tongue. All he could think about was her mouth swallowing around his cock, milking him, allowing it to slide nearly from her glossed lips, before she swirled her tongue over and around his bulbous head, teasing it. The image alone had him ready to nut. But he refused to unleash his beast until he'd taken her to euphoria, until her knees buckled and she fell limp from an exquisite release.

Until she surrendered to him.

Until she turned everything she was over to him.

He sucked her clit harder—almost savagely, causing her pussy to ripple over his fingers. She cupped and molded her swollen breasts, then tweaked at her nipples.

"Uhhh, uhhhh…ooooh…yes, my darling…yes, yes, yessss…!"

Liquid pleasure scorched through her cunt, sending her spiraling over the edge. Marcel groaned into her, hummed his desire for her and, in that instant, fire danced through her entire body.

Nairobia's head whipped from side to side, her nails clawing at his scalp as she stood on the brink of—

Delicious sensation.

Fiery energy.

Sweet torture.

Heated pleasure.

Marcel's tongue danced at her entrance, her clit captured between his teeth, his masculine fingers plunged knuckles deep.

Nairobia stopped breathing, started gasping, her veins threatening to burst.

A waterfall surged, then erupted, spraying out of her body. Marcel drank her in, gulping in as much of her juices as his already full mouth could swallow. He sucked and licked her to the very last drop. Then rose to his feet.

His face glistened, soaked from her sex juices. He licked his lips. Sucked on his fingers. Licked his lips again. "Don't move," he commanded as he kicked off his loafers. Unfastened his slacks and stepped out of them. Off came his underwear. His heavy dick sprang upward, pointing out like a tree branch.

Nairobia's body still quaked from her orgasm and the sight of him only intensified her spasms. She stood frozen in place, her drenched labia throbbing for more of him. Marcel was all muscle. And long, hard dick. She didn't trust herself not to move, not to reach out for his cock, for him, so she ran her fingers over her pussy, then dug two fingers inside and gathered her sticky arousal as Marcel stroked himself.

"You want this dick between your lips, baby…?" he muttered, his hand slowly moving back and forth along his veined shaft.

She touched her soaked fingers to her mouth. She opened it, then hungrily licked.

"Yes, my darling," she muttered over her fingers. "I want. I need…"

"To suck this dick," Marcel responded. And then he swept in, spun her around, grabbed her at the waist, and lifted her up off her feet. It all happened so quickly, so expertly, that all she could do was gasp. She bent at the waist, her ass in his face, as she leaned her head in, parted her lips and sucked the head of his moistened dick into her mouth.

"Aaaaah, shit," Marcel hissed. "*Sucer la bite, bébé.*"

And she did as he commanded.

Sucked his dick as he pressed his face into her cunt.

The feast had only just begun…

NINETEEN

Nairobia opened her eyes, and stretched, feeling deliciously satiated from her torrid night of cunnilingus. Marcel had been a man of his word when he'd said he wanted to lick her to pleasure. He and his extraordinary tongue had done just that, leaving no parts of her body untouched. He'd loved on her cunt, laved on her clit, and drank in her spurting juices with so much passion that she'd felt the room spinning as he feasted on every part of her swollen sex, sending shivers over her sensitive skin.

She couldn't remember if she'd shown him out. And she couldn't remember exactly when she'd drifted off to sleep. But the minute she heard the light snores beside her, her breath caught. *Oh no, no, no. Say it isn't so...*

She slowly turned her head to the left of her. And her eyes widened. She shot up in bed.

Oh God.

It was so.

There he was in *her* bed. Naked. The sheets whirled around him. Sleeping like a baby. Lightly snoring. This was a no-no. She allowed no man to sleep in her bed—or stay the night, *ever*. And the only lover she'd had in her bed most recently had been her boy-toy, Josiah. She'd given him a taste of her *kut*, then rewarded him for licking out multiple orgasms with a generous dose of pussy as she climbed up over him, positioned his thick cock between her lips so she could slide down over him. His strong, pulsing cock had felt so good in her. It always felt good in her. She'd ridden him into her fire, burning him with each stroke, owning him, taking what she needed from him until his neck arched, his back bowed upward from the bed, and he'd released a pleasured hiss between clenched teeth as she clutched his dick and cream flowed from her body. His cry of release, the sound so masculine, so wild, so... needy had caused her cunt to spasm and wring out another climax. Then after she'd freed his balls of its warm milk, she'd kissed him deeply on the mouth, and sent him to the guestroom.

Josiah was her only lover...at the moment.

But this, this thing with Marcel was not good. Him snuggled up in her sheets, like some long-lost lover. How had he managed to stay the night?

Her gaze riveted on his chiseled back, then locked on his muscled ass. His body was divine. And his humongous cock...

Sweet Jesus.

She blinked back the memory of the sweet burn she'd experienced the first time Marcel slid it inside her. It'd taken her back to her first time with Lexington Steele when she was a virgin starring in her first porno. Lexington had been so big, so thick, so damn excruciating and deliciously good. But Marcel had been much bigger, much thicker, much more delicious. And his cock pushing past her swollen folds, stretching her slit, had been like having her hymen broken for the first time all over again. The pain had been both shocking and sweet.

It'd seared her cunt as he'd blasted heat through her, while his wife...

Marika.

She stiffened, then hissed at the thought of her being gone. That first time together in Dubai three years ago, Marika had helped guide Marcel's luscious cock into her quivering cunt, before lowering her own scrumptious pussy over Nairobia's face, then leaning forward and kissing Marcel passionately. The two of them had set her body ablaze with their raw passion, made her pussy ache with desire…for the both of them.

Oh how she'd loved having them in her chambers. Their openness about sex and sexuality was refreshing. Intoxicating. Sexy. There were so many fond memories of the two of them tracing their tongues over her cunt, their fingers diving into her wetness, their fingers sliding over and around her cunt, feeling how slick she'd become; their tongues teasing her clit, then sliding fingers deep inside her; fingers teasing her ass. Their tongues and fingers had been wild for her, craved the taste of her, the feel of her. She'd become their sweetest guilty pleasure.

And they'd become hers.

She swallowed, her gaze narrowing as she stared at miles of rich, dark-chocolate muscle that made her gasp. She hadn't been drinking last night, but surely she'd fallen into a drunken slumber sometime in the middle of the night—with his mouth latched onto her clit and his tongue wedged between her folds—for him to *still* be in her bed.

Though he had not been asked to leave, Nairobia felt violated. She felt…slightly peeved—the gall of him to invite himself to the warmth and comforts of her luxurious red sheets.

She held her breath as she slid her hand between her thighs to make sure he'd hadn't stolen her cunt in the still of the night. Relieved that her slit was not stretched wide, she breathed out. Of course she would have still felt him throbbing inside her had he'd taken her last night. The stretch and burn she remembered had always been so much more delicious the next day—following a night of slow, deep fucking.

Marcel stirred, pulling her from her reverie. She rolled her eyes, her new thought on waking him, and putting him out. But he stirred again. Eyes still closed, he rolled over on his back, his arm swinging up over his face to shield his eyes from the morning rays as they slid through the slits of her vertical blinds. The sheet shifted, slightly, and Nairobia caught a glimpse of his rippling abs…and the beginnings of a delicious morning erection.

What was a woman with virtue to do?

Instinctively, Marcel's dick spoke to her from beneath the sheet. And the answer became evidently clear. Take what was in her bed.

Her mouth curved into a devilish grin, her sex clenching greedily, as she flipped the sheet off him, exposing the lower half of his nakedness.

She took his dick in her hand, rubbing the shaft from base to tip, gripping him with both hands, stroking him to greater pleasure, before licking him, swirling her tongue over his slit, focusing her attention all on that one part of him until he grew harder and thicker and beside himself with heated desire.

Several teasing licks of her tongue over the head of his dick morphed into sweltering tongue laps down the length of his cock, over and around his balls, then back up his shaft. Then back down again. She lapped at his balls, then sucked them lovingly into her mouth.

Marcel groaned, then smiled. "Good morning, baby," he muttered, his eyes slowly rolling to the back of his head. He hadn't planned on staying the night, but now he was glad he had. It'd been so long, too long, since he'd been awakened to the erotic sounds of a wet mouth loving his cock.

He needed this sensual moment badly.

Tiny pinpricks of pleasure burst through Marcel's body, spreading through his veins as Nairobia took him in her mouth and gave him what he so desperately needed, until he was a slave to her relentless sucking and the clawing need to explode.

Blood rushed through him. He fought like hell not to erupt. But she was luring him to the edge with her slippery mouth, coaxing a nut—or two, or three—out of him.

God, he missed having his dick in a mouth other than his own. She felt so fucking good. So wet. "Aaah, shit, yeah…oooh…" He lifted his hips into her mouth, slowly thrusting in her wet, juicy jaws. In. Out. In. Out.

She fondled his balls.

"Aaah, shit…aaah, shit, baby…*ta bouche est si humide, si chaud…*" Your mouth is so wet, so warm.

She released him from her mouth long enough to speak. "You like, my darling, *oui?*" Before he could speak, she quickly lapped at the wet tip, then feverishly sucked him back into her mouth.

Marcel groaned, his back arching in the wave of pleasure. "Aaah… shit…motherfuck, baby…mmm…I love your mouth."

No avoiding the truth now. Nairobia loved his big, long cock. Her pussy spasmed as she stroked him, coaxed him, and swallowed him down into the warmth of her throat. His heat and musky scent were maddening. She dug her nails into his hips, scraping flesh as she took him deep and massaged his testicles with tongue.

He cried out, the sound both erotic and animalistic.

His heart raced, and his fingers dug into the sheets. Un*fucking*-believable. She managed to get every inch of him down into her throat. His head spun as her throat constricted around the width of him, clutching him.

He breathed through his nose, weaving his fingers into her hair, bucking.

"Oh shit, oh shit…" The pressure built in him, and he lifted his hips up into her mouth. He gasped. Growled. Gritted his teeth.

Then called out her name as he came hard, bursting flames of passion into her welcoming mouth, his semen sliding down into her neck like warm chocolate.

Like the talented vixen she was, Nairobia swallowed every drop of him, sucking him until he went soft. His wet, sticky dick plopped out of her mouth, and she looked up and grinned seductively at him. She crawled up over him, kissing her way up to his parted lips.

He groaned, and tasted himself on her tongue.

Then pulled Nairobia into his arms, wrapping a leg over her. She blinked. What the hell was he doing? She tried to unwind herself from his deliciously warm, muscled body, but Marcel groaned in protest and tightened his arm around her.

"No, my love," she said, pushing up, trying to unwind herself. "I've entertained you long enough."

Eyes closed, Marcel grunted, and his huge hands ended up splayed across her ass.

"I'm not going anywhere, baby," he whispered to her neck. "And neither are you." He squeezed her ass. "Not until you give me some pussy."

Nairobia didn't respond, because her clenching cunt would betray her every word.

Bastard.

TWENTY

"Mmmm...ooh, *ja, ja, ja*," Nairobia panted as Marcel used his fingers to open her to him. He pressed a kiss over her mound and then nuzzled deeper, inhaling her arousal, all that pink, feminine inner flesh for the taking, glazed with pleasure.

Nairobia moaned again as Marcel used his tongue like a dick, licking her from the inside out, stroking her silky walls. "Come in my mouth, *bèbè*," he said huskily, raising his head to look up at her. His eyes were dark. His gaze focused. *"Donnez-moi ce lait sucré."*

He wanted her to give him her sweet milk one more time before he stretched her sweet, tight pussy over his dick. He hadn't forced himself on her the night before. Hadn't pressured her to let him be deep inside her. She wanted his tongue lapping her cunt. And he'd respected her wishes. But today was a new day.

He wanted inside her.

And he planned on fucking her, making sweet love to her, all in the same measured strokes.

Her wetness melting like honey on his tongue, Marcel sucked in Nairobia's clit, and she dissolved into pooling heat, arching her back and mewling out. She pumped her hips against his mouth and clutched his shoulders, moaning.

Nairobia was a dominant, powerful woman and Marcel loved seeing her lose herself to him. But she was nothing like Marika— not that he should be comparing the two. However, Marika had always given of herself willingly to him, submitted to her desires for him endlessly, whereas Nairobia was defiant. Brazen. And she refused to submit to any man.

But Marcel would break her, if it was the last thing he did. He would teach her how to lose herself to him, his pleasure. He bit down into one nipple and pinched her clit, and Nairobia cried out, her warm juices sliding out of her body.

But that wasn't enough for him. He wanted her to beg.

"Me dire que vous voulez que je vas te faire encule," he whispered in her ear. (Tell me you want me to fuck you.) "Beg *pour cette bite…*" (for this dick).

Nairobia would have laughed in his face if her cunt wasn't clutching and she weren't so caught up in sweet rapture. She begged no man for his cock. Not when she had an abundance of hard, willing dick at her disposal.

She'd give into the lust. Give into the pleasure. But she'd give over nothing to a man. He'd be here all night—and the rest of the year, for that matter—if he longed for that.

Marcel sucked her other nipple between his lips, scraped it with his teeth, then bit into it. She moaned as her breasts swelled. "Aaaaaah, yes…yesssss…"

It killed him not to be inside her, but he knew what her body needed. He wanted to hear her say it. Wanted to hear her cry out for it. He pushed a thick finger inside her. Then two. Then three.

She became unbelievably wet. And hot. Her heat burned into his hand, singed down his forearm, then surged over his stomach, before settling around his balls. His dick ached for her fire.

"Tell me you want this dick, *bèbè*," he murmured close to her ear.

Nairobia shivered as he rubbed circles into her G-spot. Eyes rolling helplessly around in their orbs, she arched off the mattress, groaned out, and soaked the sheets. Marcel fucked her with his fingers in a pulsing rhythm that made the room spin. She found herself panting in time to his fingers, her body humming in pleasure. And, yet, she still snubbed him. Refused to call out his name. Refused to beg for him.

His dick throbbed in frustration. He wanted to fuck her and fuck her now.

But...

He needed her to want it more.

Nairobia closed her eyes, and felt her body stretching apart, her orgasm spreading through her like a wildfire. Her pussy juices splashed out as Marcel's fingers fucked her hard and fast. *Splish-splash, splish-splash, splish-splash...*

Wetly, her cunt clutched his fingers, then he turned his hand and pushed hard to the back wall of her pussy, and she screamed hard and loud, her climax coming from somewhere deep.

Marcel wanted her to surrender to him. Just fucking beg him so he could feel her melting over his cock. Her defiance was unnerving. Her refusal was maddening. Fuck it. He needed to be inside her before his balls exploded. He reached for the condom he'd slid under his pillow the night before—just in case. He ripped open the gold foil and rolled the Magnum on in a matter of seconds, before grabbing her by the hips and dragging her over the sheets toward him. He covered her with his body, anchoring his arms on either side of her.

Nairobia's dark tresses fanned out over the silk sheets, and she looked like a goddess. Fucking beautiful. Marcel groaned, positioning himself at the mouth of her cunt. She toyed with her nipples, spreading open her thighs to him.

"You want my *kut?*" She licked her lips. Closed her legs. Then opened them again. Teasing him. "Then take it."

Aroused, on fire, burning, a low growl sounded in Marcel's throat.

He couldn't wait another second for her. He had to have her. Now. She'd won.

It was his defeat.

Marcel planted the palms of his hands on the inside of her thighs and pressed them apart. Then came the thick head of his cock, sliding over Nairobia's swollen clit. She moaned, thrusting her hips up to him.

In that moment, Marcel wished he had a smaller cock, one not as thick or as long—something like nine inches, maybe eight—so he could enter her in one smooth thrust. But his dick was too enormous for that. He wanted to make love to her, fuck her ever so sweetly. Not rip her insides out and kill her.

Nairobia sucked in her breath and slowly released it in a long exhale.

"You want this dick," he rasped, sliding himself back and forth over her flesh. Nairobia moaned again, softly, the feverish ache in her pussy stinging sharply. "I want you to beg for this dick, baby," he said in a strained voice. "But you're too fucking stubborn..." He pressed the head of his dick into her wet opening and pushed in. "But it's all love, baby. I'ma have you moaning and coming on this dick in a minute."

Marcel pushed forward; the plum-shaped head slipping past her tight folds. Nairobia whimpered. Slowly, he continued to work himself inside her, fucking her with the tip of his dick. He pulled back, his head dragging over throbbing flesh. Her pussy lips pulsed, her slit puckered, and pussy juice slid out.

"Uhh...mmm...fuck my *kut*..."

Marcel grinned. "That's it, baby. Beg for this dick."

He slowly moved his hips, pushing in and out, pulling the head out, then easing it back in. He wanted to be in all the way to his balls. She had his body overheating. But he was determined to take his time, until he worked every last inch of him inside her, until he bottomed out in her.

"Fuuuuck," he growled at how tight she was. He grew slick with her wetness; slowly, her body opened to him and he pushed six inches, then pulled out.

"Take my pussy," she hissed, reaching between them and stroking her clitoris. She closed her eyes and moaned.

Marcel pushed back in. Slowly worked his hips, his dick sliding in and out of silky heat.

Eight inches in…

Nairobia moaned louder. "Uhhhhh…mmmm…*neuk* me…"

Marcel kissed the hollow of her neck.

Nine inches in…

She gasped. He was thicker than her arm. The burn, the sting, made her pussy wetter. She rolled her hips. "Mmmm…aaaaah… *Ja, Ja, Jaaaaa…*"

"Fuck your pussy on my cock, baby," he murmured. "Aaah, yeah…"

He pulled out again, slowly retreating, her pussy quivering around him. He slid back in. Then out. Leaving her with nothing but the head of his cock inside her. Fucking her with the tip, he bit down on his bottom lip, enjoying the slick, tingly sensations.

She came and he felt her muscles sucking in his head, fluttering and shuddering all around him. He let out a moan, pushing back in, deeper. And she gasped.

Ten inches in…

Pain. Burn. Sting. Unrelenting pleasure.

She was everything Marcel needed.

He waited for her slit to close around him. Covered her mouth with his. Slipped his tongue in. Then pushed his dick back in. Nairobia's mouth opened in a soundless scream, her breath escaping from her lungs.

She'd said the night before she wouldn't give him her pussy, but this morning a switch in her body flipped. And he could have it. All of it. Every inch of her cunt he could fuck inside out.

Now.

Sweet pressure. Unrelenting fire. Dark arousal.

He was everything Nairobia wanted.

Everything her body yearned for.

Eleven inches in...

Her breaths rushed from her nostrils, and she felt herself gasping, gulping in mouthfuls of heated air. Marcel scorched her senses as he grabbed her tenderly around the hips and thrust forward, going in deeper. "Yeah, baby...open that sweet pussy up to me..."

Twisting his fingers through her hair, Marcel tugged, then bent to spread kisses along the side of her neck. With slow, sensual licks, he lapped his way toward her ear, nibbling, kissing, and licking. Then his mouth found hers again, making her body shiver as he licked her lips and enticed her to part them. His tongue swept into her mouth and her body opened up to all of him.

Thirteen inches in...

She was full. Stretched. Sizzling.

Her toes curled. Fire wrapped around the inside of her pussy.

Marcel took his time. Rocked his hips into her body. "Yeah, that's right, baby. I'm all in. Yeah, I feel you...aaah, yeah...wet pussy... aaaah, shiiiit...got that pussy all on this dick...give me that nut, baby... *Je voudrais sentir cette noix sucrée fonder partout dans cette grosse bite, bèbè...*" (Let me feel that sweet nut melt all over this big dick, baby).

Arms locked around his neck, her long legs wrapped around Marcel's lower back, and she welcomed him into her erupting flames, taking his slow, sweet, torturous thrust with abandon, her head and eyes rolling. Stretching around him, she clawed her nails down his back and came over and over and over, her orgasms shattering around him, soaking him. Torching him.

Her whole body shook.

Then he cried out. Her name. *Nairobia*. It was a sweet melody, a cry of triumph and release escaping his lips as he continued his slow thrusts into her body. He stayed inside her heat, inside her clutching wetness until he came again…

Flooding his condom.

TWENTY-ONE

"Naaaaairobia, *daaaaahling*," Zeus, the office manager for the trendy salon, Nappy No More II, cooed the minute she stepped through the sliding glass doors into the reception area of one of L.A.'s hottest hair salons on the West Coast.

He stood up and greeted Nairobia with two cheeky air kisses. Nairobia smiled at the high-heeled gender-bender as he took her in. He smiled at her. The diamonds around her neck and wrists instantly came alive under the recessed lighting. "You look scandalously fabulous as ever."

Nairobia tossed her hair. "Thank you, my love," she said, her oversized Birkin bag hanging in the crook of her arm. Zeus took in the crocodile leather and the diamond-studded clasp—ten-carat diamonds set on a bed of white gold, and drooled. As far as he was concerned—next to diamonds, a hard dick, and a popping lip gloss, a gorgeous handbag was a diva's best friend. And he longed more than anything to have the coveted Hermès bag in his possession.

Even though Pasha paid him a handsome salary as her office manager, it was nothing compared to the price tag of that handbag. He'd have to suck about thirteen hundred dicks at a rate of one hundred dollars a nut in order to afford the six-figure purchase, he mused before gazing back into Nairobia's sparkling eyes. He lived for her. She was an icon. A legend. And he'd watched every last one of her movies in hopes to one day become half the seductress she was. He secretly aspired to become a porn star himself and had already made several of his own home videos, which he'd posted up regularly on Snapchat, and several sex sites. But he was nowhere near Nairobia's caliber. And he suspected he and his homemade sex videos never would be.

Still…

He could dream.

Zeus looked his idol over, and bit the inside of his lip to keep from gushing. If he'd ever craved fish, she'd have been the first he'd try to fillet. Unbeknownst to anyone, some of his best orgasms were had from watching—with his lovers—Nairobia in her award-winning movie *Clitty-Clitty, Bang-Bang*, where she'd tied three hunks up—their hands and feet tethered to posts—and fucked and sucked them nearly unconscious, her cunt stretching down and over the length of them, making their horse-hung cocks magically disappear in and out of her body. He loved watching their dicks vanish in her wetness.

Zeus blinked. Then smiled at Nairobia. "I'll let Pasha know you're here." He smacked his lips together. "While you wait, would you like a glass of wine, champagne…?"

Nairobia shook her head. "No, my darling. Thanks. A lady never drinks before three."

He pursed his lips. "*Mmph.* Isn't it just past three on the East Coast?" He winked at her. "I'd say the lady deserves a *cock*tail or two…"

Nairobia glanced at her timepiece. 3:05 p.m. Her watch was still set for East Coast time. She smiled slyly. "In that case, my love. One glass of bubbly will be fine."

He pressed a few keys on his computer. Then within seconds, a server appeared, handing her a glass of Armand de Brignac Rose champagne. She took the glass of cava, then proceeded to take in the opulence of the salon as she took a slow sip.

She loved the stunning rain curtain that flowed from the ceiling to the black lava stones in the marble floor. She admired the custom décor and an impressive collection of art, including pieces by Andy Warhol, William Nash, and Leroy Campbell. The minute you stepped across the threshold of the ten-thousand-square-foot salon, you knew you'd stepped inside sleek sophistication.

"Nairobia," Pasha called out as she walked toward her, her smile wide, her eyes bright. "It's so good to see you."

The two women embraced. Nairobia air-kissed both cheeks, then stepped back from her. "You look delicious, my darling."

Pasha waved her on, blushing. Her five-carat diamond hooped earrings sparkled against the lighting. "Girl, stop. Not as fabulous as you. C'mon to the back."

Nairobia followed her down a long hall with glass walls to her station. Pasha was a sweet piece of ass. And she eyed the way her hips swayed in her Emilio Pucci printed, silk, lace-up dress and wondered just how sexually liberated she was.

She was tempted to extend Pasha an invitation to The Pleasure Zone to see just how far she'd be willing to allow her limits to be tested. But she quickly thought otherwise, deciding if she ever wanted to indulge her desires, then she'd inquire about her club on her own.

Nairobia had heard—no, no…she'd uncovered during her inquiries about the wealthy stylist—that she'd once been married to a notorious drug dealer and had come into millions of dollars from an unknown source after he was found murdered.

Bless her heart.

Nairobia admired her strength, raising her two young children alone—well, with the help of nannies and…

Marques Houston's "Always & Forever" floated through the speakers, slicing into Nairobia's musings. She found herself humming along as he crooned about not being able to stop thinking about his love interest. Nairobia imagined herself positioned between his legs, and him staring down at her, her face so very close to his dick and him urging her to suck it. Slow and deep.

She shook her head at the absurdity of her being *his* type no matter how delectably irresistible she was. Still, she grinned slyly at the memory of boldly kissing him on his succulent lips and sliding her hand over his crotch at a private release party some years ago.

When they arrived at Pasha's private workstation, Nairobia took her seat in the plush chair, and Pasha snapped the black satiny cape around her neck. "So how's life over on the East Coast treating you?" Pasha asked her as she slowly spun her chair around.

Nairobia loved the excitement and energy of New York. But it was congested. Dirty. Had rats the size of raccoons. And the beaches were filthy. It didn't matter that it was one of the world's financial meccas, or that some of the most powerful shakers and movers lived and breathed there.

It lacked culture. Lacked sophistication. Lacked the openness and carefree spiritedness of Europe. Her heart was torn between her estate here overlooking the Pacific Ocean, and the palatial villa she owned in the South of France. As far as Nairobia was concerned, setting up a permanent life in the Big Apple would never be.

New York was simply a temporary pit stop.

"It's interesting at best," she said.

Pasha smiled knowingly. "Ohmygod. I almost forgot to thank you for the beautiful gift basket. It was a wonderful surprise. But you really didn't have to."

Nairobia waved her on. "Nonsense, my darling. It was the least I could do to show my appreciation." She licked her lips. "Hopefully, you've found use for some of the goodies, no?"

Pasha blushed. The basket had been filled with an assortment of dildos and vibrating butt plugs and beads and G-spot apparatus, along with whips, paddles, a pair of diamond-encrusted handcuffs, and edible panties from Nairobia's Nasty collection.

"A lady never kisses and tells," Pasha teased.

"But a tramp, my darling," Nairobia cooed, her eyes dancing with mischief, "will confess her dirty desires. And live out her deepest fantasies. Let the tramp in you out, my love. She's dying to be released, no?"

Pasha felt her cheeks heat. She wondered if Nairobia knew of her whorish, dick-sucking ways. Wondered if she knew how she'd gotten aroused, so deliciously wet, from plotting the demise of Jasper and his goons—the men who'd fucked her throat raw and held her captive down in a basement for days at the orders of Jasper. Wondered if she knew how she'd fucked her own husband's cousin as part of some twisted revenge, then carried his seed in her womb, giving birth to his son. And if Nairobia knew all of this, she wondered how the hell she'd found out. Wondered how long she'd known.

Then she thought better of it and said to herself to hell with it. So what if she knew. She owed her nothing but top-of-the line salon service, nothing more, nothing less.

Her personal life was none of her—or anyone else's—concern.

Yes, she had at one time in her life been compulsive, almost obsessed with giving head—and lots of it. She simply loved dick. Loved sucking it into her wet, silky mouth. Loved the way it hit the back of her throat and pushed past her uvula—her *other* clit. Loved the feeling of it stretching her neck. Spit and drool splashing out of her mouth while being face-fucked. She loved, loved, loved...sucking dick.

She was able to admit that. She was a cock and cum whore. But, these days, she wasn't out here sucking dick all reckless; she wasn't brandishing her dick-sucking skills on random men. Those days were over. That was a part of her past. A past she was devoting her life to, not ever forgetting, but accepting as a consequence of her own choices.

So to hell with what people thought about her. She was rich and fabulous. Had two beautiful children. And had a man in her life who adored her. The only regret she had was marrying Jasper.

But he had given her, her firstborn, Jaylen. And, in spite of everything he'd put her through, she'd walked away from *that* life with peace of mind knowing justice had been served for everything Jasper had put her through.

And she'd walked away with her life, and…millions.

And there was nothing he could ever do to her again, because he was dead.

So she was happy. Very.

Pasha smiled, then whispered, almost conspiratorial, "Well then. The tramp in me thanks you for the treats. I love the Clit Licker and the Pussy Pounder."

Nairobia smiled. "Well, it's simply a small token of my appreciation. Your referral has turned out to be more than I'd ever hoped for."

Pasha returned the smile. "So, I take it Lamar's services are working out well."

Nairobia moaned her approval, seductively sliding a fingernail between her teeth. "Yes, my darling. His services are quite delightful. I find him most…*mmm*…"

Pasha inhaled. She'd grown fond of Lamar during the six months he'd worked for her, and was forever indebted to him for all he'd done for her during his employ with her. He had been eye candy for the women who'd come into her East Coast salon, but for her, he was more than just a handsomely rugged sexual object. He'd become her lifeline when she'd needed it most.

He was a good man. Loyal. And she knew unequivocally that he would have done anything for her—without word, without question. And he'd proven more times than Pasha could count that he would.

And he had.

A part of Pasha felt guilty for using him the way she had. He'd been simply a pawn, a means to a greater cause. It had been a time in her life when she was desperate to get from under her then husband Jasper's vicious grasp. Sucking dick had become her obsession while Jasper had been incarcerated—and it had become the root of her troubles with him. She'd become the infamous Deep Throat Diva.

And, as a result, Jasper had proven himself more dangerous and deadly than she'd ever imagined. He'd beaten her and tried to have her killed more than once. And she wanted him handled before he succeeded at putting her in a coffin.

She had a son to think about.

So when Lamar told her that he would "ride or die" for her, then licked his lips—in that moment she saw the hunger in his eyes as his gaze roamed over her body—she decided to test him.

"Come eat my pussy," she had told him over the phone.

And he'd come to her, his mouth, his tongue, his fingers, causing heat to flare through her pussy. Pasha felt shivers traveling through her body as the recollection of Lamar's pussy-eating skills slid through her memory. They'd been heavenly. And so had his smooth, dark dick. Delicious. Thick and curved. Nestled in a thick patch of black pubic hair.

She felt drool gathering in her mouth as she remembered the way she'd cupped his balls. Massaged them. Then slipped them into her mouth, slathering them with lots of spit. He'd loved his dick sucked sloppily. Her mouth had become luxuriously wet the first time she'd sucked him into her mouth, his dick pushing past her tonsils, the warmth of her throat heating his cock until he spilled his hot, creamy seeds into her mouth, and down in her throat.

From that moment on, a bond between the two of them had formed, something scandalously decadent and disturbingly beautiful. Lamar had taught her things about who she was, who she thought she'd never become. He'd kept her dirty secrets. Had promised to take them to his grave with him.

And she owed him so much for that.

Still, sucking and fucking him was only meant to be a means to an end. A good fuck for a greater cause, until he helped her carry out her plan.

Destroying her husband Jasper. Blowing up stash houses, taking him for everything he was worth—millions. Lamar had been there every step of the way, willing to do whatever, whenever...for her.

Even covering up murders.

And in the end, she'd found love in her heart for him. And made a true friend.

Pasha swallowed back the painful memories...and the naked images of Lamar. Her past was bittersweet. But her present was full of blessings.

Nairobia cleared her throat. And when Pasha blinked her into view, she was staring back at her in the mirror, head tilted.

Pasha blinked. "Oh, I'm sorry. What were you saying?"

Nairobia raised a brow. "I was telling you about Lamar, my darling. How fascinating I find him."

Pasha swallowed again. "Yes, that he is. Speaking of him, where is he?" It dawned on Pasha that she hadn't seen or spoken to him since she'd referred him to Nairobia. She made a mental note to call him first chance she got.

"I traveled light this time," Nairobia said. "I didn't need my *body* guarded, so he has the next two days off, doing whatever fine hunks of man meat like him do."

Pasha smiled. "Lamar's a great guy. He's loyal. And…"

"A delicious piece of chocolate," Nairobia added, before allowing Pasha to finish her sentence. She lowered her voice. "Oh how I crave to taste him, to have him in my sheets." She feigned embarrassment, placing a hand to her neck. "Oh my. How scandalous of me."

Pasha almost choked on her spit. "Ohmygod, Nairobia! You're a mess." She laughed.

"No, my love. I am a woman who knows what she wants. I take what I want. I demand my own pleasure, my darling. And I deny myself nothing. And I am sure you have not either, no?" She gave Pasha a knowing glance.

Pasha smiled, but said nothing. She tilted Nairobia's chair back, placing her head under the spigot, then began running water through her hair. "You do know," she hedged, moving the conversation away from Lamar, "you don't have to fly way out here just to have your hair done. My salon in Jersey is right across the water and…"

Nappy No More II was nothing like the salon and spa Pasha owned back on the East Coast. Nairobia had never stepped foot inside of that particular establishment, but she'd heard through the grapevine that that location catered to the hood trash and ghetto-fabulous, the wannabe divas and trap queens.

Pasha was a doll. And came highly regarded in the hair industry as one of the world's top stylists. But Nairobia never would have stepped foot inside her salon if she catered to that element here, too.

Nairobia's lashes rapidly fluttered. "Oh, no, no, my darling. As wonderful as I'm sure your other salon is, I am sure it doesn't cater to the same clientele as the one here does."

Pasha chuckled. "It has its moments. It's a more eclectic mix."

Nairobia heard the translation in her head: street trash with light coin. She pursed her lips. "And I, my darling, require a more—how do I say?—homogeneous experience. I need to be surrounded by good coins."

Pasha laughed, applying shampoo and lathering up her hair, lightly massaging her scalp. "Point taken." Pasha pushed a digital button on the arm of the chair, and, within seconds, the chair came alive, vibrating and pulsing.

Nairobia moaned as Pasha's fingers tantalized her scalp. "Mmm, yes, my darling, yes…that feels good. Your fingers are delectable. This chair is orgasmic." She closed her eyes, and moaned again. "I'll fly to the heavens and back for such treatment, my darling."

Pasha smiled wide. She loved catering to her wealthy clients. Loved giving them her personal touch. Hell, she'd massage their feet; maybe even lick their toes if it kept them coins coming in heavy. Nappy No More II had been open for two years now, and had already grossed nearly $5 million, thanks to the personal and attentive care paired with her highly talented styling team committed to providing one-of-a-kind service to her salon's exclusive clientele.

Nairobia had been coming to the salon since its grand opening, and she was a loyal customer who had no problem paying top dollar to look her best. She also tipped extravagantly and had graciously referred several of her wealthy friends—including a few porn stars, her way. So Nairobia would always get the red carpet treatment.

"I aim to do whatever it takes to keep my best customers coming back," Pasha said earnestly as she combed conditioner from her new hair care line through Nairobia's hair, then blasted it with a cold-water rinse for several seconds.

Nairobia cooed. "And I do believe I am *coming* in more ways than one, my darling…mmmm…yes…I already feel my juices pooling between my thighs."

Pasha chortled as she wrapped a towel around her head. Raised her up from the sink. Then reached for her boar-bristle paddle brush and blew-dry Nairobia's luxurious mane.

"So how's the new club? Is it everything you dreamed of? I've heard it's fabulous."

Nairobia's lashes fluttered. "It's *every*thing, my darling. And more. Perhaps you'd like to unleash your desires and step into the world of decadence, no?"

Pasha bristled at the thought. Sure she had a freaky side. Who didn't? But she'd rather unleash her alter ego behind closed doors, in the comfort of her own home. Still, there was no denying. She was a bit curious, but not enough to feed it.

She smiled. "Oh, no, girl. I'll have to kindly decline. Thanks for the invitation, though. But I have a cousin back home who mentioned in confidence that she bought a membership. However, she hasn't used it yet. Silver level, I believe."

Mmm. She'd only have access to the first two floors. That's what the five-thousand-dollar membership card afforded her. She'd need to dig a little deeper in her purse if she wanted more exclusive privileges. For another five grand she could upgrade. Gold level would allow her access to the first three levels. And for those able to foot the twenty-thousand-dollar bill for a Platinum level membership, they'd have full access to every level of the club, along with special invitations to special events.

Nairobia smiled. "I do hope your darling cousin comes to indulge herself soon."

"Oh, trust. She already has. Out of her two sisters, she's the more daring. The more sexually liberated."

Nairobia pursed her lips. "So she isn't afraid to unleash her freak."

Pasha chortled. "I'm never one to gossip, but…that's putting it mildly."

"Oooh," Nairobia cooed as Pasha curled her hair. "I think I like her already. Tell her to be sure to introduce herself to me the next time she steps across the threshold."

"I most certainly will."

Thirty minutes later, Pasha unsnapped the cape from around Nairobia's neck, then handed her the handheld mirror. Nairobia shook her hair, and regarded herself, moving her head from side to side, her glossy hair swinging to and fro. "It's fabulous as always," she said, handing Pasha back the mirror. She stood, running her fingers at the nape of her neck and through her hair. It was silky as ever.

Pasha took her in, admiringly. *Oooh, she's a real flossy bitch.* Pasha's Nappy No More Glossing conditioner had Nairobia's hair shining bright like a diamond. *Yassss, bitch, yass!* "Girl, I know women who would kill to have your mane…and that body of yours."

Nairobia glanced at her over her shoulder and smacked her ass. "Nothing artificial, nothing added, my darling. It's all natural."

Pasha couldn't help herself from laughing. As classy and upscale as Nairobia was, she was surprisingly just as down-to-earth. "When I grow up," Pasha said, "I want to be just like you."

Nairobia shook her head. "No, Pasha, my love. Be better than me." She grinned. "Always better. If you dare."

TWENTY-TWO

Everyone desired pleasure.

And Nairobia was an expert at using her femininity to get what she wanted. Call it manipulation. Call it being cunning. Call it whatever you liked. Nairobia called it the art of seduction. She knew all too well how to seduce. How to lure the object of her interest in, then slowly have him/her eating out the palm of her paraffin-smooth hand. And she planned on sharing that knowledge with the world in her next Tell-All.

She believed women should know how to smile more, play more, flirt more, and tease more. Not be so uptight. Not be so combative. Not be so dependent on the attention of a man. She found most women carried lots of unnecessary baggage. And were too needy and disturbingly clingy. It made them ugly. Made them appear broken and weak.

Nairobia despised broken, weak women. And she pitied women who didn't know how to embrace their sexuality, their sensuality, and their femininity.

As far as she believed, no quality man wanted a woman bearing those flaws, or scars of insecurity. He needed a whole woman—a *sensual* woman, a *sexual* woman, one who knew how to embrace her strength and her femininity, while still allowing him to be a man.

Still...

A woman needed to keep a man guessing. She needed to be

bold and daring. Needed to know how to have a life outside of having a man. She needed to know how to live life on the edge… just a little. Throw caution to the wind and give into her desires, responsibly, of course. But not be so accessible to a man—*all* the time.

Make him wait. Just a little. Give him something to yearn, something to dream about. Women needed to know how to say, "Come hither" or "Here I am, my love" in her dress, in her eyes, in her body language, without ever opening her mouth.

There was an art to throwing oneself at a man without seeming… *thirsty.*

In Nairobia's opinion, thirsty women were unattractive and depressive, which was probably why she had no females in her inner circle that she could honestly call a *friend.* Acquaintances? Why of course. She had plenty of those.

But a true girlfriend in every sense of the word, she did not exist in Nairobia's world. She found most women backstabbing, conniving, and petty. Rich or poor, women could be messy. And Nairobia had no time for drama and mess. Period.

And any woman smiling in her face usually had an ulterior motive, especially one whose smile didn't quite shine in her eyes. Like the one plastered over Lenora Samuels' lips. She was the head of one of the world's top literary agencies in the publishing world—LS Literary Agency—and, yet, she always came across as fake. Like now, as she sat across from Nairobia—at a cute Afro-Asian restaurant in Harlem, sipping her cocktail, while trying to convince Nairobia to allow her to shop her next book, *Sweet Pleasures.*

Nairobia stared at her, blinking every so often. Lenora Samuels was two screws short of crazy if she thought she would be foolish enough to let her represent her literary interests. Her last two books had both landed on the *New York Times* bestseller list and earned starred reviews from critics from around the globe, as well as selling over three million copies to date. Nairobia would never help fatten her bank accounts.

"Nairobia, my darling, I think we'd make a fabulous team," Lenora pitched, swiping her bangs from her eyes with a manicured finger. "There's no one else in the literary industry who'll have your best interests at heart more than I, my darling." Lenora flashed another smile. "I'm a relentless beast who gets lucrative results, my darling."

Nairobia matched her smile with one of her own, forced and fake. But she said nothing. Sure, Lenora was *one* of the best in the literary world, but she wasn't *the* best. She was gossipy. And despite all of her friendly overtures, Nairobia had taken an immediate dislike to her.

"I know—" Lenora started again.

Nairobia's cell phone rang. She ignored it.

"You were saying?" Nairobia said, more out of courtesy than anything else, because the fact of the matter was, she didn't give a damn.

"Well, Nai—"

It rang again. Nairobia pulled it out of her bag and glanced at the screen.

It was Josiah.

Lenora hiked up one eyebrow. "Do you need to take that?" She sounded annoyed that her pitch to sign on as her agent was being interrupted.

Nairobia tossed her phone back into her bag. "No, no. I'm fine. Continue."

"Well, like I was saying. I know a darling editor over at M&M Publishing who would simply stain her undies to sink her teeth into your manuscript. I'm telling you, my darling, she'd love to have you onboard."

Nairobia bristled. M&M Publishing had been Marcel's wife's publishing house before she'd…

Nairobia shook her head, and said, "Let's be clear, darling. I already have an agent who I adore immensely. Besides, poaching contracts away from another agent is underhanded and tasteless. It's unethical, no?" Nairobia tilted her head, and raised her brow for effect. She didn't wait for her response. "I, my darling, would *never* entertain doing business with a thieving agent."

Lenora blinked in surprise, swinging her weave. *"Thieving? Poaching?* Ha! I beg your pardon. I do no such thing. I've not climbed the ladder of success by stealing, my darling. I've climbed up the ladder and smashed open the ceiling of opportunity by taking what I want. I make things happen. I make careers, lovey. And I can snatch them away." She snapped her fingers. "Just like that. My name rings bells."

Nairobia rolled her eyes. "Lenora, darling, bell ringing or not, you're ruthless and delusional." She pulled out the diamond-tipped pins that held her hair into a sleek chignon, then shook it free, tossing her own mane over her shoulder. "What you're trying to do is steal another agent's client. Call it what you will. But, if you're trying to pilfer another agent's contracts, you'll try to steal *my* coins. And, *I*, my darling, have the resources, the connections, *and* the coins to ruin you if you dared." Nairobia snapped her fingers, mimicking Lenora. *"Snap.* Just like that. And, trust me. My bells ring louder."

Lenora picked up her glass and took a slow sip. The corner of her mouth lifted. "Now, now, let's play nice, Nairobia, darling. No need to get catty. There's no reason why two successful, beautiful black women, like yourself and I, can't—"

Nairobia laughed, cutting her off. "No, no, no. Let's not toss skin color into the ring, Lenora, dear. And let's not sit here and try to eat the elephant in the room. Last I heard, you'd said I wasn't a *real* black woman. Whatever that meant."

Nairobia had gotten that tidbit out of the mouth of an editor who'd sworn her to secrecy. Hearing that type of ignorance from other black women sliced under Nairobia's skin. Granted she was half-black. But she identified with her West African ancestry open-heartedly. Because of her exotic looks, she often found it oddly amusing how, at first glance, people assumed she was Moroccan or Egyptian—or from some *other* Middle Eastern country. It amazed and saddened her to no end that so many people did not know Egypt was a part of North Africa—and not some "other" Middle Eastern country.

She was African. And Dutch. But she lived her life as an ethnic woman. Black. And she despised other women who thought themselves the expert on what being a *real* black woman meant. Light-skinned or not, she had more African blood running through her veins than half the women who'd ever dared challenge her *blackness*.

Lenora gasped, sending her a look of horror. Then went utterly still. "I said no such thing."

Nairobia put a hand up to stop her. "Lies. Your mouth spews nothing but the froth of half-truths. You live and breathe in lies, darling. Every time you open that big cock gobbler of yours."

Lenora placed a hand to her chest, feigning insult. "I'm appalled."

Nairobia gave her a look. "Don't be, Lenora. If being a half-white and half-black woman who embraces both of her heritages doesn't make me a *real* black woman, then so be it. But know this. I'm a *real* woman in every sense of the word. There's nothing fake about me. No Botox, no silicone, no acrylics, no weaves, nothing. Can you say the same?"

Nairobia tilted her head. Her phone buzzed, and she ignored it.

"See now. There's no need for hostility, dear," Lenora said calmly.

"I invited you out today so that we could break bread and, perhaps, unite as one. Now let's get down to slicing the meat from the bone. I like you, Nairobia. Always have. You're talented. Feisty." She took another sip from her drink. Licked her lips. Then sipped again. "And…"

Nairobia looked over to her right and saw a few cameras flash in her direction. She was certain said photos would be all over social media in a matter of seconds. She brought her attention back in the direction of Lenora, and said, "And I have no intent on climbing in bed with a barracuda, my darling," Nairobia added, locking her gaze on Lenora. A slow smile worked over her mouth as she reached over and placed a hand over Lenora's. "Not unless said barracuda licked *kut*." Of course Nairobia detested her. But she'd love nothing more than smearing her cunt cream all over the cougar's stiff, cosmetically enhanced face.

Lenora's eyes widened. "I beg your pardon? *Lick* what?"

"Don't play coy," Nairobia chided, swiping the tip of her tongue over her glossed lips. She squeezed Lenora's hand. "You like wet, juicy cunt, no? Would you not like to suck my clit into your mouth?"

Lenora looked mortified as she chanced a peek over at the table to the left of them, where a handsome, middle-aged white man with sparkling blue eyes—who looked large and virile—sat with his much younger Asian companion. The couple seemed too caught up in their own conversation to care one way or the other about the goings-on at her table. Relieved, she dragged her attention back to Nairobia.

"I beg your pardon. I will not stand for this sort of talk. In public of all places."

"Then shall we have it in private?" she asked, casting her a saucy smile. "I've heard of your lascivious ways, Lenora. You might have the face of a goat. But I've heard you have the tongue of a lizard.

And rumor has it you've taken several young lovers—male *and* female—over the years, no?"

Lenora gasped. "You shut your filthy lies," she hissed. "I will not have you slander my good name." She gulped down her drink.

Nairobia's lips tipped upward, satisfaction glinting in her eyes. "Lies, Lenora, darling. Lies. You want something from me. I want something from you. You want a piece of my luscious royalties. And I want you to lick my *kut*. My cunt swells with desire for you, Lenora, darling. Come. Let me ride your face. And drown you in my juices. I'm always so wet for you every time I see you."

It was a lie, of course. But Nairobia loved making men and women squirm. She slid her foot out of her Manolo and eased her foot up between Lenora's legs. "Tell me, darling. Are your panties wet for me? Does your *kut* cry out to be filled with my fingers?"

Lenora choked on her drink, fluid shooting out from her mouth and nostrils. She coughed and slammed a hand to her chest. Satisfaction gleamed in Nairobia's eyes as she sat back in her seat, letting go of her hand and watching the old bat choke. Nairobia eyed her as she snatched up her linen napkin and covered her mouth and nose.

Nairobia bit back a laugh as she slipped back into her heel, then stood and opened her Judith Leiber clutch. She pulled out a shiny black embossed card that resembled that of a credit card and said, "You need a night of hot, sweaty decadence, my darling. Let me help you unclog your loins." She tossed Lenora the card. "The climax is on me."

Shell-shocked, Lenora sagged in her chair and watched the sultry sway of Nairobia's hips as she sauntered her way out of the restaurant, carefree and flamboyantly sexy, as more cameras flashed, leaving her with the bill.

And her hands curled into two tight fists beneath the tablecloth.

That slutty bitch!

TWENTY-THREE

S tepping out into the afternoon sun, Nairobia's cell phone rang. She fished it out of her bag and picked it up immediately, thinking it might be one of the three interviewees she was scheduled to screen for membership into The Pleasure Zone. She figured one of the three would be calling her to cancel their appointment. Wouldn't have been the first time someone got cold feet and wasn't ready for the heat. So she almost expected it.

She frowned when she saw Marcel's name as the incoming call. Why would he be calling her...now? Had she not already been generous with her time? Had she not allowed him to stir her loins and caress her clit with his fingers and tongue? Had she not allowed him to stroke himself into her juicy mouth with his cock? Had she not allowed him to fuck her deliciously numb?

So what could he possibly want with her now?

More of her—they *always* wanted more.

"I wanna see you again," he said the minute she answered. "Have dinner with me. Tonight."

Nairobia's brow furrowed. What in the world was he up to? "As in a *date?*" she shrieked. God, she hoped not. She didn't date. Never. Ever. She met for cocktails. Met for dinner. And met for a night of salaciousness. Dating was not in her DNA.

She sighed inwardly. "Or is this some sly way for you to have your way with me again?"

Marcel laughed. "Damn, baby. Would it be so wrong if I said I wanted both?"

She reached her shiny black Rolls-Royce and her driver tipped his hat as he opened the rear door. She slipped inside, then said as the driver shut the door behind her, "No, my darling, you'd be foolish to think I'd give you another night of stretching my *kut* out. It was a delicious treat, but—"

"I can still taste you," he interrupted, husky and hot. Nairobia shivered from the memory of melting on his tongue. She could see him licking his lips, his eyes glimmering in heat. She could still feel his tongue sliding over her pussy lips. Oh how delectable he looked between her thighs.

Nairobia's driver pulled away from the curb, glancing at her in the rearview mirror. She caught his thick-lashed gaze and, subconsciously, licked her lips, causing him to quickly avert his eyes. Nairobia smiled. She liked him. Samson. She'd even considered being his Delilah, just for a night. Fuck him hot and dirty in the backseat of this car, or her Bentley. Oh, how she'd be his whore, his prostitute, for the night.

He walked like a man packing heat between those strong, long legs of his, signaling to all those watching that he was a man who knew how to use it, too.

Nairobia didn't doubt it.

"*Je veux plus chatte*, baby," Marcel spoke in French, pulling her from her lusty thoughts. Nairobia could almost feel the heat of his breath as he whispered those words—"I want some more pussy"— into her ear.

"You naughty man, you," she cooed. "My *kut* is on holiday *van al die grote lul.*" (from all that big dick). "So no more pussy for you."

Marcel laughed. "Was it not good?"

Mmm. Yes. Nairobia swallowed back the memory. She didn't

need the recollections heating her blood. She looked up at the rearview mirror and captured the eye of her driver again. It was then she caught the desire in his dark brown orbs, and knew she held the power to unleashing his hidden yearnings. She decided she'd extend him an invitation into The Pleasure Zone for a night of wickedness.

Nairobia slid him a seductive wink, then said to Marcel, "It was the sweetest torture, Mar*Sell*, my darling," she admitted, remembering the feel of his lush, sensual mouth on her clit. "But I will not surrender to it, to you. Or to the delicious memory."

Marcel laughed lightly. "So is that a yes or a no?"

"To what?" Nairobia asked coyly.

"To dinner. To drinks. To me having you in my bed tonight."

It was on the tip of her tongue to say no flat out. But whom was she kidding? Lust fanned out between the two of them like a roaring fire. She'd felt it in his touch and in his tongue strokes. And had seen it in his eyes, full of heat and power.

Still…

That did not mean she had to give in to his want, his desires. And she wouldn't.

"It's a *maybe*," she said, smiling despite herself. "But not tonight."

"Okay, then. Tomorrow night?"

"Sorry, my darling. My calendar doesn't permit for deep fucking tomorrow night, either. I'll call you when it does," she said firmly.

No wasn't a word Marcel embraced. So *maybe* was promising. But it still wasn't good enough. He was a man who got what he wanted, when he wanted it. And he wanted Nairobia. He wasn't an obsessive man—but, for some reason, he found himself fixating over her. He hadn't felt this way about a woman, since his college days back at Howard University. The day he'd laid eyes on Marika.

Marika had been his soulmate, his everything. But when she

was murdered, every part of his soul had died along with her. He felt empty. Dead inside.

But his night—*and* morning—with Nairobia had stirred, no *awakened*, something inside of him. Hell. That was a lie. Something shifted in him that morning in his Rolls when he'd exposed himself emotionally and Nairobia had slipped between his legs and sucked his dick. He couldn't quite put his finger on it. But it was there. He'd felt it when they kissed several nights ago. And he'd felt it, this surge of electricity, even stronger the second he slid his dick in her. It wasn't love. Yet, it was deeper than lust.

Nairobia was bold and wild and full of passion. He wanted another round with her. Wanted to suck her toes. Tongue her ass. And taste every delicious inch of her. All day, he'd sat in his office, at his desk, distracted, his dick brick-hard.

The source of his preoccupation: *Her*.

Her body.

Her lips.

Her touch.

Her mouth.

Her cunt.

Goddamn. That sweet pussy was divine.

And he wanted more.

Nairobia glanced at the diamond-encrusted watch on her wrist. It was nearly three o'clock. She motioned for her driver to speed it up. Her first interview was in another half hour and she dared not be late. She prided herself on being prompt for business. She wasn't a believer of making someone wait…not in business.

Pleasure was a whole other story.

Sometimes it had to simmer. Slowly build up.

"Where are you?" Marcel asked, his voice dipping dangerously low.

"En route to the club. Why?"

"Swing by my office so I can suck the walls out that juicy pussy."

"No," she said firmly.

"Nairobia," he murmured. She closed her eyes as he purred out her name in a way that made her cunt clench. "Don't make me beg, baby."

"Beg, my love. I love a man who grovels," she teased.

"I wanna coat your walls with my nut, baby, then lick that beautiful pussy and all between your thighs clean." Marcel loved creampies. He enjoyed the taste of himself inside of a woman. And he wanted nothing more than to clean Nairobia's pussy out with his tongue, licking out her juices along with his own warm semen.

Instant arousal swept through Nairobia. She loved a man who loved cunnilingus. There was something so incredibly erotic, insanely provocative, about watching a man, licking, feasting, sucking, sliding his tongue inside her pussy and all over her plump, juicy folds and distended clit.

And Nairobia loved even more seeing her juices glistening a man's lips and his chin, and him licking his tongue over his lips, removing the traces of her slick release. Oh how she loved coming in a man's horny mouth, drenching him with her sweet cream.

But this freaky business of Marcel wanting to flood her cunt with his nut, then lick it out of her had her clenching. Damn him.

A wave of desire washed over Nairobia. She sucked in a huge, steady breath, but Marcel's heated, evocative words had already licked at her cunt and made her clit twitch with an urgent need.

Oh he was greedy. Insatiable. And Nairobia was tempted.

Just for a moment.

"Good day, Mar*Sell*," she said—a smile easing over her lips, just before disconnecting the call.

TWENTY-FOUR

"These just came for you," Josiah said as he walked into Nairobia's office, carrying a floral arrangement almost as wide as his broad shoulders. "Where do you want them?" he asked behind the exquisite arrangement of pink cymbidium orchids and white and pink roses.

Nairobia's breath caught. The flowers were simply gorgeous. She pointed over toward the credenza in front of the window. "You can sit them over there." She stood up and walked over as he set the large crystal vase on the table, breathing in *him* and the flowers, both intoxicating scents making her almost lightheaded.

He hadn't shaved this morning, and the light brown formed a shadow on his jaw, the light stubble giving the pretty boy a sexy rugged look.

Nairobia liked it. A lot.

Through the veil of her dark lashes, she drank in the sight of him a little longer than she probably should have, feeling her body tingle with desire.

"Thank you, my love," she said, circling him, running a hand over his chest, then up and down his muscled arm, before sliding her fingertips along his back. He wore a black PLEASURE ZONE T-shirt that molded perfectly to his chiseled chest and a pair of black jeans covering his long, muscled legs.

"It's been days since you've pleasured me, my sweet Josiah. You wish to make love to me, no?" she asked, her eyes flashing with lust, her gaze settling on his crotch.

He smirked and eyed Nairobia up and down. "You haven't had time for me, lately." He hadn't meant to say that, but it had been on the tip of his tongue for over a week now. She'd been summoning him less and less since the club's opening. And he was beginning to wonder if she'd found herself someone else to toy with, perhaps that new security/bodyguard of hers. Even behind those dark shades of his, Josiah had seen the way Lamar looked at her with raw hunger in his eyes.

Josiah was young, but far from silly to believe he'd ever be her only lover. Though he'd had hoped that eventually what they shared would, could, evolve into something more meaningful than mere fucking. He felt like a piece of meat on display for her nourishment.

And he was.

There to feed her hunger, whenever, however—on demand, at her beck and call.

Still, he no longer liked his station in her life as her boy toy. And he didn't necessarily like how Nairobia treated him as if he were *privileged* to get her attention—*any* attention. He wasn't a submissive, per se. He wasn't into groveling for attention, or begging to be humiliated. And he wasn't into pain. But he didn't mind role-playing if that's what she wanted. He loved pleasing her, loved submitting to her desires.

And he loved fucking her.

He was a man—all man. With a big dick that grew hard as granite. And he knew how to fuck—thanks to her. Nairobia had made him the incredible lover he was. And he wanted to take what she'd taught him to greater sexual heights, with no one else but her.

Sure he'd been with a few girls his own age, but he'd found them sexually boring. Nairobia, on the other hand, was spontaneous and exciting and uninhibited. She'd taught him how to surrender to pleasure, and how to pleasure a woman. She'd pushed him sexually. Tested his boundaries. He had become hers, to tease, to taunt, to toy with. To bring her pleasure when she required it, demanded it, expected it.

When Nairobia looked at him, all he saw was heat and passion and raw desire. He saw nothing else when he looked in her eyes. However, he was acutely aware of her insatiable libido. Her sexuality oozed from her pores. Her sex drive was always in overdrive, so he understood the rules. That she'd take more than one lover, whenever, wherever, she felt the burning urge to. Josiah had been fine with that. But, over the last several months, he found himself growing, evolving. He found himself wanting to bend the rules, some. Wanted to build a relationship with someone. Maybe one day have a family.

He wanted that with only one person.

He wanted that with Nairobia.

He had already admitted to himself his need of her. He wanted her, no doubt. Not only sexually, emotionally as well. He was committed and unapologetically loyal to her. But he knew Nairobia wasn't there with him. And she'd probably never get there. So he knew he'd eventually need to make some decisions about this arrangement they'd been sharing over the last several years. Not today though. Today he'd stay in the moment…until he was no longer able to stand.

Josiah slid his arm around Nairobia's waist and pulled her into him, almost possessively. She wrapped her arms around his body, melting into his muscled heat, loving the feel of his hard pecs and rippled abs. She felt her pussy warming.

Before another word was exchanged between them, Nairobia took him by the wrist, bringing his hand between her thighs. As usual, she wore nothing beneath her dress. On contact, Josiah groaned as he cupped her there, the base of his hand against her clitoris.

"Give me your fingers," she urged. "Right here, right now. Finger out my juices."

Josiah closed his eyes, slipping his middle finger between her folds and inside her. He licked his lips. She was hot and slick.

"You feel what you do to me, my love?"

"Yes," he breathed.

He wanted to believe that. That he was the reason for her perpetual arousal. But he knew better. Nairobia's juices flowed without cause. She stayed wet and ready.

Nairobia's breath hitched. "You like how I feel, no?"

"Yes." He slid his index finger inside her, and she moaned her approval. He maneuvered his fingers in and out of her body, alternating from one finger, to two, then back to one, causing her cunt to clench hungrily.

"You keep my *kut* wet," she said in a sultry tone. "So very wet for you."

Nairobia would never deny how Josiah's heated touch always brought bliss to her body. No matter where he touched her, she would surely come. She nibbled on his ear, then moaned when he added a third finger inside her. "Ja, ja…mmm…faster. Finger me, faster…"

Nairobia's folds dripped, her juices dripping out over Josiah's hand. She'd already had two mini orgasms in less than five minutes. Now she was on the verge of another, this one with more heat, more force; a rising tide of an orgasm so powerful that she felt it flooding her body. Her orgasm shot from her clit to her toes, then back up over her body. She closed her eyes, and moaned low in her throat, squeezing Josiah's wrist as she shook with pleasure.

A silent moment later, Nairobia caught her breath. Josiah nearly groaned when she took his wrist again and removed his hand, his fingers, from her body. She brought his hand up to his lips and watched him—without prompting—lick his fingers clean.

Nairobia leaned in, and kissed him lightly on the lips. "My darling, Josiah. What would I ever do without you?"

Josiah looked her in the eyes. God, she was incredibly beautiful. He took a breath, and said, "Replace me for another." He leaned in and kissed her on the side of the mouth. "But hopefully not anytime soon."

Nairobia smiled at him as he turned to walk out of her office, before plucking out the white envelope nestled in between all the beautiful pink and white flowers.

Thinking of you. I'm already missing you, baby. Longing for your touch. Your sweet kisses. Stay beautiful.

Marcel

TWENTY-FIVE

An hour later, Nairobia was at her desk interviewing a strikingly beautiful woman wearing a print wrap dress that bared a hint of cleavage. Nairobia kept her gaze on her as she crossed her smooth legs. She was petite, but shapely. The woman already held a silver membership, but wished to upgrade to the next level. She had access to the first two floors, but decided that wasn't enough for her. She wanted access to the Love Tombs. From what her application had stated, she was new to BDSM, and wanted to explore her Domme side more; something she wasn't able to do at home.

Nairobia glanced down at her application, then back up into the woman's eyes. "So tell me, Persia. What do you desire most, sexually?"

She licked her lips. "Well, as you can see from my application, I have no sexual hang-ups, but what I want most is sexual freedom."

Nairobia glanced at the three-carat diamond on her ring finger. "And your fiancé? Does he not fulfill your desires?"

Persia swallowed. "Not all of them. Don't get me wrong. I love him. Royce—that's my fiancé—he satisfies the vanilla part of me, and some parts of my freaky side, but my dark side, no. That part of me goes unfulfilled."

Nairobia nodded, understanding flickering in her gaze. "So he does not know about your membership here?"

Persia shook her head, clutching her neck as if she were reaching for a set of pearls. "Ohmygod, no. He'd lose his mind if he knew."

"How often do the two of you have sexual relations?" Nairobia pried.

"Twice a week; sometimes three times a week if I'm lucky."

"And it is good, no?"

"Yes. Remarkable. Royce is a good lover."

Nairobia tilted her head. "But?"

Persia sighed. "But it isn't enough. I need more. I want more. If it were up to me, I'd want it morning, noon, and night. I just love sex. And I love sex with him more."

Nairobia stared at her almost pathetically as she wondered how she could ever expect her marriage to last with lies. No judgment. Her indiscretions and dirty secrets were none of Nairobia's business, or concern. Most of the club's members had spouses and/or significant others at home who knew nothing about their partner's dark desires. They, like the woman in front of her, lived double lives. And, sadly, in Nairobia's experience, nothing good ever came out of it once their deceit was discovered.

Curiosity pushed Nairobia to ask, "So you are fine with sleeping with married men, no? You do know most of the club's members are indeed married or—like yourself—*happily* involved."

Persia uncrossed her legs, shifted in her seat, then crossed them again; right over left this time. "I'm not looking to disrupt anyone's home situation. And I'm not looking for anyone to try and disrupt mine. At the end of the day, when it's all said and done, I'm going home to my man. Satiated and completely satisfied.

"So to answer your question, I am more than fine sharing another woman's man. Man sharing is nothing new for me. In fact, my sisters and I used to…" She paused, shaking her head. "Oh, never mind. Let me not go there."

Nairobia's brow raised, her eyes flashing in curiosity. "Please, my darling. Do tell."

"Well, simply put, my sisters and I used to share men…"

Nairobia's lips curled. "As in *dating* the same man?"

Persia shook her head. "No. We never dated any of them. We sexed them."

Nairobia licked her lips. "Man swapping?"

Persia nodded. "Yes. Threesomes, foursomes—mostly threesomes, though, since one of my sisters usually preferred to watch while she masturbated."

Nairobia's mouth watered. "Mmm. Sounds decadent."

"It was." She reached inside her purse, and pulled out her checkbook. She giggled. "I have a confession. Anytime my sisters and I were sexing a man, we'd always use aliases. I was—well, I still am—Pain. And my two sisters were Passion and Pleasure. Pleasure, well my sister, chose her name after *you*. You inspired her. You inspired all of us. We used to watch your movies."

Nairobia smiled, touched. "I'm so glad to know I was able to touch the three of you in some way. I want to empower women to never be ashamed of their sexualities. To be comfortable in being their own freaky sexual selves."

"Oh, you've definitely done that. The three of us shared a very unique bond."

"To say the least," Nairobia agreed, watching as Persia wrote a check out for another five grand. When she was done, she slid Nairobia the check across the desk.

"My mouth is already salivating at all the nasty things I'll be able to explore with access to the lower level."

Nairobia's lips curled upward. "Indulge your desires, my darling. This is what we are here for." Check in hand, Nairobia stood to her feet. "Give me one sec, my darling." She walked around her desk and over to a wood panel. She punched in a code, then pressed her palm up to another security pad. She walked inside. Moments later, shutting the panel behind her, she returned with a new membership card.

"Here you are, my love."

Persia stood, taking the coveted gold card in her hand.

"Are you wet with desire, my love?" Nairobia wanted to know.

Persia's eyes flickered. "I'm always wet."

Nairobia smiled walking her to the door, then following her down the hall. "It was a pleasure..." She paused, suddenly remembering Pasha telling her about a cousin who shared men with her sisters, and was a member at the club.

So this was she?

She decided not to mention that she knew Pasha. If she wasn't going to make mention of it, then neither was she. It wasn't important for her to know.

They reached the sliding glass doors.

"It was a pleasure seeing you again," Persia said, extending her hand.

Nairobia shook her hand. "Likewise, my darling. Will you be using your card tonight?"

"No, God. My fiancé and I have plans tonight. But if I can get away tomorrow night, I'll be here. Latex and all."

Nairobia placed her hand up to the security panel, and the doors hissed open. They walked out together. And just as they were rounding the corner, they bumped smack into Lamar.

"Oh my bad." He looked at Persia. Then Nairobia. Then back at Persia. "What's good?"

Persia smiled, but it didn't reach her eyes. "Hi."

Although she didn't know him personally, and didn't have a problem with him knowing that she was a club member, it still felt awkward knowing he'd seen her in action on stage several weeks back.

Nairobia noticed the look between the two. "Is everything all right?"

"Yes, of course," she simply said.

"I used to work for her cousin," Lamar said evenly. He glanced at Persia. "Tell Pash I said what's up."

"I sure will," Persia said, eyeing him.

He brought his attention to Nairobia. "I'll be up on the fifth floor if you need me."

She nodded, then escorted Persia toward the club's foyer. She glanced over her shoulder, then said in low voice, "Tell me, my love. How well do you know Lamar?"

Persia shrugged. "Not well at all." A sly grin curved over her lips. "But I'd love to see him strapped to a Saint Andrews cross."

Nairobia licked her lips.

Now wouldn't that be a delightful sight.

TWENTY-SIX

Nairobia took the three steps that led up to the deep marble tub already full of mint and eucalyptus bubbles. She dropped her robe, then dipped her toe in, testing the water. It was deliciously hot, but not scalding.

A sigh of pleasure eased from Nairobia's lips as she slowly slid in, the steam and heat enveloping her. She leaned her head back on the inflatable pillow attached to the edge of the tub as Marsha Ambrosius' "Late Nights & Early Mornings" played low in the background.

The last week had been exhausting. Between the club, and flying out to Spain for an International Adult Film ceremony to only return for a meeting in L.A., Nairobia was drained. She needed this…this moment to do absolutely nothing.

She swept her gaze around the bathroom aglow with candles, then closed her eyes and inhaled. She didn't know what she was doing here, but she'd allowed herself to be enticed into coming over with the promise of nothing more than a massage.

"Nothing more, baby," he'd assured her.

So how could she say no to that?

Now here she was. Wondering if she'd made a mistake. She didn't want to give the wrong message. Smearing her sweet juices over his lips and letting him stretch open her *kut* was one thing, but this…

Marcel stood in the doorway, his eyes appraising the sight before him. She didn't know he was standing there, watching her. Adoring her. He didn't know what was happening with him, but he felt himself...changing. He felt lighter. Freer. And it was because of Nairobia. She'd done that to him.

Unlocked something inside of him.

He wasn't sure what would come of this...this thing—whatever *this* was—he was feeling. But he wanted to pursue it, to see where it took them. He just needed Nairobia to open her mind to the possibility, to explore with him.

She'd been ignoring him the last week. Not taking his calls. Basically avoiding him. And he wasn't feeling that. He wanted her. And being ignored wasn't something he took lightly to. Today, he'd tried her cell again, and when she answered he'd convinced her to come over for a night of relaxation. No sex. Simply her allowing him to pamper her and worship her in the way a beautiful woman deserved to be catered to.

But fuck if he didn't want to be inside her, to tie her to his bed and have his way with her all night, his legs wedged between hers, spreading her until her legs rested against his outer thighs, his dick slowly easing in and out of her body, stroking her walls until she orgasmed over the length and width of him.

Marcel felt himself growing hard.

Goddamn.

He wanted her to feel his cock pulsating inside her as it shot his nut, filling her, coating her walls with his semen as her pussy convulsed around his girth. Marika was gone, but he still wanted a family. Something they'd hoped for in the very near future, something that sadly didn't come to be. All future plans shot down, literally and figuratively.

His chest burned from the memory. He closed his lids for a brief moment, willing his emotions from taking over. This wasn't the time. His focus needed to be on the beautiful woman soaking in his tub.

Nothing else.

Taking a deep breath, he opened his chocolate brown eyes. His mouth curved slightly, his eyes warming with a look of satisfaction and approval. Seeing Nairobia in his tub with her eyes closed, looking peaceful, was a beautiful sight. He stepped inside the bathroom. Even though he knew how skittish she was about relationships, he wanted her. He wanted to possess her in mind, body, and soul. And he wouldn't rest until he had all of her. He was a patient man. He'd take it slow. After all, he hadn't gotten this far in life not being enduring.

But God, he wanted to fill her to the rim with everything he had. Not with just his throbbing cock—his hands, his mouth, his lips, his fingers, his love.

All of him. Every part of him. Filled deep inside her.

Floetry's "Getting Late" oozed out of the speakers as Marcel eased forward, bare-chested with his hard dick trapped beneath boxers and lounge pants. He wouldn't get naked for fear of not being able to keep his promise. He was a man of his word, but tonight, if he stripped out of his clothes, he'd take her.

No questions asked. He'd take her for himself, greedily and hungrily.

"Here you go, beautiful," he said, his voice full of fiery heat as he neared the tub.

Nairobia opened her eyes, and looked up at him. She saw the flute in his hand. Saw the fire in his eyes. Her mouth went eerily dry, but her pussy suddenly felt wetter. She sat up and took the flute from him. "Thanks, my love."

She took a sip, then set it up on the ledge of the tub. She looked at him. "Are you not drinking?"

He grinned crookedly. "Nah, baby. Not tonight." He thought it best that he didn't. He didn't want anything altering his judgment, or his resolve to not fuck. "Tonight, it's all about you. Are you ready for your bath?"

Nairobia smiled at him. She hadn't been asked that—"are you ready for your bath?"—since she was a young child. She leaned her head back against the pillow, and closed her eyes. And waited. There was her answer.

Smiling, Marcel rolled his pant legs up as high as they would go, then sat on the edge of the tub. He grabbed a loofah sponge and started with her legs, gently lifting one at a time. Then with infinite care he washed her feet, licking the soles of each foot, before sucking her toes into his mouth. He'd wanted to indulge his foot fetish with her for weeks now. Nairobia had pretty feet and toes. Suckable. Lickable. And he'd wanted them in his mouth.

She squirmed.

The sensation tickled, and aroused her all in one, sending quivers of pleasure dancing through her body. She couldn't remember the last time she'd had her toes inside a man's wet, warm mouth. And Marcel was doing such a magnificent job. He made love to each one, his hot tongue wetly lapping over every part of her foot, before licking over her ankles. His hands slid up her calves, along her thighs, then brushed lightly over her sex.

Nairobia let out a soft moan.

"You like that, baby?"

Her only response was another moan as his hands glided up the sides of her body. Nairobia felt herself melting under Marcel's searing touch. Her eyes fluttered open and she found his gaze, hot. Their eyes stayed locked as his hands dropped down, delving into the water, gliding up along the sides of her body, then back down, grabbing her hips. He slid his hands over her breasts, his fingertips grazing over her tightened tips. They burned. They ached. He teased her there, caressing and stroking, his fingers magically dancing over every nerve ending.

She visibly swallowed, her breath hitching.

Then his thumbs flicked over her nipples, causing a stream of heat to ripple through her. She felt her body craving him, deep inside her. She wanted to scream out to him, "Fuck me now! Take my pussy and have your way with it!" But she dared not. She bit into her bottom lip instead, arching her body.

His hands sensually slid up and down each arm, then moved to her hands, massaging each finger, stroking between the base of her fingers and knuckles. Nairobia let out a sigh of unrelenting pleasure. She opened her eyes and watched as Marcel interlocked their fingers and used his thumbs to massage her palms up to the base of her fingers in slow circles.

He saw the flicker in her eyes—desire and heat and feral want— and smiled.

"You want me inside you, don't you? *Vous voulez me donner cette chatte douce*, no?" You want to give me that sweet pussy.

Nairobia panted. She couldn't stand it any longer—this, this, sweet torture. "Yesss," she murmured. "*Neem me, mijn liefde. Neuk me.*" Take me, my love. Fuck me.

Satisfaction flowed through Marcel. He loved the way her body was responding to his touch. By the time he finished with her, she'd be sated, her body floating and still rippling from the after-effects of her climax long after he was done with her.

He reached for a spray nozzle and wet her hair, then sensually massaged her scalp.

Drake's "A Night Off" swept around the bathroom licking at Nairobia's eardrums, causing her to slowly roll her hips. She moaned, her body seeking relief.

Every erotic touch pushed her closer to the edge. He still hadn't touched her *there*—over her sex, and her cunt was clenching wildly.

"Let it go," Marcel rasped. *"Donne-moi. Donnez dedans, bébé."* Give it to me. Give into it, baby. "Stop fighting me, it. Surrender to it, *bébé…*"

By the time Jamie Foxx's "Freakin' Me" started playing, Nairobia felt Marcel everywhere. His hands melting into her flesh as he caressed her skin, her body. She hadn't expected this. Her ability to think—long gone, she burned with desire. Felt her insides aching with a need so intense that her whole body shook.

Her body arched, and she cried out.

He'd given her an orgasm.

TWENTY-SEVEN

The air was electric. "Maybe" by Alina Baraz & Galimatias seeped through the speakers as bodies erotically bumped and grinded. Libidos were in overdrive. And Nairobia was in her glory as she sauntered around the third floor of her club in her signature attire—something slinky, something see-through, something that gave her easy access to her pussy and her plump nipples. As she walked through the club, women admired her. Men lustfully eyed her as they fucked their lovers. Nairobia found herself slowing her pace and sensually winding her hips taking in all the erotic sights.

To the left of her, a beefy Italian was down on his knees, his face pressed in between the ass cheeks of the wife of a NBA basketball player. He stroked his thick, yummy-looking sausage while he licked in between her slick folds.

Nairobia's eyes stayed fixed on the width of his dick as it slid in and out of his fist. It was the thickest piece of meat she'd seen on a white man in a long time. And she enjoyed watching every moment of him pleasuring himself while his tongue—relentless against his lover's cunt—licked his way to her core. The heat and seductive-ness of his tongue strokes made his sex mate quake for more. And watching it unfold before her eyes made her mouth water for a taste of his tongue, his cock. Made her want to reach between her own thighs and pinch her clitoris.

The cocoa-brown basketball wife was bent over the back of one of the many plush leather sofas, her pussy stuffed with tongue, her mouth full with hard, black dick. Nairobia's mouth watered as she watched spit splash out of Mrs. Basketball Wife's mouth as she was being face-fucked. Her hunky lover's dark-chocolate dick sliced into her mouth, hitting the back of her throat. She gulped and gagged and groaned, her neck rapidly gliding back and forth. Her mouth moving with a ravening hunger.

Ooh, scandalous.

Get your swirl on, my love.

Nairobia grinned.

The rumors had been true all along.

Maya Ellerson loved waving her freak flag.

Mr. Italian Sausage removed his hand from his dick and placed both of his hands on the Basketball wife's ass, pulling her open, his tongue skimming over her enflamed pussy. She bucked, moaning in ecstasy.

"Yes, my slutty, little darling," Nairobia whispered as she passed by, "let them bring you to sweet orgasm, then fuck you to no end."

She looked over to the right of her and licked her lips at the sight of a busty redhead—blindfolded and gagged, on her knees, her shiny pink cunt being savagely fucked to shreds by a thick-dicked, tatted Mandingo with braids. He wrapped a hand in her hair and snatched her head back, slamming in and out of her, her groans of pleasure muffled by the gag in her drooling mouth. He slapped her ass until it stung and bruised, leaving his hand print in her reddened flesh.

"Fucking, white cunt bitch!" he spewed, rapidly thrusting in and out of her, stretching her tight slit beyond her imagination. Her lover promised to beat her pussy down to the seams, to fuck her until she passed out. "You like big, black dick, huh, cheating-ass whore?! You like your pussy-ass husband watching you get your guts fucked in with all this black dick?"

Tears sprang from her eyes as she nodded her head, and grunted. Her bleary-eyed gaze stayed locked on her dark-haired banker husband of fifteen years, watching her, lovingly, as he stroked his long, thin cock. He wasn't particularly handsome, but there was something rough and wild about his look that made him primitive. His brown eyes widened in delight as his wife's tatted lover pulled out of her, his cock wet from her sticky orgasm and his.

Mr. Banker was on the verge of begging the tatted sex beast to feed him his wife's juices from his veined shaft. He wasn't a cock-sucker—per se, but he'd do anything to see the look of pleasure in his wife's loving eyes, even if it meant being choked by a big, black dick; his nose savagely pressed deeply into the jungle bush of hair that sprouted out from her lover's groin. As long as it pleased his wife, he was delighted.

It turned him on. Seeing his wife completely satisfied.

He groaned his approval when his wife's next lover, a light-skinned Hispanic with lots of cock and foreskin, stepped behind her and pulled open her cheeks. Her asshole puckering in antici-pation as he slowly penetrated her vagina, then grabbed her ass in the palms of his hands, rotating it while he thrust his dick deeper inside her warm pussy.

Her Latino lover tossed his head back, grabbed both her shoulders, then rapidly pounded her body, pulverizing her swelling cunt.

Nairobia swallowed back a mouthful of moistened lust as she watched the redheaded vixen take on one lover after another, each man emptying his loins in her, coating her walls with his creamy load. Nairobia grew wetter, her lips swelling between her thighs. She wanted to spread her legs, to open herself to the beautiful men and women around her.

Her pussy ached.

She bit her lip.

"Panther" by Made In Heights oozed from the speakers as the redhead's husband groaned long and low. *"Uhn! Uhhhhhn!"* His cock became surprisingly longer, and almost reminded Nairobia of a long twig. She grimaced, almost feeling bad for him and his skinny pecker. She couldn't fathom ever having a broomstick poking in and out of her *kut*, no matter how much wealth and power were attached to its owner.

Nairobia skimmed her eyes over Mr. Banker's lean, perfectly tanned body before looking back over at his wife, who was in the throes of heated euphoria. Her pleading eyes begged for more. She whimpered and groaned over the leather ball trapped in her mouth, flicking her long hair from side to side. Her whole body thrashed anew every time another hunk pulled out of her body, then another one slammed himself inside her, filling her with the length and width of his cock, fucking into her soul.

There were eight more muscle-bodied men still standing in line, stroking their cocks and waiting their turn for a piece of her tight, white pussy.

"Oh, God, yes!" her husband cried out over Marsha Ambrosius' "69." "Fuck my wife, you big-dicked bull! Fuck her! Oh, God, yes! Fuck her! Fuck her! Fuck her! Aaah, yessss! *Fuuuuuuck!"*

Nairobia's insides quivered. She couldn't deny the prickles of heat building between her thighs, or the way her now erect nipples brushed teasingly against the flimsy material of her halter. There were so many married couples who had cuckold fantasies; men who desired seeing—or were forced to watch—their wives being stuffed with the dick of another, more well-endowed man; men who couldn't satisfy their women sexually, so their wives sexual pleasures from another man vicariously became theirs.

Cuckolds were usually submissive men, who either suffered from premature ejaculation or had painfully small cocks, and enjoyed being sexually humiliated.

Oh, how sinfully delicious it was for a woman to deny her husband her pussy, his only access being to clean up the ejaculate of the lover(s) she'd chosen to fuck in front of him.

Such was the case for Mr. Twiggy Dick who grunted and groaned and exploded his thick load in less than twenty hand strokes the minute his wife hobbled over to him on shaky legs, and lowered her swollen cunt over his face, her slit oozing load after load of creamy milk.

Nairobia watched, a mixture of disgust and fascination pooling in her eyes, as he extended his tongue and took his wife's offering, licking and gobbling her cunt into his wet, greedy mouth.

Watching the vile, yet erotic vision, made Nairobia's clit throb. She lived for these salacious moments, reveling in the forbidden thrills of others. She cupped her mound as Twiggy Dick slipped a finger in his wife's ass while drinking in her pussy as if it were a vanilla shake. Nairobia's gaze took in the erotic sight and a rush of liquid warmth flooded her loins as she massaged and kneaded, running her fingers in little circles over her clit. She caressed the slick and swollen folds of her pussy, before slipping a finger inside. Her overheated lips sucked in her finger. She worked her finger in and out of her slick opening, teasing it, toying with the beginning of an orgasm of her own. She used her thumb to flick over her clit.

Nairobia bit back a moan as an exquisite rush of heat roiled over her flesh. She looked across the other side of the room as The Weeknd's version of "Drunk In Love" played. She felt her hips slowly rolling. She needed, wanted more. She thrust two fingers deep inside her, but it still wasn't enough. She wedged a third finger in, pumping hard and fast. She felt sets of smoldering eyes on her and her husky groans turned sharp with desire.

She felt the need to be slutty, to get filthy with it.

She swore she'd never fuck any of the club's patrons. And she wouldn't. But who said she couldn't give them a sultry show?

She could make them all come without touch, without words. Her curves alone made men drool, her lush ass beckoned them to kiss it, taste it, fuck it.

She pulled her fingers from her slit and sucked them into her mouth, then untied her dress. The slinky garment fluttered to the floor as the deejay segued into The Weeknd's "Enemy."

Feeling the slow burn building up inside her, she backed herself up against a wall. Widened her stance. Raised her hands up over her head. Then slowly twirled her hips, and slid down the wall. She worked her way back up, sliding her tongue over her lips. Her body was bathed in candlelight as she swayed back and forth in a slow seductive dance.

The former *Playboy* model and porn star was in her glory as she thrust her hips and tantalized the onslaught of male admirers, making them groan. She made her body talk to them, every fluid movement of her hips, every roll of her belly, promising them a night of unadulterated bliss—even if it was an illusionary offering.

She spread open her thighs, slid her hands over her shimmering body, then down between her smooth thighs. She pulled open her glistening folds, giving them a glimpse of her beautiful pink cunt.

She knew all they really wanted was a wet pussy and a good fuck. The sight of her pretty pussy made their dicks harden. She slid a lusty glance over at a tall, muscular and very handsome hunk of white chocolate who stood naked, his thick, seven-inch erection in his hand, stroking himself as he watched her. Nairobia could tell by the look in his blazing blue eyes that he hungered for her.

Look my hung darling, but do not touch...

Her seductive moves were making the men standing around her hornier and hornier by the second. And she found herself becoming equally aroused and caught up in the moment.

She closed her eyes getting lost in the music, then slowly opened them. Her long-lashed eyes fluttered as her bodyguard came into view. He was oh so thuggish. Rugged. Tatted. She bet he liked it hard, rough and to be in total control, fucking down and dirty, balls deep. And Nairobia longed to get a sampling of his hood dick.

He wore a black short-sleeved tee that clung to his defined chest, a pair of black baggy jeans that hung just so—hiding what she still believed to be a big cock.

Nairobia felt herself grow hotter as he eyed her from behind his dark shades. He was making his rounds through the club when he came up to the third floor and stumbled on *her*. He knew he should have kept walking, but curiosity and his own secret desires that he wasn't prepared to deal with kept him there.

Goddammit. This was just what he *didn't* need. To see his client naked and seducing a bunch of horny motherfuckers—including himself. *Fuck.* She had them all entranced by her seductive wiles. It was bad enough he'd been working for her close to two weeks now and struggled to keep her out of his own head. She was mesmerizing. But she was fucking forbidden fruit.

And he knew it.

Nairobia licked her lips. And he swore she was licking them at him. And damn if he didn't find himself, in that moment, wishing like hell that same tongue was licking around the head of his dick, tonguing the moistened slit in the middle until he shot his load down in her throat, and all over her face. He wasn't a porn star, but—if he weren't on her payroll and opportunity had presented itself (another time, another place), he'd fuck the living shit out of her dick-teasing ass as if he were one.

"What the fuck, man?! he thought, scolding himself. *This is just this freaky bitch's M.O., teasing muhfuckas. She likes fucking with niggahs…"*

And she was fucking with him. He felt it deep in his gut. And he didn't appreciate it one motherfucking bit. She'd never catch him slipping, though—not if he could help it. He wasn't some soft-ass mofo. He wasn't about to get played for a sucker. And he wasn't about to let her sexy-ass or his throbbing dick fuck up his money. He had restraint. Self-control. And he intended to use every ounce of it to keep from getting lured into her snare.

He shook his head as Drake's cover of Jamie Foxx's "Fall For Your Type" started playing. How fucking apropos.

Nairobia Jansen was fucking off-limits. Period. As far as he was concerned, he wasn't about to make the same mistake twice. He'd willingly offered his last client more than just his company's security services. And he quickly found himself caught up in more than he was prepared for. He hadn't fallen in love with her. But he'd fallen in love with her head game. She sucked his dick and loved on his balls with her tongue, making his toes curl and him spit his nut faster than any other woman had ever done.

She'd been a dick-sucking beast and he couldn't get enough of her neck work. Anytime he'd see her lips, his dick would come alive. The rumors had been true. She'd been trolling online for dick, and took to sucking random cats while her then fiancé was behind the wall, serving a prison bid for drug dealing. Then he released from prison and she'd married him. To only end up leaving him, and ruthlessly bringing her man down with the help of him and others she'd meticulously lured in with her charm and seductive wiles. She'd been known as the Deep Throat Diva, and lived up to every part of her name, sucking his heart and soul out through the slit of his fat dick.

However, truth be told, attached to that wet, juicy mouth of hers had come with it a whole lot of unnecessary drama that'd caused him to take a bullet for her, and have to boot up and get down and dirty for her cause, doing things he'd cared not to rehash.

He wasn't complaining—just remembering. It had come with

the territory. Protecting a woman who'd been married to a major drug dealer. Trying to keep her safe from him at all costs. Still, because of how he was built, he'd do it all over again—for *her*, if he had to, because that was how he got down. He was loyal. And he knew if Nairobia needed him, for *anything*, he'd more than likely have her back too.

She was a fucking temptress.

That was a problem.

And his hard dick had the potential to be an even bigger problem if he didn't stay in control. He wasn't about to sign up for any drama. But fuck if he didn't want to split her yams open one good time, and push his dick up in her guts; just once.

He looked over at her one last time, before navigating his muscular frame through the crowd. He made a mental note to check her ass. ASAP. He touched the earbud discreetly plugged in his ear, relieved when someone from his detail radioed in for him to come down to the club's main level.

Nairobia watched him as he walked off and grinned slyly as he disappeared from her view.

You can run, but you can't hide your desires, my darling. I will have you in my bed. Soon. And melt my cunt all over your cock...

She threw her head back.

And climaxed.

TWENTY-EIGHT

Aside from stacking his money, Lamar had three weaknesses: beautiful women, good pussy, and superb head—and not necessarily in that order. He simply loved beautiful women. He loved fucking. And he loved getting his thick, black cock sucked, sloppily, deep and wet.

Shit.

And he had no problem getting either of the three.

But working at The Pleasure Zone was really starting to become a challenge for him. Temptation swirled up all around him. It hovered over him like a noose, swinging, waiting to slide down over his head, around his neck and strangle the shit out of him.

He decided that he had to get away from it before it lured him in, and had him strung the fuck out.

This club.

Nairobia.

Fucking Nairobia!

Not that he was afraid of her. He wasn't afraid of any broad. And he definitely wasn't afraid of pussy. No. He was afraid of himself. He was afraid of giving into the temptation and then becoming hooked on this shit around him at the club.

All this fucking and sucking, all this pussy and ass on display, had his head spinning.

The shit was better than watching porn.

And it kept his dick hard.

He'd never been addicted to anything other than making money. Period.

But desire was fucking with him.

The devil was fucking with him.

Nairobia was fucking with him. Her and that body, and those sexy-ass gray eyes of hers could tempt him to...

Lamar shook his head.

She was sin draped in diamonds. She was wickedness dipped in sweet honey.

She was...

Goddamn mesmerizing.

She was a walking wet dream.

Fucking porn-star bitch!

A fucking disaster waiting to happen!

He knew it.

And he had to keep telling himself to not let his aching dick fuck up his bread. Had to keep reminding himself that she was a motherfucking potential problem.

She was hellfire personified.

And every time he was around her, flames engulfed his balls, licked at his dick, and had him ready to nut on himself.

Motherfuck, he wanted to beat her pussy up so goddamn bad. The thought alone made heat inside him rise. He knew what a broad like her needed. She needed a good fucking, a hard, balls-deep pounding. She needed his curved dick deep in her ass, gripping him like a fist, her ass clenching hard around his thick cock.

Yeah, that's what she needed. For him to bust her ass wide open. That would teach the sexpot not to taunt a cat like him.

Gritting his teeth as he pressed the call button and waited for the elevator to descend to the main level of the club, Lamar glanced at his watch.

4 a.m.

The club would close in another two hours. But the place was still packed with club-goers starving for a night of untamed pleasures.

Lamar couldn't believe how many nasty-ass mofos there were out there, looking for any way to unleash their hidden, freaky desires. Hell, he'd be the first to admit he loved getting freaky with it. But, goddamn. These motherfuckers up in here took the word *freak* to a whole other level.

And the shit fascinated him to no end.

But, again…there was this one caveat.

Nairobia.

The stunning bombshell with the deep, raspy voice whom he'd witnessed, firsthand, toy with men, then devour them with her cunningness. She could eat a man whole. Literally. Yet, the things about her he wanted so desperately to avoid were the same things he found himself drawn to.

She was focused. She knew what she wanted. And when she had her sights set on something—or *someone*, she was unyielding. And had no problem going after it. He found himself attracted to her aggressiveness. She could be extreme and uncompromising…and that shit turned him the fuck on.

He'd done his homework—used his resources and connects to uncover whatever he could about her—before he handed her the contract to employ his company's services.

In addition to providing security detail, his company also provided background checks. And, yes, like with all his potential clients, he had a file on Nairobia. Thin as it was, it told him what he needed to know.

There was nothing shady about her, nothing remotely askew. Aside from being a freak, she engaged in no unsavory business practices. In his report of her, there was very little info surrounding her childhood. Her mother was Dutch royalty, and her father a Nigerian diplomat. From ages twelve to seventeen, she'd attended an all-girls' boarding school in Switzerland. Strangely, there was no record of her for almost a year after that until she emerged, again, at age eighteen, appearing in her first role as Pleasure in the movie *Sweet Pussy*.

Yeah, he'd bet his left nut her pussy was as sweet as it looked. Shit, shit, shit…

What the fuck was wrong with him?

He had a girl. Someone he'd been seeing for the last six months. Lana. She had nice, big cantaloupe-sized titties and a fat ass. And he dug her. He'd met her on his flight from Atlanta to Newark. They'd talked it up the whole flight back to New Jersey that by the time the plane had hit the tarmac, he'd gotten her number. And by the time they'd reached baggage claim, he'd had a date lined up for later that evening.

He liked her easy, laid-back vibe. She had a good head on her shoulders. Was into sports, like him. Was easy to talk to. And didn't come with a bunch of drama. He liked that. And he appreciated how she made him wait for the pussy. He'd sadly admitted to himself it wasn't really worth the two-month wait, though.

It was wet, sure. But far from juicy. And it wasn't spectacular. And, though she sucked his dick, her head game needed work. But he'd given her a pass for her enthusiasm, and her willingness to get better. Still, after six months of practice, she'd still scrape up his dick with her teeth.

And, besides being stingy with the sex, she still ran from the dick after more than thirty minutes of him inside her, doggy-style. Truthfully, she lacked the kind of sex drive he needed in his life. He preferred access to pussy—or head, or both—every night. However, she had thought that too excessive. But agreed to sex three times a week.

Still, in spite of those shortcomings, she was a cutie. And, although he couldn't say for sure he loved her, he did, however, enjoy spending time with her. She was a good girl who didn't drink or smoke, or curse, not even while being fucked. She was definitely a more reserved type.

Classy.

But her ass was far from a freak in the sheets. He needed, wanted, a mixture of the both. A chick who was classy in the streets, but knew how to bring it in the sheets. And Lana fell short. So, hell yeah, he was sexually frustrated. He hadn't really cheated on her—did getting head count?—since they'd been together. But it was becoming torturous not going back to his philandering ways.

And working here—with Nairobia—was fuel to an already burning need.

He couldn't get the image of her dancing up against that wall earlier in the evening out of his head, the way the light from the candles and torches illuminated her smooth mocha-coated skin. Fire had speared him as he stood there in back of the crowd and watched her, his eyes locked on her every move from behind his dark shades, as she seduced her captive audience—a bunch of foaming-at-the-mouth motherfuckers—as if her pussy had superpowers. The way she glowed. The way her hips swayed. The way she stood there in her come fuck-me heels—naked!—taunting her prey as they ogled her like a bunch of horny frat boys; pulling herself open to them, baring her beautiful tits, that fat, juicy ass—and her bare pussy.

Jesus Christ!

That freaky bitch had a fat-ass pussy.

And he had to keep reminding himself that it'd been fucked inside out by a slew of nasty motherfuckers on and off the screen. That porn stars were just overpaid whores, no more, no less.

Still...

This bitch was bad as fuck.

And she was about her paper. Getting that bread. She was a

hustler. And he dug that about her. So he couldn't hate on her for using what she had to get what she wanted. Hell, he couldn't front like he hadn't been known to trick up his money on strippers and hoes, even taking his share to one of the private rooms for some head, or taking a ho or two to his whip and fucking their lights out in the backseat.

He'd blown thousands of dollars on tricks and hoes who'd gladly offered up a night of pussy and head.

So who was he to judge?

When the elevator doors opened, he stepped in. Then pressed the button for the fourth floor. He couldn't wait to get this shit over with. He needed to set boundaries. He needed to check Nairobia's ass and set the record straight once and for all, so he could do his fucking job without all the unnecessary distractions.

This wasn't personal.

It was business.

And if she didn't like it, then hell…she could fire him. And, if necessary, terminate the terms of their contract. Yeah, right. He sighed, shaking his head. Who the fuck was he kidding?

It wasn't just about him. True, he could remove himself from the situation and replace himself with one of his partners, or with another member from his security team. Quick fix, for sure. But was that what he really wanted?

He couldn't be sure.

But what he was sure of was, losing this contract would mean the people under him losing bread. He couldn't have that. Many of them had families, had mouths to feed, and loads of bills. They needed this. So he wasn't about to fuck this up for them.

The thought of being caught up in her web of seduction unnerved him and made his blood boil. He found himself wondering if he'd done the right thing not giving this assignment to his boy, his partner in crime, Mel, instead of taking it on himself.

Regardless, limits still needed to be set. Clear, defined lines needed to be drawn in the proverbial sand.

And, tonight, before the sun rose, Lamar planned on making it clear to Nairobia what his role in her hire *would* or *wouldn't* be.

Period.

The elevator doors opened, and Lamar stepped out, making his way down the carpeted corridor, passing several *play*rooms. He did his damnedest not to stop and revel in the debauchery around him. Instead, he kept walking, keeping the sexually explicit go-ings-on up on the fourth floor locked in his peripherals. It was what he was trained to do. Be on alert. See everything around him at all times. And, right now, all he saw were tongues on pussies— on clits, mouths on dicks…and people climaxing.

He walked past a condom and lube station on the right of him, followed by the Cognac lounge, whirls of cigar smoke floating around the space. To the right of him, sultry music seeped out from beneath the closed door. Some side ho anthem he couldn't recall the name of. He wasn't sure what the hell that large space was called, but he called it the Stripper Room because of its three stages and stripper poles. All he knew was the room was filled with a bunch of horny broads taking turns up on each stage, embracing their alter stripper egos, and whatever else.

He made a quick left down another hall, then stood in front of thick sliding glass doors. He stared at the keypad to the right of the door, then punched in his four-digit passcode. He hadn't had to use it before, until now.

A split-second later, the doors slid open and he stepped through, the doors sliding shut behind him. Instantly, quietness followed in behind him. He realized then that the area was soundproofed. The walls were painted red. Red lights shined overhead. Dramatic. Sensual. He found the color fitting since the owner of the club was hot like fire.

He breathed in the heat as he made his way toward her office, toward the flames.

Her office door was slightly ajar. He heard the moan before he reached it.

He blinked.

Took a step closer. Then another. And peered in, hovering just behind the crack in her door.

Oh shit.

What the fuck?

Nairobia was atop her desk—fucking butt-ass *naked*, her body bathed in the glow of low lighting, playing in her pussy.

Pleasuring herself.

He couldn't believe this shit.

What the fuck is wrong with her? he thought as he sucked in a breath and eyed her breasts. And those mouthwatering nipples! Hard nipples. Sweet. Chocolate, melt-in-his-mouth nipples he wanted to feel dissolve onto his wet tongue.

As if she sensed his presence, knew his thoughts, Nairobia bowed her head and cupped her breasts and gathered them up toward her long tongue, swiping it over each thick, distended nipple.

He blinked. Bit back an unexpected groan.

Lamar's hungry gaze slowly skimmed over her taut body. Goddamn. She had a body that would put most broads half her age to shame. This wasn't good. Seeing this. He hadn't been standing here any more than a few seconds and she'd already managed to have him unfocused.

He had to quit. Had to get the hell out of here. And stay far away from her. Before she had him all fucked up in the head. Still his legs didn't move.

No broad had ever had him like this. Wanting to lose himself inside of them. Teetering on the edge of—

Nairobia murmured something in Dutch, her whispered voice sending jolts of electricity through him, zapping every nerve ending in his body as he stood and watched her fingers glide between her legs.

Why was this bitch fucking with him?

She was in the habit of yanking motherfuckers by the balls and dragging them by their dicks, that's why.

He gritted his teeth.

Nairobia did her best to hide a sly smile as she threw her head back, lowered her lids, and peered through her long lashes at the sight of him watching her. She feigned unknowing. "Mmm...*ja, ja, ja*...fuck me...mmm...oooh...my wet *kut*...uhh..."

Her pussy gushed, making the puddle beneath her wetter, bigger, as she finger-fucked herself and flicked a finger over her clit.

Lamar was beside himself. Crazed with lust. He needed, wanted, to be inside of her. Fucking the shit out of her. He groaned inwardly, his eyes fixed on the silhouette before him. The sound of her pussy, full of warmth and wetness, filled with juicy intense pleasure, swooped around him. The smell of her was sweet. It wafted around her office, then floated through the crack in the door, and settled on his chocolate lips. He could almost taste her.

Goddamn, motherfuck, *shit!*

This was some fucked-up shit. Standing here. Stalker-like. Prying.

He knew this shit he was doing was all sorts of fucked up. Knew he should turn away. Leave now. But he couldn't. The erotic sight of her pleasuring herself was too enthralling to walk away from. So he stood there and let his hungry gaze eat up the view. Of her pussy, her delicate fingers, strumming a wet symphony between her slick glistening folds.

His dick throbbed.

His balls ached.

Nairobia's lashes fluttered, but she managed to keep her lids nearly shut; just enough so Lamar would be none the wiser. That she knew he was there. That she felt his eyes on her, his gaze brushing over her breasts, lingering on her nipples, skittering over her rippling belly, latching onto her clit, so wet, so sensitive, so ready.

She felt the heat.

Felt the burn.

Lamar's gaze flickered as his eyes caressed her wet flesh, her fingers splashing in and out of her slit. He found himself fantasizing. Imagining the satiny feel of her soft hands on his hard dick, stroking up and down his pulsing shaft. He imagined the feel of her silky mouth as he fed her his dick, filling her jaws with his babies.

Then suspicion crept up his spine, and his mind started to race.

Why the fuck was this broad propped up on her desk like that, diddling in her cunt, with the door ajar for fuck's sake? Had she wanted to be seen? Was this some twisted fuckery she'd staged? Had she known he was coming up to speak to her?

The thought, the possibility, made his blood boil.

Nairobia moaned, and the heat roiling through his veins instantly went from anger to a smoldering want. He felt the urge to grab at his dick, to pull it out, and stroke it. He needed some pussy, some head, some ass...*something* before he fucked around and caught a rape charge.

This shit he was doing was...*creepy* as fuck!

Yet, there he stood. His imagination taking him places he hadn't wanted to travel. His gaze simmering with a desire he'd never known possible.

In that instant, he hated her for that. For fucking with his resolve. For having him so fucking aroused that the head of his dick leaked, soaking a wet stain in his boxer briefs. This scandalous bitch was trying to incite an orgasm inside his pants without even trying. Or was she?

Trying to have him go caveman on her ass, kicking in the door, dragging her off that pussy-stained desk by her fucking hair, then bending her over and pounding the shit out of her from behind?

Was that what she wanted?

His dick rammed between her sweet, bouncy cheeks?

He groaned again, this time low in his throat.

It was bad enough his dick was overly sensitive from all the blood rushing to it. Now his fucking jeans were sliding against the head making it nearly impossible to keep from busting all over himself.

He needed to spin off. Get away from the door. Now.

Move, muhfucka, he told himself.

As if hearing his thoughts, Nairobia spread her legs wider and moaned again, this time much louder, more urgent, her fingers plunging deep inside her cunt with unrelenting strokes. Her hips thrashed.

And Lamar…well, he did what any straight, horny, curious motherfucker would do.

Stood there.

Waited to see what would happen next.

Nairobia's fingers went deeper in her cunt. And he smelled the heady, wet scent of her arousal.

"Come fuck me, my love…mmm…ooooh, *ja, ja, ja*…"

Lamar's body stiffened. Wait? Was she talking to him? Had she seen him all along, lurking?

Was she purposefully enticing *him?*

"*Mmmm*…fuck me," she begged. "Fuck *mijn kut*…oooh…yes, yes, yessss…lick *mijn kut*…uhhh…"

Lamar groaned inwardly again, and forced himself to remember the girl he had at home—well, *home* at *her* own crib, waiting for him. Still, it did nothing for the raw itch he had to push open the door and drag Nairobia to the edge of her desk, throw her legs up over his broad shoulders, and sink his dick deep into that perfectly tight-looking pussy of hers.

He swallowed. Cursed under his breath. *Leave now, muhfucka! Spin off. Go home to your girl and fuck her brains out.*

"Oooh…I'm so wet…so horny…*mmmmmm*…"

Her catlike purring made his dick hard all over again, seized him by the balls, igniting his blood. She had his pulse racing. Had him breathing so hard he could hardly see straight. Lamar swallowed against the lust and took a step back. He had to bounce now before his dick—the shit felt heavy, like it was filled with cement—caused him to do something he'd regret later.

There were only two options.

To fuck, or not to fuck…

Nairobia increased the tempo of her fingers over her clit.

Lamar cursed under his breath again. Then eased back from the door. He was leaving, but not the same way he'd come in—with a hard, throbbing dick.

Nairobia cried out. Her body thrashed. Adrenaline spiked, searing through her body as she orgasmed.

She was determined to have the sexy, rugged, bouncer/bodyguard/pussy punisher in her bed, and between her sultry thighs. Oh, yes. Lamar was going to be a deliciously painful challenge. One she was determined to conquer. *Patience*, she warned herself. *Reel him in slowly*. She just needed to ensure he stayed around long enough for the ride.

Her trembling cunt clutched around her fingers. She grinned, closing her eyes, and moaning. She swore she'd own him, his cock… and that beautiful mouth of his.

If it was the last thing she ever did…

TWENTY-NINE

Nairobia whisked inside the entrance of Nappy No More II, lifting her shades over her head. She greeted Zeus with customary air-kisses. "Hey, diiiiiva," he cooed, getting up and assessing her attire. Once again, she'd come in and slayed him with another scrumptious handbag. Dior. And he was sick with envy.

But she gave him life every time she served him.

"Oooh, yass, boo, yass. You are too fabulous."

Nairobia smiled at his exaggerated antics. She found him simply adorable. Her mind wandered to the left, and she found herself wondering what his lean, toned body looked like underneath that little skimpy top and those skinny jeans. Her filthy mind flooded with salacious thoughts, trying to imagine him naked in a set of heels with his cock hanging between his legs. She wondered if he had a long, smooth cock, a short stumpy one, or if it was the size of an itty-bitty sausage link.

Oh how she adored him, in all his femininity. She swallowed. She wanted to lick over his cock like a clitoris. Oh, how scandalous. She should be ashamed of herself wondering and thinking such filthy thoughts.

Her lips curled into a naughty grin. "Zeus, my love. It's always so good to see you."

He smiled wide. "You, too. Pasha should be coming out shortly.

She should be finishing up with her eleven o'clock." Nairobia glanced at the time. It was quarter-to-twelve. She was fifteen minutes early.

"No, worries, my love. I can wait," she said, pulling out her buzzing phone.

"I'm going on a quick break. I'll be right outside if you need anything," he said, before grabbing his designer backpack, then sashaying his way out of the door.

Nairobia answered her phone on the third ring. "Hello."

"I wanna see you. Make time for me."

She felt her body heat. "Sorry, Mar*Sell*, my darling. I'm out of town."

He groaned. "Damn. How long?"

She'd come out to California to meet with her agent, then spend some needed office time at her production company. Things were getting busy there, and she wanted to have her finger on the pulse of everything happening with the production and release of several new porn titles. It was Monday, and she knew she had to—unfortunately, return back to the East Coast by Thursday early evening, before the doors to The Pleasure Zone opened.

She sighed. "Not until sometime Thursday."

"Oh, aiight. Damn. Where are you?"

She frowned. This business of being asked her whereabouts did not sit well with her. Was he trying to keep tabs on her? Or was he simply asking because he genuinely wanted to know?

"I'm in L.A.," she told him.

Marcel grinned on the other end the phone. "Shit. That's even better. I have some business out there later on in the week. I'll just fly out earlier than planned. I'll have my pilot fuel up, and be there by ten o'clock your time."

Nairobia blinked. "Mar*Sell*, my love. You can do whatever your heart desires." But that did not mean he'd be doing her.

He lowered his voice. "Does that include you, baby?"

She smiled. "Not tonight, *mijn liefde.*"

Now tomorrow?

Maybe…

Nairobia spotted Pasha walking toward the front of the salon with a strikingly exotic-looking woman, who looked almost Indian, holding a baby in her arm. Her skin was the color of cinnamon, and she was holding the hand of a caramel-skinned boy with a head full of curly hair. The little boy looked to be about four or five, and—with the exception of their different skin tones, bore a remarkable resemblance to the woman.

"Yeah—"

Nairobia cut Marcel off. "I have to go. Call me when you land."

She ended the call, sliding her phone down into the inside pocket of her bag.

Pasha met her gaze, and smiled. "Hey, Nairobia, girl. I'll be right with you."

"No rush, my love," she said, eyeing the woman with her as they made their way to the reception desk. Their eyes met, and the woman's gaze ran over Nairobia's body, before she smiled. She didn't need an introduction to know who Nairobia was. She'd found her husband's stash of porn before they were married, and a few times they'd watched some of her movies together. Then clawed at one another like two wild beasts, fucking until the sun rose.

The little boy looked at Nairobia and smiled, waving.

Nairobia smiled and waved back. "He's beautiful."

The woman smiled, then looked down at her son. "Thanks."

"Mommy, that lady over there," he said, pointing over at Nairobia, "is pretty like you." She glanced back over at Nairobia, then said, "She is, isn't she?"

"Can I kiss her?" the little boy asked.

Nairobia almost choked on her saliva. She said she liked to train them up young, but goodness. It seemed like he was already getting his training from home.

"Boy, no, you're not kissing her."

"Then can I kiss her toes, like Daddy does yours?"

"Boy, no. Don't have me smack you butt. What I tell you about that. You can't go around puttin' ya lips up on everyone, especially strangers. And you better not let me catch you sucking on anyone's damn toes. You hear me?"

He nodded, then looked back at Nairobia. "But she's sexy, Mommy."

Nairobia blinked back her shock at hearing that.

Pasha shook her head in disbelief. "Ohmigod, girl, how old is he again?"

"Four going on twenty-four."

Pasha laughed. "Well, what in the world does he know about someone being *sexy?* And toe-kissing?"

The woman sucked her teeth. "He hears his father's dumb-ass sayin'." She shook her head. "I keep tellin' Alex stop talkin' around him like that, but he thinks that shit's cute. He's got him too damn grown."

"Mommy, no bad words, okay?"

Nairobia eyed the little boy. He had diamond studs in both ears and a fancy watch way too expensive for a boy his age. His mother looked down at him, rubbing her hand over the top of his curls. "Yes, Zaire. Mommy's sorry."

Zaire, Nairobia thought. *What a beautiful name for a little boy.*

Nairobia's gaze locked on the infant boy in the woman's arms, drooling and cooing and staring at her over his mother's shoulder. He was a little ball of milk chocolate that made her want to go over and ask to hold him.

Nairobia gave him a little finger wave, and he squealed, bouncing himself up and down in his mother's arms. She shifted him. He bounced and squealed again, laughing. The woman glanced over her shoulder, then cooed, "Boobie-bear, what you laughin' at, huh? Who you see over there, huh?" He squealed again, trying to twist back around to look over her shoulder.

"He's gorgeous," Nairobia finally said. "How old is he?"

She smiled, her eyes glowing with love. "Thanks. He's six months."

Nairobia returned the smile. "You have a beautiful family."

"Thanks." She turned her attention back to Pasha, and dug her wallet out of her purse. She pulled out a credit card, handing it to Zeus who was talking on his smartphone.

"Oh, before I forget," Pasha said. "Nairobia, this is my realtor Katrina. She's the one responsible for finding me this place."

Nairobia smiled. "Nice." She asked her how long she'd been in real estate.

"Four years," she said.

"Katrina, this is Nairobia. She recently opened a club back in New York. The Pleasure Zone."

Katrina regarded Nairobia with a smile, then said, "I've heard of it. My girl back home, that's all she talks about. She has a membership. And trust, she's gettin' her money's worth."

Nairobia smiled. "I'm glad she's enjoying the club's...*amenities*. We aim to keep people coming back."

Katrina smirked. "Girl, Chanel's hot ass is a freak. She'd come over a trash bag if you let her."

Pasha laughed as she handed back her credit card, then handed her the receipt to sign.

"Mommy, can I take my baby brother to Trisha's birthday party?"

"No, sweetie," she said, handing her signed copy back to Pasha. "You're not takin' your brotha wit' you." She stuffed her wallet and the receipt down in her bag.

"How come, Mommy? I want Cassie to see him."

"He's not goin', hun. Now stop askin' me. And who is this Cassie chick?"

"My other girlfriend," he answered.

"*Whaat?*" she shrieked. "What other girlfriend? How many you think you have?"

He counted off on his little fingers, then said, "Six."

She yanked his hand. "Girl, let me get out of here before I have a stroke."

Pasha chuckled. "Bye, girl. You're gonna have your hands full with him. He's definitely gonna be a heartbreaker."

She sucked her teeth, dragging him toward the door. "Girl, please. His lil' fresh butt gonna have me put a lock on it. He on his way to becoming a manwhore if I don't watch him closely."

The little boy looked back at Nairobia and waved. Then did the unthinkable.

He blew her a kiss as he walked out of the door.

Nairobia clutched her neck. "Oh, my."

Pasha laughed. "Girl, that one right there is too much. C'mon back so I can lay my hands in that luscious hair."

Nairobia smiled. "Pasha, my darling, you can lay your hands wherever you like. For the next hour, I'm all yours…"

THIRTY

"Yo, we need to talk."

Nairobia looked up to see Lamar standing in the doorway of her office two days later. His tone was even, his face expressionless. But behind his dark shades, his dark-chocolate orbs were filled with lust. He didn't know what the hell was going on with him. It was like the more he was around her, the more drawn he was to her.

He knew it was all kinds of wrong, which is why he hadn't gone out to L.A. with her. He needed to put some distance between them. Keep their interactions strictly at the club. If she needed protecting outside of the club, he'd decided to assign one of his partners for the job.

The shit with her was fucking up his flow. Had his mind all over the place.

And that vision he had of her up on her desk playing with herself didn't help any. He played that night over and over in his head nonstop, his dick hardening at the imagery stamped in his brain.

Lamar was pissed at himself for not having better control over the situation. He'd never let a broad get up in his head the way Nairobia had in such a short time. She had to be into some sort of voodoo bullshit, witchcraft, or some other type of trickery to have him becoming obsessed with her. He was certain of it. The bitch was a sorceress.

She just had to be.

He also blamed his weakening resolve on the lack of pussy and head in his life lately. It'd been four days since he'd last bust a nut. Thanks to his girl being on the rag. He always loved fucking his girls while they were on their menstrual. But Lana wouldn't have any of that. She thought it nasty. Unclean. And disrespectful to be asked to indulge in such acts. She was bugging. And her prudish-ass was starting to wear Lamar's patience thin. It was bad enough he was still ticked off at her for not being considerate enough to top him off with some head last night.

Pure fucking selfish!

Bottom line, Lamar was on edge. And he knew if he didn't blow a load soon, he was going to explode.

Nairobia's eyes twinkled as she took in the sight of him. Hands clenched tight, she knew he was packing a weapon in the small of his back, but she was dying to see the one that hung between his legs.

"About…?" she said coolly. Then she boldly licked her lips.

"This assignment," he replied, his tone clipped. He tried not to inhale too deeply. He smelled her sweet scent. And the smell of her excited cunt from three nights ago still stained his senses.

Nairobia motioned him in and Lamar sauntered toward the desk, closing the door behind him. If he were coming in to quit, he had another thing coming if he thought she'd take lightly to that. She would not hear of it. Period.

"What about it? Do you not like the work environment?"

"It has its moments."

Nairobia raised a brow. "Meaning what?" She pinned him with an inquisitive stare as he took a seat across from her.

"Meaning, the fee you're paying us is serious. And I appreciate that, for real for real. But, on some real shit. I don't know if this is the right fit."

Nairobia tilted her head. "Oh, it's the right fit, my darling. *You* are the right fit. This is where you need to be. And it's where I *want* you to be." *Among other places.*

"And that's cool, yo. But…"

"No 'buts,' my love. Your services are all I need."

Lamar sighed. "Yo, listen, I'm cool wit' workin' wit' you. But I'm not checkin' for all the extras."

Nairobia's brow shot up. "Extras, like? I do not know what you mean by *extras.*"

"Like you tryna throw the pussy at me," he said bluntly. "That shit ain't cool, yo. I mean. I'm flattered; don't get it twisted. I'm a man. And, I'd love nothin' more than beatin' that thang up, word is bond. But, I'm tryna run a professional business 'n' it's like you tryna sabotage shit. Tryna make it hard for me to do my job. I'm not diggin' that, yo."

Nairobia's cunt clenched at his street vernacular. He was so roguish. Yet, Nairobia instinctively knew he was also so deceptively gentle behind his tough exterior. She'd been around enough men to know a man with a heart. She wanted to crack open his shell, and drink him in.

She studied him thoughtfully. Then smiled. "The only thing I want to make *hard* for you, my darling, is your cock. Not your job. Have I failed you?"

"I got a girl," he stated, circumventing the question. Of course he was hard. His dick started swelling the minute he'd stepped through the door and sat down. Lamar sensed he didn't need to confirm or deny it because she already knew the answer when her gaze flitted to his crotch, then looked back up and smiled. He knew she knew. He didn't know what it was about her, but she had some type of overpowering effect on him. She was a sexual magnet. And she craftily pulled him in every time he was near her. "She's a good girl," he said, not sure—at that moment, if he were trying to convince her or himself of that. "I'm not tryna fuck things up."

Undeterred, Nairobia stared at him; her eyes alight with curiosity and amusement. "That's nice, my love. But does she appreciate you? Is she eager to swallow you in her cunt? Does she make your toes curl? Does she love being down on her knees worshipping your cock?" Nairobia sensually slid the tip of her tongue from between her lips, then slowly licked over the top of them. "Does her cunt stay wet and hungry for you?"

He winced. No, of course she didn't do any of that shit! And, hell no, she wasn't eager about sex the way he was! That was one of the fucking problems. And, truth be told, it was slowly starting to eat away at him, like acid, corroding his senses. Cheating in the past had always been easy for him. He did it with no thought, or no regard for anyone else. But, nowadays, he was trying to do something different, trying to be different. But the shit was getting harder by the moment, right along with his fat dick.

"We get it in," he said, crossing his right ankle over his left knee. The words were forced. But he managed a straight face when he said them.

"How many times a night?" Nairobia inquired.

How *many* times a night? Ha! Was she fucking kidding him? He was lucky if he got it every other night, and that was a reach.

She didn't wait for an answer. "A young, virile man such as yourself, my love, should have his cock sucked into a warm mouth, and his seeds milked daily."

Lamar's dick, heavy with arousal, jumped in his lap. He felt his nut swelling in his balls. He felt himself go tense, drawn, his body prickling with sexual awareness the way she looked at him. Those sinful gray eyes of hers threatening and promising pleasure like he'd never experienced.

He was tempted, so, so, very tempted. His resolve was hanging by a thread, a very thin one at that. It was stretched to the limit. But it'd hadn't broken…yet.

Lamar took a deep breath and tried not to inhale, along with air, her mind-numbing scent. Foot back to the floor, he subconsciously opened and closed his legs. Opened. Closed. Opened. He fanned them out wide, then shut them tight, pressing his balls together, drawing Nairobia's gaze back to his crotch.

He stopped.

"Listen, real talk, ma. I can't keep workin' under these conditions. If we can't come to some type'a understanding, I'ma need to assign someone else to manage your security needs."

There went that rapacious smile of hers. Again. "I would hate to lose you, my darling. But if you must, then fine. Just as long as you manage my sexual needs before you walk out that door. Let me wrap you in my warmth, my love. Just one night."

Lamar groaned. His hunger, his overwhelming desire, his gnawing frustration evident in the fists at his side and the clenching muscles in his jaw. "You like fuckin' wit' muhfuckas, I see."

"No, my darling," Nairobia purred. "I love *fucking* men who I desire. Men who moisten my cunt long before they ever touch me. *You*, my darling, moisten me."

Lamar bit down on his bottom lip to keep from roaring out a growl, roiling energy circling all around him.

"Be clear, my love," Nairobia said straightforward. "I don't want to marry you. I want to *fuck* you cross-eyed. And I want you to *fuck* me blind. Then I want you to continue doing what I pay you to do. Provide my club's security. And, to be on-call for whatever other security details I may need you and your company for. Nothing more, nothing less, my love." She stood up from her seat and, with a sway of her hips, prowled around toward him, sliding a finger over the top of her desk as she did so. "Now remove your shades, my darling," she demanded softly.

"For what?" Lamar asked with a scowl.

"Because, my love." She ran a hand over his back, then massaged his shoulders. Lamar tensed. Then relaxed under her touch as she caressed his shoulders, then leaned over him and slid her hands up and down the length of his arms, feeling every bulge of muscle. He sat stone still, trying like hell to not seem fazed by her soft touches, or to let her see how aroused he was slowly becoming. Nairobia nipped at his ear, then whispered, "I want you to look me in the eye, like a man should, and tell me you don't want to feel the inside of my *kut*."

He swallowed. "Nah, yo. I'm good on that." The lie stung the tip of his tongue as he said it. But he needed to make a point. The point being—

"Is your cock hard for me?" she boldly asked, sliding her hands down over the front of him, her fingertips flitting across his chiseled chest, then down to his six-pack. "My pussy is so wet for you. Do you want to *neuk me*." Fuck me.

He hissed in a shocked breath, then silently cursed. He knew he should shut her the fuck down, to stop her before he gave in and gave her what she'd been begging for since he'd taken on the security detail. A hard fuck.

But her scent, her touch, her smooth, soft hands…

Shit.

The truth was, he *wanted* to rip her back out. Wanted to *give* her the dick the way she wanted it. How many cats from around the way would be able to say they'd actually fucked a real live, famous porn star?

He grabbed her wrists, removing her hands from his body. "Like I *said*," he reiterated sternly. "I gotta girl."

He released his grip on her wrists, and Nairobia smiled, straightening herself. She walked in front of him, her nipples jutting out on display. "And I've already told you my intentions, my darling. Your *girl*—as you say—can have you." She took him in, and licked her luscious lips. She eased back on her desk, and spread open her thighs. "I don't want *you*. I *want* your cock…"

Nairobia widened her thighs, and Lamar's gaze descended, his eyes flickering over her cunt, before narrowing intently. No matter how hard he tried, he couldn't deny his throbbing erection straining to be free, or the fire burning through his gut.

He felt himself unraveling by the second. He kept telling himself *fuck* the job. Just get up and leave. But something kept him seated, that *something* being the sight of her pussy. He eyed it as she peeled open two puffy petals of flesh and showed him her pink insides. "I'm so wet for you, my love. You want to taste it, no? Lick it? Sniff it? Fuck it?"

She wanted *him*. Inside *her*. Now.

He groaned inwardly. He had no fucking control with her, needed to get away. Fast. He mentally yelled at himself for sitting there and allowing this shit to go on. It bordered on disrespectful. It was blatant sexual harassment. But who the fuck was he kidding?

He didn't want to file complaints. He wanted to plow deep in her. The shit had his dick harder than granite. He rose to his feet as if unfazed by her lewd behavior, as if he had women flashing him all the time.

His cock pulsed again, stronger, harder.

Nairobia eyed him like he was her dinner for the night, like a starved predator eying tender prey. She'd seen the long, heavy length of him. Her pussy clenched for it.

His glare still riveted to her glistening sex, Lamar struggled to keep from licking his lips. He didn't eat pussy, not that he hadn't.

He just didn't eat anyone's. And he rarely gave his girl head, mostly because she wasn't serving up any herself. But Nairobia's deliciously sweet-looking pussy, splayed open on display, made him want to dive in tongue deep.

He swallowed, hard.

Nairobia smiled at him. "My *kut* yearns to feel your tongue on it, to feel your cock and fingers in it. But I won't taunt you, my love."

She closed her legs. Lowered the hem of her dress. Then stood to her feet.

Feeling robbed, Lamar's jaw tightened.

Shit, shit, shit!

"Nairobia," he rasped. "I'm warnin' you, yo. Stop wit' the bullshit 'n' just let me do my fuckin'—" He stopped himself. The ache in his hard, throbbing dick was making it difficult for him to think straight. Fucking Lana, man! Of all the broads he could have been with, why the fuck had he ended up with one who acted like a church secretary? No—scratch that shit. A goddamn nun!

"Let me love you with my mouth," Nairobia offered, the hunger in her pupils darkening. "I want to taste your semen on my tongue…"

Lamar groaned. "I can't keep doing this wit' you, yo," he grated. He finally removed his shades, and his hooded eyes flicked over Nairobia's face.

"You can't keep doing what?" she asked, stepping in to him. "Denying yourself what we both know you ache for?" She ran her hand down over his chest again, then over his abs, before her palm descended lower.

Oh my…

He was hard and thick as she imagined he'd be. She dragged her hand over his erection. Instead of removing her hand, all he kept thinking was why the fuck Lana couldn't be as hungry, as aggressive for him as she was? Why didn't she just give him some head when he'd needed it the most? His balls were aching; he couldn't think about anything else. But release.

"Tell me, my love," she purred, stepping in closer, surrounding him with her heat. Her lips were inches from his. "What can't you keep doing?"

"Wanting you. Imagining you," he pushed out, surprising himself at the answer. His voice had gotten huskier. "You keep fuckin' wit' me, ma."

Her cunt clenched. She liked the way *ma* rolled off his tongue.

"Indulge your desires, my love." She reached for his fly. "And free yourself to the pleasure…"

He gritted his teeth. "I'm telling you, yo. Stop fuckin' wit' me."

Nairobia swallowed, beginning to pant. "Or what?" she challenged, palming him again, squeezing his dick.

This fucking broad was relentless. She wasn't going to quit until he had her bent over her desk, with her ass in the air. But what was he really doing to stop her?

Not a goddamn thing!

His zipper went down.

Fuck. This shit was all Lana's fault. Nairobia's hand went down into his jeans. *Fuck.* He needed somebody to blame for what he was considering. Lana should have been on her job at keeping her man happy. Should have given him some pussy, some head…*something*, instead of leaving him with blue balls. Lamar sighed. Maybe— for a greedy, unguarded moment, he could break Nairobia off some dick just this one time. That's it. Dick her good so she could fall back from her BS, and let him do his fucking job without all the extras. No harm, no foul. Right?

He was a grown-ass man with a hard-ass dick.

She was a grown-ass woman with a fat-ass, wet pussy.

They were both two consenting adults.

So what he had a girl?

She wasn't fucking him right anyway.

Afterward, he could blame his indiscretion on a moment of weakness, the result of a horny, throbbing dick and a lack of reasoning.

Masculine heat and testosterone pulsed around them. He gave her a look, so raw, so primal that it made Nairobia's simmering juices pool in the center of her cunt.

THIRTY-ONE

He'd been hanging onto that thin thread, trying desperately to maintain his composure, but she'd kept fucking with him until he'd snapped. Suddenly Lamar was against Nairobia, panting in her face. "Is this what you want, huh?" He growled low in her ear, grinding himself into her. "This hard dick?"

He tried to use restraint. But it was too late. He was beside himself. Drunk in lust. He was staggering in need. He knew his delusions of staying away from her and not fucking her had been wishful thinking. She'd pushed him to the edge. And now he was determined to bring them both over the sexual cliff.

Before he could think straight—talk himself out of it, he had her pinned up against the wall. Her arms up over her head, he held both wrists in place with one hand, restraining her, trying to tamp down his fury and desire. "I warned you to stop ya bullshit, yo. But you wanna keep fuckin' wit' me. You like teasin' muhfuckas, huh?"

"Fuck me," Nairobia goaded. "Fuck me senseless, if you dare."

She saw heat and anger flash in his eyes, and her pussy clenched. Fearlessly, she moaned. She wasn't afraid he'd hurt her. She *wanted* him to hurt her. Wanted him to rob her of her juices and steal her soul. She knew he was open and voracious for her. She knew it wouldn't be long before she'd break his resolve.

And she had.

Now she had him right where she wanted him. His body pressed against hers, between her thighs, smoldering need enflaming them.

And she was looking forward to the delicious repercussions.

"I'm warnin' you, yo. You playing wit' fire."

She dared him with her eyes, blazing in raw passion. "*Mmm.* Burn me, my darling. My *kut* is already in flames. Slide your cock in my heat. Burn me with your hard thrusts. Take my pussy. And let's go up in flames together."

She licked at his face.

Lamar tightened his grip on her wrists. She thought this a game. Thought he was some fucking toy. And that knowing only incensed him more. With his free hand, he ripped her dress open, baring her breasts.

Nairobia's heart stopped at the sound of tearing fabric. She wasn't going to resist. She welcomed it. And had he been lucid enough to realize that fact, he would have surely seen she wasn't fighting him. That she'd manipulated this—this sordid encounter.

Lamar grabbed the slit of her dress and yanked. The thin, silky fabric tore open, exposing her bare pussy.

Her left breast exposed, Nairobia moaned as her nipple peaked. "I told you to fall the fuck—"

Lamar never finished the thought. Hands pinned tightly against the wall, Nairobia leaned in and crashed her mouth against his and prowled inside, kissing him with a ferocity that snatched his breath. He didn't kiss random broads. Ever. But here he was, caught up in her wicked kiss, his tongue searching greedily for hers. She bit down on his lip. Dug her nails into his flesh. And that sent him reeling, barreling over in aching lust.

She was a whore, for fuck's sake! Of course she wanted it rough. That's what whores liked. Rough, dirty fucking. He'd been chained to vanilla sex for far too damn long. Now he wanted something different. Nairobia had pulled a beast out of him from somewhere he hadn't known existed.

Somewhere dark.

Letting go of her wrists, Lamar broke their heated kiss and stepped back from her, savagely ripping off her dress, the garment finally fluttering to the floor around her feet. He took in her naked body, and something flared in his eyes. Obsession.

He wanted her. His dick ached for her.

"I'ma fuck the shit outta you," he growled, impatience and need thrumming through his veins.

Nairobia taunted him with a sexy grin. "Promise, my love?"

His nose flared. "I'm not fuckin' playin' wit' you." He yanked his shirt off over his head and threw it across the room.

Nairobia's lips curled into a devilish grin. "Then give me what I want. *Neuk me, klootzak! Mijn honger kut voeden met je harde lul.*"

Lamar's jaw tightened. "What did you just say to me, yo?" His dark tone made Nairobia shiver. The way his eyes darkened made her body burn.

"I said *fuck* me, *motherfucker!* Feed my hungry pussy with your hard dick."

Her words shocked him. But why should they? He'd heard her curse in her films. Knew she liked dirty talk. He'd watched enough of her movies to know. As classy as she was, she still liked it filthy. Still, he hadn't expected it, completely. Yet, it turned him on.

Surprising her and himself, Lamar picked her up, shoved her back against the wall and took her mouth fiercely, giving her a hot, dirty kiss; the kiss blanking his mind as her tongue melded into his. He knew he'd regret this in the morning. But, this very moment, he didn't give a fuck. He had to have her.

Breaking from their long, hot, tongue-lingering kiss, Lamar bent to her breasts and sucked them into his mouth, one after the other, hard. Nairobia groaned in pleasure, arching toward him, digging her fingers in his locks, and raking her nails in his scalp.

Lamar groaned as he sucked her nipples. Then slowly bit into each one. Nairobia cried out, her hips slowly winding, grinding her wet pussy into him. She was so caught up in the heat and the moment that she didn't know when he had the time to unfasten his jeans and pull down his boxers before she felt his dick. It was thick. And heavy. And deliciously curved.

Her pussy clenched for it.

"Yes, yes, yes...you sexy, motherfucker...mmm...*u grote lul* thug..."

She called him a big-dick thug, but all he understood was the word *thug*. "Yeah, baby, I'ma thug, muhfucka. You want this thug dick, huh," he gasped as he tore his mouth away, breathing roughly. Heat bubbled in his veins. "You want me to bust ya guts up...?"

She didn't speak. She trapped him with a wrenching glare instead, sending Lamar's blood boiling. In one swift motion, he reached under her right leg and pulled it up over his arm. He slammed his dick in. Rough, uncaring. One motion and he was balls deep inside her. And Nairobia gasped. He pushed her leg further back, her toes touching the wall. She was unbelievably flexible. And wet. So fucking wet.

Lamar groaned, his hips pressing against hers, causing a delicious heat against her clit. He felt his dick at the mouth of her cervix, and nearly lost it. Her pussy was maddening. Lifting her other leg up, he pinned her firmly against the wall. And stroked himself into her clutching heat. He felt himself on the verge of explosion.

Already.

He pulled out. And then it hit him. He wasn't wearing a condom. Fuck.

It was too late to turn back now. He was already teetering, dangerously unraveling. Already being reckless. He'd already felt her raw insides. And he wanted more of it. Gripping her hips, Lamar probed her slick, creamy cunt with his cock, the head pooling with pre-cum, tickling the center of her slit. He pushed his way back in. She was tight, so goddamn amazingly tight, tighter than he imagined. How could that be?

Her cunt had tons of dick miles on it and, yet, here she was tighter than his girl. He hadn't even been back inside her more than a minute and already the base of his spine tingled. Her snug walls created a sinful friction that made him dizzy.

He had to blink back the stars floating around him. He shut his eyes tight. Then opened them.

Nairobia grabbed his dick, her walls milking his shaft. "Fuck me," she whispered, her gaze locked on his. "Give me your thick, black dick, my love...oooh...yes...yes...give my *kut* your cock and cream..." Her body opened to him, welcoming him. He entered her deep. Pleasure burned his gut, clutched his balls, and made him weak-kneed.

Stroking, stroking, stroking, he was becoming lost in pleasure, lost in her. "Aaah...oh shit...yeah, baby...uhhh...you so mutha-fuckin' wet..."

"*Ja, ja, ja*...take my *kut*, fucker...dig your cock deep in me..."

He slammed in her. "Oh, you wanna talk shit, huh, *bitch?*"

Whap!

Her hand came hard across his face. Being called a *bitch* excited her. Slapping him was to anger him so he'd call her out of her name again.

Lamar's face stung. His pupils flared. He pulled out, and slammed harder inside her, his curved cock boomeranging around her walls, hitting every nook, every crack, of her core. Each thrust slammed her back into the wall.

He grated, "Is this"—thrust—"what"—harder thrust—"you want?"—*unrestrained* thrust"—"Me bangin'"—deeper thrust—"your muthafuckin'"—*savage* thrust—"guts out?"

Nairobia couldn't stop moaning if she wanted to. He felt too good inside her, his curve, his thickness…so delicious. Her cunt grasped and pulsed around him, milking him, as his cock swept around her walls. Curved cock was divine. *He* was divine.

"This what the fuck you wanted, right? Huh, bitch? A hard fuck?" he bit out, pummeling deep inside her, fucking her mercilessly.

She dug her nails into his shoulders, and he hissed. "Motherfuck. I didn't wanna give you this dick"—two hard thrusts—"but… uhh…you wanna"—three hard thrusts—"keep fuckin' wit' me… aaah…shiiit…"

Nairobia's breath, hot on his neck, burned his flesh. His throat. She couldn't keep her eyes off the thick tendons and the way his Adam's apple moved. She sunk her teeth into the column of his neck. Bit his lips. And called him every dirty name imaginable.

Lamar's pulse spiked. Everything about her was paralyzing. She had him practically shivering. "You have me so fuckin' hot for you," he rasped. "Got me cheatin' on my fuckin' girl. Fuckin' scandalous *bitch.*"

Whap!

She slapped him again, her pussy wildly clutching around friction and heat.

Lamar growled. "Fuckin' whore…slut…uhh…good muthafuckin' pussy…shiiit…" He slammed in and out, in and out, harder, faster.

"Choke me, *vreemdgaan* motherfucker," Nairobia hissed, calling him a cheating motherfucker. "*Ja, ja, ja…*"

Lamar's hand went to her neck, and he pressed until her eyes widened. Until she clawed at the wall, until the mouth of her cervix snapped at the head of his cock, until she soaked him and a delicious pleasure swirled up and around his balls. An avalanche of raging desire swelled in his cock. He thrust in and out of her body, his strokes relentless.

Lamar moaned as his climax neared. Nairobia reached for his pebbled nipples and pinched them as she orgasmed around his cock. His muscles bulged. Electricity soared through him. He threw his head back and let out a ferocious growl that vibrated through her body. His legs shook. A moment later, his seed gushed hotly inside her, and his world nearly went blank.

THIRTY-TWO

Sure he'd climaxed quick. But the way his curved cock swept around in her cunt, Nairobia wouldn't hold his speedy release against him. Lamar's cock had so much potential that she wasn't the least bit agitated that he'd not been able to last long. Though she'd hoped he could handle her slick heat, she really hadn't expected him to. In fact, most men couldn't. Not the first time anyway.

So there was no surprise there.

She chuckled to herself as she eyed him wiping his sticky cock with a warm, soapy cloth that she'd handed him, then drying his cock and balls off with a plush towel before stuffing himself back into his underwear.

Nothing was said between them.

He'd fucked her hard, every controlled thrust bursting with power, his cock claiming her wetness, his balls slapping at the back of her. Yes. The cock was good, so she already decided she would allow him an opportunity at redemption. Until then, she would let him stew in his failure. Let him wallow in his disappointment.

Lamar finished dressing, unable to look at her.

His dick wasn't little by any means, but he felt small. His pride shriveled.

He was disgusted with himself for being weak, for fucking her. But more overpowering than that was his embarrassment. He wasn't a minuteman, but in a matter of a hundred-and-fifty-strokes or so, she'd managed to reduce him to one.

What the fuck?

All that fine ass and he couldn't deliver the pounding he'd threatened her with. He'd had her up against the wall, pinned up like a real live pinup poster, fucking into her tight, wet heat when something snapped inside of him. She'd slapped him and pinched his nipples and that made him lose it. He exploded. The nut was good. Damn good. But that wasn't the point. Yeah, he wanted to nut. Needed it. But, he still wanted to make sure she knew he'd been up in her. He wanted to pound her insides out. Make her feel his hard dick still throbbing in her long after he was done and gone.

And he'd failed—miserably.

Fuck.

He'd never had pussy that damn good in his life. The way her walls grabbed his dick, all that wetness, all them juicy slurping sounds it made…like his dick was being sucked while he was fucking her. Pussy that good was dangerous.

But he wanted another round. Just one more time to show her what he was really made of. Not some fast-nutting whimp. He was a man. A *muhfucka* who made broads' jaws lock and had them running from his deadly curve. But Nairobia was a professional dick taker. She hadn't run from shit. She'd molded to it.

And made him nut quick.

Yeah, he was sulking. He knew his dick game was on point. He knew how to dick a broad down right. So what the fuck happened?

Lana's non-fucking ass happened. He'd been too backed up and too goddamn overheated. Yeah. That's what had happened. He suffered from sexual neglect. And the end result was a fast nut. Period.

Still, there was no fucking way he'd ever mention this shit to any of his boys. He'd be the brunt of every joke under the sun for at least a week or more.

Shit.

Lamar reached down and scooped up his crumpled black T-shirt. He didn't remember ever taking it off, but there it was strewn on the floor. He pulled it on over his head, hoping like hell the wrinkles would stretch out over his muscled chest.

Nairobia watched him intently. She knew his ego was bruised. But she wasn't about to soothe him with words of encouragement. He should have pulled out, changed positions, given his nut time to roll back in his balls, something. Not keep pounding into her *kut*, like he was Batman. But she knew he couldn't help himself. He'd been too greedy for her. Now look at him.

Head hung low.

Ego deflated.

Lamar picked his shades up from the carpeted floor and slid them back onto his face. Nairobia glanced at the time. It was a quarter to nine. The club would open soon. She felt herself becoming aroused all over again at the thought of another night of free-spirited debauchery.

"See you downstairs, no?" Nairobia inquired, staring at his back as he made his way toward the door; the words: The Pleasure Zone stretched in gold lettering between his shoulder blades.

"Yeah," he said over his shoulder.

Nairobia smiled, and the sight of her plump lips still swollen from their heated kisses made him groan inwardly.

He'd really fucked up.

"*Vergeven jezelf,* my darling," she called out to him.

Lamar paused in the doorway, turned around and stared at her. He scowled. "Excuse me?"

"I said, *forgive* yourself."

His throat tightened. He swallowed the knot.

"For what?" he asked, his hand on the doorknob, already knowing the answer.

Nairobia gave him a look, one filled with compassion, then said, "For losing yourself to me."

Lamar said nothing, simply walked out, closing the door behind him.

Poor thing.

THIRTY-THREE

Fuck.

Fuck.

Fuck.

Lamar locked the bathroom door, then made sure all the stalls were empty, before going to the sink and turning the water on. He rubbed his temples and sighed as he stood in the mirror and stared at himself. He'd fucked up. Royally. *Motherfuck.* He should have never let his emotions *and* his underserved libido get the best of him. But he had. And now he felt like shit.

Not even a full fifteen minutes of fucking. That's all he had been able to deliver. What was it about that broad that had him coming fast and hard?

Lamar was pissed that his dick had failed him. Right when he needed it to be at peak performance, his motherfucking cock flopped. *Now this bitch thinks I'm some lame-ass muhfucka.* He gritted his teeth. *Muhfucka, you shoulda kept ya dick in ya pants. That's what ya dumb ass get!*

Yeah, he loved pussy. But he wasn't weak for it. At least, he hadn't been. He hoped not to ever be. But what was it about this fucking broad that had him off his game?

That fucking ass of hers, those hypnotizing eyes, them sexy-ass lips, her soft, curvy hips…and oh, fuck. The way she talked all dirty 'n' shit in whatever language she'd spoken in his ear.

It had his head spinning.

He wanted to blame his current predicament on Lana's ass for being all stingy with the pussy. But the shit was all on him. He knew it. And it made him feel like such an ass. He'd screwed up. Not her.

Now he'd have to crawl up in bed with her and look her in the face and hope like hell she never asked him if he'd cheated on her. Getting head was one thing. But straight up fucking another broad was a whole other thing. He'd be forced to give her the truth. Raw.

The way he'd given it to Nairobia.

He groaned.

Fuck.

Muhfucka, you all kinds of crazy! Goin' in raw. What the fuck is wrong wit' you, yo? He swallowed back the memory of how deep he'd felt inside her. So damn deep. The way he'd driven into her hard and fast. And how wet and hot she'd felt around him.

He shook his head, and cursed under his breath.

The bitch obviously knew she affected him.

He dragged a hand over his face.

He needed something to relax him. Badly.

And then it hit him.

He hadn't smoked in over a month. *That* coupled with not getting pussy on the regular was what had him on edge. Had him vulnerable…and all fucked up.

He needed a blunt.

He let out a breath and closed his eyes tight. Everything about what went down up in Nairobia's office was all types of wrong. But the pussy felt so good. The way she'd opened up to him. Took in his massive curve. Grew wetter around him. The way her touch had his body on fire. No broad had ever made his blood boil the way she had. The way she always did, from the minute he'd laid eyes on her.

All that shit felt so fucking right at that moment, no matter how dead wrong he was for having her pressed up against the wall like that. No matter how much he enjoyed being inside her. The shit was wrong. Dead wrong.

But, oh so fucking good!

He opened his eyes again, and when he looked back into the mirror, he hated what he saw even more. Fucking clients wasn't his M.O. Not usually.

But he'd done it twice already. With two separate clients.

And with either of them, he did nothing to stop it. They'd asked for it. And he wanted to give it to them.

But this time was different. He had a girl.

Shit.

Not for long, though, if she didn't start fucking him right. In the streets, Lamar could be ruthless. Gully. And dangerous. But there was another side of him when it came to women, especially the ones he took an interest in. He'd give them the shirt off his back if they needed it. And he'd gladly give them his hard dick, on call, if they wanted that too. Anything they needed, anything they wanted, he'd make it happen. No questions asked.

He leaned in and splashed cold water on his face. He had to get his head in the game. He had a job to do tonight. There was no time to let this shit fuck up his paper. Period. He reached for one of the white complimentary face cloths and dried his face, then shut the water off. He stared at his reflection again. He thought back on the first time he'd linked up with Pasha. She'd sucked his dick like no other female had in his life. She'd spun his top so good that he'd come in her mouth in less than eight minutes, then had staggered backward, collapsing on her bed.

He clenched his jaw. Nairobia and Pasha both had a way with making him nut fast. The shit wasn't a good look.

I ain't no fuckin' minuteman!

Lamar's cell buzzed in his front pocket. Pulling it out, he sighed. Speaking of the devil in designer heels. His voice was hoarse when he answered, "Yo?"

"Well, hello, stranger," she said sweetly. "I haven't heard from you in a while. Thought I'd give you a call to let you know you were being thought of."

His expression hardened. "Yo, Pasha. Why the fuck you put me on to this broad, yo?"

She blinked, taken aback by his harsh tone. Then her eyes widened. "Ohmygod, no." She gasped. "Tell me you didn't…"

He hesitated.

"Yo, my dick got hard," he said, sighing. "What the fuck else was I supposed to do when all she does it flaunt all that ass up in my face?"

"You take a cold shower. You go home to your woman," she ticked off. "You lock yourself in a bathroom stall and jerk off."

"Yeah, fuck a cold shower. And fuck a bathroom stall, yo. And Lana's dumb-ass not fuckin' this week. So what the fuck was I s'posed to do? I needed my dick in somethin' wet."

Pasha laughed, not surprised that Nairobia had finally had her way with him. She just didn't expect it to happen so quickly. She thought Lamar would be able to resist temptation. Then again… he hadn't been able to resist her, either, when she'd summoned him to her, the first time. "Ohmygod, you're a mess," she said.

He groaned. "Don't remind me, yo. How you 'n' the boys?"

"Oh, no, little daddy," she said playfully. "I'm fine. And my sons are fine. But you do not get to change the subject."

He groaned. "Nah, fuck that. I'd rather we did."

"Not until you tell me. How was it?"

"Yo, word is bond, Pasha. That bitch is deadly."

And the fucked-up thing was…

He wanted her again.

THIRTY-FOUR

Candles flickered about Nairobia's living room.

Staring into the flames, she held up the only picture she had of her father. Oba Chukwu. She didn't know why she'd held on to it. But she had. Taking it everywhere she'd ever been, hidden in a jeweled lockbox in her traveling trunk.

He was the first man Nairobia had had wrapped around her fingers, the man who'd showered her with adoration and kisses and fabulous gifts. Up until the moment he'd turned his back on her, she'd been the center of his universe. Then—*snap*—he'd disowned her. Just like that. Because she hadn't conformed to his expectations of what—and *whom*—he believed she *should* be.

His dreams for her hadn't been hers. And she'd refused to allow him to decide her life for her. That had been a defining moment for Nairobia. As a result, she'd carved out her own path in life. Not once, ever, looking back.

She wished more women were like that. Determined. Unyielding. Not allowing a man to define them. Or confine them.

But most weren't.

She'd forgiven her father a long time ago for breaking her heart. Yet, they still hadn't rebuilt a relationship. And, deep down, she was okay with that.

Him not being in *her* life had been *his* loss, not hers.

And now he was dead.

He'd died over six years ago in a plane crash flying out of the Democratic Republic of the Congo. He'd been there on business. The accident had been ruled foul play. But the authorities had not been able to identify who had been behind the deadly crash.

Though they'd been estranged, the news had still had come as a shock to her. Nairobia had been on stage accepting another Adult Film award when her mother had tried to reach her. It wasn't until several hours after the plane crash that she'd finally learned of his tragic death.

She'd listened to her mother's wracking sobs and had tried to console her best she could. But walls had been painfully built, and she'd felt nothing. And there'd been no tears shed.

The only thing she'd felt was relief. She could finally let go of the idea that one day he'd find it in his heart to love her again. His death made it final. He wasn't ever coming back, wasn't ever going to welcome her back into his heart again.

So with that knowing came no tears. Perhaps because she'd already buried him the day he'd told her she no longer was his, that he'd disowned her.

He had been her first experience with men. He'd showered her, almost eighteen years of her life, with love. And she'd spent the remaining eighteen years of her life, avoiding it—at all costs, from anyone else.

So why had she dug out her father's photo of him holding her in his arms. It'd been a proud moment for him, her birth, so she'd been told. Yet, he'd blamed her for breaking his heart, for ripping out his soul and tossing it to the dogs.

She'd never believed that. Not one moment. Thank God. But she could see how some other young, impressionable girl would. He'd tried emotionally blackmailing her. But it hadn't worked. She'd been too headstrong. Too determined to live her own life. And make her own way.

She had.

And she made no apologies for doing so.

Still, there'd been times when she'd wondered how a father could turn his back on his child, his daughter. Unless he'd never really loved her in the first place. But, then, somewhere along the way, she'd stopped wondering. Stopped caring.

What that experience had taught her was that men were manipulating. And only loved with conditions. She stared at the photo of her father once more, hoping she'd feel something, anything, before burning it.

But she didn't.

The penthouse phone rang as she neared the edge of the photo over the candle's flickering flame. She pulled it back, and let it flutter to the table, next to the burning candle. She went to retrieve the ringing phone.

"Hello."

"Good evening, Miss Jansen. This is Stewart."

She smiled. "Hello, Stewart. Is everything all right?"

"Yes, yes. There's a…" He paused. Nairobia heard him ask, "Sir, what did you say your name was?"

"I didn't," she heard a gruff voice in the background say. "Just tell her I'm here. And want to see her, *now*."

Nairobia scowled. She didn't like the sound of the man's tone. How dare he be rude and demanding?

Stewart returned to the phone. "Ma'am, there's a gentleman down in the lobby, refusing to give his name. He said you'd be expecting him."

Nairobia frowned. She wasn't expecting anyone, especially tonight. "There must be some mistake," she said. "Are you sure it's *me* he's asking for?"

"Yes, ma'am."

Baffled, she flipped through her mental Rolodex searching for a hint of who this nameless scoundrel might be. "Has he been here before?" she asked, wondering who in the world would dare come to her home, refusing to give his name to her dear Stewart.

"No, ma'am. Not that I can recall."

"Well, what does he look like?"

"Well, ma'am. Tall. Well-dressed. Dark as night—no offense, Sir."

Nairobia scowled. "Thank you, Stewart. But you can send Mister Dark As Night on his way. He isn't welcomed here."

She hung up.

Seconds later, the phone rang again.

"Yes, Stewart?"

"I told you I'd find you, sexy," a deep voice said into the phone. "Didn't I tell you to be ready for me?"

Nairobia blinked. No. It couldn't be. "Coal?"

"The one an' only, baby."

Her breath caught. "How'd you find me?"

He grinned. "I have my ways. I told you I have eyes everywhere."

She found nothing flattering about a stranger showing up to her building, practically admitting to watching her. She didn't like the predatory edge to his voice. "Are you *stalking* me?"

He laughed. "Nah, baby. I don't stalk. I seek out. Come have dinner with me."

Nairobia glanced at the time. It was nearing nine p.m. Oh, he was good and crazy to think she'd flounce herself out from the comforts of her home to dine with some stranger—even if said stranger was tall, dark, and dangerously handsome; even if she'd practically creamed on said stranger's cock in the middle of a dance floor.

"I will do no such thing, my darling. You want to see me, you'll have to return at a respectable hour and try again."

His rich laugh boomed through the phone. "Oh, okay, okay. I

see you, baby. And I tell you what. I'll be back tomorrow. Noon. How's that for respectable?"

"That's a start," she replied. "But still not acceptable. Perhaps I am not free for you at noon. Or any other time."

"Then make time. We have some unfinished business. Don't think I forgot how good you felt in my arms."

She smiled. "Nor should you have."

"Tomorrow. Noon," he repeated. "Be ready for me."

"Sorry, my love. I'll be at the *shooting*"—she made sure to enunciate that part—"range."

"That's even better. I gotta big gun that needs to be fired off."

"Good night."

The line went dead.

THIRTY-FIVE

Squaring her shoulders, her hair swept into a sleek, side-parted ponytail, Nairobia sauntered out the sliding glass doors, wearing a black Emilio Pucci ruffled, one-shouldered sheath dress and a pair of black ankle-strap heels. She stepped out in the July heat, baring her long, sexy legs and smooth back. The look was chic. Classy.

She spotted him. Leaning up against the driver's side door of a black Range Rover—watching her, in a white Gucci T-shirt and a pair of white jeans. The stark contrast against his dark skin was sexy. There was something about a deep, dark-chocolate man donned in all white that made her toes curl.

He smiled, his eyes appraising her as she strutted toward him, her oversized clutch tucked beneath her arm. "Damn, baby," he murmured, stepping forward and pulling her into a hug. She turned her head, his lips suddenly catching the side of her mouth. "Damn, you smell good." He took a step back, his dark brown gaze running up and down her body. "Damn, you sexy. But, uh, a little over-dressed for the range, aren't you?"

She tilted her head, lifting her black Dior shades. "No, I'm actually *under*dressed, my love." And she'd meant that in every way. Sans a bra, she'd worn lace crotchless panties. Her gray eyes glinted. "Now, shall we go? I feel like shooting."

He grinned. "No doubt, baby. You're talking my talk." He started toward the other side of the SUV, but stopped when Nairobia didn't budge.

Hand on her hip, she pointed toward the rear passenger door. "I'll sit in the back. Please and thank you, my love." She had no intentions of sitting up front with a man she'd only met once, under a bunch of flashing lights, in the near darkness of a club.

No, no. She'd sit in back of him in case she needed to open her clutch and…well, it paid to be armed and ready. One could never be too safe nowadays.

He frowned. "You buggin', right? You expect me to ride you 'round like I'm some chauffeur?"

She tilted her head. "You wish to be in my company, no?"

He narrowed his eyes. When he didn't respond right away, she waved toward a sleek black Benz, the sun beaming down on its sunroof, and out stepped her driver, Samson. "As you can see, my darling. I do not *need* you to chauffeur *me*, anywhere. I'll chauffeur *you*."

And with that, she walked off.

He blinked. Then shook his head, and grinned. He was definitely digging her style. She was topnotch. Definitely the type of woman he wanted on his arm.

Word is bond, I'ma bag that…

She stopped and glanced over her shoulder. "Well? Are you riding? Or shall I meet you there?"

He pressed the key fob and armed the alarm to his truck, then followed behind her, his eyes taking in the voluptuous and mouth-watering curves of her body.

Goddamn.

Samson tipped his hat. "Afternoon, Miss Jansen." She smiled, then kissed him on the cheek. "Good afternoon, my love. Samson, this here is…"

"Coal," he answered for her. "What's good?"

Samson gave him a courtesy head nod, but gritted his teeth as he eyed him slide his big body inside the cabin of the car.

Nairobia smiled. "Be nice," she whispered, before sliding in after him. Samson shut the door behind her, then opened the driver's side door and slid behind the wheel.

"Where to, Miss Jansen?"

"The shooting range, please."

He nodded, then pulled away from the curb, adjusting his rear-view mirror and eyeing the intruder in the backseat with his fantasy girl.

"So damn, baby. What's good with you? I bet you thought I forgot about you, huh?"

Nairobia shifted, angling her body so she could take him in. "I'd actually forgotten all about you," she said honestly. She wasn't one to pine over a man for longer than a night, maybe two. After that, it was out of sight, out of mind for her.

He laughed. "Damn. Straight like that, huh? Cool, cool. I dig that. Well, I didn't forget you, word is bond."

Nairobia stared at the four-carat diamond in his ear, then glanced over the diamond-encrusted necklace around his neck, then skittered her gaze over the Rolex on his wrist. "What do you do for a living?" she asked.

He caught her gaze. "As I told you in Vegas, me an' my uncle own several businesses. We have several detail shops and about eight Laundromats."

She raised a brow. "Legitimate, no?"

"Oh no doubt."

Samson's gaze rose to the rearview mirror. *Yeah right, motherfucker.*

Coal met Samson's gaze, and scowled. *What the fuck, muhfucka? Hatin'-ass pussy.*

"Hm." Nairobia said. "And how many lovers do you take to your bed a night?"

He laughed. "Damn, baby. You don't eff around, I see. You get right to it, huh?"

"Life is too short not to, my darling."

"I feel you. I do my thing," he said, stretching his arm along the back of the seat.

Nairobia gave him a look, then eyed his arm. "And what exactly is this *thing* you do?"

He grinned, then leaned into her ear, and said, "I'd rather show you than tell you."

"I'll keep that in mind. Are you a cunt licker, my darling?"

He frowned. "Nah, nah. Not my thing. I'll beat that thing up, but I ain't licking on it."

Nairobia raised her brow. "But you like your"—she ran her hand over his crotch—"your cock licked, no?"

He spread his legs, and grinned. "No doubt, baby."

Hm. Selfish lover, no?

He glanced up and caught Samson eyeing him again. His jaw clenched. "Yo, fam. We good up there? You keep eyeballin' me an' I ain't diggin' it. So wasssup? We got beef I don't know about?"

"Nah," Samson said stiffly. "No beef."

"What, you tryna suck on this dick or sumthin'? Say yeah, so I can break your jaw, bruh."

Nairobia's breath hitched.

Samson frowned. "Not my thing, Sir."

"Aiight, then. So how 'bout you keep ya eyes on the road an' let me handle what's going on back here."

"Now, now. Play nice, my love." She reached over and touched Coal's knee. "Samson is protective, that's all. As he should be."

Coal's nose flared. "Well, he ain't gotta worry. You in good hands when you wit' me, baby. Believe that. So how 'bout"—he reached over and pressed the privacy window's button—"a little more privacy." He eyed Samson as the window rolled up, cutting off his view.

Samson smirked, pressing a hidden button for the cabin's monitoring system. He might not have been able to see what was going on, but he'd damn sure hear everything being said.

Once they arrived at the Rifle & Pistol Range, Samson opened the door and held his hand out for Nairobia, helping her out. "Thank you, my love."

He gritted his teeth as Coal slid out of the car. He flicked a dollar bill at him. "Bitch-ass," he mumbled low enough for him to hear.

Samson slammed the door, his jaw twitching.

Coal trotted up the stairs behind Nairobia, his eyes locked on her ass.

"Okay, baby, let's see what you got," Coal said smugly.

Safety goggles on, Nairobia tossed her hair over her shoulder. "No, my love, you first." She stepped back to a safe distance.

Coal smirked. "Aiight, then," he said, putting on his earmuffs. He aimed his Glock and fired six bullets into the Silhouette target. Three in the head, two in the heart, and one in each kneecap.

Coal stepped back, pulled off the earmuffs, then turned and faced Nairobia. "Don't worry, baby. I'm warming up. Now let's see what you got."

Nairobia smiled, slipping her earmuffs over her ears. She stepped into the booth, and tossed her hair.

Coal licked his lips. Hands down, she looked smoking hot in her form-fitting dress and those sexy-ass heels with a gun in her hand.

He felt his dick harden.

Feeling his gaze on her ass, Nairobia raised her weapon and

shot six bullets into a fresh target. All six in the center of its groin, causing Coal to wince and think twice if he'd planned on trying any funny business. She stepped back, then faced him, removing her earmuffs. "No worry, my love. I'm still warming up," she mocked, smirking.

He laughed. "Oh, so it's like that, huh? Oh, aiight, aiight. I got you, baby. Let's go. It's on now." He stepped back in place, raised his gun and fired off, this time emptying his magazine into his target, each bullet—one after the other, bull's-eye.

Nairobia walked up and kissed him on the cheek. "Impressive, my darling."

Satisfied, he smirked. "Now let's see your work, baby."

Earmuffs back on, she raised her 9mm and shot another six rounds into another fresh target—all six bullets in the head, between the eyes. She pulled her earmuffs off, then removed her glasses.

Coal whistled. "Damn, you good, baby. Where'd you learn to shoot like that?"

She smiled. "A lady never kisses and tells, my darling."

His eyes went liquid as he stared at the beautiful set of lips of hers. He licked his own, stepping forward and pulling her into his hard body. "You ain't gotta tell me nothing, baby, but this: Do *you* kiss?"

She looked up at him. She didn't say no, so he lowered his head and leaned in for a kiss. She moved her head, and he ended up kissing the corner of her mouth instead. Damn, twice already he'd tried to get those lips and she'd denied him.

He groaned in disappointment. He could almost taste her. Fuck, he wanted to taste her sweet lips. Wanted to know what that hot, wet tongue felt like against his. Wanted to feel—

"You have not earned my kisses."

Nairobia and Coal returned two hours later, with the two of them standing outside her building, with cars and people streaming by. "Yo, I dug chillin' with you. Wasn't exactly what I'd had in mind, but it was kinda fly."

"I enjoyed myself as well," she said, meaning it. She didn't bother asking what *he'd* actually expected. She was only interested in what she was willing to give.

Her gaze trailed over his body—hotly. She was tempted to invite him in for an afternoon romp, but thought better of it. Instead, she pulled him into her and whispered against his cheek, "You take care, my darling." She kissed him there and hugged him, feeling his body heat matching her own.

He grabbed her by the waist to keep her from stepping back.

"It's still early, baby. I'd hoped to have you to myself the whole day. No driver. Just you and me."

She shook her head. "Not today, my love." She stepped out of his embrace, and he shoved his hands down in his pants, trying to conceal the thick bulge in his pants.

He sighed. "Damn, so you really gonna send me on my way?"

"Yes."

He shook his head, pressing the key fob to disarm his truck. "You sure?" He grinned, opening his door. "Going once, going twice… going once again…going twice again…"

Oh how tempted she was. Her body burned to know what his naked body felt like over hers. But her curiosity wasn't strong enough to change the fact that she knew he'd come to her expecting for her to slide down on his cock, expecting to be pleasured by her, expecting her to be the good little whore. No, no. Nairobia whored on her own terms. She gave her sex to no one who expected it. Besides, he didn't lick *kut*. Oh no. He could do nothing for her. She dare not ever give her good pussy to a selfish lover.

She waved him on. Then watched as he slid behind the wheel, started his engine, then shut the door. She walked off toward her building.

He rolled his window down. "Damn, baby. So when I'ma see you again?"

She glanced over her shoulder, and thought to say, "When you learn to pleasure a woman." Instead, she settled on what he'd told her, "I'll find you."

The translation simple:

Don't call me. I'll call you.

THIRTY-SIX

F ierce and on fire, Nairobia stepped out of the elevator donned in a red corset and lace thong wearing a pair of six-inch pumps, holding a bullwhip in her right hand. She wasn't sure what she planned on doing with the lash, but she knew she'd find a reason to make good use of it sometime before the night ended.

She sauntered through The Pleasure Zone's first four levels, before making her way down and around the circular stairs. She looked up at the three cages hanging from the ceiling, and swallowed in the delicious sight of two women sixty-nining in the middle cage. The top one was a beautifully tanned blonde and the bottom one had rich ebony skin and a long tongue. The blonde's ass was pulled open wide while her ebony lover slid her tongue in and out of her pink pussy, sweeping and seeking out her orgasm.

It was a splendid sight.

The cages on either side of the two orally obsessed women were lowered, the gates opened. Two naked, busty brunettes stepped inside the cage on the left with a six-foot-two, blond-haired Channing Tatum lookalike. Both women immediately dropped down to their knees and began laving his meaty cock and sucking his balls. Hands on hips, he threw his head back, his eyelids sweeping closed from the pleasure.

A bare-chested man wearing a pair of black leather chaps, his dick and ass out on display, stepped into the cage on the right, followed by two androgynous females with smooth skin and high cheekbones—their breasts swollen, their nipples tightened peaks, their glowing purple cocks jutting out from leather harnesses.

Nairobia's cunt clenched.

She eyed the two cock-wielding vixens, the promise of dirty, raw fucking flickering in their eyes as they followed their male lover inside the cage, eyeing his muscled ass.

Switchblade Symphony's "Clown" played as the gates slid shut, then each cage slowly ascended, hovering midway in the air.

Nairobia pumped her pelvis to the beat, threw her whip up and swung it in the air, then...*whoosh*...brought it down, its lashes striking across the floor.

A wave of applause swept around her as everyone in view of her presence clapped in excitement at the exquisite sight that stood before him or her. Nairobia smiled. Cracked her whip again. Then continued her descent down the stairs.

Candles flickering, moans and gasps floating through the air, The Mission's "Slave to Lust" poured softly from the lower speakers as Nairobia winded down into the Love Tomb. Firelight flickered over the rounded walls as she eased her way down one of the passageways, heels clicking toward a cluster of chambers.

Out of the corner of her eye, Nairobia saw a light-skinned woman on her knees, sucking the cock of a hooded man, standing in front of her. Though the man's face was obscured behind the leather, his eyes looked like liquid amber through the slits of his hood as he ravished her mouth with his cock, fucking into her throat, hard and fast.

Across from them, there was a couple stretched out on a bench in the throes of something hot and sweaty. Nairobia stopped and marveled at the two horny lovers. Bald, excessively tanned and slightly wrinkled, he had to be in his late fifties, but his erection protruded out like that of a man half his age. His balls were small, but his cock was long and thick. His much younger companion, an Italian brunette, moved down his body, removed his cock ring and slipped a condom over his throbbing erection. She crawled back up over him, then positioned herself over his cock. She tilted her hips forward and took him all the way in. With each thrust of her hips, she took him in deep. Deeper. Her hair swayed about her bouncing breasts as she ground her body down on him, scraping her clit against the base of his cock.

Nairobia stood transfixed watching his young lover lift her hips and allow him to thrust upward into her wetness, closing his arms around her waist, his hips beating up against her bouncing ass. He had rhythm. He had thrusts. He had power. Nairobia watched as his cock pummeled and hammered inside her, disappearing and reemerging wetter with each thrust.

By the time Switchblade Symphony's "Chain" started playing, Nairobia's hand flitted to her thong and found it soaked. She licked her lips. It'd been years since she'd fucked an older white man, the last time being in her movie, *Daddy Cock*, where she'd fucked a roomful of old, married businessmen in suits.

She was nineteen.

Petting her wet panties, Nairobia gave the lovers one last glance, then reined in her growing desire to join them. Ordo Rosarius Equilibrio sang about tying a lover to a chair, kissing her neck and pulling her hair as Nairobia passed the pool with its shimmering blue water. An array of colorful, sordid sex played out in and around the pool.

Yes, my darling, Nairobia mused, licking her lips as she swayed her hips toward the passageways. *Show me the secrets of the tortured garden*.

The Love Tomb was more than a playground for kink. It was

where pain and pleasure swirled into one. Each chamber held a St. Andrews Cross, a rack, bondage cuffs, an X-bar, several spreader bars, and more painfully delicious assortments of kink equipment. Vanilla play was not ever allowed down in the Love Tomb.

A guttural moan from one of the chambers drew Nairobia's attention, and she moved toward the direction of the deafening sound. Inside there was a beautiful woman the color of maple syrup wearing nothing but a black thong and knee-high leather boots. In one hand she held a flogger. In the other, a leather paddle.

A mocha-colored Latina was hoisted up in a sex sling, legs spread, knees bent. Her husband was bent over and tied down to a spanking bench. His skin was sweating, his face etched in burning pleasure.

Swoosh!

Maple Syrup delivered a stinging kiss to the sexy Latina's cunt causing her to scream out, her head snapping back. Nairobia found herself staring delightfully at the sight of her juices pooling out of her slit.

Nairobia licked her lips, imagining herself licking into the Latina's sweet, tangy cunt sauce to soothe her, to bathe her searing labia with wet laps of her tongue.

Swoosh!

More screaming. More arching. The Latina was awash in pain, bathing in pain, scorching in pain, breathing in pain. *Swoosh!* Maple Syrup's flogger went down across her sex again, and her hips thrust up to greet the flames. An exquisite burn that singed followed the sting into her swollen sex. Passion boiled up into the pit of her pussy, then burst out the tip of her clit.

Her slit flared open and juices spurted out.

Her husband groaned as he lifted his head and fought against the restraints, and the pain.

Whap!

He yelped.

Maple Syrup swung the paddle across his ass, its heat dancing over his reddened flesh. His cock pulsed, pre-cum leaking from its slit. Nairobia licked her lips at the exquisite welts spreading over his skin. Fluid dripped from the tip of his dick. And Nairobia longed to slink into the chamber and lick the wet streaks of pre-cum on the leather bench.

Mr. Paddle Prints growled, and raised his ass higher, pleading for more. Maple Syrup gave it to him harder, faster.

Whap!

Whap!

Pop!

He gritted his teeth—his ass a bright, blistery red, tears springing from his eyes. The ache in his cock amplified the throbbing across his ass. Maple Syrup whacked him again. Spittle flew out of his mouth as he begged for more.

Whap!

Whap!

Nairobia's cunt clenched with each strike of the paddle as it struck across his ass like lightning. And then Maple Syrup was back in front of his wife, her flogger up over her head, bringing it down over and around.

Swoosh!

The Latina cried out as the lashes bit into her clit, the suede ribbons slapping into her sex as "Glory To Thee, My Beloved Masturbator" played over her moans.

Maple Syrup pushed the Latina's thighs wide and opened her up with her fingers. She leaned in and licked the nectar that flowed out from her slit while her husband looked on in sweet agony. She lapped at her, sucked in her sensitive nub until she panted.

Her husband groaned, lifting himself, pumping his hips in the air until his cock thudded upward. He pressed his hips against the bench and ground his horny cock into the leather until he orgasmed.

Maple Syrup abandoned the Latina's pussy long enough to deliver three more rapid strikes across her husband's ass. The man cried out, his hips pumping a mile a minute. "Aaaaah, aaaaah...uhh-hh...! I'm coming!"

More semen spurted out of his cock, and Nairobia's mouth instantly watered. The sight of his gushing milk made her think back to a movie'd she starred in back in her earlier porn-star days, *Cum Gushers*. She'd been encircled by ten men—five white, three black, and two Latino—who jerked their cocks until they were hosing her down in thick streams of their warm, sticky cock cream in her face, over her breasts, in her mouth.

Groans reaching an ear-splitting crescendo snatched Nairobia from her reverie, and forced her to look over toward another chamber. Drawn to the cacophony of sound, she sauntered over and peered inside.

There on an unforgiving wood floor, a strawberry blonde knelt between the legs of a deliciously dark-tanned Italian, his muscled back and ass covered in raised welts on his otherwise spotless flesh. He'd been flogged with a knotted leather flog that left his back a crisscrossed mess of welts.

His body strained against her hand as she burrowed her fingers deeper, deeper, wriggling them inside him, spreading him wide.

Nairobia's mouth fell open as the woman fucked her long, slender fingers into his ass; her deep strokes were neither too slow, nor two fast. Just right. And deep. Oh so deep. Nairobia waited with bated breath, wondering if she'd curl her hand into his ass and fist him.

He closed his eyes and let her have complete control of every part of him. He was the CEO of a Fortune 500 company. He was a powerful man—a man in control of every aspect of his life personally and professionally. But tonight, he relinquished his control. Allowed his lover to inflict the sweetest torture upon him. He wanted to submit, but never had the opportunity to do so in his daily life. Until tonight.

"The Pleasure of Sin" by Athamay whirred out from the speakers. Nairobia clutched the whip in her hand and gasped as she watched the woman push her fingers into the welts on the man's legs while fucking him in his ass. He groaned, his thick, meaty cock stretching forward, bobbing up and down. His face was flush with desire and desperation as her fingers thrust inside of him.

His strawberry-blonde lover poked and probed and slammed in and out of his long-limbed body with her fingers, wrenching out loud grunts of discomfort that eventually roared into gasps of pleasure as she stroked over his prostate.

More pre-cum. More groans. His lover opened him up wide, and pressure built up inside his stomach and hips. "God, yes," he growled, close to orgasm. His lover had coupled pain with pleasure and he'd become unable to distinguish between the two, knowing only that he yearned for them both. He loved them both.

Finally, on the brink of delirium, the married CEO and father of three begged his lover for release. His balls ached. His cock burned from the strain of fighting back his climax. His breath hitched. He closed his eyes and bit down on his lip.

Nairobia wasn't a fan of fucking her fingers or tongue into a man's ass. But being the sexual being she was, she understood the overpowering sensations brought on by prostate stimulation and anal play.

Still…she'd rather not. But this wasn't about her.

It was about—

Mr. CEO cried out again, his eyes snapping open pleadingly.

He couldn't hold out any longer. His lover's sweet torture was killing him. He needed release. And he needed it now. He begged her for it.

Finally his lover gave him permission. And the instant she twisted her wrists inside of him and used her free hand to dig her fingers into his raw back, his body shivered and shuddered. But it still wasn't enough, so she reached for his balls and squeezed and twisted, the pain

His hips bucked. Oh fuck yeah…he was coming. And coming. And coming.

A smile curved Nairobia's lips. *Now he can go home and fuck his cock into his wife slow and sweetly.* Completely overtaken, sated, satisfied. He'd come for a night of pain and pleasure, both all in one act.

And he'd found it.

At The Pleasure Zone.

THIRTY-SEVEN

"Yo, word is bond, son," Lamar said into the mouthpiece of his headset. "That pussy good as hell, yo." He was on his cell talking to his right-hand man and business partner, Mel. They were both loyal to Pasha. And, though neither of them had ever spoken on it—they knew without it needing to be said that they'd both experienced Pasha's deep throat specials. The difference now was, Mel was still getting blessed with her skills on the low. Not as often as he'd like, but enough to keep him wanting to hang around.

Lamar had been on the phone the last thirty minutes filling him in on what had gone down with him and Nairobia in her office over two weeks ago.

And…sadly, three nights ago he'd fallen victim to the pussy—*again*.

But he'd conveniently left out the part about how she'd had him crying out like a little bitch—a *first* for him—when she'd licked down the trail of hair that led down from his navel to his dick.

He'd hissed out a heated breath.

Then closed his eyes as Nairobia inched her warm tongue back up his body, reaching his brown-pebbled nipples. "Oh, shit," he'd pushed out as she closed her mouth around his nipple and sucked as she lightly pinched the other, causing him to cry out.

That shit had never happened to him. She'd caused a burning, boiling need to roil over his body, as she tasted him with her tongue, slowly exploring the brown ridges of each nipple, and making his toes curl.

And when she'd wetly licked her way down his chest, then swirled around his navel, a fire built in his body. His abs tightened as she dipped her wet, hot tongue inside. She'd made his body shake. And when she'd palmed his cock, he made a growling sound. Nairobia's sensual flicks of her tongue had awakened erogenous zones he hadn't known existed.

"Ahh, yeah…I don't know what the fuck you doin' to me…"

Her lashes swept upward and she'd looked at him, full of heat and desire, setting every nerve ending ablaze. By the time Nairobia's tongue made its way down to his dick and flicked over the bead of pre-cum that seeped out—swiping her tongue along the tip, tasting his arousal, before sucking him into her mouth—a guttural sound had roared out from the back of his throat and he'd begun rocking his hips in a sensual rhythm, his body arching up to the maddening pleasure.

She'd teased him with her mouth and tongue, her hot breath cascading over his twitching cock, then abruptly stopped.

"*Ahh!*" he'd yelled, rolling his hips. "Damn, yo. Why you fuckin' wit' me? C'mon, suck on that dick…"

"No, no, my love. You want my wet mouth feasting you? You want my tongue loving you? Then tongue my insides. And taste my cunt."

She'd caught him off guard with that request, no demand.

She hadn't been kneeling in front of him as he'd had liked to see her, but having her between his legs while he lay on his back with one leg draped over the back of her sofa was sexy enough.

And as bad as he wanted to bust in her pretty-ass mouth, he wasn't about to reciprocate and put in any tongue work, especially knowing how she loved to fuck. But he'd be remiss if he hadn't acknowledged the fact that Nairobia had a beautiful-looking pussy. And he had wondered if it tasted as good as it looked. He knew what it felt like raw—he was still tripping off that. That was some real live reckless shit on his part. But damn if he hadn't loved the way his dick was wrapped in nothing but wet, silky heat. Still, his freak flag wasn't waving high enough for him to want to indulge in licking her out.

So he hadn't.

As a result, Nairobia had left him with his dick aching for her mouth. Yet, that hadn't stopped the sensations from shivering their way through his body. In fact, that only had made him want her more.

He'd known he should have stopped it. But how, when he'd wanted it, *her*, so goddamn badly? He hadn't gone over to her penthouse for pussy. She'd summoned him. Said she needed to go over some security issues with him that couldn't wait until the following day, or be discussed over the telephone.

But when the elevator doors opened to her apartment and he'd stepped into her foyer, there she stood. Naked. That teasing allure of hers called out to him, taunting him. What the fuck was he supposed to do after seeing all that body? Bad enough he'd wanted another round with her in order to redeem himself.

And there she was offering pussy up on a platter to him. So he did what any man with a dick would do: he threw his arm around her and lifted her against him. Saying nothing, Nairobia had wrapped her legs around him and kissed him as if she wanted to taste ever bit of him, savoring and memorizing every part of his mouth.

No, he didn't kiss. But he'd kissed her *again*. Had his tongue swirling around hers, probing inside a mouth that had probably sucked a nation of dicks and licked more cunts than a country of hungry, sex-starved men.

Mel laughed. "Muhfucka, what happened to not fuckin' the clients, huh?"

Lamar groaned. "Yo, man, fuck that. I tried, bruh. But she kept throwin' that shit at me." He leaned against the door of the black S-600 with the tinted windows, and kept his eye trained on the Valentino entrance. Her fifth boutique and counting, Nairobia had been inside the expensive Fifth Avenue boutique for close to an hour in search of the perfect dress for a Hedonism party she'd been invited to host in Jamaica tomorrow night. She hadn't wanted Lamar to come inside, and he was fine with staying outside, waiting.

"Yo, you got issues, fam," Mel said, still laughing at his boy whom he'd known since elementary school. Truth was, they were more like brothers than anything else. They'd been through thick and thin together. Knuckling up together, hustling together, and fucking broads together.

Lamar grunted. "Nah. What I got is a hard, horny dick, muhfucka. My shit stays on rock." He shook his head. "Yo, I'm tellin' you, fam. This club shit is killin' me, yo. The shit that goes down up in that muhfucka is…" He paused, then swallowed. "Man, listen. It goes down up in there."

"Well, damn. You sound miserable," Mel teased. "Let me put you outta ya misery. Let's swap. You come out here 'n' let me handle the club shit."

"Hell, nah, fam. I'm good right where I'm at." Lamar scowled when a bike messenger sped by almost running into the side of a cab. *Dumb muhfucka.*

"Yeah, aiight. That's what I thought. But, word is bond, yo. Nairobia bad as hell, so I already know you beatin' that thing up. On some real shit, I'd probably be tryna knock it down, too. No doubt."

Lamar cringed, looking back over toward the entrance of the high-end store. "Yeah, you already know, playa." Yeah, he'd fucked Nairobia good, at least that he wanted to believe. Yeah, she'd moaned.

And her pussy—*goddamn, that pussy*—had flooded with warmth. She hadn't faked that. Nah. Not possible. Yeah hell, he'd bust that shit down. But he still hadn't been able to beat that shit down the way he'd been known to do with his shorties from around the way. This had been the third time he'd come fast, and hard. The shit wasn't cool. And it was fucking with his ego. But he damn sure wasn't about to tell his boy how the pussy was fucking up his whole stroke game. The shit was crippling.

And it was fucking with his head.

He took a deep breath. If Nairobia ever threw him the pussy again—all he needed was one more go at it, he knew he'd need to double-wrap and be smoked out if he really wanted to fuck her until she tapped out. But he didn't need to worry about that now since he didn't plan on fucking her again. He didn't plan on having another moment of weakness. Three times was enough. So it was all good.

Now that he was single again, he'd be sure to keep his dick sucked and fucked to keep his balls on *E*.

Problem solved.

"But, yo, fam, I'm sayin' though," Mel said. "What's good wit' you 'n' shorty? Y'all still together?"

Lamar raised a brow. "Nah, son. I had to dead that." He gave him the shortened version of why he and Lana were over, then glanced at his watch. *What the fuck?!* Yeah, he was getting paid well to stand outside and do nothing, but this shopping shit was getting ridiculous.

"Damn, man. Sorry to hear that."

"Nah, man. Don't be. I knew she wasn't for me; I just didn't have the heart to let her know it. Shit happens for a reason, feel me?"

"No doubt."

Lamar swallowed as Nairobia finally walked out—her hair sliding down her back and blowing up in the wind, headed toward the car, empty-handed. Men stared at her as they walked by, their necks snapping to keep their eyes on her even as their feet moved. Women glanced her way, some amazed at her beauty; others sneering. Head up, Nairobia slung her hair unfazed by their burning gazes.

Lamar frowned, wondering where the hell her shopping bags were. But it wasn't his concern so he returned to his call.

"Yo, I gotta bounce, fam, but I'ma hit you later."

"Cool, cool. No doubt."

"Bet—"

"And, yo…"

"Yeah, wasssup?" Lamar said, eyeing Nairobia as she stopped to take a photograph with a middle-aged couple.

"Try keepin' ya dick in ya pants, muhfucka!"

The line disconnected as Nairobia reached the luxury vehicle. Lamar opened the back door for her. She smiled at him, then leaned in to him so only he would hear and said, "I'm so wet."

She slid in, and pulled her designer shades over her eyes.

Shaking his head, his breath hissed. He felt himself growing excited at the thought of her wet pussy. Remembering oh so well how wet and juicy it could get. He shook the images, thinking of something less pleasant, like why the fuck she didn't have shopping bags. She'd been inside for mad long, so what had she been doing all that time inside? Fucking? Was her pussy wet from being fucked in the back of the storeroom? Had she let some horny-ass salesman finger her? Was she laid out on some mink coat 69ing with some thirsty motherfucker?

With a muttered curse, Lamar closed his eyes for a split-second, and shook his head again. This shit was crazy. *Try keepin' ya dick in ya pants, muhfucka!*

A moment longer, he groaned inwardly, finally easing into the car and shutting the door behind them. It was inexplicable, this burning urge that came over him every time he was near her.

Yeah, he was in way over his head, this time.

As he sat beside her he watched her from his peripheral vision. And all he could think about was the feel of her tight heat, and how her sweet pussy clutched and fluttered around him. Arousal splintered hot and fiercely through his body.

And then he felt it.

His dick swelling painfully hard.

THIRTY-EIGHT

"Y ou still have not come to my club," Nairobia said as she eyed Marcel. He sat across from her, cutting into his steak. They were having an early dinner. Not a date. She'd driven her own car. And he'd driven his. And now they sat, finishing up their meal, sharing a cozy table for two.

"Why? Do you not wish to see the inside of sweet decadence?"

Marcel wiped his mouth with his napkin, and regarded her with a smile. He was proud of her success with The Pleasure Zone, and had this been another time in his life, he'd been there with his libido and hard dick in hand ready to indulge in his sexual proclivities. But since Marika's death...that part of his life had died too. He had no desire for sex parties or clubs, things he and Marika had enjoyed together. These days, he preferred the comforts of behind closed doors to pander his desires...hopefully, one day, with one special someone.

"I've already felt the inside of sweet decadence," he murmured. "Inside you."

Nairobia felt her cunt tingle, and herself warming from the inside out.

Damn it all to hell. And damn him. The man was unapologetic. Relentless.

She dismissed his comment. "How is my darling Carlos doing?"

Marcel raised a brow. "Would you like his number to call him?"

He smiled, but his eyes had gone dark as sin. She stared at him unsure if he was pulling her chain, or serious.

Was that jealousy she saw flash in his eyes?

She'd bet her gun's license and second-degree black belt—something many had no knowledge she possessed—that it was.

Feigning a shrug, she said, "If you wish for me to have it, my love."

His body stiffened. "I'll tell him to call you," he said blandly.

Nairobia reached over and placed a warm hand over his very large, long-fingered one. She smiled. "I don't ever need another man to do my work, my darling. His number is at my fingertips whenever I want it." She tilted her head. "Tonight, I dialed yours, no?"

Marcel regarded her in kind. True, tonight she'd called him, a pleasant surprise to say the least. Finally, they were turning a corner...or maybe not.

She still had up so many walls. He thought he was guarded. But, goddamn. She had the walls of Jericho erected around her. But he was more determined than ever to climb over them, one layered-brick at a time.

He nodded. "Yes, you did."

"Then let's not dilly-dally over nothing. Stay right here—with *mij*, in the moment."

He smiled. "Have I told you how beautiful you are?"

She had her long hair elegantly pinned up in a French twist, and still wore the faint traces of a burgundy-wine lip gloss over her plush lips. Marcel's gaze dropped to her cleavage, and he licked his lips.

Tonight, she'd worn something a little less...revealing. Still sexy, still seductive, yet, far from scandalous, she'd worn a black dress, with lace sleeves and lace cutouts on either sides of her. The dress hugged her in all the right places, still leaving room for one's imagination to roam freely, filling with salacious thoughts.

She cocked her head to the side. Then a slow smile worked over her mouth. "No, *mijn liefde*, you have not. Not in"—she glanced at her diamond bracelet watch—"the last hour or so."

He laughed, his brown orbs sparkling, his dimples deepening. "Then let me correct that now. Nairobia, baby, you look beautiful. Edible. And I'd love nothing more than to take you home and eat you alive."

She felt heat brush over her skin. God how she loved his deep dimples, his infectious laugh. He was everything she should want. That she *would* want, if she were on the market in search of a life partner.

She slid out of her heel and extended her leg, sliding her foot over the inner part of his thigh. The left. Where his dick usually rested. Marcel smiled, and leaned back in his seat, spreading his legs wider, welcoming the press of her warm foot against him.

He felt the question simmering on his lips. He felt it burning the tip of his tongue. So he asked her—point-blank, "When are you going to stop running from me?"

Nairobia's lashes fluttered. "What do you ever mean?"

"Don't play coy with me, baby. You know exactly what I mean. Why are you running from me?" She felt his dick thicken and stretch the fabric of his pants against the sole of her foot. Her mouth watered at the feel of him coming alive.

She licked her lips. "I-I'm not running, my love."

Marcel pressed his legs shut around her foot. "You feel that, right? It's all yours, if you want. Stop running from me, Nairobia."

Oh yes. She felt it. The answer twinkled in her eyes, hitched in her breath. Her toes kneaded the head of his dick as her eyes swept over his face. He licked his lips, his eyes darkening. A decadent ache pulsed over her clit. Why did he have to be so damn fuckable? Why couldn't he simply leave her be?

Why, oh, why did he have to come into her life trying to dig up feelings she never knew existed, feelings she hadn't believed she was capable of?

Nairobia bit that lush lower lip that drove Marcel crazy with want. *"Maudite, bébé,"* he hissed. Goddamn, baby. *"Je veux faire l'armour à la bouche."* I want to make love to your mouth.

She felt her lips curl upward, before she licked her lips. Before she felt a sweet ache building up deep inside the walls of her cunt swelling her lips and clit.

"You naughty boy."

Marcel's eyes glistened. "All for you, baby. How about we head back to my place for dessert?"

"And what exactly, my darling, Marcel, will dessert be?"

Hunger flashed in his eyes. *"You."*

THIRTY-NINE

"Yo, we good?" Lamar asked walking into Nairobia's office, shutting the door behind him. She'd been acting shady toward him over the last two weeks and he wasn't feeling the energy between them. He'd felt the change over a week ago, but planned on letting it slide. After all, he wasn't there to be friends, or her fuck buddy.

Still, he had to work with her. And he *wanted* to keep things running smoothly between them. Not that he needed the paper. He'd been sitting on stacks long before he'd started his security firm. But when she'd dismissed him from her office yesterday without so much as a glance, that didn't sit well with him.

"Hmm." Her warm gaze sizzled over his body. He wore a pair of loose-fitting black jeans, boots, and his muscle-molding black tee. His locks were down, and he looked scrumptious. "Let's see, my darling. We fucked. We came. And we've moved along. Why wouldn't we be, *good?*"

Lifting his hands, he said, "I don't know. You tell me. You seem kinda—I don't know…distant ever since…you know…"

"Ever since your cock melted inside me?" she finished for him.

He bit out something under his breath. "I shoulda pulled out." He took a seat in front of her desk. "My bad."

Nairobia leaned back, twisting her chair from side to side as she seductively licked her lips. "You couldn't help yourself, my darling."

Lamar bristled. *This fuckin' broad, yo.* She was being smug. He wasn't feeling that shit. But she was right. He couldn't. And he still felt like shit for not being able to beat down her guts right. He hadn't delivered his best performance. And now that's all she would remember, him busting a fast nut.

Giving into the temptation had been a blessing and curse for him. It had opened his eyes to the fact that Lana wasn't the one for him. And he'd gone to her a few days later and ended it with her. Sure, it hadn't gone well. But he'd tried his damnedest to hold on to all the things that were right about her to stay with her.

Sadly, it hadn't been enough.

He just couldn't see himself spending the rest of his life laid up with a broad with subpar pussy. Of course he hadn't told her that. He wasn't callous. He'd simply told her, "It's not you, ma. It's me. I'm not built for a relationship right now. You deserve better than I can give you."

She'd cried and screamed. And demanded to know, "Who's the bitch you screwing?"

"There's no one else," he'd told her. That was partly true. There wasn't. But there was Nairobia who had confirmed what he'd already known. He needed someone who had the same hungry sex drive as him, someone who loved to suck and fuck as much as he loved fucking and getting sucked. Lana wasn't it. So she had to get chopped.

And he had Nairobia to thank for it.

"I'ma keep it gee wit' you, ma. I hadn't had pussy in over a week. My stamina is usually through the roof."

Nairobia's mouth curved. "Okay, if you say so, Lamar, darling," she said nonchalantly. "No explanation needed. Most men can rarely control their desires before spilling their loins in less than ten minutes. You, my love, lasted almost nine minutes longer the second time."

Lamar cringed inwardly. So basically he'd only dicked her down for eighteen-minutes-and-some-odd-seconds before he'd popped his cork inside her.

What the fuck?

She'd timed him.

He guessed he should have considered that an improvement—eighteen minutes of fucking, considering that the night he went in raw he'd come in a little under fifteen minutes. Three extra minutes, whoopty-fuckin'-doo! He still hadn't delivered.

His scowl deepened. "I didn't know you had me on a time clock."

"I didn't. Is it my fault my *kut* is platinum? Did you not know I was good pussy, my love?"

Lamar's jaw tightened. He didn't like how she was making him feel, like a pathetic chump.

She smiled at him, amusement dancing in her eyes. "If it's any consolation, a hundred-and-fifty strokes of hard-pounding cock was able to give me multiple orgasms. That's more than others." On their second night together, he'd given her an extra twenty strokes, fast and hard.

She'd fucked up his stamina.

His stare hardened. "I'm not like other muhfukas, yo. So don't compare me to none'a them. I don't bust quick…"

"But you had, my darling. Twice," Nairobia heard the voice in her head say. She wouldn't remind him of it, though. She wasn't a callous lover.

"Not until you," Lamar continued. He inhaled deeply. All of a sudden, all he could smell was *her*: Her hair, her breath, her skin; the wild needy scent of her wet pussy all somehow flooding his lungs.

He needed to fuck her again, and just get it all out of his system.

Nairobia smiled again, slowly taking him in. She sensed his still bruised ego and decided to stroke it. Just a bit. "You have a thick, curved cock that felt delicious inside me, so hard, so deep. It throbbed inside me both times you wedged yourself inside me. You kept me hot and wanting, melting all over you. So do not fret that your performance had not been longer. It was the best it could have been in those very short moments. Know my pussy is still wet for you. So if you wish to indulge yourself, if you wish to slide your cock back in me to redeem yourself…say so."

He groaned, the memory of dumping his nut inside her, then not being able to feel his legs afterward still fresh in his mind.

And she smirked.

"Oh, you think that shit's funny, huh? I ain't no minuteman, yo."

She shrugged. "I never said you were. You are only what you believe you are."

"Yeah, aiight. But you tryna imply it."

She leaned forward in her chair, and eyed him thoughtfully. "Remove your shades so I can see your eyes."

Hesitantly, Lamar removed his sunglasses, and held them in his hand. "Okay, now what?" he asked, his voice husky.

"I find you adorable, my darling."

He scowled. *"Adorable?* Gee, thanks."

"Yes. I find you adorable enough to want to give you the pleasure of my mouth, to allow your cock to feel the velvet lash of my tongue…"

Lamar fanned his legs open and shut, feeling his blood quickly rushing to the head of his cock. He'd been in need of some head—some super soaker-making-his-toes-curl type of head. He needed to feel his dick down in a throat.

He'd already predicted she'd be a problem. Now he saw her more of a challenge. And that was a turn-on to him. Fuck staying away. He'd already fucked that up the first time he'd slid his dick in her. He wanted like hell to say it'd been a mistake. But it hadn't been. For him, there was no turning back. Not now. The pussy was too fucking good. So if she wanted to offer up some head, he would damn sure slide into her mouth and rock her neck back.

He licked his lips. "Oh word? So when we doin' this? I wanna see what that mouth do. I need that in my life, for real for real."

Nairobia's eyes took on a wicked gleam that made Lamar's dick twitch, throbbing in demand to unload. She hadn't even touched him and his dick was already aching. She had his balls ablaze. Everything inside of him boiled. He was so ready to bust.

What the fuck is wrong wit' me?

His gaze locked on her rising chest, the swell of her breasts, Nairobia's nipples tightened and stretched toward him. He licked his lips and groaned, dragging his hands over his face. The tension between them was so thick that Lamar found it almost too hard to breathe. His hunger for her had his dick straining against the button-fly of his jeans.

"Is your cock hard for me?"

"What you think," was his only reply.

"Stand up," Nairobia challenged.

He stood, and her breath caught at the sight of his bulge. She licked her lips.

"Lock the door. Then remove your clothes."

"Nah, yo. That ain't how this goes." He frowned as her phone rang. She stared at the caller ID. Marcel. "You want this dick. You come get it." He sat back down.

Amusement curled her lips. She could see the burning desire he had for her roiling in his eyes as she untied the strings to her wrap dress. Lamar watched as her dress opened. His hooded gaze fixated on her breasts, her nipples. They looked succulent. Edible. Not just her breasts, her nipples, every goddamn part of her.

His gaze dropped to a thin strip of lacy red silk covering her pussy. She spread her legs. The damp spot at the center of her thong made his mouth go dry. The sight slammed scorching heat into his chest, making it hard to breathe.

"Do you think about me, Lamar…?"

Hell yeah, he thought of her. Ever since that night, there in her office, he'd thought about her. Shit. She'd been on his mind more than once, more than twice; almost every fucking waking moment she crossed his mind. That truth shocked and irked him. Lamar was pragmatic. Calculating. He thought everything out—*first*, before acting on it. He kept shit in check. He wasn't impulsive. Being in his line of work being impulsive could get you—or someone else—killed. So he was always in control, of everything.

Until now.

Fuck. Somehow Nairobia had managed, in such a short time, to unravel every fucking thing he stood for, every goddamn thing he was. In all the years he'd been fucking, there hadn't been a woman yet who tempted him to let go of his control the way she did.

He didn't know Nairobia. Didn't know shit about this pornstar bitch. He knew of her, true. Through her films, through her books, and, now, through her club, but he didn't know *her*.

"Do you dream of fucking me?" Nairobia asked in a husky voice as she prowled over to him. The erotic aroma seeping from her pussy was making it hard for him to think straight. It was bad enough his brain, and blood, was already soaked in lust for her.

She was fucking with him again. And he was in no mood for her fucking game playing. Not tonight.

A low growl rumbled in Lamar's throat and he swallowed it back as he rose abruptly and fisted her hair in hand, forcing her gaze up to his.

"Stop fuckin' wit' me," he growled.

Nairobia took him by his wrist, bringing his free hand between her legs. Instinctively, Lamar cupped her there, the base of his hand against her clitoris.

"Put your finger inside me. Feel how wet I am."

He slipped one finger between her folds and inside her.

Nairobia's pussy clenched. "Is that what you want"—she ran her hand over the front of his crotch, then grabbed his dick—"to *fuck* me?"

Lamar's jaws tightened, as did his grip on her hair. His finger moved in and out of her. She was so warm, so wet. "Yeah, I wanna fuck you."

Nairobia smiled, sending him a challenging stare. She palmed him again, squeezing his cock. "Then fuck me."

"Shit," he hissed, feeling blood pump and pool into the shaft of his dick. His dick felt painfully tight strapped in by a jockstrap and boxer briefs. Why the fuck was she making him reckless? Why was he letting her? He'd never felt such an intense need to fuck, or experienced such a surge of…unbridled arousal.

Nairobia's lips curled up into a seductive grin. Her burning eyes scorching over his muscled body.

Lamar's chocolate eyes darkened to nearly black. She knew exactly what she was doing to him. There was no mercy in her eyes as she stroked his dick over his jeans, just lust. Sensations pounded all through his body.

This shit was crazy. He couldn't understand how or why she had this overwhelming effect on him. He'd told her week's back that she was playing with fire. But standing here now, her gaze fierce and hot on him, his dick on the verge of exploding, he knew more than ever that *she* was the fire. And he was about to go up in her flames.

FORTY

"Spread your legs," Lamar demanded as he removed his gun from his lower back and bent Nairobia over her desk and kicked at her ankles until she parted her smooth, silky thighs. He slapped her ass.

"Yes, yes. Ram your cock inside me," Nairobia hissed as Lamar opened his jeans and pulled his dick out of his underwear. She shook her ass, taunting him as she made each ass cheek pop. "Search and seize my *kut*. Fuck me, Lamar. Fuck me hard."

Lamar reached between her thighs and ripped off her thong, tossing it aside. Nairobia's clit tingled at the aggressive act. She was driving him crazy with lust. She was everywhere he fucking breathed. He tasted her in his lungs. Felt her on his skin. His dick ached for her. He couldn't wait any longer.

He needed in.

He positioned the head of his dick at the mouth of her pussy. He let the tip rub up and down her wet slit, then penetrated her with one hard stroke. Nairobia let out a moan.

"Ja, ja, ja…take my *kut*…fuck *mijn zoete gat, mijn liefde*…" Fuck my sweet hole, my love.

With a jerk of his hips, Lamar pulled out and slammed back into her again.

His hips ground against her ass. He spread her beautiful flesh open, and watched her juices soak his shaft as he slid in and out of her folds. "Aaaah, shit…"

Pleasure and pressure built up inside his balls. He began thrusting hard and deep. Faster. Deeper. He was on the verge of coming already. No. Too fucking soon. "Aaaah, shiiit…"

Lamar knew he needed to pull out before his nut erupted.

But she felt so fucking good.

Too good.

Her pussy was so tight and creamy. His eyes rolled in his head. In all his years of fucking, he'd never felt anything so goddamn good in his life—her warm pussy grabbing him, exploding over him with each pulsing orgasm. He could feel his nut swelling and boiling low, filling his balls with an ache so powerful that he felt his body sizzling and his legs shaking. Withdrawing and slowly pushing back in, he slowed the pace, working his cock in and out of her pussy in slow, easy thrusts.

Whap!

Lamar slapped her ass. Slid out to just the tip, and slowly moved the head of his dick in and out of her slit. He watched in amazement how her muscles grabbed and slurped at his dickhead. He loved the way her sex sucked greedily at his cock. He wanted to fuck her pussy raw. Feel her wet heat and bust his nut in her guts again.

Pleasure burned in his chest. He closed his eyes. And slammed back in, the head of his dick bumping her cervix. Feeling possessed, he growled. Groaned. Grunted.

Slick sounds mingled with their panting breaths.

"Fuckin' bitch," he hissed, slapping her ass again. He was in balls deep. But he couldn't be in deeper. He wanted to be swallowed up in her wetness, drowned in her liquid heat. His thrusts kept coming faster…faster. Harder. She had him losing control. "Sweet whore pussy," he murmured huskily in her ear. "You like feelin' this thug dick up in you, huh? You like teasin' muhfuckas…flauntin' all this fat ass in muhfuckas' faces, huh…?"

His teeth sank into her shoulder. And Nairobia let out a long, erotic moan. She mewled out like a wildcat in heat. Her breasts bounced. Her nipples tightened. Her cunt pulsed. Ecstasy swept through her. She rocked her hips and pumped her pelvis in greed to get more of him inside her, gripping him hot, tightly, every thrust sending *him* and her spiraling closer to the edge. "Mmm," she moaned, savoring the pleasure. *"Geef me je harde lul…"* Give me your hard cock.

Tightening his hand on her hips, Lamar began fucking her in deep, hard strokes, his curved dick brushing over her walls. He couldn't get enough of her lush body, her deep well of sensations. One thrust after another, banging harder, he couldn't think, couldn't see anything except…fire.

An inferno blazing up around them.

Whap!

He slapped her ass again. Harder.

Nairobia let out another moan as his hand left behind a heated sting that had her gasping. He leaned over and draped his hard chest over her and wrapped one arm around her quaking body. Her cunt opened to him, clutching and milking, growing wetter around him as he reached under and found her clit, distended, swollen, sensitive. He slammed in her. His heavy sac tightening as it slapped at the back of her pussy.

He gripped her hips, demanding she hold still while he invaded her cunt with rapid-fire shallow plunges of his dickhead into her opening. He teased her there, and she gripped him as she reached back and spread open her magnificent ass—her heat and scent surrounding him, making him insane with need to nut in her. To take what he needed. Her pussy, her ass. To own her.

He couldn't believe how incredibly wet she was. He nearly burst with feverish need. Heat spread over his skin. Lamar bit at her neck, before slamming back inside her body. Nairobia still hadn't given him the dick suck she'd promised him earlier. And he wanted inside her mouth.

Now.

But his dick was engulfed in so much of her heat that he couldn't pull out. Her pussy entrapped him, her clutching walls holding his cock hostage. Nairobia rocked her hips back against him, glancing at him over her shoulder, seductively licking her lips, her gaze full of desire, full of hot need. She was burning up on the inside and wet enough, he could hear her juices splashing as he moved in her.

She murmured something inaudible in Dutch, swiveling her hips, only sending him further over the edge of an orgasm. She pulsed inside and all around him, driving him mad. His dick loved the feel of her, but he hated her. He'd never been inside a woman—any woman—and wanted to stay inside her hot wet hole all day and all night, fucking her, stroking her.

Fuckin' dick-teasin' sorceress bitch!

Pussy so muthafuckin' good!

Lamar's eyes rolled back in his head again. "Aaah, shit...aaah, muthafuck...this muthafuckin' pussy...uhhh..." His thighs shook from the endless thrusting, his dick was so hard it ached. Nairobia egged him on, whispering dirty words in Dutch, taunting him from over her shoulder.

A spasm wracked Lamar's entire body. He quickly pulled out, leaving her aching and empty. "Get on your knees and suck my dick," he growled, his eyes watering from the rush of sensations. He wanted to bust in her mouth.

But it was too late.

Before he could get his condom off, he came with a rush, with a fierce spasm, a force so powerful that his entire body shook.

Nairobia laughed to herself. Silly man he was.

Demanding she kneel and suck his cock. Ha. She knelt before no man. And she sucked when she wanted, not when summoned.

Nairobia looked at him, taking him in—*all* of him, standing there, his eyelids fluttering, his chest heaving, his jeans open and shoved down, his sheathed cock exposed, wet and sticky, and curving to the right. What a delicious sight.

So decadent.

So masculine and erotic.

Lamar stumbled back and collapsed into one of her office chairs. She smiled slow and easy and seductive, then leaned in and brushed a gentle kiss over his lips. Lamar's brain was mush. He couldn't see or think straight.

Nairobia sauntered off toward the bathroom, her juices sliding down the inside of her thighs—leaving her heat and musky scent and him sitting there, dazed and confused.

Lamar closed his eyes, and shook his head as his pulse finally steadied.

He knew.

He was in too deep.

Beyond the point of no return.

And in some serious fucking trouble.

Shit.

FORTY-ONE

A few days later, Nairobia was snuggled into Marcel's sofa, her bare feet curled underneath her as she stared at the flames flickering in his fireplace. It was the middle of a sweltering July, but never too hot for a gorgeous fire.

Marcel stepped into the room barefoot in a pair of lounge pants, and settled onto the sofa beside her. He pulled Nairobia into his arms and she snuggled against him.

She gave a soft sigh, then lay against his bare chest, the top of her head resting just underneath his chin. Marcel pulled her in closer, and breathed her in. She smelled of mangos and coconut. He loved the way she smelled. He ran his hand up the length of her arm and pressed his lips to her hair, inhaling even as he kissed her head. The scent of her hair was intoxicating. He wanted to stay like this for as long as humanly possible, just breathing her in.

He'd needed to see her.

And she'd wanted him to.

They hadn't seen each other since the night they'd had dinner, several weeks ago. Between her travels back and forth to L.A., the club, and her other engagements. She'd also been very busy… avoiding Marcel.

But tonight, she'd finally decided to make time for him.

Surprisingly, she'd finally admitted to herself that she really did enjoy his company. That he called to a part of her soul that frightened her. He made her feel things she never fathomed. But she couldn't lose herself in him.

In doing so, she feared she'd lose everything, her voice; every part of who she was. And she wouldn't allow that.

Marcel had told her over dinner to stop running from him. But Nairobia wasn't running. She was simply preserving, protecting herself. Self-preservation was all she had. It was what had kept her from heartache thus far. Letting go of it would make her susceptible to getting hurt.

A man had already sliced her in the heart once in her life. She vowed to never, ever, allow another man free reins to her heart. Maybe her years as a porn star had made her too detached, incapable of fully loving anyone other than herself.

But she felt something for Marcel, a fluttering in her heart.

Unfortunately, she couldn't quite put a finger on it, couldn't quite describe what the feeling was. She just knew it was there, chipping away at her.

And she didn't like it.

"I'm not her," Nairobia finally said, breaking the momentary silence between them. Her voice was barely a whisper as she glanced over at the sixteen-by-twenty oil painting of Marika hanging on the wall. "I'll never be."

"I don't want you to be," Marcel said earnestly, following her gaze. "I want you to be you. That sexy, beautiful, free-spirited woman you are. That's whom I'm attracted to, baby. That's whom I want to spend my time with. Not some facsimile of my wife. There was—and will *always* be—only one Marika. I'm not looking for another."

Nairobia turned her eyes from the stunning portrait and gazed directly at Marcel.

"Then what are you *really* looking for?"

Marcel inhaled sharply, scrubbing his hand over his face. He thought he'd already made it clear what he wanted. He wasn't into the dating game. He actually felt out of touch. And the prospect of being on some online dating site was something he couldn't wrap his mind around. The thought of dating after having been married for so long actually made him uneasy. And he wasn't into multiple sex partners—anymore. Well, not really. Well, he hadn't been since Marika's death. And he seriously doubted he ever would be again.

"I'm looking for someone who I can spend my life with. Some-one whom I can travel the world with, someone I can wake up to, make love to, and fuck whenever, wherever, however." He smiled at her. "I'd like to think I already found what I'm looking for. *You.*"

Nairobia sucked in her breath and let it out in a long exhale as she tried to picture herself spending the rest of her life with *him*—with *anyone*, for that matter.

She couldn't see it. And it saddened her. It simply wasn't there. And she couldn't force something that wasn't obtainable.

"I can't do—"

Marcel put his hand up to stop her.

"Ssh. Please. Don't say anything right now. Think on it. I'll give you all the time and space you need. No pressure."

There was nothing to think about. This couldn't happen. It wouldn't happen.

"Mar—"

He leaned over and covered her mouth with a kiss, shutting her up. When he finally pulled away, she had to catch her breath.

"Baby," Marcel began and paused. Nairobia's heart stopped. What-ever words would come next, she knew for certain her entire world would most likely never be the same again once they were spoken.

She braced herself. "Yes?"

"*Je t'aime…*"

Let me love you.

FORTY-TWO

Marcel wasn't used to being put on hold by *anyone*—not for long, anyway. He'd told Nairobia to think about what he'd wanted from her.

To love her.

He said he'd give her space, while she thought it over.

But that was close to fucking three weeks ago.

He hadn't considered she'd take her slow, sweet-ass time. A few days, tops, should have been sufficient enough for her to decide whether or not she wanted to pursue more with him. It wasn't a difficult question. He hadn't asked her to marry him, or to jump off a cliff with him. So what the fuck was the problem?

And why was she avoiding him?

This waiting-around shit was driving him crazy.

He grunted, shaking his head. *Look at you, man. Obsessing over a damn woman. Pull your shit together. If she ain't beat for you, then let that shit go…*

He sighed, and leaned back in his chair. The problem was, he didn't want to let go. He wanted *her.* No one else.

Nairobia was the one, the only one for him.

He knew that. Felt it in every part of his soul. Marika…

He looked up toward the ceiling, and closed his eyes.

She'd come to him in a dream, and had given him permission to find love again. She wanted him to be happy. And to be with someone who would, could, love him for the man he was.

Marika had been the only woman who had done exactly that. Loved every part of him. And he knew no one would ever love him in the way she had. And he also knew he'd probably never be able to love another woman as deeply as he had her. But that didn't mean he wasn't capable of loving again.

He wanted love.

He still had so much more of it to give.

And he had a big, hard dick with lots of nut that he wanted to share with someone special. He didn't want random pussy from a bunch of faceless women. He wanted to be able to look in a woman's eyes and see, feel, the pleasure he was giving her every time he touched her, looked at her, or simply made love to her.

He didn't want a woman he had to fuck, simply because she wasn't someone he found worthy of being made love to. He wanted substance. Something meaningful. What he wanted was a love of his own.

Was that too much to ask for?

Marcel sighed.

Shit. Maybe it was too much to ask for.

Hell. He was starting to think *maybe* something was wrong with *him*. He was motherfucking Marcel Kennedy reigning over an entire empire of music and media. He was the motherfucking man. He had sex appeal, a large bankroll, and mad swag. Hell, his motherfucking name rang bells in the industry. He could have any woman he wanted. He knew this. Hell, he'd bedded down some of the baddest ones out there. His name *and* his dick always made lasting impressions.

And, yet...

He was still alone.

He leaned forward, and covered his face in his hands. This shit was so fucked up. "Why'd that bitch have to kill you, baby?" he whispered into his palms.

He felt so fucking helpless without her. Yet, he somehow found hope in his memories of her. He couldn't tell anyone that she spoke to him, not only in his dreams but while he drove, while he showered, while he sat alone at home or in his office. Marika came to him. Sat and talked with him. He could see her clear as day. Smiling at him. Weeping for him. Praying for him. She was everywhere, watching over him. He felt her presence. Could still feel her touch. And smell her in the air.

Maybe there was something wrong with him.

He didn't know.

All he knew was, Marika had come to him and had told him that Nairobia was the one. She'd given him her blessing. But had warned him to be patient with her.

Sadly, time was ticking away.

And his patience was running out.

He'd give her two more days, that's it. Then she'd need to make up her mind.

Him.

Or nothing at all.

FORTY-THREE

Nairobia found herself straining for release. She was coiled tighter than a hymen. And she needed to break free.

From the club.

From Marcel.

Even Josiah—whom she adored, was getting on her last nerve. She felt like she was being strangled. And she didn't like it one bit.

Oh, don't be mistaken. She loved The Pleasure Zone and all of its debauchery, and hedonistic energy. It was truly a den of iniquity. And she loved owning it. But what she didn't love was the work that went along with it. It was becoming mind-numbing, and mundane. She hadn't opened the private club to be chained to a desk, *managing* it. No. *That* was not what she'd envisioned for herself when she opened the extravagant club. To *work* long hours. To be holed up in an office, save from being bent over her desk with a hard cock seesawing in her cunt. Other than that, that was absolutely not the plan she'd had in mind.

Yet, here she was—*still*, poring over vendor invoices and sorting through an assortment of member profiles. Suffocating. Shutting her club down was not an option. Ever. She still had not found anyone to manage her club—not that she'd been looking aggressively, but she still *needed* someone.

Something had to give. Soon.

She sighed—heavily.

She was not an optional kind of woman. She was not ever the white-picket fence type of woman, but somehow she felt like that's what Marcel was trying to make her into. Not that he'd said it. It was what he didn't say.

He was commitment oriented. He loved the idea of being married and waking up to someone every day for the rest of his life. She was—well, she was allergic to the idea of being committed to one person. She didn't know what that felt like, since she'd never dated anyone. Sure she'd been seen with men. Even rumored, over the years, to have been in several torrid affairs with many celebrities, and a few world leaders.

No. She'd fucked them, probably. But having *affairs?*

Absolutely not.

Well, unless you wanted to consider what she'd shared with Josiah an *affair*. She saw him, as with all the others, including Lamar—whose cock she'd ridden the night before—as sex objects. Boy toys. Fuck buddies. Pleasure seekers.

They all desired something from her. And she'd given it freely, because she had wanted it herself.

Pleasure.

Unadulterated bliss.

Nothing more, nothing less.

And she was the happiest when she was in the throes of sweet, searing pleasure, or seeing others become engulfed in it.

Lamar pushed open her door and knocked as he walked in, cutting into her reverie. "Hey, these were dropped off for you…"

She looked up at him, and saw a very large, long white box under his arm as he stepped into her office. "Where do you want 'em?"

She pointed over toward the sofa. "Over there," she said, sounding distracted. "Please."

Lamar looked at her. "Yo, e'erything aiight?"

She inhaled sharply, then exhaled. "Everything's fine, my love. Thanks."

"Oh, aiight. If you say so."

She forced a smile. "I do."

He frowned. She wasn't looking at him lusty-eyed, wasn't being her flirty-self. He knew something was up, but he wasn't going to pry. He knew when to fall back, and mind his business.

"Please close the door shut, on your way out."

He glanced over at her again. "No doubt. I got you."

She waited for him to walk out, and shut the door, then pushed back from her seat and walked over toward the sofa. She pulled apart the red ribbon tied around the box, then slowly lifted the lid. She gasped. There were three-dozen red roses inside with a card.

They were absolutely beautiful.

Nairobia picked up the card and read it:

Beautiful flowers, for a beautiful woman. I can't say I'm in love. But each rose represents the love that flows through my veins and fills my heart. All you need to do, baby, is let me share all that I am, with you. Marcel

P.S., I'm waiting to hear from you. Please don't keep me waiting.

Nairobia stared at the card several moments longer, and reread it twice before setting it in the box. She picked up a single rose and brought it to her nose. Her heat thudded in her chest as she inhaled.

She thought she had it all figured out. But now she felt herself second-guessing herself, questioning her wants, her needs, her own desires.

This was not good. It wasn't her. And she felt herself slowly coming apart. She was starting to feel like her freedom was slowly being taken from her and she was beginning to feel like a caged bird. Trapped.

She didn't like it. And she didn't know how much more of it she'd be able to take, before she'd finally come undone. She was starting to lose control—of herself, her life, everything. She felt it. And it frightened her.

Her whole life had been about control. *Her* control. *Her* power. Every part of her existence, *she'd* controlled, *she'd* been responsible for staying empowered.

Nothing, or no one else had ever been able to take that from her.

And now a man—not just any man, but *the* man of most women's dreams—was trying to disrupt the very order she'd spent her entire life maintaining.

Her cell rang. She lifted it from her desk, and stared at the screen. Speaking of her looming demise.

It was Marcel.

Again.

She shook her head. "No, I can't do this with you," she muttered to herself. "Not now, Mar*Sell*."

She let the call roll into voicemail.

It had been three weeks since she'd told him she needed time. Time was relative, no? So she hadn't been specific in defining the length of time she actually needed. Truth was, she tried not to think about it. But everywhere she turned, *he* was there.

In the news, on the radio…in her thoughts, on her voicemail, all over her skin, she couldn't get away from him.

But she needed to.

She had to.

God, help her if she didn't.

FORTY-FOUR

"Hello, Miss Jansen?"

"Yes, Stewart? Hello."

"Hi. Mister Kennedy is here to see you. Shall I send him up?"

Nairobia blinked. Pulled the phone from her ear, and stared at it. Why hadn't he called her first? Well, he had. She hadn't been taking his calls.

Still, what business did he have to come to her home unannounced?

The gall.

She placed the receiver back to her ear, and sighed. "Yes. Send him up."

This was as good a time as any. She glanced over at her packed bags.

She had a lot to sort through. She needed to get away. To regroup, and recharge.

Only for a while, maybe a few weeks or so.

She couldn't be away for too long. She had businesses to manage. Then there was The Pleasure Zone that she still needed to look after. Business was thriving in such a short time, and it had her thinking of opening one in Europe, perhaps over in Belgium, or France.

First, she still needed to find someone able to manage the one here, before she pursued the opening of another club. But it would happen.

Nairobia was a woman who made things happen.

For now, The Pleasure Zone wouldn't be taking on any new memberships until she returned from her travels. She knew she was being foolish, whisking off like this.

But, damn it all to hell.

This was about her. It always was about her. Her wants, her needs, her desires.

And, right now, she wanted and needed and desired to be…

Her breath caught as the doors to her apartment slid open and Marcel strode in, pausing midstep when he caught sight of her opened travel trunk in the center of the floor. He glanced over at her other bags. Marcel burrowed his brows, then looked at her. "Going somewhere?"

Before she could answer, her cell started ringing. Lamar's name appeared on the screen. Holding Marcel's gaze, she answered, "Yes." Then spoke into the phone. "Hello."

"Yo, you sure you don't need me to go with you?" She'd told everyone at the club that she'd be on travel for a few weeks. That she'd still be reachable by cell if anything arose that couldn't be managed without her. Otherwise, it'd have to wait until she returned.

Josiah had wanted to go with her. And she was tempted. But she restrained herself. Told him she needed him here.

"No," she said as she watched Marcel watching her. "I'll send for you if anything changes."

"Aiight, then. You be safe out there. I got you, aiight?"

"Thank you."

She smiled, and her cunt tingled as memories of him slumped over on her bed resurfaced. Oh, how last night had been a delicious goodnight, goodbye fuck. She'd told him it would be his last night of pleasure with her. And, finally, he'd delivered—one sumptuous hour of deep-stroking-curved-dick-slinging pleasure that had them both clawing at the sheets.

And he'd come like he'd never done before. She wasn't sure what he'd been on, but whatever it was, he'd finally redeemed himself.

Now it was time to move on. Nairobia had done her part.

Fulfilled his fantasy of fucking a porn star…her.

Pleasure.

"Yo, take special care of ya'self, aiight?"

"I will. *Zie je snel, mijn lieveling.*" See you soon, my darling.

He had no clue what she'd said, but he had a lopsided grin on his face when she ended the call..

A muscle ticked in his Marcel's jaw as he counted the bags neatly lined along the wall.

Six.

Where was she going with *six* goddamn bags?

He wouldn't have to ask. He already knew the answer.

She was running from him.

"Where you going?" he asked, walking further into the apartment.

"On travel."

He raised a brow. "And you weren't going to call, or see me before you left?"

She shifted her gaze.

He scowled. "Damn. So fuck me, right?"

She shook her head. "No. Not fuck you. I adore *fucking* you. That is part of the problem, my love. It is why I simply need a moment of *me* time. Away from you."

He gave her a perplexed look. "I don't see the problem. You dig me. I dig you." He stalked over to her, and pulled her into a possessive hug. He kissed her on the forehead. "You love this dick. And I love giving it to you, baby. So what's the problem? Explain it to me."

Nairobia sighed, looking up at him. She couldn't stop looking at him, his very sexy, toe-curling self. She'd been with a countless number of sexy, beautiful men; but no one as free-spirited or as unnerving as Marcel. Every part of him is succulent. Tempting. Highly addictive.

He was a dangerous drug. One Nairobia had no intentions of becoming hooked on.

"You are the problem, Mar*Sell*," she said softly, her voice in almost a painful whisper. "You." She reached for his hand. "Come, sit." She pulled him over toward the sofa, then sat. She on one end of the sofa, he on the other end, Marcel already felt the divide between them. She was pulling away from him.

Maybe he'd pushed too hard.

Fuck.

Marika had warned him to take it slow with her. He thought that that was what he'd been doing. Taking it *slllooooowww*. Excruciatingly slow. Any slower, the clock would stop ticking and he'd be dead.

He took a steadying breath. "So what exactly are you saying here, baby. Tell me something. Because right now I'm at a loss." He scooted over closer to her, closing the space between them. Still not satisfied, he inched closer.

There.

Now she was only an arm's length away.

Nairobia's pulse quickened. She shifted.

"I'm not ready for what you want."

Marcel reached over and tugged her into the crook of his arm. "Come here, baby." She didn't resist him as his strong, dominant arm encircled her. He held her for a moment, allowing the heat between them to radiate.

Then he said, "How do you know that? You haven't even given it, *us*, a try. At least sample the ride, before you throw in the key."

She swallowed. Then inhaled. She smelled him in the air. He smelled of soap and a hint of something with a woodsy, very masculine scent.

"Maybe you can't see it yet. Maybe you don't want to see it. But we're meant for each other, baby. I can't stop you from running, but eventually, you're going to have to find a way to stop hiding from the truth."

She looked up at him. "And *what* truth is that, Mar*Sell?*"

He circled her waist with his arm. "That *you* know what *I* know. That we belong together, baby."

She swallowed, broke free of him, and stood to her feet. "Why are you trying to convince me to be something I can never be? Why, Mar*Sell?*" She paced, then turned to face him. "Tell me. Why are you trying to change me, when you know I am not the type of woman to be chained to a man?"

Marcel blinked. He felt himself precariously close to dropping to his knees, begging—for what he didn't actually know. But goddamn it! That's what he felt like doing. He was willing to strip himself—emotionally, mentally—bare before her.

What the fuck was going on here?

If she didn't want him, fuck it. No foul, no harm. He'd get over it; over her.

Right?

Wrong. He didn't *want* to get over it. He didn't want to walk away from something that could be beautiful. And real. Why the fuck couldn't she see that he wanted her exactly the way she was? That she was lovable exactly how she was.

That she was...

Perfect.

For him.

He felt his heart pounding in his ears. "Hold up, baby. I'm not trying to change you, or convince you of anything. I'm not that kinda man, to try to change a woman. All I'm saying is, you've come into my life, and given me purpose to love again."

Nairobia swallowed again. Love was *not* in her life plan. It had never been.

Marcel held out his arm, wanting to feel closer to her. He gave her a faint smile when she slid down next to him, burrowing into his side so he could wrap his arm around her again. He did. And he could feel her melting into him as he anchored her against him.

Nairobia felt overwhelmed. Everything about Marcel was so intense, so damn…demanding. He wanted her. But did she want him?

She honestly didn't know.

She thought she did. No-strings-attached wanted. That Marcel was simply an occasional good fuck when her cunt craved the stretch of a jumbo-sized cock.

But Marcel had disrupted the balance in that. He'd changed the rules without her permission. He pushed his way into her life without the decency of a proper request.

Did she want *this*? Did she want *him*?

At one point—hell, before he stepped over the threshold, the answer would have been absolute—a definitive *no*. But now she was uncertain. She'd allowed Marcel to get inside her head planting seeds of hope and promise; hope that would somehow come up short, and a string of promises that would surely be broken.

How could they not be?

Here was a man still stuck between the past and the present, trying to stubbornly wedge his way into her future. She couldn't, she wouldn't, give into the illusion that there'd be some happily-ever-after.

She didn't believe in fairy tales.

And she wasn't the type of woman who wept and sniveled over the loss of a man when things went terribly awry.

And Nairobia didn't do uncertainty. And she didn't indulge in fear.

Yet, at this very moment, she felt uncertain, and deathly afraid.

He dared her to dream. Dared her to let a man—*him*—into her heart. And she didn't know what to do with that. Being single gave her that autonomy to live her life, on her terms, by her rules, no one else's. She never wanted to be under the thumb of a man. Never wanted to be defined by a man. But relationships had a way of stifling one's independence, had a way of stripping them of their identity. No, no. She wouldn't stand for that. She didn't want to ever lose herself…to anyone.

She'd never been in a relationship. Never had to be accountable to anyone, except herself. And she'd been fine with that.

She still was.

Wasn't she?

She pulled away from him—again, and stood. She paced. She was so confused. She didn't do confusion. And, yet, she'd didn't know if she were coming or going. Something she was never known for. But Marcel was, he was…

Damn him.

He was making her weak.

And she despised weak women.

Marcel rose to his feet.

She eyed him, and he gave a pained look that seared her soul. She averted her eyes from his gaze. Why was he doing this to her?

He crossed over to her in less than two steps and cupped her face in his hands, pressing his forehead against hers.

"God, you're so beautiful," he breathed out. "Why can't you let me in?" He looked at her, deep in her eyes. "I'm not a perfect man, Nairobia. But I'm a good one. And I'm loyal, baby." He tenderly kissed the side of her mouth, then his mouth moved over hers, his tongue teasing over her lips, before pushing its way into her parted mouth. He kissed her deeply, with a hot need that burned through her body.

When he pulled away, she was breathless, and feeling helpless to resist him. But she had to. She would never be the woman he needed, the woman he deserved. Devoted to only him.

"You can trust me with your heart, baby," he said, his voice cracking as if he'd been reading her thoughts.

She swallowed the lump in the back of her throat. "It's not you I don't trust. It's me. I can't do this with you, Mar*Sell*. I wish I could, my darling. But…" She shook her head. "You overwhelm me. You complicate my life."

"That's the last thing I'm trying to do, Nairobia. I want you. *You*. But I'm not going to throw myself on you. I think I've done enough begging. If you're not ready for love, then I can't force it on you." He sighed, his heart aching. "God, I want you. But I'm not going to pressure you. I want you, when you are ready to be wanted. When you're ready for me, baby. I'll be here. When you're ready for a good man, a real man, to love you, baby, you'll know where to find me."

She leaned up and pressed her lips against his, grabbing him by the back of the neck and kissing him in a way she'd never kissed a man. Any man. Suddenly, she was kissing him with her heart, her whole mouth over his, devouring him, tasting him, savoring him, as if this would be their very last kiss—with a passion she hadn't wanted to admit she had for him.

He did this to her.

Made her feel weak with want, with desire.

She didn't like this feeling of feeling open and vulnerable.

But he had her becoming undone.

One last sweep of her tongue against his, Nairobia pulled away, and Marcel groaned out his disappointment. He'd felt it too. The finality.

She was leaving him no other choice. He'd have to let her go.

They both stared at one another.

He leaned in and pressed his forehead against her, one last time. Then pulled back. "Go do you, baby," is all he could say. Nothing else would matter. Her mind was made up. And he wasn't about to stand in her way. If she wanted *him*, she'd have to find her way back to him.

End of story.

Nairobia stared at him, blinking, as he let go of her. She stood there and eyed him as he turned from her and walked out the sliding doors. It was in that moment she felt herself blinking back tears. Maybe in another life, she could be the kind of woman he deserved. The kind of woman he needed. Maybe in another life, in another place, she could allow her heart to open to him.

But for now, she loved being her own woman. Loved endless pleasure. Loved the freedom of doing whatever she wanted, with whomever she wanted, wherever she wanted—answering to no one.

Maybe, in another life, she could fall in love.

Be in love.

With *him*.

Maybe.

ABOUT THE AUTHOR

Cairo is the author of *Dirty Heat, Ruthless, Retribution, Between the Sheets, Slippery When Wet, The Stud Palace* (original ebook), *Big Booty, Man Swappers, Kitty-Kitty, Bang-Bang, Deep Throat Diva, Daddy Long Stroke, The Man Handler,* and *The Kat Trap.* His travels to Egypt inspired his pen name.

IF YOU ENJOYED "THE PLEASURE ZONE," BE SURE TO CHECK OUT
MARCEL, MARIKA AND NAIROBIA'S FREAKY PAST IN

By Cairo
Available from Strebor Books

TEN

Marika

The black-suited driver rolls the stretch Bentley with its tinted windows through the ornate iron gates of the Beverly Hills mansion where tonight's extravaganza will take place. He slowly pulls in front of its circular driveway, then stops the car and slides out of the driver's seat, walking around to open the door for Marcel and me.

Marcel leans over and kisses me lightly on the cheek. He takes in my white draped, sleeveless Azzaro Capricieuse jewel dress with its plunging V-neckline and long slit in the middle, revealing my inner thigh. I'm wearing the six thousand-dollar dress—that is sure to catch the eye of many of tonight's elite guests, shakers and movers in the movie and music industry as well as some well-known sports figures—with a pair of white Valentino Garavani six-inch, rock-stud sandals.

His gaze drops down to my perky nipples peeking from underneath the thin fabric of my dress, then onto my smooth, shimmering thighs.

He licks his lips. "Damn. You look sexy as fuck, baby."

I smile, breathing in the scrumptious scent of his cologne, Creed Royal Oud. Every time he wear this, it drives me wild. "Thank you. You don't look too bad yourself." The glint in the diamond studs in his earlobes is blinding. He's donned in an elegant, black-fitted Valentino suit with a matching pair of loafers. "And you smell delicious, I might add." My hand slides between his legs, finding his meaty dick. I gently massage it until it starts to thicken.

"Yo, c'mon, baby," he says, grinning while trying to pull away. "You better stop before shit gets serious back here 'n' I end up ripping that dress off you 'n' beatin' that fat pussy up in this backseat."

"Ooh, yes, daddy," I coo into his ear. "Beat this pussy up. Fuck it until it stretches and burns. I want to feel you still inside of me throbbing and pulsing long after you've pulled out."

Marcel leans in, and whispers, "Hold tight, baby. By the end of the night, I promise. I'ma be doin' just that. *Putain la gueule d'ya cul sexy.*" Fucking the shit out of ya sexy ass. "But, for now, let's save the foreplay for inside."

I press my thighs together, reluctantly retrieving my hand from his hard dick.

The back passenger door swings open.

Marcel winks at me, grinning. "You ready?"

I lick my lips as sordid scenarios of lewd sexapades flash through my freaky mind, causing heat to creep inbetween my thighs. My clit tingles, causing my pussy to instantly moisten.

"I'm always ready."

"So, what…or should I say *who*…are you in the mood for tonight, baby?" Marcel asks as we maneuver our way through the maze of designer-clad and diamond-studded guests, giving customary smiles and head nods, along with generous hugs and handshakes.

"I'll know when…." ·

There are several VPs and A&R executives from various record labels and numerous A-list celebrities and athletes milling around the room, drinking flutes of some of the finest champagnes while mingling, flirting, groping, and sidling up to their objects of desire as bare-chested waiters wearing black bowties and tuxedo pants circle with champagne on silver trays.

"Ooh, the two of you are simply delicious together," says a sultry voice in back of Marcel and me. We both look over our shoulder and our eyes flicker into the face of Nairobia Jansen—the half-Dutch, half-Nigerian author, model, and sex goddess who has graced the covers of both *Penthouse* and *Playboy* and has built a multimillion-dollar empire with her adult toy line.

"Mmm," she purrs, running a finger lightly down my spine, causing a burst of sensations to erupt inside of me. She's dressed in a scandalous white sheer dress sans bra and panties, brazenly revealing the assets she's most famous for—her voluptuous breasts, curvaceous hips, and beautiful round ass. "I'd love to have the two of you in my chambers tonight doing all sorts of naughty things."

"Nairobia, my darling," I say saucily, casting my gaze to the swell of her breasts, "you're looking irresistibly scrumptious as always." I lick my lips at the outline of her dark areolas and thick chocolate-tipped nipples.

She air-kisses both my cheeks, then hungrily eyes Marcel as he leans in and kisses her lightly on the lips, cupping her delightful ass.

He licks his lips, then says, "Good to see you, baby."

Gray eyes lit with mischief, Nairobia stands on her tiptoes and whispers, "And it would be even better to *feel* you deep inside me again." Before giving Marcel a chance to respond, she presses the mounds of her breasts against him and nibbles on his earlobe, taking his hand and sliding it between the long slit in her dress, placing it between her legs. "I've missed the feel of you inside my pussy."

Marcel gives her a lopsided grin. "Oh, word? You miss this long, hard dick, baby?"

She moans in response, pulling me into her, cupping her hand at the base of my neck for a tender kiss. My pussy moistens. She parts my lips with her tongue, while her other hand finds its way to my breasts. She brushes her mouth against the column of my neck, her warm breath heating my skin.

My hand slinks between her legs to join Marcel's. Index and middle fingers brush lightly against her slippery nub while Marcel's fingers get lost deep inside her heat. The scent of her pussy, wet and hungry, flows freely over Marcel's hand.

My mouth waters for a taste of her sweet nectar.

In between gasps and moans, Nairobia says, "I want…mmm…both of… you…*fucking* …me…in my *mouth*…my *pussy*…my sweet, tight *ass*…"

Marcel's thick fingers open her, wide and wanting, making room for my two slender fingers to slide in alongside his. Together we finger-fuck her. I can feel the silken swell of her cunt as she nears orgasm. She's getting wetter with each stroke.

Marcel leans in, kisses me, tongues me, then does the same to Nairobia. She hums deep in her throat, her cunt contracting around our probing digits, causing my own pussy to pulse. And thicken with desire.

"Spread your legs wider," I urge. She is close to coming. I can smell it, feel it, around our fingers as she thrusts her hips; four fingers fucking into her juicy cunt. The sound of wet pussy swallowing our fingers causes a deep throb to take root inside of me.

"Yeah, baby, nut on these fingers," Marcel murmurs, his voice deep and husky. "Bust that pussy for me, baby…"

And she does.

Like a tidal wave, warm juices erupt, washing over our fingers, soaking our hands. Nairobia squirts and shudders and gasps. Her skin flushes hot. And then she comes again.

A few seconds later, when her body is no longer trembling, when her cunt is vacant from our prodding fingers, Nairobia kisses us both, whispering promises of sweet, nasty things to come, then floats away.

"Damn, I love how wet her pussy gets," Marcel says, kissing me, then pressing his cum-slick fingers to my lips, offering me Nairobia's cunt juice. I suck his fingers into my mouth, sweeping my tongue around his fingers.

He smiles, and I moan as he pulls his wet fingers from my mouth. "Mmm, and she tastes so good."

Across the room, there's a set of eyes watching us. I'm not sure who spots him across the room first—me or Marcel, but when my eyes land on him I know he's the one I want eating my pussy alongside my husband.

He's gorgeous. And tall, at least six feet five, with a shock of dark, wavy hair and dark, piercing eyes. From where I'm standing, he looks as if he's been sculpted from a delicious batch of caramel, then drizzled with hot fudge.

"Him," I say, sliding my sticky fingers into my mouth, then licking them as I would a hard dick. "He's who I want for us tonight."

"Yeah, that muhfucka's real sexy, baby. Good choice."

He doesn't shift his gaze when he sees us looking back at him. He smiles. I smile back. Marcel acknowledges him with a head nod. "Yo, I think he likes what he sees."

"And so he should," I say, feeling my skin heat at the thought of sucking his dick and licking his balls while Marcel fucks me. I pick up a crystal flute off one of the trays. I hand it to Marcel, then grab a flute for myself.

Marcel smirks. "Let's hope the muhfucka doesn't have a lil'-ass, infant-size dick. I'm not tryna see them pretty lips wrapped around no tiny-ass dick, baby."

I clink my glass with his. We both take slow sips. The fact that Marcel enjoys seeing my mouth wrapped around another man's dick, the fact that he revels in the sight of seeing my lips painted with another man's semen, is what makes me desire him even more. Not many men could or would handle having their women—let alone giving her permission—to suck another man's dick. And he damn sure wouldn't be willing to kiss her with another man's cum on her tongue. But Marcel…he's uninhibited. Freaky. And secure enough in his manhood to enjoy it. Encourage it. And indulge in it.

"Oh, no," I say, eyeing Mr. Sexy across the room. "The way he's standing, all wide-legged and confident, tells me that whatever is hanging between those long legs of his is quite substantial."

"Yeah, well. It'd better be."

I grab his dick. Squeeze the head a few times. Then tell him I'll be right back. He kisses me on the cheek, his hand gliding over the globes of my ass. "Go get 'im, baby."

"I plan to," I say, gulping down the rest of my drink, then pulling Marcel into me. "For the both of us." I reach up and press my lips against his, parting them easily, my warm tongue prodding around his mouth before breaking free and prowling in the direction of the mystery man.

The smell of wet pussy and freshly fucked ass wafting around the room is intoxicating.

The thing I love most about sex clubs and private parties, there are no pretenses. No judgments. No limits. No shame. No room for games. No space for confusion. Everyone is always here for the same reasons, to fuck and be fucked shamelessly. To explore rapturous fantasies with whomever they choose. To be sexually fulfilled.

"You are one fine man," I say, walking up to him. I am already wet, but now I've become wetter with eager anticipation. I set my empty glass on a nearby table.

He flashes a megawatt smile, revealing straight, white teeth. "And so are you, beautiful. I enjoyed the show."

I smile, reaching for another flute of champagne as a bare-chested waiter in black tuxedo pants saunters by with a full tray. "Oh, there's a whole lot more to see," I assure him, my tone full of seduction and promise.

"Hmm. I love the sound of that." He places his empty glass on the tray, taking another one full of bubbly. "So who's the man I've watched you work the party with?" I tell him it's my husband. He grins and nods his head in approval. "Aah. And he doesn't want to join us?"

"Not at the moment." My gaze, full of fire and hot desire, skims his body, pausing over what looks like a growing bulge, thick and heavy. "But he will, trust."

He grins. "I look forward to it. The more the merrier." He pulls in his bottom lip, slow and seductively.

I give him a knowing smile. "So, what shall we drink to?" I ask, reaching up and pulling the diamond hairclip from my hair, letting my hair cascade over my shoulders.

"Why not to a night full of endless possibilities," he says with a wink.

I toss my hair, shamelessly flirting with this fine hunk of man. "Well, my husband and I"—I nod my head over in Marcel's direction—"would love to end the night with *you* in our bed."

He waits a beat, then glances over in Marcel's direction, lifting his flute. Marcel returns the gesture, along with a head nod. He smiles, returning his attention to me.

"Oh, and what an endless night of possibilities it shall be." His eyes scan my entire body, from head to toe. "I have a thing for pretty feet," he says, licking his lips. "And beautiful, open-minded women."

I grin, holding his gaze. "And I have a thing for fine men who aren't afraid to indulge their desires. That's a real turn-on. What are your desires, uh…I didn't get your name."

He grins back. "I didn't give it. Names aren't necessary. Just know I'm a freak, here looking for a good time. And I have a whole lot of energy for more than one round."

"Okay, Mister-No-Name-Freak-Looking-For-A-Good-Time, what do you desire tonight?"

He glances back over at Marcel, who is being entertained by two buxom vixens wearing nothing but glitter and gold body paint over their gym-Pilates-toned bodies.

A sly smile eases over my moist lips as I eye Marcel slide both his hands in between each of their legs. The two sex kittens lean in and kiss. And I swallow, imagining the feel of their warm flesh against his fingers, imagining the taste of their wetness on my own fingers, on my tongue.

A vision of sharing the two vixens with Marcel causes my pussy to spasm and my nipples to peak hard.

"For starters," Caramel says, bringing my attention back to him, "to answer your question. I desire a night with *you*." He tears his stare from mine, glancing over at Marcel. "And *him*. But for now…" He eyes my feet again. "I'd like to taste them pretty toes." He slides his lusty gaze back up to meet mine. "Then lick you to climax."

My breath catches.

Then, without another word, he's whisking me off outside toward a row of cushion-padded benches. The backyard is dimly lit with gaslight sconces and tiki torches.

The walls of my pussy literally tremble as I watch this tall, sculpted hunk of a caramel-coated man gulp down the rest of his drink, then drop on one knee, unfasten the straps of my heels, remove them, then gently fold his large hands around my ankles, lift a foot to his face. He kisses my feet with warm lips. Then runs his tongue along my arch, kissing the tips of my toes, then putting them into his mouth. I can't help but moan as his tongue slides around, and in between, each toe as his hands slip up the back of my calves, my thighs, then back down. He sinks all five of my toes inside his mouth. And I feel myself melting into the sensation. Erotic and sensual, my clit tingles.

I arch forward, aching for him, devouring him with my eyes. He sucks and licks my toes as if he's sucking and licking on my clit, sucking and licking on my cunt, sucking and licking on my swollen lips, sucking and licking as if each toe were a tiny, hard dick. Heat dances over my body. Spreads out over my skin. And stirs my simmering lust.

"Do you want to taste my pussy, too?"